WICKED PURSUIT

Welcome to the

BLACK ROSE AUCTION

In **WICKED PURSUIT** by Katee Robert, a Little Red Riding Hood remix, a mob princess with a taste for doing things she shouldn't acquires a stalker who will kill anyone who touches what's his…

In **DIVINE INTERVENTION** by R.M. Virtues, a Goldilocks remix, a witch must work with her ex's father (who she betrayed) and an angel to steal a magical chalice from the auction floor. But things get scorchingly complicated when all three agree that revenge is best served in the bedroom…

ALSO BY KATEE ROBERT

Court of the Vampire Queen

DARK OLYMPUS
Neon Gods
Electric Idol
Wicked Beauty
Radiant Sin
Cruel Seduction
Midnight Ruin
Dark Restraint
Sweet Obsession

WICKED VILLAINS
Desperate Measures
Learn My Lesson
A Worthy Opponent
The Beast
The Sea Witch
Queen Takes Rose

The

BLACK ROSE AUCTION:

WICKED PURSUIT

WICKED PURSUIT

KATEE ROBERT

sourcebooks
casablanca

Published by Sourcebooks Casablanca, an imprint of Sourcebooks
P.O. Box 4410, Naperville, Illinois 60567-4410
(630) 961-3900
sourcebooks.com

Originally self-published in 2024 by Katee Robert.

Cataloging-in-Publication Data is on file with the Library of Congress.

Printed and bound in the United States of America.
LSC 10 9 8 7 6 5 4 3 2 1

To H. D. Carlton and Cate C. Wells.

Without Haunting Adeline and Nicky the
Driver, this book wouldn't exist.

FOREWORD

When we set out to create the Black Rose Auction series, we knew we wanted it to be luxe and dangerous and sexy! The premise is that there's an annual auction, presided over by the mysterious Reaper, where anything can be purchased for the right price. It's a place to make statements, to auction off the services of some of the world's most exclusive sex workers, to find priceless artifacts that the general public has only heard rumors of. Within these books, you'll find dangerous men, powerful women, and a heist or two! Be sure to check out read.sourcebooks .com/blackroseauction or scan the QR code to get an introduction to all six authors and their work!

The moment we chose the premise for the series, Katee's face lit up with a delicious idea. "Next Gen Wicked Villains" would've been enough to have me frothing at the mouth. (Belle, Beast, and Gaeton's grown-up brat daughter?! Uncle Hook?! Meeting the rest of the Wicked

Villains' offspring?!) But when Katee said it would be a Little Red Riding Hood stalker romance, I had a feeling she was going to do something truly bold.

I knew it would be dark, and I knew it would be sexy. I didn't know it would snatch me by the throat, drag me into a dark alley, and leave me begging for more. This is unquestionably one of my all-time favorite Katee Robert books. She's a writer at the top of her game, and this stands as proof that she's willing to keep challenging herself and taking risks. I bow down to how fearlessly she wrote this story, and I just know her readers are going to be as blown away by it as I was.

I dare you to try to put it down once you've started.

Jenny Nordbak

CONTENT GUIDANCE

TROPES: Stalking romance.

TAGS: Stalking, Mafia, dubious consent, bad girl so damn tired of being good, skull masks are sexy and no one can tell me otherwise, murder is foreplay apparently, auctioning myself off sounds like a really good call that couldn't possibly backfire, why yes I will incite my stalker to increasingly violent acts, jealousy can be sexy, you can fuck who you want but at the end of the night I'm reclaiming *my* pussy, second generation Wicked Villains, no I do not want to go to a kink club where my parents hang out, FFM scene, MMF scene, in this house we support women's wrongs, antiheroine, antihero, breath play, primal play.

CONTENT WARNINGS: Dubious consent, stalking, murder, assault, violence, blood, choking without prior discussion, cheating, consensual nonconsent, explicit sex, attempted sexual assault (not the hero), breeding (epilogue).

PLAYLIST

Throughout *Wicked Pursuit*, you'll find footnotes referring to songs that inspired a scene, might be playing in the background of a scene, or may otherwise enhance your reading experience. We encourage you to queue up these songs so they're ready to play whenever you see them referenced. For a handy Spotify playlist tailored to each book, go to read.sourcebooks.com /blackroseauction or scan the QR code and search for *Wicked Pursuit*.

LITTLE RED RIDING HOOD—aeseaes

WHISPERS—Halsey

BODY IN MY BED—VÉRITÉ

MY HEART'S GRAVE—Faouzia

CRUEL—Jackson Wang

BREAKFAST—Dove Cameron

FORGIVE ME—Chloe x Halle

PRAY—Xana

VIRTUAL REALITY—rey

DREAM GIRL EVIL—Florence + The Machine

USE ME (BRUTAL HEARTS)— Diplo feat. Sturgill Simpson and Dove Cameron

BABY SAID—Måneskin

WHEN YOU SAY MY NAME—Chandler Leighton

FEEL—Måneskin

TOUCH—July Talk

BOYFRIEND—Dove Cameron

SHE CALLS ME DADDY—KiNG MALA

DE SELBY (PART 2)—Hozier

MERMAIDS—Florence + The Machine

THE GARDEN—July Talk

MONSTER—MILCK

HOWL—Florence + The Machine

DEVIL I KNOW—Allie X

SHACKLES—Steven Rodriguez

SPIDER IN THE ROSES—Sonia Leigh and Daphne Willis feat. Rob the Man

DEVIL DEVIL—MILCK

MONSTER—Meg Myers

MACHETE (ACOUSTIC)—SPELLES

WOLVES—Selena Gomez feat. Marshmello

BREATH OF LIFE—Florence + The Machine

CALL ME QUEEN—Ndidi O

TALK—Hozier

NEW FEARS (BEDROOM RECORDING)—Lights

HOLD ME DOWN—Halsey

BLUE EYES BLIND—ZZ Ward

LIKE YOU MEAN IT—Steven Rodriguez

HEAVY IN YOUR ARMS—Florence + The Machine

LAST LAUGH—FLETCHER

SMILE—Maisie Peters

STRUT—EMELINE

THE DEVIL WEARS LACE—Steven Rodriguez

WATER—Tyla

1121—Halsey

WHAT THE WATER GAVE ME—Florence + The Machine

HOW VILLAINS ARE MADE—Madalen Duke

ARSONIST'S LULLABY—Hozier

DARK MATTER—Seratones

EVERYTHING WE DO IS WRONG—Tuvaband

SAVAGE (RAIN RECORDING)—Lights

ISLAND—Miley Cyrus

I OF THE STORM—Of Monsters and Men

THE DEVIL IS A GENTLEMAN—Merci Raines

I PUT A SPELL ON YOU—Annie Lennox

FEELING GOOD—Nina Simone

NIGHT CRAWLING—Miley Cyrus feat. Billy Idol

ANIMALS—Nickelback

MOVEMENT—Hozier

shouldn't be here.[*]

I told Luke I was going out with Michelle and some of our other friends, but that wasn't the full truth. I made a stop first. I needed to get out of the increasingly oppressive atmosphere of our apartment. Of the silences that grow more and more strained as the weeks pass and it feels like we're no longer the people we were when we met.

I love him. I think. Or at least I used to.

It feels like a lie right now, while I'm sliding down another man's cock.

The man in question...I can't remember his name right now, not with desire and shame and alcohol fuzzing my thoughts. He's handsome in the way so many men in the life are, harsh and cruel with scars on his knuckles and tattoos creeping up his wide neck.

"That's right, baby. Ride my cock."

* LITTLE RED RIDING HOOD—aeseaes

"Shut up," I mutter. But I don't stop. He's got my dress rucked up around my waist back in this private booth that really isn't that private. Not that it matters. Luke is a good man. He wouldn't be caught dead in a bar like this. One where the floors are sticky, where smoke lingers in the air, where every person is carrying. A bar frequented by the most dangerous people in Carver City.

No, Luke prefers bars that are frequented by professionals in business suits sharing a drink as they decompress from a long day at the office. Places where the emphasis is *networking*. Where the music is never too loud and is intentionally palatable. Where the drinks are named fancy things that hint at prestige but are made with well alcohol.

Luke is a lot like those bars. He doesn't incite dramatic passions, and the most exciting thing he does is travel incessantly for work. These days, being with him is as comfortable as a well-worn sweater. And as coma inducing.

No. Holy fuck, *no*. I am *not* thinking about him while I'm doing this.

I snake a hand down to stroke my clit. If I'm going to be a horrible, cheating girlfriend, then I'm at least going to get off while I do it.

It doesn't take long. It never does when I'm doing something that good girls don't do.

Not that I was raised with that kind of bullshit, but I've had the sword of Damocles hanging over my head since I was old enough to be aware of what it means that my aunt, the leader of our territory, has no children. Of the fact that my mother only has *me*. That math only adds up to one solution, and it's one that's never sat comfortably on my shoulders. I never asked to be heir. I don't really want the title or the responsibility.

Even so, there's a part of me that strives to not disappoint the people in my life. I went through school without a single bad mark on my record. I got good grades and didn't bother to date much, because no one was brave enough to face down the required family dinner. After high school, the wildest I got was using a fake ID to get through the door of the Tower, our favorite club in town. I had my first taste of freedom there, of what life might be if I were just another rich girl, no responsibility chaining me to a future I didn't choose for myself. It was heady and amazing and addicting.

Then I met Luke on my twenty-second birthday.

He doesn't know what my family does. He's not from Carver City, didn't grow up here with the oppressive "family" culture—really just another way to say "mob" culture. He looked at me and saw the girl I'd always strived to be, good and kind and always coloring inside the lines.

I'm not being good right now.

I stroke my clit faster, the shame that's coating me driving me over the edge and into an orgasm that might not change my life but feels good nonetheless. I ease off the stranger's condom-covered cock and stagger to my feet. Coming here was a mistake, but fuck if I don't feel at home in my own skin for the first time in years. Maybe ever.

The man reaches for me, his brutal expression relaxed. "Where you going, Red? I'm not done with that pussy yet."

Red isn't my name, but with my crimson-dyed hair, the guy

didn't question it when I gave it to him. I pull the skirt of my dress back down over my hips and easily dodge his hand. "Thanks for the good time. See you never."

"Hey!"

I ignore him and stride out of the private booth. The bar is much the same as I left it, dingy and dark and filled with people who live and work in the shadows. The enforcers who keep rulers like my aunt in power. People like my fathers, with blood on their hands. People like I'll eventually be when I take over the Belmonte territory. The clock ticking in my head was silent while I was fucking the stranger, but it starts right back up again. My parents may have given me space before cramming me into the heir role, but it's only a matter of time before they tire of my resistance.

But it won't be tonight.

I pull my phone out and text Michelle.

Me: When will you be there?

Michelle: Girl, I AM there. Where are you?

Guilt flares. I didn't set out with the intention of cheating on my boyfriend, but as I was walking to the bar to meet Michelle, I saw *this* bar and…I stared at that grungy front door and neon sign and could see an alternate universe where I was a different woman, a more dangerous one. The kind of woman who could walk into a bar, crook her finger at a man, and fuck him with barely another word.

And then I did it. And it felt *good*.

I swallow hard and type out a response.

Me: Be there in two.

I hitch my purse more firmly onto my shoulder and stride out the door. It's not particularly late, so there's plenty of foot traffic. I fall in with a group of chattering college students. There was a time when Carver City was split more intensely, but years of peace have changed things. Now college bars nestle right up next to places where seedier business is arranged. There's an unspoken agreement—the lieutenants of the various territories stay away from civilians, and if a normal person wanders into the wrong business, they're sent on their way without any violence. It works. Mostly.

The small hairs on the back of my neck lift.

Someone is watching me.

I glance over my shoulder, certain my ill-advised partner has followed me. He's nowhere in sight. In fact, no one seems to be paying me much attention. That's almost enough for me to brush off the feeling, but I've been trained too well.

Growing up the way I did, even while dodging my responsibilities as heir, there was no way I could avoid certain realities. Carver City may be at peace, but that doesn't change the danger inherent in our life. Violence could erupt at any moment, at least in theory. As a result, Da taught me to trust my instincts. If they say run, then I run. If they say hide, then I hide. Better to be overcautious than to end up dead.

Right now, they're saying that someone is following me.

I pick up my pace, hurrying to the bar where Michelle is waiting for me. She's a perfect mix of her parents, short with generous curves and a thick waist, her skin medium-brown and her hair dark and wavy. Tonight she's wearing a pair of paint-ed-on jeans and a cute flowery top that does wonders for her cleavage. "About time you got here!"

"Sorry, I got held up." I'm still not quite sure how I feel about what happened... No, that's a lie. My nerves are alight, and my skin feels too tight. I want to *move*. To dance and scream and chase this feeling of being alive. "Is anyone else coming?"

"No." She makes a show of pouting. "The only person who returned my text was Zayne, and only to tell me that he's got work in the morning and isn't interested in being hungover for it."

I drop into the chair next to her. "That sucks. I haven't seen him in ages." He's not an heir like Michelle and me, but like Michelle, he's one of the only people in this city I consider a friend. Or at least I used to, before I started dating Luke. The rest of the heirs and spares range from friendly acquaintances to those who don't give me the time of day. But at least none of us are enemies. We've all grown up the same, with the importance of peace in Carver City drilled into us from an early age.

"You'd see him more if you came out more."

I shrug because she's right. Luke and I used to come out with them when we first started dating, but then his job got more demanding, and I convinced myself I liked the chill nights at home and...here we are. "Tell me about this new girl you're seeing. When do I get to meet her?"

"Oh, you know." She waves that away, happy to flit to a new subject, just like I hoped she'd be. "It's not that serious. So probably never. But I just heard the juiciest gossip."

My phone buzzes.* I motion for her to keep going as I glance at it. Unknown number? Frowning, I pull up the message.

Unknown: Someone's been a bad girl.

I scoff. *And someone has never heard an original line in their life.* I'm about to put down my phone when it buzzes again. This time, it's a picture message. The lighting is dim and the framing is strange, as if it was taken through a gap in a door. Even so, I recognize what I'm looking at immediately.

My dress, held up around my hips by hands with scars on their knuckles.

My bare ass, lifted just enough for someone to see that I am most definitely fucking the man I'm straddling. The man who isn't my boyfriend.

And, in the mirror behind the booth, *my* face.

Another buzz.

Unknown: What would your boyfriend think?

"Is something wrong, Ruby?"

I startle and nearly knock over the glass of wine the bartender just set down in front of me. "No. It's fine." I don't sound convincing, even to myself. Sure as hell not enough to get past Michelle.

She narrows her pretty green eyes. "We lie to other people. We don't lie to each other. What's going on?"

My resolve to keep my earlier activities to myself crumbles.

* WHISPERS—Halsey

I'm not ready to talk about whoever the fuck is texting me—I'll deal with *that* later—but cheating on Luke? That knowledge is a stone in my stomach.

I cast a look around the place. It's a completely different crowd than the last one, even though only a handful of blocks separate the bars. We're firmly in neutral territory here, and while there hasn't been war between the territory leaders since before I was born, everyone still breathes a little easier when they're in the shadow of the Underworld. Whoever took that picture of me isn't here. I'm sure of it.

Mostly sure.

I shiver. "I...uh...just had sex with some guy in a private booth at the bar down the street. That's why I was late."

Michelle lets out a whoop that turns several heads in our direction. "So you finally broke it off with the wet blanket. That calls for a toast and some shots."

For the first time, guilt takes proper residence inside me, overriding the other emotions. "We didn't break up."

She freezes. "*Ruby.*"

"I know."

"No, I don't think you do." She nudges my wine toward me. "Look, I get it. Luke is hot as fuck, and he knows his way around a clitoris. So do a lot of people. You're bored with him. Worse, in my opinion, you're *boring* while you're dating him. Or at least you are lately."

I jerk back, stung. "Wow, tell me how you really feel."

"I only do it out of love." She sips her wine. "I understand the urge to play daddy's little girl, especially since you have two dads, but aren't you tired of pretending to be someone you're not? I threw that shit away years ago."

Yeah, Michelle did. The second we turned eighteen, Michelle buried her last give-a-damn and went to town. She partied everywhere except the Underworld—there are some lines not even she was willing to cross—and slept her way through half of Carver City.

I was so jealous, I could barely breathe past it.

There was nothing stopping me from doing the same thing. Nothing except myself and the expectations I set up. As if by carefully not stepping out of line, I could keep my parents from intervening and pushing even harder for me to take up my role as heir. I never realized that the strongest chains a person can be bound in are those of their own making.

"It's different."

"If you say so." She shrugs. "Look, I understand exactly how exciting it can be to do something you're not supposed to. You get no judgment from me there. I just don't understand why you're staying with Luke if you're out riding someone else's cock."

I toy with my wineglass, not sure if I can fully explain what I don't entirely understand. "I care about him."

"See my last point—you don't care enough to *not* cheat on him."

My phone buzzes on the bar and I shudder. "I don't know, okay? I'm just not ready to break up with him." I drop my phone into my purse.

"Is it your parents? You know they aren't going to think less of you that the first boyfriend you ever had isn't your end-all, be-all."

She's being logical, and there's nothing about this situation that's logical. "If I break up with him, there will be questions. I'll have to move home, and then Aunt Sienna will be in my business. She already doesn't believe he's good enough for me, and if she thinks he did something, because she'd never believe *I'm* the issue..."

Michelle grimaces. "At that point, we might as well kill him and save him from her locking him up in her murder basement and torturing him for months."

"It's not a murder basement," I say faintly. "It's a lab."

"Two terms, same result. Besides, the alternative is for you to stay with Luke forever, becoming the cliché of a bored housewife. What's next, sleeping with the pool boy?"

"We don't have a pool in our apartment complex." The protest is weak, even to my ears.

"Then tennis coach, tutor, fill in the blank. You know what I mean." She nods at my glass. "I think we need something stronger to continue this conversation."

I'm already motioning the bartender over. "Agreed."

———

Several hours and far too many shots later, I still don't have a good answer for why I'm climbing the stairs to the apartment I share with the boyfriend I...love?* I don't know if that's even the right word.

When Luke and I first got together, we were like a wildfire. I was drunk off the freedom of living on my own and having hot sex with a partner who showed every evidence of being completely obsessed with me. He was handsome and sexy and wanted

* BODY IN MY BED—VÉRITÉ

me more than anyone ever had. We couldn't keep our hands off each other, and there were more than a few times we were caught fucking in places we shouldn't have been. I don't know when things changed. Maybe when we moved in together. Maybe when he got his new job and started working longer hours and traveling out of town for extended periods of time, selling insulation to companies. Things are *fine*, but fine feels tepid at best.

Maybe my standards are too high. Look at my parents after all. They've been together for nearly thirty years, and they still flirt and play grab-ass and make regular trips to Hades's kink club. The fire never burned out between them, and gods help me, but I want that fiery love.

I thought I had it with Luke. But then, I was never completely honest with him, was I? It's no wonder we fell apart along the way.

I stumble through the front door and stop short. I expected the apartment to be bathed in shadows. He has an early morning tomorrow. A meeting with…someone. He definitely told me, and I definitely forgot as soon as the conversation ended.

Except he's not in bed like I expected. He's sitting on the couch with a tumbler of whisky and a paperback. He's so fucking handsome that the first time he approached me, I couldn't believe he was even talking to me. Now I wish he were less perfect. A few scars. A crooked nose. Something to make him feel *human* and fallible.

Is it any wonder I went seeking sin just to be able to breathe? Except that's not fair. It's not Luke's fault that I'm a shitty, cheating girlfriend. The blame lies solely with me.

"Hey, Ruby." He holds out a hand, and maybe it's the alcohol making me foolish, but I'm crossing to him and taking his hand before I realize I really shouldn't.

I jerk back. "Sorry. The bar was so damn crowded, and I'm covered in perfume and cologne. Let me take a shower and we can chat."

"I was just going to bed. I was reading and lost track of time." He rises easily and brushes a kiss over my lips. "Glad you got home safe."

"Me too." I don't know what the fuck I'm saying. I stand there, numb, and watch him walk into our bedroom.

It's only when I set my purse on the counter that I remember the weird messages. Luke and I don't go through each other's phones, but there's no reason to leave out clear evidence that I was up to no good. My stomach drops when I click on my phone and see the series of texts.

Unknown: You can ignore me, but do you think HE will?

Unknown: I'm feeling generous after the show you gave me, so I'll give you until three to respond before I send that photo to the boyfriend.

Unknown: Clock's ticking, Red. And I'm not a patient man.

I glance at the clock. Five minutes until three. I should ignore it. There's no reason to engage with this weird-as-fuck interaction. He called me Red, just like the guy at the bar. Maybe it was one of *his* friends who somehow got my phone to get my number. Except that doesn't make sense. My purse was right next to me the entire time. It's more likely that whoever this is, they were close enough to hear the guy call me Red.

I bite my bottom lip. It's hard to think through the film of drunkenness making me feel loose and reckless. "Fuck it," I mutter. I type a reply.

> **Me**: Pretty pathetic to get your jollies watching other people fuck. Get lost, loser.
> **Unknown**: Baby, you keep talking to me like that and I'll wash your mouth out with soap.

I blink. "This motherfucker is out of his godsdamn mind. Does he think I'm *flirting* with him?" Now's the time to walk away. Put down my phone and call...well, not my mom. Not Dad either. They'll ask too many questions. Da may, too, but he'd at least take care of the creep first.

Except I don't.

> **Me**: This game is over. If you know who I am, then you know who my parents are. My fathers will bury you somewhere no one will find you.

A pause, long enough that I let out a sigh of relief.
Then my phone buzzes.

> **Unknown**: Daddies' little girl, huh? Do they know you've been haunting Mafia bars and rubbing your pussy all over the trash that hangs out there?

The blood rushes to my head. Or out of my head. I can't tell if I'm furious or terrified.

Me: Who the fuck are you?

Unknown: Here's what's going to happen. You're going to be a good girl and send me a picture of those perfect tits. In return, I won't tell your boyfriend that you've been a dirty little slut behind his back.

I stare at the text, my mouth hanging open. "The *audacity* of this motherfucker." My nails click against the screen as I type too hard.

Me: June, two years ago. If you're good enough to get my number, you're good enough to find that picture.

I'd let Michelle convince me to join a wet T-shirt contest. It was a wild time. It was also the night I met Luke for the first time. We'd been flirting for hours, and after that contest, we ended up in the parking lot, and he ate my pussy right there against my car.

Unknown: It's a nice picture. I want one that all of Carver City hasn't seen.

Shame heats the back of my neck. I got quite the lecture after the contest pictures were posted—all three of my parents got a word in edgewise about it. Our family has a reputation after all.

No one talks about the fact that my parents engage in public kinky behavior every Saturday night, but I show my tits once and it's the end of the world.

I don't know if it's the shame or the alcohol or the kernel of fear growing in my stomach. Whatever the cause, I find myself in the bathroom. I jerk down my dress and raise my middle finger as I snap a photo.

Me: Choke on that, douchebag.

His response is nearly instantaneous.

Unknown: Good girl. Now get some rest. You'll need it for what comes next.

2

The next morning, I'm filled with all kinds of regret, mostly for the sheer amount of alcohol I imbibed.* The memories sit in my sour stomach and my pounding head. And the texts on my phone.

I scroll through them again, alone in my bed, Luke's side long since gone cold. I'm not even sure when he left. He said he had an early day, and now that I'm sober, I'm nearly certain he *didn't* give me the details. Oh well. We're ships passing in the night, always. The more pressing issue is the fact that I have acquired a stalker.

I read through the texts a third time. There's no clue, no hint to his identity. And I sent him a picture of my breasts. Brilliant. I delete the text thread with a curse. I could go to my fathers with this. Or, if not them, my mother. They would fix this little problem inside twenty-four hours.

* MY HEART'S GRAVE—Faouzia

But then I would have to admit what I've done. I'm not ready to do that.

If I get a little thrill from the threat this stranger poses...well, I'm in a free fall. What's another weight added to my legs?

I haul myself out of bed and get ready. A hangover has never been enough to make me late for work before, and it won't be today either. I drive onto the Belmonte estate with minutes to spare. Mom has been petitioning for the family to move to a proper office for years, but Aunt Cordelia insists on tradition. The house is easier to defend, the large property ringed with heavy fences and armed guards. It doesn't matter that neither have been necessary for as long as I've been alive. There was a time when they *were* necessary, and that's enough for my aunt.

I let myself in through the front door and walk down the wide entrance hall to the east wing, where the offices are kept. Mine is right next to my aunt's. She pokes her head into my office and waves. Aunt Cordelia is a fierce woman, and she only seems to get fiercer with age. She and my mother share the same coloring—dark hair, dark eyes, olive-toned skin that harkens back to our Italian ancestors.

She smiles. "There are some reports on your desk, Ruby. Could you have them back to me by end of day?"

"Of course."

Her smile falls away. "Is everything okay? You look a little pale."

"I'm fine. I was out with Michelle last night."

Cordelia's smile goes a little tight. "And how is she?"

"Good." I keep my voice bright. Michelle's parents are the

same age as mine and still in good health, but my aunt never forgets that Michelle is the heir to their territory. A change of power is always rife with potential challenges. If Carver City is to fall back into war, it will happen then. It's not something I like thinking about. So...I don't. Instead, I do the books and pretend the family isn't backing me into leadership, and they allow me some element of freedom. But someday Michelle and I will be dealing with each other not as friends but as leaders of our respective territories. I shudder at the thought and cover the motion up with a cough. "Well, I'll get to work."

"Sounds good."

My phone pings as Cordelia steps back into the hall. I jump. "Godsdamn it."

It's probably Michelle. Or maybe Luke. Except when I flip over my phone, it's a text from an unknown number. Again.

Unknown: I like you in red.
Unknown: Fitting.

I glare at my phone. I'm too hungover for this shit.

Me: Fuck off.

The response is almost instantaneous.

Unknown: What did I tell you about using language like that?

Here, in the fortress that is my family household, I actually laugh.

Me: Come get me then.

What is *wrong* with me? Last night, I had the excuse of alcohol, but that's not the case right now. "Enough of this." I reach for the landline at my desk. I'll call Da and let him handle this.

My phone buzzes.

Unknown: Can't stay hidden and safe there forever. You'll wander eventually.

I stare at my phone for a very long time. I know what the smart, normal response to this man would be. Allow my fathers to do what they do and take care of the threat.

But…

I tap my desk with a single finger. That feeling, the one that blossomed into existence over the course of the past few months and culminated in me going to that bar last night? It's still there. Stronger even. As if by giving in to it once, I've fed a beast inside me that slumbered previously.

It's awake now. And there's a fizzling in my veins, a thrill that makes me shift in my seat. This stalker is *dangerous*. Then again, so am I.

Me: If you come for me, you're dead.

———

The day passes uneventfully. There's a big deal in the works, the kind that happens once a decade, so everyone is wrapped up in the details. I already ran the numbers and compiled the reports, so my part in the process is done until Cordelia has signed on the dotted line.

My stalker has been silent for most of the day.* That won't last.

I walk into my apartment and look around. The lights are all off, just like I left them. Luke must not be home yet. I glance at my phone. He's late. But then he's been working late more and more often in recent weeks. The business trips have increased too: long weekends and sometimes entire weeks. Maybe he's having an affair. I examine the thought from different angles. A year ago, the very possibility would have sent me into a spiral. Now I just feel...tired. We're going through the motions, and we're not even doing a good job of it.

I toss my purse onto the counter and shrug out of my jacket. It's time.

It takes me a few minutes to stage the photo the way I want it. I take a few extra photos for good measure. Yeah, that will work. I look sexy as fuck with my red dress hiked around my thighs and falling off one shoulder. Not enough to expose me fully, but the promise of more is there. I send it to the unknown number and type.

Me: You want to wash my mouth out with soap, fucker? Come get me.

* CRUEL—Jackson Wang

That reckless feeling inside me gets stronger, strong enough to make my head spin. *You're calling his bluff. That's it.* I'm normally a better liar, even to myself.

I shove up from the couch and stalk to the kitchen. There's a safe hidden in the cabinet above the fridge. I have to drag a chair over to get to it. Da would yell at me something fierce if he knew; a weapon is only as good as your ability to use it, and if I were under attack, I'd get myself killed before I'd be able to reach the gun.

But when would I be under attack? My life is so devastatingly *normal* that it makes me want to scream sometimes.

I drag my finger over the pad, and the safe pops open. It's second nature to pull the gun out, eject the magazine, and ensure the chamber is empty. Then I load it and test its weight in my hand.

It feels good.

I'm not a fool. I know the cost of war, that conflict in Carver City would mean being on opposite sides of a line from Michelle and the other families. I don't actually *want* that. But I crave... more. I don't even know what that *more* looks like.

I look at my phone again, but there's no response. Trust a stalker to run away the moment his victim stops playing the scared little girl. If he wanted someone to whimper and run to hide, he chose the wrong woman.

Even though I know better, I pull down the bottle of good whisky and pour myself a healthy glass. Then I bring both glass and gun back into the living room and drop onto the couch.

Still no response.

"Coward," I mutter. I tell myself what I'm feeling is relief, not disappointment.

My phone rings.

I stare at it blankly for a beat too long. At the **UNKNOWN** flashing across the screen. He's…calling me. I lift my phone to my ear cautiously, as if he might somehow physically reach through it. "Hello?"

"Are you trying to provoke me, Red?" His voice is deep and filled with gravel.

Gods help me, but it sends a shiver that isn't entirely fear down my spine. "That's not my name."

"Isn't it? It's the one you gave last night."

I lift my glass to my lips and pretend my hands aren't shaking. "Is that you, baby? I didn't catch your name last night. On purpose. Learn to take a hint."

He laughs, low and mean. "No, Red. You didn't have sex with me last night. But you won't get a chance to fuck that piece of shit ever again."

I set my glass down too hard, spilling whisky. "Wow, big talk for a coward who won't actually face me."

"I'll see you when I'm good and ready, Red."

"That's not my name," I repeat.

"Sure it is. You're Little Red Riding Hood, wandering off the path and away from your protective family."

I lick my lips. "I suppose that makes you the Big Bad Wolf."

"Sure." Another of those menacing chuckles.* "I can't wait to eat you right up, bite by bite."

"Why wait?" Even as I speak, a little voice in the back of my mind is screaming at me to shut the fuck up and call my parents. But I don't hang up. I don't call for help.

* BREAKFAST—Dove Cameron

I just stroke a finger down the barrel of my gun and relish the adrenaline surging through me. Maybe I am a fool after all. There's no other explanation for me leaning back against the couch and letting my voice go soft and crooning. "I'm right here, all alone and helpless."

He snorts. "The second I walk through the door, you're going to shoot me. I don't think so."

I jerk straight. How the fuck does he know I have a gun nearby? "Are you watching me right now?"

"I wouldn't be a very good stalker if I weren't."

I curse and surge to my feet. "You know what happens to the Big Bad Wolf in that fairy tale? He dies." The curtains are mostly closed, but I snap them all the way shut.

"Am I peering through your window?" His voice lowers even more, gaining an edge. "Or am I already in your apartment?" He hangs up.

True fear overtakes me. I shove my phone in my pocket and snatch the gun. He's not here. He can't be. Surely he wouldn't be that reckless...

I take a deep breath and down the rest of my glass of whisky. If he's here, I'll deal with it. Simple. End of story. I may be a sheltered Mafia princess, but I *am* a Mafia princess, and I have the training to match. I'm not helpless. Da made sure of that.

I've been in my living room and kitchen. This apartment is bigger than it has any right to be, courtesy of Dad refusing to allow me to pay for it. He wanted me in a good part of town, and while my pay from bookkeeping for the family business is solid, Luke's income isn't much, even with the recent job change.

There's no way we could afford this place on our own. I think it bothers Luke that we take a handout from my parents, but letting them pay our rent is better than the alternative—Dad and Da coming in weekly to ensure nothing horrific has happened. I know for a fact they have an in with the building's security and keep tabs on me. It goes with the territory.

I hold the gun loosely at my side as I check the bathroom and wrench the shower curtain back. No stalker hiding there. Of course. That would be cliché. Next is the laundry room. Also empty. This is bullshit. He's bluffing. Probably. Hopefully. As much as part of me relishes the confrontation, I'm not a total fool. Egging on a stalker is a bad idea. It only ends in one of two ways.

Either I kill him.

Or he kills me.

The fear shadows my steps, still in the driver's seat. Words are on the tip of my tongue, the temptation to call out, as if *that's* ever a good idea. The bedroom suite is the last place left to check. I find myself holding my breath as I ease open the door.

At first glance, the bedroom looks exactly as I left it this morning: The bed is unmade on my side. My shoes, tossed off last night, are in proximity of the walk-in closet.

Except there's one difference.

In the center of my pillow is a small jewelry box.

"Maybe it's from Luke." Even as I say it, I know I'm reaching. When we first got together, Luke did the normal boyfriend thing of buying me jewelry for holidays. He quickly realized that my taste is incredibly eclectic, and while I appreciated the thought, I never wore what he bought me more than once or twice before it ended up in a drawer. These days, he buys... Fuck, I don't even know. The ridiculously expensive coffee I like. Sometimes we go out for meals to places I want to try. Thoughtful little things that prove he really knows me and understands what I like.

Gods, but we're boring.

Either way, there's no possibility that he suddenly started buying me jewelry again.

As tempting as it is to go straight to the box, I make myself check the closet, jerking my dresses to the side, and then the bathroom. Both are empty.

Only then do I return to the bed. I keep hold of the gun as I stare at the box; I'm not ready to let myself be even a little defenseless yet. I flip open the lid, half expecting a bomb.

It's a ring.

"What the fuck?" I sit on the bed and stare at it. It's beautiful. A large ruby nestled into a woven gold band. The band looks a little like... "Teeth." Sharp and predatory and designed to rip into prey. I snort and take it out of the box. Teeth around a drop of blood. It's pretty and over-the-top and exactly something I would have picked out for myself. "Who *is* this fucking dude?"

My phone rings, and I drop the box. I know without looking that it's *him*. I should let the call go to voicemail, but I find myself picking up the phone all the same. "What a hideous little gift."

"You love it."

I would if it were from anyone else, and that pisses me off. "I don't fuck with costume jewelry."

His chuckle makes me grit my teeth. "Nothing but the best for you, baby. This ring is special. Did you know that?"

Despite myself, I can't help perching the phone between my face and shoulder and tugging the ring out of the box. "Don't tell me you're proposing. The answer is no, Wolf."

"You haven't earned the right to be my wife, Red."

That stings, and it has absolutely no right to sting. I glare at nothing and slip the ring onto my finger. Just to see. It fits perfectly. "Fine. I'll bite. What's so special about it?"

"You'll find out." A pause. "I can't wait to see it on your finger in person. Soon, baby." He hangs up.

The front door opens.

I don't stop to think. I jump to my feet, my fear and adrenaline surging to the fore again. I knew this motherfucker was arrogant, but to walk through my front door? Absolutely not. I charge through the bedroom door, gun raised—

And nearly shoot Luke in the face.

He ducks. "Holy fuck, Ruby!"

"Sorry! Damn it, I'm sorry." I take the time to unload the gun and set it on the kitchen counter. "You startled me. I thought you wouldn't be home until later." It's not really the truth, but it's the best I can come up with on the fly.

"I wrapped the job up early." He approaches me cautiously and presses a kiss to my temple. "Is everything okay? You seem tense. I didn't even know you *had* a gun in the apartment."

"You know how my parents are. Overprotective and all. But it's just work stress." I don't exactly mean to lie, but if I tell him someone is bothering me, then I might have to admit what started it and... Fuck, Michelle is right. What are we doing? I cheated on Luke, and I don't even feel bad about it. I'm entertaining a fucking stalker because it makes me feel more alive than dating Luke does these days. "Luke...this isn't working."

To his credit, he doesn't seem surprised by me blurting out that statement. He gives me a sad smile. "No, it's really not, is it?"

"I'm sorry. I love you, but—"

"It's not like it was." He drags his hand through his thick dark hair. "*We* aren't like we were."

"No."

His expression is devastatingly sober. "I don't want to fight, Ruby. I love you too, but I don't know how to fix us either. Not like we've been going."

My chest feels tight, but there's too much relief to get this train off the tracks. "I'm sorry."

"Yeah, you keep saying that. Me too." He sighs. "I'm going to need some time to find another place. I guess I can sleep on the couch..."

"No, that's silly. This might be ending, but there's no reason to be dramatic about it. I promise not to jump you in the middle of the night. You can stay here until you get another apartment lined up."

He nods slowly. "Okay." Luke takes a step toward me and then shakes his head again. "Sorry, habit. I'm going to take a shower."

It's only when he walks away that I realize there was a smudge on his collar. Was it lipstick? I have absolutely no urge to investigate. If he slept with someone else, well, it's nothing more than I've done. Those in glass houses and all that.

3

The next day, there's a giant display of flowers sitting on my desk when I get into my office. My stomach drops. Luke was gone when I got up again, and he hasn't given me any indication that he's changed his mind about breaking up. Why would he buy me flowers?*

I circle the vase warily. This feels wrong the same way the ring—still on my finger—felt wrong. That doesn't stop me from approaching and plucking the card from the arrangement. Before I can open it, I see something else. A little rectangle nestled into the petals of one flower. I pick it up and go cold.

It's a bar of soap.

"Fuck." I drop it onto my desk and pick up the card.

We'll be using this later, dirty girl.

* FORGIVE ME—Chloe x Halle

"In your dreams, asshole." I will *not* be washing my mouth out with soap. Ever.

I pick up the vase and drop it into the trash. The bar goes in after it, followed by the card. I shouldn't be entertaining this guy, shouldn't be accepting gifts from him, no matter how perfectly suited to me they are.

I grab the ring and try to pull it off, then whimper when fiery pain erupts. "What the *fuck*?" I tug on it again and have to bite down a second whimper.

"Ruby?"

I drop my hand and straighten so fast, my head spins. "Oh, hi, Da."

My fathers have similar coloring—dark hair and pale skin—but that's where the similarities end. Dad is about my height. Da fills a doorway. He's doing that right now, his dark eyes concerned. "Did you hurt yourself?"

I am *not* about to explain that I was trying to take off a ring that apparently has prongs set into it to prevent removal. I guess I know what's special about it now. "No, not at all. Just tossing this in the trash."

He eyes the flowers. "Trouble in paradise?"

I stare. He sounds almost...happy. But that doesn't make sense. "I thought you liked Luke."

"I do." He shrugs, not even bothering to deny his tone. "He's a good kid, but that's the problem. He's not like us. And you might be a pampered Mafia princess, but you're not like him either. It was never going to last."

I stare. "But you've treated him like you're ready to walk me down the aisle to him."

"*You* liked him. That was enough for us as long as he treated you well. You seemed happy enough." Another shrug. "It's all a father can ask for."

Somehow I think Dad has a different standard. If Da gave Luke a fair chance, Dad never did. Not that he said much about it, but he doesn't say much about anything. "Well, we broke up. He's looking for another place right now."

He walks to me and pulls me into his arms. "I'm sorry, honey. I know you cared about him, even if he ultimately wasn't a good fit. You'll be okay in the end though."

I let myself sink into his hug. He has a way of wrapping me up that drowns out whatever has worried or scared or bothered me. It works now too, beating back my conflicting feelings about my current situation.

It's enough for me to take a deep breath. "What are you doing here so early?"

"Oh, that." He gives me one last squeeze and steps back. "One of our guys was killed last night. Or the day before. Hard to say."

A chill slides down my spine. "We're not at war with anyone."

"I know." Da shrugs. "But people are going to people, and he was a mean motherfucker. He probably just pissed off the wrong person, and they dealt with it. But he was one of ours, so I'm looking into it."

My mouth goes dry, but I can't stop myself from asking, "Who was it?"

"I don't think you'd know him, honey. It was Rafe, one of our newer enforcers."

The timing seems suspicious in the extreme. I can't remember the last time violence broke out in our territory, let alone murder. There are bar fights from time to time, but even the most trigger-happy of enforcers doesn't go too far for fear of bringing the territory leaders down on their head.

A coincidence. Has to be a coincidence. I don't know the name of the guy I fucked, but surely he's not the same person. We were in neutral territory, so he could easily belong to any of the territory leaders. I didn't recognize him, but that doesn't mean much; I don't interact with our enforcers.

I force a smile. "I'm sure you'll find out what happened."

"Sure will." He pulls me into another hug. "If you want to move home—"

"No, Da."

"If you want to move home," he repeats, "you know we have space for you. You don't even have to stay in your old room. We have an entire empty wing that you could redecorate to your heart's desire."

If I do that, then it's only a matter of time before Cordelia starts pushing different partners on me. She's been respectful since I started dating Luke, but I know she'd prefer me to be married to someone in the life and ideally popping out a baby or two as quickly as possible to secure the line of succession. If I move home, she'd take it as a signal that I'm ready to dance to my family's tune. I love them, but I'm not doing that.

Not yet.

I still have life to live before I'm forced to take on that role. I've spent too much time in the past two years settling. But Da means well, so I just say, "I'll think about it."

"That means no." He steps back but smiles as he says it. "It's okay, honey. We're here however you need us. And if Luke gives you any trouble, Dad and I will deal with it."

Considering how they'd do that, I'm not giving them even the smallest excuse to step in. "I have it covered. It's all being dealt with very politely."

"Politely." He snorts. "Then he's not the one for you, Ruby. Any person worth having in your life will fight to stay there, even if it means fighting dirty."

Da would know. He and Dad played all kinds of dirty to end up with Mom, but I heartily prefer not to hear *that* story. Again.

He seems to realize it. His grin is almost sheepish. "If you need help with anything, just give us a call."

"I will. I promise." I give him one last hug, and then he leaves.

I barely wait for the door to close before I rush to my computer and log in to the family database. It's a heavily encrypted monster of a program, with all the information one needs to run a criminal enterprise. Including our employee files.

It takes me thirty seconds to find the enforcer who was killed. Rafe. "Well...that's not good." I slump back in my chair, staring at the man I had sex with a few days ago. "A coincidence," I murmur. My stalker is all bark and no bite. Surely he didn't kill someone just because I fucked them. That would be...

Gods, I'm a monster. There's no other explanation for the

twin bolts of fear and desire that go through me at the thought. The feeling of pure *power*.

I shake my head, shrugging off the feeling. It's not real. It's not who I am. I may be a monster in my own way, but I'm not a murderer, and certainly not of someone who didn't deserve it. Sure, Rafe was an enforcer, so he's hardly a saint. Even in peaceful times, it's not like we're running a perfectly legal business. Which isn't to say that he deserved to die, but he definitely wasn't a civilian.

Now I'm talking myself in circles.

I pick up my phone and then set it down. "No, what am I doing? Engaging in this fucked-up game isn't okay." I need to pass this over to people who are more qualified than I am. It's time to end things with the stalker. Except... No, this isn't my fault. I may be a cheater, but I couldn't have had any way of knowing what I did would lead to someone dying.

If this is my stalker's doing.

"Only one way to find out."* It's an excuse and not even a good one. I don't care.

Me: Do you know Rafe?

It barely takes him five seconds to respond.

Unknown: Don't be a coward now, baby. What do you really want to ask me?

* PRAY—Xana

I glare at my phone. He's so *irritating*.

Me: Did you kill him?
Unknown: Your parents would have done the same thing if they saw his grimy hands all over their precious princess.

He's not entirely wrong, and I hate him for it. My parents have a firm "no enforcers" rule. At least not for hookups. It complicates things, tempts people to think they're outside the chain of command because they're in my bed. A relationship is one thing, but for casual sex, the boundary is firm. I was never tempted to break it…until that night of acting wildly out of character.

Me: You didn't answer my question.
Unknown: What do you want me to say, baby? That I slit his fucking throat for touching what's mine? That I'll do the same to anyone else who puts their hands on you?

I shiver. He's bluffing. He's got to be… Except I don't believe that, do I? I can't tell what I'm feeling. It's like my body and brain are at war. My brain is screaming that I'm playing with fire and the only way this ends is in pain and death. My body? It's got its wires crossed.

Me: Not sure what response you're looking for with that dramatic proclamation. Do you want a cookie?
Unknown: Haven't you figured it out yet, baby? I want YOU.

———

I come home to an empty apartment, but that's nothing more than I expect. It's become the usual these days. What *isn't* usual is my ensuring there's no stalker hiding in a closet before I drop my purse onto the kitchen counter and pour myself a strong glass of whisky. There's a part of me that wants to keep my wits about me...but there's a stronger part of me, buried deep, that wants an excuse to behave badly.

I don't have to pretend I'm a good person who has the right priorities when I'm seven sheets to the wind. Whatever that fucking saying means.

I take my whisky and phone into the bathroom and set them on the counter. A long scalding-hot shower does wonders on the knots forming between my shoulder blades. I'll have to get a massage soon, because there's only so much I can do to combat the tightness on my own.

By the time I turn off the water and wrap a fluffy towel around my body, I'm feeling loose and somewhere in the vicinity of relaxed. Luke still isn't home, so I drop the towel on the floor and stretch out on our bed. The sheets smell faintly of him, of us, and my guilt raises its irritating head.

The guilt's also mixed up in frustration and shame and, yes, lust.*

I don't make a conscious decision to slide my hands over my warm, naked body, but the touch feels good, so I keep going. I have a lot of pent-up tension, and this is a surefire way to release some of it. I cup my breasts and pluck at my nipples. Warmth curls through me. *Yes*, this is what I need.

* VIRTUAL REALITY—rey

I tease myself, dragging my fingertips over my stomach to my pussy. I spread my legs and circle my clit lightly. Delicious tingles start low in my stomach. I want to take my time with this, to really work off my stress.

My phone rings.

I open my eyes. I'm not even sure when I shut them. "I should have put the damn thing on silent." I ignore the call until it goes to voicemail...and then the phone immediately starts ringing again. "Motherfucker."

I grab it with my free hand and curse even harder when I see **UNKNOWN** as the caller. Now's the time to put my cell on silent or even turn it off. I don't do either.

Instead, I answer. "You're interrupting."

His slow chuckle makes things low in my stomach clench. I could pretend it's because I'm still circling my clit, but that's not entirely the truth. "Do you think you deserve an orgasm after how you've been acting, baby? Fucking mobsters and running your mouth every chance you get."

I circle my clit faster. What the fuck is wrong with me that his almost threats make this hotter? "As if you're not just as bad as a mobster."

"You're right. I'm worse." Another of those delicious low laughs. "Why don't you let me fuck you instead? I'll do a better job of it."

My curtains are closed. There's no way he should be able to see what I'm doing. He's bluffing. "I'm not fucking myself."

"Not yet," he agrees easily. "Stop teasing that clit and give your needy pussy your fingers."

Again, my fear rises. Again, it makes my desire deeper, hotter. "Are you watching me, Wolf?"

"Always, baby."

Either he's bluffing…or he's got cameras in my room. It's possible. Probable even. He was here to leave the ring, so he had the opportunity. Bastard. "You're a creep, you know that?" I put my phone on speaker and drop it onto the bed next to me. I could blame this on the whisky, but I'm barely buzzed. No, it's *danger* I'm drunk on. "You want to fuck me, Wolf? Come do it."

I roll over onto my stomach and knees, the new position putting my ass in the air. It feels extra vulnerable, which makes me work my clit harder. It's not enough, but I knew it wouldn't be. I slide two fingers into my pussy, almost shocked at how wet I am.

He hasn't responded. I've startled him. *Good.*

My orgasm is close, flirting with the edges of my awareness.

"You want me to fuck you, Red?" His voice is different. Even more ragged. I think there's an accent, but I can't be sure. "You want me to give that pretty cunt all the things you've been too much of a good girl to ask for?"

I finger myself harder, faster. This isn't real. He's not here, for all that his presence saturates the room. "Big words for a guy who isn't even in the room," I gasp.

"Give your clit some love, baby."

Without having any intention of obeying, my fingers move from my pussy to my clit. I'm so sensitized, it's almost too much. "Fuck."

"That's right. Come for me, Red. Say my name when you do."

I can't give him that. I *won't*. My orgasm rises and crests, and with my last little bit of willpower, I moan, "Luke!"

A beat of silence. "You're going to pay for that."

"Prove it." I roll onto my back. It was a good orgasm, but it wasn't enough. I'm not satiated in the least. My body is one throbbing knot of desire, and my fingers aren't going to get the job done, no matter how many times I come. Damn it. I drag in a rough breath. "Did you put cameras in my bathroom too, Wolf?"

He makes me wait for his answer. "No."

I shouldn't trust him, but strangely, I do. He hasn't lied to me yet. "Goodbye."

"Red."

My finger hovers over the red button to hang up, but I hesitate. "What?"

"Let's stop playing this coy shit. Friday. Eleven. The Broken Tree. The first guy who talks to you will be me. I want you in that bathroom with your skirt up and my cock buried inside you within five minutes."

I can barely breathe. I may have fucked Rafe under nearly identical circumstances, but I could at least pretend I didn't know he was a murderer. Wolf has blood on his hands, and he's not even trying to convince me otherwise. "Now who's playing coy? Friday is days away, and I just whetted my appetite. Who knows what I could get up to in the meantime?"

"You know what happens if you let someone else touch what's mine."

"You keep saying that as if I'm a sure thing. I'm not." Probably.

He laughs harshly. "Yes, baby, you are. The only question

remaining is how many people you're going to get killed while you pretend otherwise."

"I'm not meeting you."

"See you Friday. And leave the panties at home." He hangs up.

"Mother...*fucker*." Am I breathless at his audacity or because the thought of obeying makes my pussy clench?

I don't know.

The ache in my body only gets worse as I mentally play through the scenario he painted. Of *his* rough voice in my ear as he picks me up and sets me on the bathroom counter. Of his possessive touch as he flips up my skirt and fucks me like he owns me. I hate it and love it in equal measure, but it gets me so hot, I can barely stand it.

I spread my thighs wide. "If you're watching, Wolf...enjoy the show." I don't stop for a very, very long time.

4

The tension of waiting for Friday is getting to me. Luke is gone more often than he's home again today, and I think there's another trip on the horizon. Not that it's my business anymore. Wolf has been remarkably silent since I masturbated on the phone with him. I should be grateful for the small reprieve, but I can't help feeling like this absence is the calm before a storm. I still haven't decided whether I'm going to answer his summons or not, and I have just over twenty-four hours left.*

Either way, I'm pathetically grateful for the distraction of Michelle inviting me out.

I keep a wary eye on my phone as I get ready. It should be a relief not to hear from Wolf today—maybe he's gone off to terrorize some other Mafia princess—but I find myself checking my cell more than is wise. And every time there's nothing from him, my stomach dips a little.

* DREAM GIRL EVIL—Florence + The Machine

My phone buzzes, and I get another of those awful dips when I realize it's Michelle video calling. I give myself a shake and paste a smile on my face. "Hey, girl."

"I forbid you from cancelling."

That surprises a laugh out of me. "Who says I'm thinking about cancelling?"

"Call it my best friend superpower." She looks amazing, as always, her hair pulled back in a wet look that gives fuck-me-in-the-shower vibes. "Check out this dress." She turns the camera to face a full-length mirror, and I actually gasp. The dress is stunning, a slick bodycon masterpiece that hugs her generous curves and looks almost transparent. She moves, and I realize the translucence is a trick of the light and fabric. Clever.

"There's no way your dad is letting you out of the house in that."

"I'm an adult and can make my own clothing decisions." She sounds startlingly like her mother when she says it. Michelle flips the camera back around and glares into it. "My superpower was right. You're not even ready."

"I just need to put on my dress." I spent entirely too much time on my makeup and hair, fighting my straight tresses into some semblance of waves and pairing subtle smoky eyes with crimson lips.

She frowns like she doesn't believe me. "What dress are you wearing?"

"I don't know now. You're going to show me up," I say teasingly.

"Yeah, yeah, I show everyone up." She closes her eyes, and I get the distinct impression that she's going through my closet by memory. Michelle has inherited her mother's fashion sense but not the desire to create clothing for other people. "The sheath dress. The black one. Don't wear anything under it but your best lingerie. We're getting you *fucked* tonight, my friend."

The dress she's talking about actually *is* sheer. The cut is loose and high along my throat, but it barely hits the tops of my thighs, and while it hangs dramatically wide, it's meant to be worn with a shift underneath. "Bold statement."

"On all counts." She grins, completely unrepentant. "Also, Zayne is coming out. I couldn't convince Guinevere to join us, and Cassim never returns my calls, so he didn't get an invite. Jo is busy doing...something...with Kiley and Sunara. Probably playing checkers with how boring those three are. Talia said maybe."

"Talia always says maybe and then doesn't come." The heirs and spares of Carver City all attended a private school on neutral territory in our formative years. I think the goal was to create a bond between us so that the peace would last past our parents' generation. It worked with me and Michelle—and Zayne, though he's a spare. The rest? We're friendly enough when it's required, but I wouldn't call us friends.

"Hope springs eternal. I called you a car. It will be there in ten, so you better be ready. Love you. See you soon." She hangs up before I can curse her out for being bossy.

I grab the dress she recommended though. And while I throw on my best black lace panties, I bypass the bra entirely. Instead, I take a minute to use some makeup to make my nipples appear like hearts. Michelle wants to get me fucked tonight? I'm going to make sure it happens.

What happens if Wolf kills them?

I shove the thought aside. I can't even prove he killed Rafe, for all that he acted like he's responsible. He might have been bluffing.

The reasoning feels flimsy, but I don't let that stop me from yanking on sky-high heels and hurrying down to the sidewalk to meet the car Michelle called. As it pulls from the curb, my phone dings with a text.

Wolf: Going somewhere?

I glare at my phone. So he *was* watching me today. He just decided that I didn't deserve attention. Well, fuck that. If he won't give me attention, then someone else will. I snap a picture of myself, ensuring he can clearly see my heart-shaped nipples. I send him the photo.

Me: I'm going to get fucked.
Wolf: Baby, you try my patience. Friday is tomorrow.

I grin even as my heart beats faster.[*]

Me: I already told you I'm not showing up.
Wolf: Liar.
Me: You're just my stalker. You don't get to tell me what to do.
Wolf: Wrong on both counts.
Me: Do you like my dress, BABY?

[*] USE ME (BRUTAL HEARTS)—Diplo feat. Sturgill Simpson and Dove Cameron

Wolf: Flashing your tits at anyone who looks. You're about to make me have to blind the whole damn club.

I snort.

Wolf: Don't try to call my bluff tonight, Ruby. You won't like what happens.

I stare at my phone. This is the first time he's called me by my actual name. The warning is a big flashing neon sign. It makes me wet.

I don't know what the fuck is wrong with me. At this point, I've made my peace with it. I've spent my whole life unaware of how deep my well of recklessness truly goes—at least until recently. Now I'm in a speeding car with no brakes. Crashing is the only way to stop.

You could ask for help.

"I'm not ready for it to be over," I whisper. I send a quick reply.

Me: I guess we'll see, won't we?

I drop my phone into my purse without waiting for a response. He left me hanging all day. It's only polite to return the favor. I decide to ignore the small voice pointing out that I'm treating my stalker like there's something between us. There's not. Or at least nothing I want to explore. He's bringing out something toxic and dangerous in me, and if I had any sense, I'd cut him out of my life the way I'd cut rot out of an apple.

It's a quick drive to the Tower, a club that brings in an interesting mix of college students, businesspeople lingering after happy hour, and a scattering of people in the life. I don't know that we consciously picked a club in Yasmina's territory as the place to congregate, but this choice ensures there's no friction with the various territory leaders. My parents never feel perfectly comfortable when I end up in Ursa's part of town. They haven't forgotten the threat she represented in the time after my grandfather died.

The club itself is exactly as it used to be when I'd come here all the time, first with a fake ID that Zayne sourced and then legally at twenty-one: bumping music, a packed dance floor, and a VIP section that circles the top and is filled with private booths that allow us to people watch like modern-day royals looking at our subjects.

Michelle appears in front of me, looking even better in person than she did in the video. She pulls me into a tight hug. "You really came."

"I said I was going to."

"Yeah, but this is twice in a week. How many times have you cancelled in the last year?"

Shame heats me as I realize she's right. I've been going through the motions in more ways than one.

I give her a bright smile. "All that changes now. I'm here. Let's do it like we did in the old days." Not that I ever allowed myself to go as hard as she did. But maybe that changes now. I'm single, stalker or no.

"That's my girl." She hooks her arm through mine. "Zayne already claimed our customary booth. Drinks are on the way."

I lift my brows. "Then what are you doing down here?"

"Just getting a closer look at the options." She grins. "But it's early yet. We have time to do our picking later."

Michelle practically drags me to the dramatic staircase leading up to the VIP section. Our booth is right in the center, though there's more than enough privacy to encourage getting up to illicit deeds. Zayne lounges in the middle of it, arms outstretched across its curved back.

He smirks when he sees me, the pretty bastard. "Look who the ball and chain let out."

"No more ball, no more chain." Michelle releases me to drop down on one side of him, and I sink onto the other side.

He looks at me with interest. Zayne is built just like his father, athletic, with medium-brown skin and thick dark hair, and he's got his mother's beauty. He's downright *pretty*. Tonight he's wearing a black suit with faint dark purple pinstripes that elevate the look.

"It's recent," I say into the silence that stretches. "I'm still getting used to it, and he hasn't moved out yet. That's why I haven't told you."

Also the fact that we don't talk as much as we used to. We haven't since Luke and I started dating. Initially it was out of respect for my new boyfriend, because Zayne and I fucked a very long time ago before deciding we were better as friends. He flirts outrageously with anyone who comes into his sphere, regardless of their relationship status. Then the space was just...easier.

Which is kind of shitty, now that I think of it.

I clear my throat. "How have you been?"

He shrugs. "Same old, same old. Got a promotion to COO, which irritates Cassim to no end, but I've put in the work. He's CFO now, but he'll take CEO when Mother retires... If she retires."

"She'll retire." Michelle leans against his side and props her head on his shoulder. "Just like eventually my old man will get tired of all the bullshit and step down. Cassim might think he wants that, but it just means more work for him."

"Sometimes I think he gains sustenance from work."

"And Sunara?" All the heirs and spares are clustered in age except for Cassim, who's the oldest. But Zayne, Michelle, the twins, and I are the same age. Kiley, Sunara, and Michelle's sibling, Jo, are the youngest. Only by two years, but I can't help seeing them as the babies.

He shrugs. "Same old, same old. Her nose is always stuck in a book, and she avoids every party our parents host." His dark eyes sharpen with interest. "That's a cool ring. Where did you get it?"

I have to fight the urge to shove my hand behind me. There are a dozen reasons I've kept the ring on, each flimsier than the next. The truth is that I could suffer through some scratches and remove it. I just...haven't. "Just something new. It was a gift."*

He narrows his eyes, no doubt to ask who gifted it to me, but the waitress walks up, her tray full of drinks. Instantly the threat of an inquisition is gone, and Zayne is all charm, his focus entirely on the waitress. "Thank you, beautiful. You knew just the thing I needed."

The waitress *is* beautiful, with warm dark brown skin,

* BABY SAID—Måneskin

gloriously full lips, and breasts that press against the low cut of her top. She's also incredibly familiar. She's worked here a long time, and she was definitely a regular in the VIP bar when I used to come around more often. Her name is…Natasha! That's it.

It strikes me all over again that I can flirt with—can seduce—anyone I want. I'm allowed to. I'm single.

What about Wolf?

I ignore the voice, just like I've been ignoring it all day. It's time to have some fun.

5

lean forward, propping my arm on Zayne's thigh, and give Natasha my best charming grin. "Don't listen to him. He's a terrible flirt."

The smile she turns on me is significantly warmer than the one she gave him. "I know. I've worked here a long time." She laughs. "But he tips like a dream."

"One day, you'll stop breaking my heart, Nat."

"Hold your breath. Maybe it'll happen faster." She nods at me. "Nice to see you around here again, Ruby. It's been a long time."

Michelle leans over Zayne, causing him to grumble good-naturedly, and motions at me like I'm a prize on a game show. "Ruby is newly single. Isn't that a trip?"

"Newly single, huh?" Natasha sets the drinks onto our table, lingering a little longer than strictly necessary in front of me, and then leans in. "Maybe we should get a drink sometime when I'm not on the clock."*

My mouth is suddenly dry. The possibilities make my head spin. Natasha is so gorgeous, I have to drag in a breath and pause in order to not stumble over my words. "Sure. We could do that."

Zayne waits for her to move away before he leans against me dramatically. "I changed my mind. You need to be back in a relationship. There's enough competition with this wild one." He jerks his thumb at Michelle. "No one is going to want to fuck me with the two of you as options."

"You're so sweet." Michelle presses a quick kiss to his cheek and grabs her drink. "But you're right. You can't compare. You do, however, make an excellent wingman."

"That's what they all say." He sobers. "But you're really okay, Ruby? He didn't break your heart, did he? Luke was pretty cool, but I won't hesitate to break his kneecaps."

I laugh a little, though threats of violence are never quite a joke in our world. "No, I broke up with him. He's been a perfect gentleman."

Zayne snorts. "No wonder you left his ass."

"Why do people keep saying that?"

Michelle and Zayne share another look and snort. She finally downs her drink. "Please tell me you're joking when you ask that question. You had, like, a couple years of testing the waters in college, but before you had a chance to really let your freak flag fly, Luke locked you down. You wouldn't have—" She cuts herself off at my warning look, but it's too late.

* WHEN YOU SAY MY NAME—Chandler Leighton

Zayne swivels to face me. "What happened? What did I miss?"

"It's nothing."

Michelle flags down Natasha. "Babe, we need some shots." She barely waits for Natasha to get out of earshot to say, "If you call cheating on Luke with some lowly muscle in a shitty bar nothing."

I fully expect Zayne to join in on the laughter at my expense, but his gaze goes serious. "Ruby, what the fuck?"

Shame threatens to heat my skin. It *was* a shitty thing to do, but Luke and I are over now. We weren't going to be less over if I didn't cheat on him. Yeah, that logic feels like a stretch.

I look away. "So I'm not perfect. Sue me. Are we having fun tonight, or should I just go home?"

"Don't be like that." Michelle reaches over Zayne and playfully smacks my knee. "You read me the riot act when I fucked that actress. You don't fuck up often. Forgive me if I'm conflicted by it."

Zayne tilts his head back against the booth and exhales loudly. "The actress was on a downward spiral and wanted to run off to Vegas and marry you. Forget Uncle Hook—your mother would have chopped her up into little pieces."

I give him a sharp look. "Tink wouldn't do that, and you know it." Probably. She may have bought into the life we lead, but she still keeps her hands clean of the necessary ugliness that a territory leader must be part of. Most of the time. When it comes to her kids, all bets are off.

"No, he's right. It's not just the marriage. Clary had a constant cocktail in her bloodstream. She started with microdosing, but it got out of control. She's doing better these days."

Zayne blinks. "Tell me you're not checking up on her."

Michelle's expression shutters. "That's enough talking about exes. That's a brunch conversation, and we're out for drinks."

"More than drinks. Our girl is on the *rebound*." Zayne motions toward the railing that overlooks the dance floor, as magnanimous as a king. "Pick your poison, Ruby. Who will it be tonight?"*

I rise, dodging his half-hearted attempt to slap my ass, and move to the railing. The dance floor is even more crowded than it was when I came in, bodies pressed together as closely as lovers.

My skin prickles. Someone is watching me. I scan the room below, trying to note anyone paying undue attention to me, but it's an impossible endeavor. If Wolf is here, I'd never know. There are too many people. He could be anyone.

But when I follow my instincts to the person causing my senses to ping, it's a woman I've seen around before. I can't remember her name, but I *do* remember Zayne shooting his shot with her, like, six months ago and being turned down so fast, he came back to the VIP lounge with his tail tucked between his legs. Truly, he has excellent taste. She's built like an Amazon, tall and thick, cocking a full hip against the bar as she stares boldly at me.

Her long wavy dark hair makes her pale skin stand out. Which, in turn, brings my attention to her dark red lips. And the tight pants she's wearing, paired with a lacy red bra that shows off her impressive tits. Tattoos climb up her sides, but I can't see the details of them from this far away.

* FEEL—Måneskin

She lifts her glass and tilts her head to the side. I can't tell if it's an invitation or a challenge.

I twist to catch sight of Natasha. As gorgeous as she is, it's smarter not to fuck the people who work at our favorite places. It's like pissing where you eat. "Hey, Nat, what's the tall beauty's name?"

She peeks over the railing and whistles. "You have expensive taste. That's Tatiana. She's an escort who's started hanging around the club on her time off. She's cool, and she doesn't step on toes, which Cassim was initially worried about. You could do worse."

An escort.

No wonder she sent Zayne packing before. He might be a trust fund baby, but no doubt she's here to enjoy herself rather than work. I'm just reckless enough to attempt to succeed where my friend failed. "What's her poison?"

Natasha laughs under her breath. "Macallan 1946."

Jesus. She wasn't kidding about having expensive taste. "Is that what she buys herself or what she tells assholes who want to buy her a drink?"

"Both." Natasha grins. "You have your hands full with that one."

Only for tonight. "Send her the drink and an invite to the booth, please." I turn and press a couple hundred dollars into her palm. "Put it on my tab. This is for *you*."

"At least it won't be a dull night." She pockets the money and disappears down the stairs.

I should probably play it cool, but I'm too curious to move away from the railing. I watch Natasha slide next to Tatiana and speak directly into her ear. Tatiana laughs, and even though there's no way I could possibly hear it from here, I swear I do.

Or maybe that's my phone buzzing.

I don't tear my gaze away from the woman now holding the shot glass, an amused expression on her face. I lift my phone to my ear. "I'm busy."

It's nearly impossible to hear with the loud music, yet I can pick out Wolf's words easily. "Wrong answer, Red."

A chill shoots down my spine, quickly followed by desire. His voice is just as cold as ever, but there's a thread of pure fury in it. I watch in amazement as Tatiana downs her drink as a shot instead of sipping it. Holy shit, this woman is something else. Maybe she's got a beast inside her too. I can't quite pull my attention from where her dark red lipstick leaves a mark on the glass. "It's not fun when the shoe is on the other foot, is it?"*

He pauses. When he speaks again, there's a hint of a growl in his voice. "Did you miss my texts today, baby? Feeling neglected?"

"Don't be absurd." I crook my finger at Tatiana, and she nods and starts working her way toward the VIP section. "You're my stalker. You could vanish tomorrow, and I'd be relieved."

"Little liar." He lowers his voice until I have to strain to hear him. "You're mine. Don't think that just because you broke up with that asshole you can go around giving that pussy to anyone who looks at you."

"It's my pussy. If I want to bend over and let the whole club have a chance at me, that's my prerogative."

"You really do love the color red."

* TOUCH—July Talk

I blink. "What are you talking about?"

"You know what. I'll butcher anyone you let touch you. And I'm *always* watching, Red. Anyone gets to fuck you, it's going to be me. You fuck someone else, I'm going to take it poorly."

"That's a shame. Because I have a gorgeous escort coming up here to rock my world."

He's silent for a beat, as if I've surprised him. "An escort. You mean—"

I hang up. It's petty and will no doubt incite him, but...I like it. That feeling I've been chasing ever since the reckless decision to fuck Rafe is back, and it's stronger than ever. I feel at home in my body, my adrenaline racing, my skin sensitized.

Tatiana comes to stand at the railing. She's got two lowball glasses in her hands, and she presses one into mine, standing a little too close. "For you."

I raise my brows but lift it to my lips all the same. It's a bad idea to take an open drink from someone I don't know, but I don't give a fuck. I'm in motion, and nothing can stop me now. "Thanks."

She mirrors my move, sipping the liquor at the same time. It burns down my throat, but her expression gives no indication that she's choking on fire right now. She looks even better up close, her skin luminous and her long dark hair just messy enough to suggest someone was running their fingers through it. Maybe her. Maybe someone else.

"What is this?" I hold up the glass and swirl the amber liquid.

"Macallan 1946."

I blink. "Do you know how expensive those drinks are?"

Tatiana laughs, the sound low and sinful. "Honey, I drink them regularly, so yes, I am aware. I was...touched...by your offer to buy me a drink." She sinks enough innuendo into the word *touched* to drown the whole club in lust.

I'm not immune. I don't want to be. I lean in and get a hint of her perfume: something spicy and just as tempting as every other part of her. "So do you come here often?"

"You can do better than that. I clocked you the moment you came through the door, but that doesn't mean you can get away with giving me less than your A game." She trails her long red nails on my bare arm. "I like the dress."

"Oh yeah?" I'm having a hard time drawing a breath.

"Mm-hmm." Her nails reach the sleeve of my dress and drag over the seam until she's brushing her knuckles against my throat. "I play the game for a living. When it comes to my off time, I prefer to be direct. I saw you and I wanted you. I think you want me too."

I can't tell if this is happening too fast or at exactly the right pace. I can't even blame the alcohol; I'm barely buzzed. "You're forward."

"Life is too short to be anything but what you truly are. Don't you think?"

She's not saying anything I haven't thought, and recently, but there's a part of me that still hesitates. Worst of all, I know *why* I'm hesitating. Wolf. Not even because he's threatened to bathe the club in the blood of anyone who touches me. There's a connection there, and I don't know what it means. He's claimed me, but that doesn't mean I'm *his*. We're not dating. We're sure as fuck not exclusive, murder of Rafe or no.

No. Damn it, *no*. I'm not going to let my fucking stalker decide what I will or won't do.

It still feels a little like a betrayal to lean into Tatiana's touch.

Her smile widens. "You want to get out of here?"

That's a bad idea. One even I know better than to give in to. I don't know this woman, and for better or worse, I am who I am. She could lead me right into a trap...or I could do the same to her, courtesy of Wolf.

I lick my lips. "Why don't we sit and chat for a bit?"

Her smile twists as if I've disappointed her. "Sure, baby, whatever you want."

Baby.

It's a common enough pet name, but something about the way she says it feels almost pointed. I clear my throat. "Don't call me that."

Instantly, her expression softens. "Oh. Sorry. Of course. Do you have an issue with pet names in general or that one specifically?"

"That one." More information is on the tip of my tongue, but giving it would once again feels like I'm accepting Wolf's claim on me. I'm not. Truly, I'm not.

"How about I call you lovely then? You certainly fit the bill." She finally drops her hand, and I have to stop myself from grabbing her wrist and placing it back on my throat.

"That works," I manage.

"Perfect. Introduce me to your friends." She turns and heads to our table, where Michelle and Zayne aren't even trying to pretend they're not watching avidly.

I take a step to follow her, and my phone buzzes insistently. I almost ignore it, but I know exactly who's calling. "I'll be right there. I have to take this."

Tatiana glances over her shoulder and winks at me. "Don't take too long, or I might change my mind about who I'm fucking tonight."

"Wouldn't dream of it." I head to the short hallway that leads to the bathrooms. It's only mildly quieter here, but I should be able to take the call without screaming. More, it offers the illusion of privacy, and I don't want Zayne or Michelle asking questions.

Sure enough, it's Wolf.

He barely waits for me to answer before he starts in. "Not her, baby."

I turn and look out over the VIP section. It's filled to the brim tonight, all the booths occupied. Some of the people I saw on my path to this hallway were regulars when I used to come out more, and others are new, but none of them seemed to be paying any attention to me. And none of them were on their phone.

What am I talking about? There's background sound on my side of the call, not Wolf's. He's not here. I don't know how he knows what's going on, but he's not calling me from inside the club.

I clear my throat. "Again, see the point where you don't own me or my pussy. I'll fuck who I want."

"Not *her*, Ruby." There's something in his voice again, another hint of an accent I can't quite place. It only seems to come out when he's feeling particularly intense. "If she lays one finger on you, I'll break it."

"Wow, you're downgrading. Cute." I don't know why I say

it. He's proven himself to be dangerous, and even if he's bluffing about killing Rafe, he's still more than capable of hurting someone like Tatiana. She's savvy and obviously able to take care of herself, but she's not local. The rules are different for us. "She's not one of the families." Though she might be in the life. It's not like I'd know. I can't tell if I'm bluffing or being honest. "She's off-limits."

"Your rules. Not mine."

I force myself to power through the instinctive reaction to fold. "And what if *I* touch *her*? Are you going to break *my* fingers? Cut off my tongue?"

He curses, low enough that I can't pick out the words. When he speaks again, his voice is so cold, I shiver. "You keep testing me, thinking you can get away with anything just because no one's ever taken you to task. Don't, baby. You aren't going to like what happens if you do this."

"So you keep saying. Prove it."

"If you hang up on me one more fucking time—"

I hang up. It's shortsighted and a terrible idea, but I've already made a long streak of bad choices. No reason to get smart now.

Plus, there's a small horrible part of me that wants to call Wolf's bluff, to push him into *something*. No matter what the response is or who's hurt by it.

6

Back at the table, Tatiana has made herself at home with my friends. Zayne is hanging on her every word, practically salivating at her proximity. Michelle has her arms crossed over her chest and her expression shuttered again, but she's smiling. It's her lying smile.

She catches my eye and shakes her head at my questioning look. Apparently we won't be talking about whatever's bothering her tonight.

I sink down on Tatiana's other side, and she reaches over without looking at me and sets her hand on my thigh. *High* on my thigh, her pinkie skating underneath the hem of my dress, close enough to my panties that my pussy clenches in response. She's not fucking around.* I like that.

Zayne clocks the move and grins. "You have excellent taste, but you can't blame me for shooting my shot last time. You're gorgeous."

* BOYFRIEND—Dove Cameron

"I know." Tatiana laughs. "But I'm not really a one-person kind of woman. More is better." She glances at me. "As long as you don't have a problem with it."

Fucking a stranger who might get murdered by Wolf and fucking one of my few friends in this world who might get killed are two different things. It says ugly things about me that I think that way, but I am who I am.

But that doesn't mean we can't get creative.

I twist a lock of her long dark hair around my finger. If Zayne fucks Tatiana, then there's no reason for Wolf to want *him* dead. "More is definitely better." I meet Zayne's eyes over the top of her head. "It's important to me that my friends are happy, and I think making you come would make Zayne *very* happy."

Michelle stands abruptly. "I have to go."

I start to follow. "Do you want me to—"

"No, I just don't feel well. Have fun, Ruby. You deserve it. Truly." She squeezes my hand, and then she's gone, heading down the stairs.

"What was that all about?"

Zayne shrugs. "She's been acting kind of weird lately. She'll talk to us about it when she's ready."

"In the meantime..." Tatiana slides her hand higher on my thigh and cups my pussy. "I'm sure we can find a way to entertain ourselves."

"Definitely." Zayne stretches his arm over the back of the booth and leans down to kiss her throat.

We're doing this...here.

The high walls of the booth provide an element of privacy,

but ultimately we're in public, and anyone who's interested could wander over and see Tatiana tugging my panties to the side to drag her knuckles against my bare pussy. It's a light, teasing touch, designed to seduce.

It works.

I lean back against the booth and spread my legs a little. Her chuckle is low, and she wastes no time zeroing in on my clit and lightly circling there. Then Zayne reaches over to follow her lead. *No.* I grab his wrist, and then, when they both pause, I guide him to the front of her pants. "I'm not greedy. There's enough to go around."

He doesn't hesitate. He unbuttons her pants and shoves his hand inside. The material is thin enough that I can clearly see him stroke her, can see him change the angle as he presses his fingers inside her.

Tatiana shivers. "Don't stop." She grabs my panties and tugs them down my legs. My dress does nothing to hide my nakedness, but I'm too turned on to care. Or maybe I'm turned on *because* I'm practically naked in this club, and even if we're not entirely on display, we're not exactly hiding either.

There will be consequences for tonight, but I'll worry about them tomorrow.

Tatiana drinks me in and then turns to kiss Zayne. She pulls away just enough to say, "Get your cock out, handsome.* I want you to fuck me as I eat her pussy."

Zayne grins, obviously just as drunk on lust as I am. "What's the rush?"

"I have somewhere to be later." She nips his bottom lip and

* SHE CALLS ME DADDY—KiNG MALA

then shimmies out of her pants. The public nudity doesn't seem to bother her in the least, and it sure as fuck doesn't bother me when I get to see that she's not wearing a single thing underneath.

I can't help myself. As Zayne pulls his fingers from Tatiana's pussy, I grab his hand and suck him into my mouth. She tastes like heaven, like sin, like the best fucking night of my life.

She eyes my hand, and a slow grin spreads over her dark lips. "Nice ring."

She's on the move before I can come up with a response, kissing me and pushing me onto my back on the booth. Then Tatiana moves down my body, and I get a glorious look at her body. Zayne dazedly takes up position behind her. He meets my gaze and gives a rueful grin that I can't help but return. Even in my wildest plans for the night, I hadn't planned on getting into a threesome with one of my friends. Not that I'm about to put a stop to things.

Tatiana shoves up my dress. "Pretty pussy."

"You can say that again." Zayne does something with his hand that makes her jolt.

She twists to look at him. "Condom."

"Of course." He holds one up and rips it open. We both hold still as he rolls it on. Zayne doesn't fuck around with protection. He wants kids eventually, but on his terms, with the person of his choosing. Fucking is fucking, but kids are forever.

He grips her hips, his expression a mask of concentration as he thrusts forward. I know exactly how it feels to be fucked by Zayne, though I truly hope he's learned a thing or two since we lost our virginity to each other all those years ago. But to be stretched almost painfully by his big cock, to have his hands holding you in place...

Maybe I was too hasty in keeping Tatiana between us. In drawing the line in the sand with sex on one side and friendship on the other.

Then her mouth is on me, and there's no space to think about anything but her tongue shoving inside me. I can barely keep myself propped up on my elbows, but the view is worth the extra effort. She backs off just a little, leaving lipstick smeared on my pussy, and then parts me with her fingers so she can focus on my clit. Her gaze is wicked as she tastes me, as she watches my eyes practically roll back in my head when she finds the exact right stroke that has my toes curling.

I look up her body at Zayne again. He's gripping her wide hips and watching us as he fucks her slowly. Giving her time to concentrate on me. Or maybe fighting for his life because he's about to come. Either way, I mourn the fact that he's still wearing a shirt. I want to see the flex of his abs as he thrusts into her. Her ass jiggles a little with each stroke, and I bite my bottom lip, wanting to get my mouth on her more than anything. I simply *want*.

Tatiana licks and sucks her way over my pussy, once again descending to press her tongue into me as she strokes my clit with her thumb.

My pleasure goes nuclear. My elbows give out, and I collapse onto my back, spreading my legs wider to give her more space. My fingers find her wavy hair, and my hips start to move, lifting to her tongue and touch without my having any intention of doing so.

Apparently that was the thing Zayne was waiting for. Tatiana moans against my pussy as he starts to fuck her harder. His thrusts have her sliding against me, and I tighten my grip in her hair, grinding against her face in time to his strokes. I can't be certain, but I swear she chuckles against my clit.

My orgasm sweeps in like a rogue wave. One moment, my pleasure is building in steady strokes. The next, I'm crying out, not bothering to muffle my orgasm as I come all over Tatiana's face.

She doesn't stop. She presses my legs wider and licks me from back to front, moaning as Zayne fucks her harder. The careful coaxing is gone, replaced by a frenzy that has another orgasm cresting.

I drag Tatiana up to take her mouth. Zayne understands the goal immediately. He moves with her, pressing her down against my body as he keeps fucking her. I kiss her with everything I have.

I don't expect him to reach between our bodies and push two fingers into me. I hope to the gods no one can see what he's doing in the tangle of our bodies. It feels too good to stop.

Tatiana is so soft against me, her hands sliding down to grip my ass, to lift me to give Zayne better access. But she hasn't come yet, and I need that as much as I need to orgasm on Zayne's fingers. More, more, *more*. I'm a glutton for the pleasure being dealt right now. I couldn't stop even if Wolf were standing over us with a gun in his hand.*

The image hits me so hard, it drives what little thought I have from my head. I don't know what he looks like, but he's depravity personified, someone who might as well be a shadow but is infinitely more dangerous. I want him here. I want to shove his face

* DE SELBY (PART 2)—Hozier

in the fact that I'm disobeying his order. For him to have seen me coming all over Tatiana's face, see me on Zayne's hand. I want him to *choke* on the knowledge that they're touching me when he's not.

I snake my hand between our bodies to find Tatiana's clit. I pause when I encounter a piercing, but there's no time to try to get a good look. I circle her clit frantically. Zayne curls his fingers inside me. Oh fuck, I'm going to come again.

This time, Tatiana follows me. She sobs against my lips, her body shaking as we fuck her over the edge. Zayne's strokes go wild and inconsistent, and he presses his free hand to the small of her back, holding her down as he finishes inside her.

He eases back first and carefully holds the condom in place. "I'll be right back."

Tatiana gives me a deep kiss before she sits up. She stares at my pussy, at where she marked me with her deep red lipstick. "A picture worth framing."

I really am drunk on pleasure, because the next words out of my mouth are a gauntlet thrown at her feet. "So take it."

She smirks. "That's the orgasm talking, lovely."

The orgasm...and something infinitely more dangerous. "No, it's not." I grab my phone and pass it over. "Use mine. If I still want to send it to you in the morning, then I will."

"You're so bad." She says it like it's a good thing. Then her fingers are there, parting my pussy obscenely. She takes a few photos and hands my camera back.

I look at them, and holy fuck, they're hot. Her lipstick is smeared on my skin and almost perfectly matches her nails where she's touching me. I swallow hard. "You're good at this."

"Literally my job." She tugs my dress down, for all the good it does. I can still clearly see her marks through the sheer fabric. Tatiana holds up my panties. "These are lovely, but you look better without them."

Zayne walks back up, his pants once again in place. He presses a quick kiss to my lips and then a significantly longer one to Tatiana's.

She seems to melt into it but then reluctantly draws away. "I have to go."

"Stay." He trails a single finger down her stomach and stops just above her pussy. "That was barely more than a taste."

"A taste is all I have time for tonight." She snags her pants and pulls them on, carefully brushing his hand away. "But that *was* fun, so if you want more, I'll make room on my list for you." She produces a card from somewhere and presses it into his hand. "Thanks for the orgasm, handsome."

I get a card too. It's thick card stock and contains only an email. No phone number.

"If you haven't changed your mind by then, send me that picture tomorrow, lovely. I meant it when I said I'd frame it." She kisses Zayne lightly and gives me the same treatment. Then she's gone, striding away as if she didn't rock both our worlds.

Zayne slumps against me. "I think I'm in love."

"You say that all the time."

"I think I mean it this time." He slides down until his head is in my lap and then gives me a surprisingly sweet smile. "That really was only a taste. Want to go back to my place and fuck some of that frustration out? I know we decided our friendship was simpler without sex involved, but I'm still riled up."

I almost say yes, but not for any of the right reasons. I want to keep riding the high of Wolf's anger, the sharp edge of doing something I shouldn't. Playing those games with strangers is shitty. Doing it with my friends is unforgivable. I shake my head. "It'd be a poor substitute for what we both want."

"Speak for yourself." He laughs and sits up. "But yeah, I think that ship has sailed. Still, if you ever want to fuck someone else together again, that was fun. I'd do it again." His gaze shifts to the stairs, going contemplative. "I think I will book her though. Get her out of my system and all that."

I don't tell him it's a bad idea, that Cassim will lose his everloving shit if he finds out Zayne is frequenting an escort. He barely tolerates Zayne's fuckboy tendencies, and the Sarraf family cares about perception even more than my family does. It's because of how Yasmina ended up in power, and while Yasmina and Jafar are hardly puritanical when it comes to sex and sex work, Cassim is a stick-in-the-mud.

Saying as much won't change what he's going to do though. "Good luck."

"I hear the doubt in your voice, and I'm choosing to ignore it. I'm just looking for a good time, Ruby, not a spouse. Tatiana and I will have that good time, and then we'll go our separate ways." He scrubs a hand over his face. "Are you hanging out longer?"

"No, I think I'm good."

"I'll wait with you while you call a car."

I know better than to argue with him. And honestly, with Wolf's threats still ringing in my ears, I don't relish the idea of standing on a dark street corner by myself. "Okay."

We close out our tabs and wait in comfortable silence on the curb for the car to show up. We're headed in opposite directions, so I don't offer to share with him. And to be perfectly honest, I want some time alone to think about what happened tonight.

"Hey, Ruby."

"Hmm?"

"I'm glad you're back." He slings an arm around my shoulders and kisses my temple. "I missed having you around."

"I missed you too."

It's not until I'm in the car that the horrible reckless feeling rises again, not remotely sated by my activities of the night. It's the only explanation I have for pulling out my phone and sending that picture of Tatiana's fingers and lipstick on my pussy to Wolf.

The message changes over to Read, and I hold my breath as I wait for a response.

He doesn't type anything. Not on the ride home. Not as I'm showering. Not as I'm lying in my bed, staring at my phone. When I wake up in the morning, not sure when I passed out, he still hasn't texted me back.

7

Ruby, I know you're entering your loveable slut era, but there are lines."

I carefully apply brilliant scarlet lipstick in the mirror. "You've been to the Broken Tree before."*

"Yeah, which is why I know it's a bad idea." Michelle clears her throat. "Look, that was the one place where my dad lost his shit and stepped in. Do you know how humiliating it is to be collected by your father at a bar? Now multiply that by two, because that's what you'll be experiencing when *your* dads find out."

"They aren't going to find out." I finish with the lipstick and admire the effect. "I look *good*."

"Of course you do." Michelle actually seems worried in the video chat on my phone. "At least let me come with you."

"No." I finger comb my hair a bit to give it a just-been-fucked

* MERMAIDS—Florence + The Machine

look. "The last thing I need is Uncle Hook ruining my fun, which is what he'll do if you step foot in that place again."

"Ruby." Michelle leans back. "If you want to fuck someone dangerous, we can make that happen. You were acting reckless last night, but this is on another level. We could go to the Underworld—"

I stop her with a glare. "You know damn well why I'm not going to the Underworld, which is the same reason *you* don't go there. The last thing I want is for people who are practically family to witness me getting kinky and wild." Not that I'm overly kinky by nature...or at least I haven't explored that, because *where* would I explore that? At the Underworld, where my parents have a damn sex date every Saturday? No, thanks.

"Ruby." Michelle sighs. "Meg can be very discreet. She's set up a session for me a time or two in one of the private rooms. We could—"

"No." If the situation were different, that might actually be an attractive offer, but the one thing the Underworld doesn't have is my stalker. *Wolf.* Which should be a mark in the positive column. Safe, sane, and consensual are the hallmarks of good kink. There's nothing safe or sane about meeting a man who's been stalking me, one I suspect of being a murderer, in a bar that's decidedly *not* safe. Can't pretend it's not consensual though. He's hardly showing up and kidnapping me.

The thought makes my thighs clench, which just goes to show that I'm not acting rationally. I don't care. I'm in a free fall, and I don't know whether I'll land safely or smash myself to pieces. It doesn't matter, because it's too late to stop. "I'll text you when I get there and do regular check-ins."

Michelle worries her full bottom lip. "If something goes wrong—"

"It won't."

"You can say that with all the confidence in the world, but that doesn't mean you can brazen your way out of a bad situation." She hesitates. "What's going on with you?"

"If you want to talk about what's going on with me, then maybe we should talk about what happened last night. Were you pissed because Zayne wanted to fuck Tatiana or because *she* wanted to fuck *us*?"

Her expression closes down. "Neither. It had nothing to do with that."

"Okay, then what was it about?" When she doesn't immediately answer, I nod. "Thought so. I love you, I appreciate you, and I'll call you later."

"Godsdamn it, Ruby!"

I hang up and step back, getting a good look at myself in the mirror. Michelle's right to be worried. I'm out for trouble. My black skirt barely covers the essentials, and I left off panties, as ordered. My crimson top is a faux-leather under-the-bust corset that leaves a slice of stomach exposed and does wonders for my breasts, which are only covered in a matching lace bra. My only practical choice is my footwear; I went with chunky boots instead of heels.

The better to run for my life when this horrible plan inevitably goes south.

Why are you doing this?

I didn't have an answer when I started getting ready. I still don't have one an hour later when I walk through the door of the Broken Tree.

Michelle wasn't joking. This place reeks of trouble. It's dim and wreathed in smoke. Every single person here, regardless of gender, possesses an air of danger that has me fighting not to make myself smaller. I square my shoulders. I am *not* prey. I am the heir to the Belmonte territory, and I will not be cowed by a bar full of enforcers.

No one approaches me as I walk to the bar, but I can feel people's attention trailing in my wake. The woman behind the bar is small and has medium-brown skin and bright teal locs. She raises her brows. "You lost?"

"Taking a different path tonight."

She shrugs. "Suit yourself. What'll you have?"

"Bourbon. Straight."

She smirks a little, but she pours me a stiff drink and accepts the cash I slide across the bar. Then she moves down to the next patron without another word.

I lean against the bar and sip my drink, letting the alcohol take the edges off the fear curling through me. This was a mistake. I shouldn't be here. What the fuck was I thinking? If I leave now...

I feel the change in the bar the moment *he* walks through the door. Even as I tell myself to maintain my position, I turn and look. Wolf. He has to be.*

He's older than I expected. I tell myself it's not disappointment I feel at the silver in his long hair. He's attractive in a brutal

* THE GARDEN—July Talk

sort of way, pale skin weathered from the years. He wears a suit well enough; it's expensive and tailored to his broad body. I doubt he's one of ours, but he's obviously high up in whatever territory he owes allegiance to. His dark eyes land on me, and he doesn't hesitate to cross to stand in front of me.

I lick my lips. "Wolf?"

"Sure, baby." His voice is different, coarser, but I suppose that's to be expected when I've only talked to him on the phone.

I've come this far. I'm going to see this through. I step closer until our chests nearly brush. "I did what you told me." I lower my voice. "No panties."

He grins. "Let's find out."

My heart beats too hard as he takes my hand and leads me back through the bar to the bathroom. It's cleaner than I expected, but that's about all it has going for it. Wolf shuts the door behind him, and then he's pinning me to the counter and taking my mouth. He tastes like cigarettes, which is…not great. He palms my pussy roughly, which doesn't feel bad exactly, but it's also…not great.

Damn, this is disappointing.

"No panties," he murmurs against my lips. "I like it."

He lifts me onto the counter and sinks to his knees before me. *Okay, this is more like it.* He said he'd have me on his cock inside of five minutes, but I guess we haven't hit that time limit yet.

Wolf flips up my skirt. "Nice." Then his mouth is on my pussy, and yeah, I can get on board with this.

I relax into the feeling of his tongue dragging through my folds and then spearing inside me. Okay, this is better than nice.

At least Wolf appreciates a good tongue fucking. He moves up to suck on my clit, drawing a little moan from my lips. "*Fuck.*"

Behind him, the door swings silently open.

My orgasm is bearing down on me, and at some point, my hands found their way into his hair, so it doesn't register at first that we're no longer alone. At least until the masked man steps into the bathroom.

Did I think the silver fox with his tongue in my pussy had a dangerous aura? What a joke. My blood practically ices over the moment *he* steps into the room. His mask is a stylized skull with cheekbones that seem sharper than they should be, eye sockets deep enough that I can't see his eyes, and teeth hiding his mouth. He's dressed in a black sweatshirt with the hood pulled up and jeans, both totally nondescript. His mundane clothing doesn't detract from the menace rolling off him in waves.

This is the real Wolf.

He eases the door shut behind him and leans against it, arms crossed.

Oh fuck. I'm in so much trouble. I try to pull on not-Wolf's hair to get him off me, but he just moans and sucks my clit harder. Even with fear so thick in my throat that I can taste it—or maybe *because* of it—my orgasm rises again, sharper this time. "Stop," I murmur. He doesn't stop. And then it's too late. I come with a cry that feels like a warning. A warning he doesn't heed.

As soon as I orgasm, not-Wolf shoves to his feet, and his hands go to the front of his pants. He never gets a chance to get his cock out.

My Wolf moves. He grabs a fistful of the man's hair and

yanks his head back. I barely get a chance to scream before he slices a long knife over the man's throat. Hot blood sprays my chest and thighs and pussy.

The body slumps to the ground, and Wolf takes his place. "You've been a bad girl, Red." And that, that is the voice that's been talking low and threateningly to me on the other end of the phone.

"I—"

He grabs my hips and jerks me off the counter while spinning me around to pin me against it. In the mirror, his mask makes him look like a death god, come to punish me for my transgressions.

At my feet, the body is still twitching. *Oh fuck, oh fuck, oh fuck.*

Wolf leans down until the cool surface of his mask touches my face. "Always so eager to give this pussy away to those undeserving." He spears two fingers into me from behind.

I cry out, and I can't begin to say if it's in protest or demand for more. I brace my hands on the counter and tilt my hips, giving him better access. "I'm sorry."

"No, you're not." He wedges a third finger into me. He's being rough, but fuck, it feels good. "But you will be."

Against all reason, pleasure coils tightly inside me. He's found my G-spot, and he's working it in short, rough strokes. I can't think, can't move, can't do anything but make a pathetic whimpering sound. "Wolf, please."

He jerks his fingers out of me and flips me to face him. "Back on the counter."

I resume my position on the bathroom counter. He clasps my throat loosely with one gloved hand. It kills me that I can't see his eyes. I might as well be touched by some otherworldly being. Too much distance, yet I love it all the same.

"Open your legs for me and accept your punishment."

I don't hesitate. I spread my legs for him and moan against his hand around my throat as he shoves three fingers back into me. He circles my clit with his thumb and curls his fingers against my G-spot.

"Oh, f—"

"What did I tell you about that language, Red?" He presses down on my throat, cutting off my air even as he winds me up higher and higher.

It feels so fucking good that I attempt to drag in a breath, but there's no air to be had. I wrap my hands around his wrist, trying to get him to back off, but he just pins me harder. He's not crushing me, but I can't fucking breathe, and holy shit. Oh gods.

I orgasm. It's as if every bit of my panic transforms into pleasure, and he eases his palm back so I can drag in a long inhale of sweet oxygen, and then I'm coming even harder. It feels like my bladder is going to give out, and I squirt all over his hand and forearm. Only then does he start fucking me slowly with his fingers, in long strokes that draw my orgasm out. I look down and belatedly realize he's still wearing his leather gloves.

He never actually touched me.

That shouldn't matter...but it does. "Wolf," I rasp. "You promised to have your cock inside me within five minutes."

He slaps my pussy. Hard. "Next time, don't give away what's mine, Red." He guides me to lean against the mirror, and then he moves back. He catches my hand and lifts it, the ring he gifted me glinting in the low light. "This marks you as mine, baby. Don't forget it." Before I can find the words to make him stay, he slips out the door.

In the distance, there's a familiar voice roaring, "Ruby, where the fuck are you?"

Oh shit. That's Uncle Hook. Michelle ratted me out.

I barely have enough time to yank my skirt into place before the door flies open and in walks the man who's my uncle in every way but blood. He's nearly as tall as Da, though he's built a little leaner, his long dark hair pulled back in a messy bun and his medium-brown skin flushed with anger. "Ruby!" He stops short at the sight of me. At the dead man at my feet. "What the fuck is going on here?"

"I can explain." Except...can I? I'm still not sure I've processed what the fuck just happened. I had the wrong guy going down on me. Wolf *killed* him. And then I came all over *his* hand while he choked me.

Uncle Hook shakes his head. "Not another word. We'll take care of this."

True fear flickers to life for the first time. "You can't tell Da. Or any of them. You *can't.*"

His dark eyes are sympathetic, but he's already shaking his head. "It's too late, Ruby girl. They're already on their way to my place. They'll beat us there."

I'm going to kick Michelle's ass for this. I am in *so* much trouble.

Uncle Hook holds out his hand, his expression devastatingly kind. "Come here. Don't look down."

At the dead man at my feet. The one he obviously thinks I killed.

Didn't I?

Wasn't there part of me that knew he couldn't possibly be Wolf? The vibe had been off, and I didn't question it. I didn't *want* to question it. Maybe part of me wanted to punish Wolf for not being the first one to actually talk to me. Maybe part of me wanted to call his bluff.

Joke's on me.

There's no window to throw myself out of, and Uncle Hook takes up most of the doorway. There's no escaping what comes next. I curse myself for my recklessness and put my hand in his. He easily urges me over the dead body and whisks me out of the bathroom. The bar itself is empty but for the bartender.

She holds up her hands when Uncle Hook cuts her a harsh look. "I saw nothing."

"No, you didn't." His gaze gentles on me, but there's no opportunity to escape here either as he hauls me through the bar and out into the waiting SUV. It's only when we're safely inside and driving away that he speaks to me again. "You don't have to answer this, not to me, but if it's easier to talk to me than your parents..."

Understanding dawns, bringing with it even more humiliation. He's asking if I was assaulted. If it was a justified kill. It would be so easy to lie, but I can't. I just *can't*. Not about that. "That's not what happened." Yes, he kept going even after I tried to get him to stop, but if he hadn't been about to be murdered, I don't know that I would have stopped him. And sure, he wasn't exactly honest about who he was, but I didn't slow down enough to verify... Gods, my head hurts. Maybe it turned into an attempted assault, but that's not the real reason he's dead, and it feels wrong to pretend he died for any other reason than the selfish impulsiveness that led me to that bar with the intent to fuck my stalker.

Uncle Hook's shoulders dip the tiniest bit. "If you—" He doesn't believe me.

"Jesus fuck, he didn't do anything to me I didn't want him to. I went back there of my own free will. Things got out of control, but not like *that*."

His brows slam down, but he seems to rein himself in forcibly. Probably still wondering if I'm protesting too much. This man has been a fixture in my life since I was born. He won't believe that I killed a man in cold blood any more than my parents will.

I *didn't* kill the man in question, but that seems a small enough detail considering the fact that I'm responsible for his death. More unforgivable yet is the fact that my body still thrums from what Wolf did to me. I came harder with him than I've ever orgasmed with anyone else before. All with a dead man at my feet.

8

We make the rest of the trip in silence. As promised, Hook delivers us to the tall building that houses both his family and his crew. These days, Michelle has her own suite on a completely different floor from her parents. Part of me wonders if she'll be waiting for me too. This reeks of a shitty intervention, but that's not fair. I'm in a mess of my own making, and as angry as I am with my best friend, if I were in her position, I can't say I would have done anything differently.* I am acting out of character. Reckless. Putting myself in danger. I can't even argue that I'm not, because Wolf is proving himself to be a threat right down to his bones. He's killed at least one person. Likely more.

Upstairs, my parents wait for me with Aunt Tink. Mom rushes to me the second we walk through the door. She grabs my hands and surveys my body. No, she's looking at the blood spattered across my front. "Are you hurt?"

* HOWL—Florence + The Machine

I'm *changed*. Altered into something unrecognizable. But hurt? "No."

"Who was he?" This from Dad. He's got *that* look in his eyes, the one that promises violence to anyone who crosses those he cares about.

"One of mine," Uncle Hook says. "He's been with us for nearly a decade. He's a bastard, but she says it was consensual."

I give him a sharp look, not liking how he phrased that. "It *was* consensual." At least to start with. But explaining that means explaining what I was really doing there, which means explaining Wolf, and I'm not ready to have that conversation.

Mom surveys me with those big dark eyes that are like staring into a mirror. "Tell us what happened."

Now is the time to come clean. To confess that things got out of control with Wolf. To tell them that I have a stalker who's dangerous and violent. To explain that I encouraged him despite knowing what a shitty idea it was.

I don't know why the words won't unstick themselves from my throat. Surely it's better to tell the truth than to have them staring at me like they've never seen me before.

I'm not ready to give him up yet.

I am a *fool*. I'm the girl in the horror movie running up the stairs even as the audience screams at me to call the cops, to yell for help, to do anything but help orchestrate my own violent death.

I have to say *something* though. I take a deep breath. "Luke and I broke up. I guess I'm rebounding pretty hard, and I went looking for trouble. I was in the bathroom to hook up with that guy."

One of my fathers makes a choked sound, but I keep my gaze on my mother.

"Someone came in when we were in the middle of it. A guy I don't know. He killed...uh...the guy I was hooking up with and took off when Uncle Hook started yelling."

"The guy." Aunt Tink snorts. "Gods, Ruby, you don't even know the name of the guy you're fucking?"

Mom doesn't look at her. "What we're not going to do is slut-shame my daughter."

"Who's slut-shaming? I'm just commenting on good survival instincts." Aunt Tink shrugs, completely unrepentant. "In the future, stick to college boys and businessmen, Ruby. And get their names first."

"That's enough." Da steps between me and Aunt Tink. "Let's go home." He cuts me a sharp look when I start to protest. "Now is *not* the time to cling to your independence."

"Okay," I finally say, feeling very small.

He turns to Uncle Hook. "Do you need any assistance in the aftermath?"

"No. I'm going to keep this in-house. She was never there. He's not normally one to get into bar fights, but it's as good a story as any. You stay in this line of work long enough, and old grudges have a way of catching up with you."

They exchange a look steeped in meaning and history. "Thanks for getting our girl."

"Anytime." Hook glances at me. "Don't stay mad at Michelle for too long. She was only trying to look out for you."

Honestly, as angry as I am at Michelle, the truth is that her instincts were spot-on. I *was* in over my head and sinking fast. I still am.

Mom doesn't release me the entire way back to the estate. My parents do one of their mind melds, and my fathers peel off, leaving Mom to deal with me. The reprieve won't last, but they've obviously decided that Mom has the best chance of the three to get the truth out of me.

She barely waits for us to walk into my childhood bedroom before she starts in on me. "It's hard to lose your first love, but that's no excuse to put yourself in danger, Ruby."

"I know."

"Do you?" Her voice sharpens.

This isn't the suffocatingly soft check-in that I expected, and I'm almost relieved that this is going to turn into a fight. I drop onto the bed, feeling like I'm sixteen years old again and in trouble for sneaking a bottle from the wine cellar.

Mom narrows her eyes. "You are a Belmonte. Your actions have consequences for more than just you. If that man belonged to anyone but Hook, his death could have been enough to tip us into a conflict with another territory."

I snort. "There hasn't been war in decades."

"Exactly," she snaps. "Because people have worked hard to make that the truth. They didn't do it by being selfish and reckless."

I should feel guilty. I *know* I should. But she's standing here and judging me when I know for a fact she did some crazy shit when she was my age. And war *was* an ongoing threat at that time. "That's rich coming from you."

"I see there's no reasoning with you right now." Mom shakes her head. "We'll talk in the morning. And I *do* mean it when I say we're going to talk, Ruby. You're going to explain what the hell is going on with you." She turns and walks out of the room.

The second I don't have her strong personality to crash against, I wilt. She's right. I'm being reckless and selfish. I'm not just a normal person who will only hurt myself with my actions. If I manage to single-handedly drag Carver City into another war...

Well, not single-handedly. Wolf played his part too.

With that in mind, I grab my purse and dig through it to find my phone.*

Me: What the fuck was that, Wolf?

He doesn't make me wait long.

Wolf: You know what, baby.

I hate the way heat lances me at those four little words. I *do* know what. I've been playing with fire, and I'm too much of a damn fool to stop.

Me: You can't just go around killing people like that.
Wolf: Are you mad I slit his throat...or that you would do it all over again because you like how you came hard and messy all over my fingers?

* DEVIL I KNOW—Allie X

I flush and almost throw my phone across the room. Damn him. No one else has ever tapped into this part of me. I didn't even *know* I had the potential for this messiness inside me. This all might have started with me stepping off the path set out for me, but I had no way of knowing I'd end up lost in the woods with no way out.

Or that I might not want a way out.

Wolf doesn't wait for a response this time.

Wolf: Or maybe it's that you can't wait to do it again.

Ding ding ding, we have a winner. I hate myself more than a little for that truth. But not enough to stop.

But now that I'm standing here, my blood buzzing with shame and anger, I can't help wondering if my little stunt the other night put two more people in danger. I hold my breath as I text Zayne.

Me: What are you doing?

He responds immediately.

Zayne: Is this a "you up" text? Maybe Michelle is right and I SHOULD be worried about you.

I glare at my phone even as relief makes me lightheaded. That's Zayne all right.

Me: Just making sure you're still alive and haven't expired from wanting Tatiana.

Zayne: You're so mean. I adore it. Welcome back, Ruby. Come out with us next weekend?

Me: Sure. Text me the details later.

I want to be done, but if Wolf might hesitate to harm one of the other children of territory leaders, he seemed really determined for me not to fuck Tatiana in particular. I dig out the card she gave me and laboriously type out an email on my phone.

Me: I think I'll hang on to that picture, but I just wanted to say thanks for the other night.

Is there a good way to ask her if she's been menaced by a guy in a skull mask? I bite my bottom lip. She isn't a friend or family member. I don't want her to think I'm trying to manipulate her into seeing me again, but surely she'd appreciate a proper warning?

Me: Also, this is really awkward, but I've acquired a bit of a stalker, and he's kind of possessive, so keep an eye out, okay?

Tatiana: It's really sweet that you are worried about me, but I can take care of myself. Have a good night, Ruby.

Well, that's a clear dismissal if I've ever read one. I shove my phone back into my purse and rise. I can't dodge a conversation with my parents indefinitely, but I sure as fuck can do it right now. Maybe by the time they track me down, I'll actually know what to say. There's no avoiding disappointing them—that ship has long since sailed—but surely there's something that will make this less catastrophic?

I really wish I believed that.

I duck out of my room and hurry down the hall to the guest bedroom that has a conveniently placed window. The old oak outside is a perfect climbing tree that stretches just close enough to the wall to climb over. There's a camera on the other side, but by the time they see me on the screen, I'll be gone. I've never snuck out before, but I've imagined it thousands of times, thought of what I would do if I weren't so determined to be a daughter who makes my parents proud.

This is not the action of an adult who wants to be taken seriously, but I'm tired, my nerves are frayed, and the reckless feeling that got me into this mess in the first place is still riding me hard. I need time and space to get my head on straight, and that won't happen in my childhood home.

I catch a taxi on the next street over and go back to the apartment I share with Luke. At least for now.

By the time I unlock the door and stumble inside, my adrenaline has run its course, leaving only exhaustion. The feeling only gets more pronounced when I peek into the bedroom and find the bed empty and undisturbed. Luke spent the night somewhere else...maybe *with* someone else.

An ache takes up residence in my chest. I don't know him anymore. I don't know *myself* anymore.

For reasons I'm not prepared to face, I pause only long enough to wash my face and change into a pair of cotton panties and one of Luke's T-shirts before I walk back into the living room, grab the throw blanket, and lie down on the couch. Sleep takes me in seconds.

———

I wake sometime later, well before dawn, to the feeling of being watched. I open my eyes slowly to near-perfect darkness. What woke me?

I get my answer the moment I turn my head. He's sitting on the coffee table, his elbows propped on his knees. The faint glow of the streetlights reflects on his leather gloves and the smooth material of his mask.

Wolf.*

He's in my apartment.

"I know you're awake, baby." His raspy voice feels like a stroke of a finger right over my pussy.

I turn onto my side to face him. "You shouldn't be here."

"Shh." He raises a gloved finger to the curve of the teeth on his mask. "Don't wake the boyfriend."

I shoot a glance at the closed bedroom door. Did Luke come home after I fell asleep? True fear spikes through me. I may not love Luke anymore, but I did for a very long time. We had two years of happiness together, two years of soft moments and vulnerability and memories that I'll cherish, even if we no longer fit together. I don't want him hurt. I don't want him *dead*. Wolf is more than capable of doing both.

I swallow hard. "Why are you here?"

"Should have stayed safe behind those spiked walls, baby.

* SHACKLES—Steven Rodriguez

Instead, you defied your parents and snuck out. How was I to take that but as an invitation?" He hooks the corner of the blanket and tugs it slowly off me.

I'm perversely glad that I didn't put on pants. Even without seeing his eyes, I can feel the heat of them on my exposed skin. I feel possessed, and if I believed in magic, I'd think he put a spell on me in that first text message. That's a cop-out though. The reality is that I tasted the truth of myself when I walked into that bar and chose to cheat on my boyfriend. Everything that's happened in the wake of that decision rests solely on my shoulders. I could have put a stop to this the first night; I chose not to.

Just like I'm choosing not to stop it now.

"I should hate you," I find myself saying. Confessing into the shadows between us. Of everyone, he has the most possibility of understanding. "You're a monster. You've killed people. Stalked me. Threatened me."

"Only with the consequences of your own actions." He drops the blanket on the floor and drags a single finger from my ankle to my knee. "But you're right. I'm a monster. It takes one to know one."

"I'm not a monster." But my knees fall open under the barest hint of his touch. And then open farther as his finger travels up my thigh to stop at the edge of my panties.

"You are." He sounds so confident, as if he really believes it. As if he really knows me. "You've been wearing the mask of a good little girl for your entire life, but beneath it, your teeth are just as big as mine." He drags a knuckle over my pussy. "Even before you knew me, you were willing to let people die for a taste of your pussy."

"No."

"Yes." He presses hard against my clit, making me jerk. "You know what your parents are capable of. Do you really think they'd let that filthy prick stay among the living if they knew he fucked you?"

I open my mouth to say that of course they wouldn't kill someone for such a silly reason, but it's a lie. Isn't part of the reason I never worried about Luke the fact that he wasn't in the life, and we have rules? Those same rules apply to the people who owe their allegiance to my aunt.

My aunt watched what happened with my parents, how a romantic conflict with my mother almost lost the territory two of its best generals, and course corrected. Maybe even overcorrected. Unfortunately—or fortunately, depending on who you ask—my parents agreed with her. I think they would prefer I marry one of the spares from a different territory and dodge the potential pitfalls of elevating one enforcer above the others in our territory.

I knew that, and I didn't care. It's not as if the rules are secret. Rafe knew it too. That doesn't mean he deserved to die.

"You have to stop killing people."

He snorts. The slight tension in his wrist is the only warning I get before he pushes my panties to the side and shoves two fingers into me. "I'll stop killing your lovers when you stop fucking other people, baby. It's as simple as that."

9

As simple as that. As if giving myself over to my stalker completely is a reasonable thing to do. It strikes me all over again that he's *here*. In my apartment. If Luke were here...

I look at my bedroom door. Was it closed earlier? I'm not sure. Surely Luke would have said something if he'd come home and found me sleeping on the couch? But no, I'm thinking about this as if he's still my boyfriend. He's not. We're basically glorified roommates.

Wolf grabs my chin in a painful grip and turns my face back to him. Or to his mask. "Looking for your boyfriend to save you?"

"No, of course not."

He fucks me slowly with his fingers, even as he holds me captive with his hand on my jaw. "Liar. We haven't talked about him yet."*

Fear licks at me, threatening to smother my desire. "Wolf."

* SPIDER IN THE ROSES—Sonia Leigh and Daphne Willis feat. Rob the Man

It's difficult to talk with him holding me like this, but I force my way through it. "Leave him alone."

He's silent for several beats, the only sound the slick, wet slide of his gloved fingers inside me. "The others had your pussy. He's different. He had your heart. When I deal with him, I'm going to make it hurt."

"N—"

He shifts his grip, covering my mouth and stopping my protest. He leans forward, pressing me back onto the couch hard and pinning me there with his bigger body. "You don't get to tell me no, Red. Not about this."

My body coils tight, but I fight against the feeling with everything I have. I speak softly against his palm. "Not him, Wolf. He's an innocent in all this."

"Innocent." He makes a growling sound that has my toes curling despite myself. "Even now, you're arguing for his life. You've been riding his cock for years, sleeping next to him, giving him all those little moments that should have been mine."

"Wolf, please." I may not want to stay in a relationship with Luke, but that doesn't mean I want something bad to happen to him. "Please don't hurt him. I'll do anything."

"Anything." Again, he makes that sound that's almost a growl. "Fine, Red. I'll make you a deal. I'll leave him alone if you do one thing for me."

Relief makes me dizzy. "Okay."

"So eager to save him." He yanks his fingers out of me and flips me onto my stomach before I can do more than whimper. He drags down my panties with rough hands and forces my knees wide.

Not that he has to do much forcing.

I'm already tilting my hips, offering him my pussy, when he reaches between my thighs to palm me roughly. The leather of his glove slides decadently against my pussy lips. Then his weight is at my back, his low voice in my ear. "Would you let me fuck you right here while he's sleeping in the next room, knowing that if you get too loud and wake him up, I'll slit his throat and then go right back to fucking you?"

I shudder, and not even I can tell if it's in anticipation or terror. If I had any sense, I would try to convince him not to do this. I wouldn't be rocking my pussy against his palm, so wet that I'm dripping all over his hand and wrist.

"Yes," I whisper. I could tell myself that this is something I'm simply enduring to keep Luke safe, but it's a dirty lie. The ugly truth is that I've been panting after Wolf's cock ever since I started engaging with his stalking, taunting him, seeing just how far he'd push it. How far he'd push *me*.

"You going to let me take you bare, baby?"

Distantly, alarm bells clang through my head, but I ignore them. I'm on birth control. It will be fine. Probably. "Yes."

"What a good little martyr." He pinches my clit hard enough to make me jerk, but I manage to swallow a whimper at the last moment. Luke is a freakishly light sleeper. It won't take much to wake him.

Then Wolf's hand is gone. I hold my breath as his zipper rings achingly loud in the silence of the room. He grips the back of my neck and presses me harder to the couch, bending me down farther. His blunt cock head nudges my entrance, and I barely have a moment to tense before he shoves his entire length inside me.

I bury my face in the couch cushion, bite down to keep from screaming. It's too much, yet I've never been so close to coming from penetration alone. He's *big*. Broad and long and normally the kind of size I need plenty of foreplay to take.

Wolf doesn't give me time to adjust. He withdraws almost all the way and spears me again. Gods help me, but I have to bite down another scream. I tense, wanting to shove back onto him, but his hand on my neck keeps me in place.

On the third devastating stroke, he doesn't immediately withdraw. Instead, he snakes one hand around my hip to idly stroke my clit as he grinds slowly into me. His voice is low in my ear and barely distorted by the mask he wears. "Go ahead, baby. Scream your way through that orgasm."

I lift my head enough to gasp, "No."

"You know you come so much harder when someone is dying for that pussy."* He shifts the movement of his cock inside me, rubbing against my G-spot with each movement. "Show me your teeth, baby. Show him your teeth."

It's more tempting than it should be. I'm not the monster here, yet I am nearly far gone enough to give Wolf exactly what he wants. To scream my way through an orgasm and sentence Luke to death.

I *can't*.

I drop my head, intending to bury it in the couch cushion again, but Wolf gets there before me. His forearm, sweatshirt shoved up, meets my mouth just as I bite down. And I don't stop.

* DEVIL DEVIL—MILCK

I bite him through my orgasm, my body taking over. Maybe part of me wants to punish him too. To make him hurt even a little for exposing this feral part of me that I've worked so hard to keep under lock and key.

Wave after wave of orgasm crests and crests again as he fucks me roughly. The slap of flesh against flesh fills the room, and I'm aware enough to distantly wonder if *that* will be enough to wake Luke.

I'm too far gone to stop.

When Wolf finally orgasms, he pulls out of me, and then his come is hitting my bare ass in achingly hot lashes. He eases his arm from my mouth, and I'm horrified to note the coppery taste of blood on my tongue.

He moves my hair off the back of my neck and nips me there. "Big teeth indeed, Red."

"Wolf—"

"I'm going to text you an address. Be there at seven tomorrow night. Go to the side door. There's a skeleton key on the knocker. If you don't show, I'll consider our deal null and void and take out my frustration on your little boyfriend. After you fucked around at the club the other night and the bar last night, I have a *lot* of frustration."

I blink open my eyes, not quite sure when I closed them. "What are you talking about? What address? I just fucked you. That's our deal."

"That was pleasure, baby. This is business. You wanted to know what it would take to leave *him* alone. It's this." He gives the nape of my neck one last light bite, and then he rises.

Without his weight at my back, I feel vulnerable in a way I'm not prepared to deal with. I sit up, pull off my shirt, and wipe down my ass, watching him fix his pants. If I hoped to catch a glimpse of his face, I'm out of luck: he's already got the mask back in place. "What's at the address?"

"You'll find out tomorrow night." He seems to study me for a long moment, and if I were even a little romantic, I might think he's committing the sight of me naked to memory. "Don't try to call my bluff. I don't bluff."

"You didn't hurt Tatiana. Or Zayne."

He stills. "That mercy was a good investment in our future that I'm already starting to regret. Don't make me change my mind."

I could pretend I'm debating going, but we both know I'll show up exactly where he wants me to. I would even without the threat against Luke, without the renewed one against Zayne and Tatiana. I've never felt as seen as I do with Wolf, and it's a terrible thing, but I can't stop myself from seeking that feeling out again and again.

Wolf moves past me, and a few seconds later, I hear the front door close. I make myself count to ten slowly, and then a second time, before I rise and pad to the bedroom door to crack it open.

The bed is empty.

Luke never came home.

I don't know if Wolf was just fucking with me or if he didn't know Luke wasn't here. I guess it doesn't matter. Luke is safe. I'll make sure he *stays* safe. But that's not why I'm going to...

My phone buzzes, and I walk back to the coffee table to look at the text from Wolf. It's an address, but not one in Carver City. "What the fuck?"

A second text quickly follows.

Wolf: Check your front door.

"You motherfucker." I stalk to the door and fling it open. There's no one there. Instead, there's a package sitting unassumingly on the floor of the hallway.

I scoop it up, take the time to lock the door again—for all the good it will do—and head back to the coffee table to see what he's up to now. The box is high quality. When I lift the lid off, there's black tissue paper with a ribbon around it. I undo the ribbon and fold back the paper, and... "Damn, Wolf, you have good taste."

I lift the dress up and whistle under my breath. It's short and sheer with ropes of pearls sewn into the fabric. I'd like to think the pearls cover the necessary bits, but I'm sure the truth is that they'll act more as a frame for my breasts and pussy. I check the rest of the box, not finding any undergarments. There are, however, strappy heels. In my favorite brand. In my size. Because what kind of stalker would he be if he didn't know my shoe size?

Me: Fancy.
Wolf: Change into it tomorrow after you arrive at the address. ONLY it.
Me: I gave my word.

———

The next morning, I find a flight and hotel confirmation in my inbox. That motherfucker thought of everything and left nothing to chance.

This is probably a trap. Heirs don't travel much and for good reason. There may be peace in Carver City, but that doesn't mean there aren't outside threats who look at our prosperous city and want to take a bite out of it for themselves.

It's possible that Wolf is associated with one of those entities. Probable even. This might all be some elaborate plan to get me out from under my parents' protection and then use me as leverage to get what they want.

I google the address Wolf gave me, not expecting to find anything, but there are a few hits of interest. One is a forum thread that... "Holy shit."*

The poster alleges that the Black Rose Auction is held at that address annually. "No way." I've heard of the auction of course. Everyone has. Or at least everyone in our line of business, with ties to the shadows. It's kind of an open secret, an auction where people with money and connections can come to bid on items they don't necessarily want to be attached to publicly.

Sometimes those items are people.

Me: I am NOT going to be an auction item.

My parents will kill me. If this is what Wolf intends, to auction off the only daughter of Beast, Gaeton, and Isabelle Belmonte, the heir to the Belmonte territory...there's no way people won't

* MONSTER—Meg Myers

find out. That *everyone* won't find out. My shame will be on full display, and if I do it wearing *this* dress?

No. Absolutely not.

I glare at my phone, but other than the notification under my message changing to Read, nothing happens. He doesn't even try to text back.

Me: I'm serious, Wolf. I'm not doing this. It's too far.

Thirty seconds later, a picture comes in, and my heart drops into my stomach. It's of Luke. He's sitting at his favorite coffee shop, bent over his laptop with a look of concentration on his face. When he works, he's completely oblivious to the world around him. Wolf could slit his throat, and he'd never see the man coming.

Wolf doesn't reiterate his threat, but he doesn't have to. He's close enough to take this picture, so he's close enough to follow through on his threat.

I swallow hard, feeling sick.

Me: I hate you.
Wolf: See you soon, baby.

———

I lie and tell my family that I'm not feeling well, ignore their pointed questions about why the fuck I'm not home, and dodge some well-meaning texts from Michelle and Zayne. Then I'm at the airport and boarding a plane. Wolf booked me first class, but

I can't bring myself to appreciate it. Or the driver and car waiting for me when I land. He's thought of every detail...and I've done nothing but *think*.

I may feel seen by Wolf in a way I've never experienced before, but that doesn't mean I know him. I don't know what he looks like. He says he wants me, but it's easy to lie. It's not like I've challenged him in any meaningful way. I let him fuck me bare, for gods' sake.

The city shifts around me as we leave its limits and head into the countryside. The longer I go without hearing from him, the worse I feel. Even as I tell myself not to be so weak, I can't help reaching for my phone. This time, I don't bother to text. I call him.

He doesn't make me wait long before he answers. "You're making good time."

I look around, even though I know there's nothing to see. "Who are you, Wolf?"

He's silent for a beat. "You'll find out at the auction."

My heart skips a beat. "What?"

"Come on, baby. You didn't think I'd send you to the auction and let someone else take you, did you?"

Honestly, I hadn't been sure what to think. I settle back in the seat, telling myself I'm seven different kinds of foolish for being comforted by his words. He hasn't given me *anything*. Trusting him is downright suicidal. "And here I thought you were serving me up to whoever you work for."

"You're mine, Ruby."

I jolt at him saying my name again. Not baby. Not Red. *Ruby.* I clear my throat. "Why all the song and dance? You already had me. Thoroughly." I don't know why I ask. He's held his information close from the first moment we started interacting. There's no reason for him to be explicit now.

"Because you're mine," he repeats. "And it's time everyone knows it."

Oh. *Oh.* "So this is you pissing on my foot."

"No, baby. This is a declaration of intention. After I take you in the auction, everyone who's worth a damn in our world will know who you belong to. No more sneaking around. No more games. No pretending you're just a good girl who's been forced into being bad."

My chest feels too tight. "My parents are going to find out. You know that, right? It doesn't matter what you *intend*. They'll string you up and skin you alive."

Wolf, the bastard, chuckles. "Then I guess I better make you fall in love with me so you'll intervene on my behalf."

The rushing in my head almost convinces me that I misheard him. Lust, yes. But he's asking for *love*? Maybe I should have seen the writing on the wall with how possessive he is, how jealous. This was only going to end one of two ways—with one of us dead or with us together.

It's still outrageous that he's just saying this shit. "I haven't even seen your face. We've barely had a single conversation. You can't honestly expect me to fall in love just because you're good at getting me off."

"That's where you're wrong, baby. We don't need all the pussyfooting and small talk. We *see* each other." There's a sound in the background, and he clears his throat. "Don't fuck with the Concierge. They won't find your mouthing off as cute as I do."

"Wolf—"

"See you soon." He hangs up, leaving me spinning out. Nothing about this experience has been what I expected, but looking back, I can admit that my short-sightedness is to blame. I've been reacting to him in the moment, when it's clear he had a plan from the beginning. I wonder what he would have done if I hadn't slept with Rafe that first night. I'd bet good money he had a different angle of approach. *Bastard.*

The car turns off the main road, and I stare at the sprawling estate. We have money, but this opulence is on a different level. The place is obviously a private residence, but it's easily two or three times the size of my aunt's estate, and the grounds seem to stretch forever. I even catch sight of a boathouse in the distance, perched on the edge of a large lake.

We bypass the main entrance and circle around to the side, just like Wolf instructed. The driver doesn't speak a word as they hold the door open for me and set my bag on the ground next to the door with the skeleton key knocker. I'm still deciding if I'm supposed to thank them when they get back in the car and drive off without looking back.

"Well, I guess that answers that." There's no going back now. I march to the door and knock.

10

The door doesn't lead to a foyer but to a narrow hall. I don't bother trying to get a better look. Not when all my attention is taken up by the Concierge. They're a tall white person wearing an expensive three-piece suit that's been tailored to their lean body. I can't quite figure out how old they are—somewhere between forty and sixty: old enough to have fine lines on their smooth skin, to look seasoned in a way people in their twenties can't quite pull off, but not old enough to be affected by age in the slightest.

I can't begin to guess their thoughts as they look me over. "This way, please."*

The room I'm led to is luxurious and lovely...but there's a lock on the outside of the door. I'm also divested of my phone and bag. It's enough to make me doubt, yet again, what I've decided to do.

This is beyond playing cat and mouse with a stalker. The first

* MACHETE (ACOUSTIC)—SPELLES

rule of safety is to not go to a secondary location, and I voluntarily boarded a plane and allowed this Concierge to lock me in a cell.

"Please sign this."

I stare at the contract. "Fuck." It's huge. Too huge to read through in one sitting, even if my eyes don't immediately cross when I have to wade through legalese. We have lawyers on staff for a reason.

The Concierge is unsympathetic. "We cannot move forward until you sign."

I'm tempted to ask them for a CliffsNotes version, but there's no reason to trust they'd be telling the truth. "I need to read this."

"By all means."

I expect them to leave. They don't. They sit on the short chair across from me, cross their long legs, and...wait.

My skin heats as I page through the contract. Despite my fear of not understanding, it's relatively straightforward. The house takes 20 percent of the winning bid on me. I get the rest.

By signing this—by participating in the auction as an item—I am giving consent to whatever the winner wants to do with me. The exceptions are anything that could maim or kill me...which leaves a lot to be desired.

I look at the Concierge. "No safe words?"

"The contract is your safe word." They smile thinly. "And each room is outfitted with a panic button should such a thing be necessary."

That's...not how safe words work.

I keep reading. The contract removes the house's responsibility for any harm that befalls me. My only recourse lies in the fact that the three days I'm apparently offering at auction will happen on the premises, which means there will be someone who isn't Wolf there if things go wrong. In that time, I can cancel the contract and repay the amount I received...for a truly ostentatious fee—an added 30 percent.

If Wolf is the one who wins... He has never hurt me. Scared me, yes, but he's had plenty of opportunity to do actual harm, and he's never crossed that line.

But who knows if Wolf even has money like we're talking about here? He seems like he's thought of everything, but what if there's someone with deeper pockets than him? The security in this place is intense. He can't kill his way through the crime scions of the East Coast to get to me.

The thought makes me tingle a little. I really am a foolish monster.

I sign before I can talk myself out of it.

The Concierge gathers up the contract. "There's a showing this afternoon before the auction itself. You will be expected to be silent and still for the duration."

"Okay." I swallow hard.

The Concierge leaves without another word. The lock clicks a few seconds later. I want to ask why they're locking me in when I've consented to be here and signed the contract, but there's no one to ask.

My seclusion doesn't last long. A pair of people arrive and guide me into a different part of the building, where I'm subjected to a number of beauty treatments. A body scrub, a blowout, professional makeup. I thought I took good care of myself, have been called high-maintenance in the past, but this is on another level.

Through it all, they don't say a word. After the third attempt at getting my questions answered, I give up and just enjoy the fun parts.

Unfortunately, that's when the grim thoughts start circling. Wolf made it sound like tonight he'd claim me publicly, but he might have been lying to keep me complacent. If one of Carver City's enemies wins me in the auction...if they demand...

I shudder. I'm having regrets. Lots of regrets. Especially when I'm handed what I'm expected to wear for the viewing. "No. Absolutely not."

The person—they never gave me their name—doesn't blink. "We don't have time to argue. Either wear this or wear nothing."

I stare. Surely they wouldn't make me go naked...but that's exactly what they're saying. Not that the garment hanging from their hands is much better. It's not what Wolf picked out for me, but it covers just as little. Less even.

No choice.

I pull on the sheer sheath dress; it's a deep emerald shade that makes the most of my lightly tanned skin and long red hair. The person hands me a pair of strappy stiletto sandals, and I slide them on with only a grimace of protest.

Then it's showtime. Or viewing time, apparently.

———

There are...pedestals.*

* WOLVES—Selena Gomez feat. Marshmello

A part of me assumed that this was specifically a sex auction, but apparently that's not the case. There are a handful of people perched on pedestals, but there are even more that hold everything from a priceless diamond necklace to famous art to a strange chalice that makes the small hairs on the back of my neck stand on end to a fucking *flower*. Who auctions off a flower?

A cornflower-blue dress catches my eye, and I nearly trip over my feet when the details register. That dress has adorned Byrne women in at least two presidential inaugurations. Those bitches are like the Kennedys but even more powerful. What the hell is that dress doing *here*?

I'm not the only person auctioning themselves or being auctioned off either. There's a petite blond woman who doesn't make eye contact as I pass. She's beautiful. I bet she'll get a large bid.

I'm led to an empty pedestal near the end of the row and step carefully up to perch on it. There's not much space, so I won't be able to shift or even turn if I don't want to risk falling right off it. It's only twelve inches from the ground, but that would be humiliating.

Between one breath and the next, the lights drop, bathing the room in darkness. I have to clamp my jaw shut to keep from making a startled sound, but I hear at least a few people let one slip. It makes me feel less alone, even if I can no longer see anyone.

And then the spotlights turn on overhead. This time, I can't stop myself from flinching. I couldn't see much to begin with, but with the lights in my eyes, I might as well be onstage. I get the impression of doors opening, hear the murmur of people walking the aisles between us, but I can't detect more than the faint outline of bodies.

It's horrible...and kind of sexy.

No one tries to touch me. They don't attempt to interact with me. They just circle my pedestal and talk about me like I'm an object to be purchased.

Which I suppose I am.

Through it all, I concentrate hard, trying to pick a familiar gravelly tone out of the masses. An impossible task. It distracts me though, at least until a light voice says beside me, "Would you look at that hair. I'd love to have it wrapped around my fist."

A lower voice chuckles. "I bet you would." There's a hint of a Russian accent there. "But this one isn't for you, love. I hear the Wolf has his eye on her. You know better than to get between *that* one and his prey."

I turn my head in the direction of the voices, opening my mouth to question how they know *my* Wolf, but it's too late; they're moving away. Even knowing it's a terrible idea, I almost step down and go after them. I thought Wolf was a name I made up for him, one to give a cheeky nod to his reference to my being Little Red Riding Hood. If other people call him that, does it mean he's done this before?

Wolf promised I'd get my answers tonight at the auction, so I'll just have to ask him when I see him. Besides, I signed the contract. It's too late to back out now.

More, I don't *want* to back out.

My parents are going to kill me when they find out what I've done. I push the thought away and focus on getting through the next however long. People keep coming and coming; some don't bother to pause near me, intent on other prizes, but others do.

They comment on my breasts, my hair, my ass. Some of the bolder ones even speculate on what my pussy tastes like.

I pass the time by fantasizing about what Wolf would do to them if they tried to find out for themselves. It would be bloody and violent, and when he came to me afterward, evidence of violence all over him, he'd fuck me harder than I've ever been fucked.

Slowly, so slowly that I almost don't notice, the last of the attendees file out of the space. The lights come up, and I'm left blinking and disoriented.

A different person than the one who's spent the day corralling me about appears, dressed in the same expensive black clothing. "This way, please."

I'm led through yet another set of doors and to a small dressing room. There, my makeup is retouched, my hair smoothed, and my body shimmied into the dress Wolf provided, my feet strapped into the sky-high heels.

The last one felt indecent; this one is an invitation. It's just as over-the-top as I'd suspected. I stare at myself in the mirror—at my rosy nipples on display, at the hint of my slit between my thighs, all framed with gorgeous inlaid pearls.

With my hair down in careless waves and my makeup kept mostly natural, I look like some kind of sea nymph who just rose from the ocean spray.

One who wants to fuck.[*]

"Please wait here until someone comes for you. They'll bring you out to the stage where the bidding will take place and then

[*] BREATH OF LIFE—Florence + The Machine

bring you back here to wait until the auction ends and the details of payment are finalized. You will meet the winner in the room they book after all that's done."

My stomach feels hollow in a way that has nothing to do with hunger. This is happening. There's no going back now. Maybe there wasn't from the moment I got that first text message. Earlier even.

"Okay," I manage.

The person smiles. "We handle these things with the utmost care. Your payment will be deposited in the account you provided us before you leave this room."

"It's too bad I'm not a virgin. I'd make a killing."

They laugh a little. "You'd be surprised. Some of our clients' tastes run to the untouched, but plenty of them prefer a partner who knows what they like and is willing to experiment."

Experiment.

The word sends a zing right through me. "Right. Well, I guess that's me."

"I'll be back when it's time."

Once again, I'm left alone with my own thoughts. This time though, there are none to speak of. I sit numbly and wait for my turn, wait for my fate.

It might be an hour or mere minutes later that my door opens and the Concierge appears. Their expression is just as professionally blank as ever. "It's time."

I don't see another soul as they lead me down the hallway and into another new part of the building. I half expected them to have converted the viewing room into the stage, but I should have

known better. It's peak rich people to have an entire fucking the-
ater in their basement. I suppose I can't throw stones considering
what family I was born into, but it's honestly ridiculous.

And maybe I'm just trying to distract myself from the reality
that I'm about to be auctioned off and that I have absolutely
no control over who wins the bid. I either trust Wolf or I don't.
Maybe it's the height of foolishness that I do, but I cling to the
memory of the stranger from the viewing.

*The Wolf has his eye on her. You know better than to get
between* that *one and his prey.*

If that person knew it, then maybe others do too. Maybe
there won't even be a bidding war. Maybe I'm building this up in
my head and it will be downright disappointing.

The Concierge stops just in front of a large doorway that
stretches into darkness. "The stage is through here. Walk to the
other doorway, and wait to be summoned."

A bolt of fear makes me forget my attempt at bravery.
"You're leaving?"

"I have other auction items to retrieve. Go." They turn and
walk away.

There's nothing to do but walk through the doorway and
into the shadows. There's a piece of clothing carefully draped
over a chair nearby, and I can't help shifting to it. My eyes go
wide when I recognize the Byrne inauguration dress. Why's it just
sitting here? Shouldn't it be onstage right now, securing bidders?
Maybe the original owner changed their mind.

I could probably back out and beg for them to release me
from the contract. But my pride won't let me. Guilt rises, and

I shift from foot to foot. My pride. What a joke. I should be focused on doing this for Luke, to keep him safe, but all I've had my mind on is *Wolf*.

You really are a selfish bitch, aren't you?

Yeah. I really am.

I lift my chin, take a deep breath, and charge through the doorway. Three steps in, I realize the space isn't as dark as it looked from the outside. There's a faint light coming around a corner, and a hush of whispers reaches me as I get closer.

"Sold! For a dollar to the man of the hour. Me."

A crooning voice makes my skin go tight. It's as if sex was bottled into sound.

He laughs, low and sinful. "Get going, love. You'll need your rest for what comes next."

I stop just inside a second doorway and look out into a large room. It's hard to see because of the lighting—a theme in this place. I catch sight of a lean white woman with long dark hair walking down the steps on the other side of the stage, her head bowed and her fists clenched. She's not wearing anything but her skin.

Suddenly I feel downright overdressed.

Wait, did she just sell herself for *a dollar*?

I'm so distracted by the sight of her bare ass and the low price tag that I completely missed the other person on the stage. He's not naked, but there's something about him that suggests sex in a much more over-the-top way than the naked woman. He's a white man dressed in low-slung leather pants and little else, his long white-blond hair pulled into a bun with parts braided, a ring glinting on his sensual lower lip.

He turns and finds me unerringly. "Don't be shy, love. Come show the people what they came to purchase." He's already turning again without waiting to see whether I'll obey. "Our next auction item is something quite special. Not a virgin, so don't get your hopes up there. I have it on...good...*very* good...authority that she gets down and dirty and loves being bad."

I step onto the stage, and my lungs shrivel in my chest. I'm not a coward, but I'm achingly aware of the way my pussy and breasts are on display, the way everyone present can see me and imagine and... I shiver, and I'm not entirely certain if it's with fear or desire.

"That's right, we have Carver City's very own Ruby Belmonte, the heir to the Belmonte territory." The man smiles, flashing perfect teeth, and motions me closer. "She's been a good little Mafia princess for a very long time, so much so that I myself wondered why she'd darken *our* doors." He casts a wicked smile to the audience, which is bathed in shadows. "Yet here she is, prime for the plucking."

I don't quite make the decision to set my hand in his. It simply happens by virtue of his magnetism. If I weren't dead set on a certain man in a mask, I might be dropping my nonexistent panties just from standing next to this guy.

He gives me a twirl that ends with my back to his chest... though I notice that he very carefully keeps his hips away from my ass, not taking the opportunity to grind on me.

He releases my hand to catch my chin and bare my throat while bending me back against him and putting my body on display. "Now, look at this delicious little thing, wandered into our midst. She may think she's been bad, but we know the truth. She's barely dipped her toes in sin, and it's someone's lucky day, because they get to show her exactly how depraved we can be."

The lights haven't gotten brighter, but I'm half convinced they're spotlighting my nipples, due to the heat gathering there and at my clit.

Who knew that being on display was one of my kinks? Not me.

"How lovely she blushes." He laughs, low and a little mean. "I bet her ass will redden prettily under the right hand. Let's start the bidding at a quarter of a million dollars."

Someone with a light musical voice calls out, "Make it three hundred."

"Darling, look how eager you have them. No minimum bid for this sweet little pussy." He lifts his voice a little. "But we can do better than that. Let's hear three fifty." It's practically a command.

I had no idea bidding would start so high. Sure, my family may have a fortune stashed in the vault, but it's not like normal people have access to hundreds of thousands of dollars.

Does Wolf? Who could he possibly be to have access to the kind of money these people are throwing around?

While I'm ruminating, the bids climb quickly. Four hundred. Five hundred. Holy shit.

The auctioneer gives me a slow smile. "You've got them by the throat, love." He's not exactly trying to be quiet, but he's not pronouncing *these* words to everyone. "I bet we can get them to a million if you turn around and bend over just a bit. Give them a good look at what they're getting." He lowers his face a little, until it's almost kissably close. "We both know you're getting off on this. Let them see how much."

He's right.

My pussy is practically dripping. The voices have been calling out too fast, speaking too quickly, for me to be sure one of them is Wolf. I turn around, slowly and with a little extra swivel in my hips. As if on cue, slow, sensual music starts from somewhere.

The auctioneer whistles. "Looks like we're in luck. We get a little preview. Can I hear five fifty?"

I bend in time with the music, and I swear I actually hear the collective inhale as the icy, air-conditioned air strokes my pussy.

"One million." The voice is low with a hint of rasp, a hint of accent, and it strikes me right in my core. I *know* that voice. I've spent days taunting its owner, have spent hours fantasizing about just what filthy things he'll say to me when it's finally just us without all the games.

Wolf. My spine snaps straight, and I turn around. "Sold," I blurt.

The auctioneer laughs. "Someone's eager, but the bidding isn't over until it's over. Can I get a million five?"

"Another person makes a bid, and I'm putting a bullet in their brain, Reaper."

The auctioneer—Reaper—drops his seduction act and goes cold. "Don't threaten my guests, Wolf. You want her? Bid the highest. Otherwise, it's not my *other* guests who will be getting a bullet to the brain. This is neutral territory, and everyone here is enjoying my hospitality...as long as they obey the rules. So obey them."

The silence stretches and then keeps stretching, the threat lying heavy in the air. No one makes a sound.

Reaper curses softly. "So be it. Our lovely Ruby Belmonte goes to the Mad Wolf. Good luck, love. You're going to need it."

'm led off the stage in the opposite direction that I walked on. I can't help lingering there, wanting to see what will come out next. It turns out to be another woman, this one just as petite and blond—and naked—as the one before me. Hopefully she gets a better rate.

"Ms. Belmonte?* Please follow me."

I allow yet another staff member to gently take my elbow and guide me away. With each step, the truth hits me again and again.

Wolf was here. He won.

Was he wearing the mask when he did it? Or do all the other attendees know what I don't—what he really looks like? Reaper certainly seemed to know who he was.

The Mad Wolf.

That name tickles some memory in the deep recesses of my mind, but the recollection slips away when I try to grasp it. All

* CALL ME QUEEN—Ndidi O

I know is that I've heard the name before, a long time ago. He's not from Carver City—that much I'm sure of. If he were, I would have registered *that* nickname.

My guide takes me back to my dressing room, where I wait impatiently for the funds to clear. It seems to take forever but, I suspect, it is a very short time indeed. I'm still pacing in circles when they reappear.

They smile. "Everything is finalized. Please follow me to the room chosen for you."

Within a few minutes, I'm led through the warren of hallways to a luxurious bedroom that puts the one I spent the day in to shame.

And it's fully kitted out.

I step through the door and look around. I may avoid the Underworld like the plague, but I'm familiar with the equipment and toys that go along with some flavors of BDSM. This room has a significant number of them.

There's an open trunk that displays crops, floggers, and paddles in every shape and weight. The four-poster bed has rings embedded in it at different heights, the better to bind someone to. There's a rainbow of Shibari ropes and three different kinds of padded cuffs. That's not even getting into the spreader bar, the spanking bench, or the seat that very much looks like a throne.

I cross the room, look through a door, and find a bathroom fit for royalty, all dark glossy tile with more showerheads than any shower actually needs.

"Damn, y'all really go all out."

"Ms. Belmonte."

I turn to my escort, belatedly realizing that they were waiting for me to acknowledge them so they can leave. I try for a smile, but I'm too overwhelmed to fully swing it. "Sorry. I got a little wowed. What do you need from me?"

"Nothing, miss." They smile. "I just want to reiterate: once you leave the premises, you are agreeing to hold the auction harmless for any damages that result in the events that follow."

Damages. They would see it like that, but I can't exactly fault them. I'm here of my own free will, and I knew exactly what Wolf was capable of when I boarded that plane.

When I fucked him.

When I came all over his fingers with a dead body at our feet.

"I understand."

"Good."

Another person hurries in, faintly out of breath. They whisper in my escort's ear and then press a box into the other's hands.

My escort frowns. "This is highly irregular, but the Mad Wolf would like you to have this while you wait."

There's nothing to do but accept the box. I almost laugh at myself. As if I'm not frothing at the mouth to see what he's sent along ahead of himself. "Thank you."

"Good luck."

Before I can ask why everyone keeps saying that to me, they're gone, closing the door softly behind them. It's just as well. For better or worse, I mostly know what I've gotten myself into. I hope.

I walk to the bed and set the box on it. It's about the size of a shoebox and made of heavy wood, but aside from being polished to the point where I can see my reflection on its surface, there's nothing notable about it.

I'm stalling.

I tug on my ring, relishing the little spike of pain I get in response. Strictly speaking, I'm not a masochist, but I can't deny that a little pain adds a fun element of spice to normal sex. If my parents weren't who they are, I probably would have found my way through the Underworld's doors before now.

"Stop stalling." I flip open the lid before I can talk myself out of it. There's a flat black surface with a thick note card on it.

I want you naked and kneeling when I come for you.
Wear this.

"Well, there's one thing Wolf consistently has—audacity." I flip up the secondary lid, and my mouth goes dry. It's not the blindfold that makes my stomach erupt into butterflies.

It's the collar.

I lift it carefully, shooting a nervous look at the door. I know what a collar means when it comes to BDSM. It's a claim, a sign marking consent of ownership, of submission. This collar is gorgeous, more jewelry than utility. It's a choker that drips rubies in various lengths. I hold it up to my neck and shiver. The pattern will frame my bare breasts and shoulders when I put it on.

I'm nervous for sure, but nervousness can be a good thing. I lick my lips. "Okay, I can do this." The question is whether I obey or start pushing boundaries immediately. I look around again. "If you're going to play this way, then we need a damn negotiation first." A safe word, though the very concept seems almost laughable after what we've already done.

No, damn it. I don't have to keep being reckless just because I started out that way. Wolf is familiar enough with kink to offer me this collar, so he can damn well sit through a conversation before we cross yet another line that we can't uncross.

I carefully set the collar back in the box but don't close it. Then I return the blindfold to its place.

And sit down to wait.

There's no clock in this room, but I wait long enough that I'm heartily glad for the en suite bathroom. It has a whole treasure trove of goodies too. The tiled walls of the shower also contain sturdy anchors for bondage games. Under the sink, I find enough industrial-strength cleaners to make me laugh. As if there were any doubts about what went on in this room.

In my snooping, I find a drawer full of a dozen different kinds of lube and another with a wide selection of dildos and vibrators. Truly, it's a kinky wonderland.

I finally end up in the large chair. It's more comfortable than I'd expected and wide enough to accommodate a number of body types, with extra room so someone could slip their knees on either side as they ride...

The door opens softly, moving slowly enough that I'm half-sure I've fallen asleep and am dreaming. But then he's there, filling the doorway, his skull mask the only thing light about him.

Wolf.*

* TALK—Hozier

He steps into the room and closes the door behind him, just as softly, just as slowly. There's a faint click as he locks it, and then he crosses his arms over his chest. "I should have known you wouldn't obey."

"You haven't earned obedience."

He laughs dryly. "I just paid a million dollars for you, Red. I think I've earned plenty."

"Oh, that?" I don't lean forward, forcing my body to stay relaxed. "I thought that was for everyone else's benefit."

"In part." He doesn't move. "But it's currently sitting in *your* bank account, so take off that fucking dress and get on your knees."

My pussy pulses in response to the rough words. "Take off the mask."

"Not yet."

There's no room for argument in his voice, so I change tactics. "You offered me a collar. You understand what it means?"

"It means you're mine." Still, he doesn't move.

I am. I bite back the words before they can slip past my lips. He's too sure of me. He has reason to be, but that doesn't mean I'm not capable of digging in my heels over this. "I want a safe word. I want you to promise to respect it."

Another of those dry chuckles. "You'd only have my word that I will."

"Your word is good enough for me. Even if you haven't been completely honest with me."

Is there a hesitation in his response? I'm not sure. I don't get a chance to question it before he nods once. "Fine. Pick your safe word, baby."

"Huntsman."

"Cute. Now that that's out of the way." He pushes off the door and snaps his gloved fingers. "Take off the dress. Get on your knees."

"You're not even going to ask me what I'm into? What my limits are?"

"We covered this. I wouldn't be a very good stalker if I didn't know shit about you, Ruby." He keeps talking in that low, growling voice before I can react to his tongue forming the syllables of my name. "You like a little pain. You want to be bad, want *me* to hurt other people just to get to your pretty pussy. You want to pretend I'm forcing you into a corner, but you're so wet, you're practically shaking for me."

I lick my lips. "That's still very limited."

"You have a problem with something, tell me, and we'll discuss it."

"Just like that."

"Just like that. You're mine, baby. Wearing that collar isn't just about everyone who sees it knowing I own that pussy—that I own *you*. I take care of what's mine."

It seems too easy, but maybe I'm just looking for an excuse to push him until he takes what he wants. I might have gotten away with pretending I was being coerced before, but I came here of my own free will. I signed that contract. I stepped onto the stage.

So I stand and slide out of the heavy dress. It hits the ground with a faint thud, leaving me naked before him. Except for the ring he gave me. He points at a spot right in front of him, and after the slightest hesitation, I cross to kneel there.

"You don't follow instructions worth a damn." He moves to the bed and grabs the blindfold and the collar. Then he steps behind me and carefully lifts my hair off my shoulders.

A heartbeat later, the collar fastens around my throat. The long threads of rubies slither over my skin, making me shiver.

Wolf holds up a small key in front of me. "This is mine. Not going to make you wear this one in public, but you *will* be wearing the alternative."

My heart beats faster. "Possessive much?"

"You have no fucking idea." He wraps his fist around the key. The blindfold is next, a thick thing that blacks out my vision of the room entirely.

"Wolf, I want to see you."

"Later." His footsteps circle me, and I can't help tensing in response. "I'm going to put you on that bed and eat your cunt until you beg for mercy, then I'm going to fuck you until I fill you up. Then I'm going to do it all over again. And again. Until you don't have any confusion about who that pussy belongs to."

I can't quite catch my breath. "Wolf."

"Somewhere in there, I'm also going to fuck that tight little ass. If you're very good, at some point, I'll fuck that bitchy mouth of yours until you gag and cry for me."

"*Wolf.*"

The sound of his steps stops in front of me. "You got a problem with any of that?"

I might laugh if I could draw the air for it. "No." I swallow hard. "I haven't done much anal though. You'll have to be careful if you don't want to hurt me."

"Oh, baby, I *do* want to hurt you." His hand—his *hand*, not his leather gloves—cups my face. "But not by accident. If I hurt you, it's going to be on purpose. I'll be careful with your ass."

I can't stop shaking. He hasn't done anything but talk to me, touch me almost innocently with his bare hands. I can't stop myself from leaning my cheek deeper into his palm. "Okay."

"Good girl."* He removes his hand, but I barely have a chance to mourn the loss before he sweeps me up and sets me on the bed on my back. "Spread your legs. Let me see what a million-dollar cunt looks like."

I don't hesitate. I spread my legs wide enough that my hips ache. My pussy throbs in time with my racing heart, and my desire feels heavy in a way I can barely stand. His mouth. I'm finally going to get his mouth.

He moves away from the bed, his boots making soft sounds on the carpet. The slide of cloth reaches my ears, and I freeze. He's stripping. For the first time, I'm going to have his entire body against mine. No clothes between us. No mask. No gloves.

I reach up for my blindfold, but his harsh voice stops me. "You take that blindfold off, and I'm going to forget about being careful with you, baby. Choose wisely."

My fingers brush the blindfold, but as intoxicating as I find the idea of him doing exactly that, I don't want it for the first time it's truly just us, no one else around who'll intrude. So I put my hands on the bed and fist the sheets. A reminder to obey.

"Thought so." His voice is closer. I can't hear his footsteps

* NEW FEARS (BEDROOM RECORDING)—Lights

any longer, not over the rushing in my ears. There's no telling how close or far he is.

Then rough hands find my thighs. The grip is painful enough that it surprises a yip out of me. I don't get a chance to decide if I want to protest for real or not. His mouth finds my pussy, and then there isn't a single thought in my head beyond *more*.

He *devours* me.

It's as if he wants to imprint himself on every inch of my pussy. He licks and sucks at my folds, delves his tongue deep inside me, moves up to kiss my clit as if he can go for hours.

I, on the other hand, am a keg of dynamite about to explode.

"Wolf!"

He responds to my desperate cry by shoving two fingers into me as he works my clit. I barely have time to process the intrusion before his pinkie presses against my ass. I tense, but he goes slow there, only intruding to his first knuckle.

It's still almost too much. All I can think about is how much bigger his cock is. It scares me and excites me, and *oh fuck*, I'm coming.

My back bows, and I reach for him without thinking. He grabs my wrists with one hand and pins them to my stomach, all without stopping what he's doing to my pussy. It only makes it hotter.

I come again. Or maybe it's an extension of the first one. I'm not sure. All I know is that I need more. "Wolf, please. Fuck me."

"Already pressing me," he says against my clit. "Impatient."

Yes. Always. "Let me ride your cock. Please."

He sucks hard on my clit, but then he eases back. "Better ride it good. Can't have you disappointing me." He loops an arm around my waist, and for one disorienting moment, I'm spinning. Then I come down straddling his waist.

I was right. He's naked.

I start to press forward, intending to feel as much of him against as much of me as possible, but he again catches my arms. This time, he guides them behind my back. "Clasp your forearms."

The new position leaves me helpless once again. Especially when he grabs my hips and guides me to the broad head of his cock.

"Now, baby. Make me proud."

Even with the recent orgasm, I have to fight my way down his cock. It reminds me of... But no, I'm not thinking of Luke right now. He might have had a monster cock, but that just means I know how to take one.

One step at a time.

One sliding inch after another.

I work myself down Wolf's length in slow strokes. With my arms behind my back, he's got to have an excellent view. I wish I had it too. I *need* it.

It seems to take a long time, but eventually I sink the last inch and seal us together. Wolf mutters something in a language that sounds like Russian, but I'm too far gone to question it.

I grind mindlessly on him. It's not enough. "I need my arms."

"Fine."

I release my forearms and grip his shoulders. It's tempting to lean forward again, to rub myself on his chest, but it's clear he won't allow it. I'll figure out why later. Right now, I'm too busy fucking him.

"My perfect little slut." He tightens his grip on my hips, lifts me, and slams me back down onto him. "Always so eager to ride any willing cock that will have you."

I gasp, but his coarse words only make the pleasure coil tighter inside me. "Yes."

"Watched you fuck that enforcer as if he had any right to this pussy. Watched him put his hands all over you while he split you wide open where anyone could see in that short little dress."

I can still see the picture he sent. The damning evidence of me on someone else's cock. "Yes," I moan.

"Then you shared *my* pussy with that bitch, letting her mark you up and take a picture with her hands all over you. Taunting me."

"Yes!" I ride him harder, faster. "It felt so good. I knew it'd make you so mad."

"You keep passing that cunt out like free candy. It's like you want me to punish you. To fuck you hard and fast and reclaim what's mine." His teeth find my nipple, and it's enough to have me dancing right up to the edge.

I don't make a conscious decision to move. To disobey. It's as if my hands have a mind of their own. One moment, I'm quivering and shaking, on the brink of coming, and the next, I rip off my blindfold and look down at Wolf.

I freeze.

He's not wearing a mask right now. He's just as naked as I am, his face all harsh lines.

His...familiar face.

Because I know this face. I've seen it wearing a thousand

different emotions, seen it angry and soft and filled with the kind of lust that makes my clit throb.

Luke.

But no. That's impossible. It can't be. I *know* Luke. He's a nice guy. Respectful. Almost boring these days, though he wasn't when we started dating.

I've never seen *this* expression on his face though. He looks cruel, his blue eyes so cold that I shiver on his cock. It's as if another person is wearing his skin. I don't know *this* man. *My* Luke would not stalk me. *My* Luke would not murder someone and then finger fuck me over their dead body.

"What the fuck," I whisper.

If he says something harsh and self-assured like Wolf would, I may do the mental gymnastics to keep fucking him. Instead, he says, "I can explain." And he doesn't *sound* like Luke right now. But he doesn't sound like Wolf either.

He has a *Russian* accent.

I shove off him. I don't have a plan, but I'm nearly to the door when he catches up with me. He wraps me in his big body, and I really am a fool, because part of me wants to melt for him.

"Stop, Ruby."

"Let me go. What did you do with Wolf?" It's the only explanation. Luke and Wolf *can't* be the same person. Luke must have figured out what was going on and then stepped into Wolf's clothing.

"I'm Wolf."

"Don't lie to me!"

He braces one arm on the door in front of me. "Look."

I see what he means immediately. The bite mark on his forearm, the perfect impression of my teeth from the last time. When he fucked me on the couch and told me to be quiet or he'd kill Luke. Except *he's* Luke. "What the *fuck*?"

His hard cock presses against my ass. "What's your safe word, baby?" His accent gives the words a strange flavor, as if he's not Wolf or Luke, but someone who may be more dangerous than both.

"What?" My head is spinning. I can't think. I can't process what the hell is going on.

"Your safe word." He tightens his hold on my waist and lifts me just a little, just enough for his cock to find my entrance. "Because as far as I'm concerned, nothing has changed between us. You were happy enough that I paid a million dollars for this cunt five minutes ago. I mean to take what I'm owed."

Again, my foolish body takes over. I arch back against him, my safe word trapped on the inside of my teeth. "I hate you."

"Yeah, you keep saying that." He wedges his cock into me, one slow inch at a time. It doesn't feel like care though. It feels like humiliation, especially when my pussy blooms around him in response. "Hands on the door."

"Fuck you." But I obey. I press my hands flat to the door as he starts to fuck me again. This time, it's not like when I was riding him. It's closer to what happened on the couch.

A claim of ownership.

"When you come, I want you to say my name," he murmurs in my ear. "My real name."

"I...get that...now? Lucky me." Gods, his cock feels good inside me. I don't understand how I didn't recognize him as Luke, who I've fucked more times than I can count. But then Luke never fucked me like *this*. He was selfless to an outstanding degree, and if sometimes we got a little rough, it was always with me on top and driving things. It never felt dirty or borderline violent.

"Casimir."

Just like that, everything clicks. The name I barely recognized. The Russian accent. Casimir Romanov. The vicious fixer for the Russian branch of the Romanov family.

The Mad Wolf.

12

The Romanovs don't have a foothold in Carver City. I don't know if they ever tried to, but to the best of my knowledge, when they sent their people over from Russia to put down roots in the States, they stuck to the main port cities. Our power structure is older and more insular than a lot of other cities in the country. That remains true to this day.

But that doesn't explain what he's doing *here*. With me.

I open my mouth to demand answers, but he slaps my clit before I can speak. His voice is harsh in my ear. "Do it, Ruby. Come for me right fucking now."*

Even as my mind rails at his arrogance, at his determination to make me fold, my body is primed and ready to submit. It's everything I can do to clamp my jaw shut and keep his name trapped on the right side of my teeth. I can't stop myself from coming though. My body is too eager for the pleasure he gives.

* HOLD ME DOWN—Halsey

He curses against my ear. "Stubborn to the bitter end."

Wolf—Luke—*Casimir* pulls out of me. I don't have a chance to figure out what I'm supposed to do next, because he throws me over his shoulder and starts carrying me to the bed.

"Time to talk."

That snaps me out of it. "You son of a bitch." I beat my fists against his lower back. "You lied to me. You've *been* lying to me." For two fucking years. He must have known exactly who I was in that bar the night he hit on me, when we took shots together and ended up with him going down on me in the parking lot. He took me home that night, and within a week, we were official.

A lie.

Casimir pauses in front of the huge trunk of toys, but I don't have a chance to twist to see what he's doing before he's on the move again. He drops me onto the bed. I bounce, and then he's on top of me, straddling my stomach.

I almost—*almost*—get distracted by his massive cock right in my face. He's still hard and coated in my orgasm. I've seen his cock like this before, but it's not the same. It will never be the same again.

He slams a cuff around one wrist and, in one smooth move, clips it into a bar connected to the rings hanging on either side of the headboard. I gasp, but it's too late. He already has my second wrist bound and clipped in. "You motherfucker."

He ignores me and moves down my body to give my ankles the same treatment. I try to twist and kick him, but he easily avoids the blow. Within seconds, I'm bound spread-eagle on the bed.

Helpless.

No one even knows where I am, thanks to my lies. I didn't book the plane ticket with my credit card, so there's no record of it. I turned in my phone when I arrived at the estate, and I watched the Concierge turn it off, so I can't rely on location tracking.

I'm fucked.

Casimir climbs off the bed and pulls on his pants. Then he turns back to me. "Now. Speak. Get it off your chest so we can move on."

His audacity leaves me temporarily speechless. He's talking as if this has a foregone conclusion, as if this is a little bump on the path to our future. Delusional.

I rattle the cuffs against their rings. "Untie me."

"No."

I open my mouth to use my safe word but hesitate. Do I believe he'll ignore it? Or that he'll actually let me go if I use it? I don't know which is worse, and that speaks volumes to how fucked my head is right now. But damn it, I want answers. "How long did you stalk me before we 'met' for the first time two years ago?"

He lifts a single dark brow. "A few months. You made it easy. You put every thought in your head on social media."

My breath whooshes out. The question was a hunch; to have it verified feels...complicated. But he's answering my questions, so I don't linger on the emotions clogging my chest. "Why me?"

"You know the answer to that." He moves around the room, making the same circuit I did when I first got here, examining the toys and tools, poking his head into the bathroom.

Yeah, I guess I do. He picked me because I'm heir to the Belmonte territory—not because he took one look at me and was overwhelmed by wanting. It shouldn't matter. He's Casimir fucking Romanov. He's a fucking stalker, a murderer, an enemy; the answer to *why me* shouldn't make my chest tight and hot.

Carver City has had peace for a long time, and the territory leaders are—mostly—still in their prime and not easy pickings. But we heirs are coming of age, and most of us are taking on more responsibility, training for the roles we'll one day fill.

It'd be smart for an enemy to plant the seeds of dissent now. To target us. Whether to tee us up to be perfect victims later...or to merge with us in a more traditional format. Marriage.

I swallow hard. "How many Romanovs are in Carver City right now?"

He gives me a wolf's grin. "Smart girl."

Fuck. Fuck, fuck, *fuck*. Michelle hasn't said anything about suspicious people in her life, but she's definitely been acting strangely. I was dating a damn Romanov for two fucking years and I had no idea.* She might have someone close to her. She might be in danger. And Zayne...and the others. Fuck. "Who?"

He just stares at me, expression stony.

A slow-dawning horror takes up residence in my chest. "Tatiana. She's one of you."

"My...sister."

The horror inside me grows claws and teeth. His sister. I had his *sister's* mouth and fingers all over my pussy. I sent him a picture of it. Oh gods... "What the *fuck*, Casimir?"

* BLUE EYES BLIND—ZZ Ward

"I told you to leave her alone. You didn't listen."

I stare at him, trying to see the man I fell in love with. The features are the same—his handsome face, sensuous lips, pale eyes—but Luke never wore a cold expression like Casimir does now. They don't even *move* the same. "What was your endgame? Because from where I'm standing, it looks like you never planned to tell me the truth."

He shrugs. "Once we were married, I would have mentioned something."

"Mentioned something," I repeat numbly. "You lied to me. You've *been* lying to me from the beginning."

He gives me a long look. "Keep throwing stones, baby. You were so quick to tell me who your parents were to Carver City— who your aunt was. Oh wait, you weren't. You never did."

Because I thought he was outside the life. I thought he was something just for me. I hadn't planned on us getting so serious, moving in together, the whole nine yards. It just kind of happened, and it never felt like a good time to explain that my parents were overprotective because we're in organized crime. I tucked that conversation away in the same place I've tucked my thoughts and feelings about being heir. "That's different."

"Sure." He doesn't say it like he agrees. "Then let's do one easier. I might have lied about who I was...but so did you."

"No, I didn't. You knew my name from the start."

"Come on, Red." He picks up a flogger, and my whole body goes tight. But he doesn't approach the bed with it. He just runs it lightly over his palm, almost contemplatively. "We wouldn't be here if you were the good girl you pretended to be for years. You'd still be sleeping next to Luke, the nice guy who's perfectly safe."

"Perfectly boring," I snap.

"You never thought so when you were coming on my tongue."

I flinch. It's true. During the first year of our relationship, we were insatiable. *I* was insatiable. I'm still not sure when it all changed. "Not recently."

"No," he agrees. "Not recently. I've been distracted with work, with things back home that required my attention. I would have course corrected, but you took that option away when you…" His fist clenches around the flogger. "*You* cheated, baby. So before you get on your high horse about lies, consider that I haven't touched another fucking person since we started dating. You've done it three times."

My body flushes with shame, which only makes me angrier. Yeah, I cheated, but would I have if I'd known who he really was? The logic is deeply flawed, but I'm too mad to care. "I cheated on *Luke*, not you. Once."

"Semantics." He drops the flogger and moves to stand at the foot of the bed, his cold gaze raking over me. "Once on Luke, twice on Wolf. It all amounts to the same thing."

He's right. I hate that he's right. I could argue that I was never in a relationship with Wolf, that we never agreed on anything at all, but that doesn't feel like the truth. "If you were honest with me—"

"Then you would have gone running to your precious parents." He crosses his arms over his chest. "And your fathers would have taken exception and tried to do something about it. So I would have killed them, and we still would have ended up here."

He says it so calmly. It's not even a threat. It's just fact.

I stare. "No."

"Yes." He shrugs. "This is better."

He's been four steps ahead of me this entire time. What the hell am I supposed to think of that? I don't know. I can't *think* at all. "Did you hurt Tatiana? Threaten her?" Her email hadn't seemed worried, but I was a stranger. It's not like she'd confess to me.

He actually has the nerve to look insulted. "We're family. She might be a bitch, but she's blood. And she hardly forced you into that little threesome. That's not on her."

"Funny how you make an exception for her when you didn't for the others."

"Life isn't fair, baby. You know that better than most." He drinks me in with long sweeps of his gaze. He finally stops at my pussy. "What's your safe word?"*

"No."

"That's not it." He moves back to the cabinet of toys and tools. "You use it, this stops. But you want me as much as I want you. You wanted me as Luke, even if you weren't honest about what you needed. So I gave you what you need in the form of Wolf. You liked our fucked-up little games, or you would have put a stop to them. So now that there are no more lies between us, we're going to keep playing."

"*No.*"

He turns back around, a few things I can't quite see clearly in his hands. "Keep telling me no while that pussy practically gushes

* LIKE YOU MEAN IT—Steven Rodriguez

in anticipation. You might have a lying mouth, but your body knows who owns you."

"You don't own me." I wish I sounded more confident, especially as he climbs on the bed to kneel between my spread legs. I jerk on the bindings, but they hold me steady. Worst of all, it doesn't *hurt*. He's been very careful with me, and I love and hate that realization in equal measure. "Stop, Casimir. I mean it."

"No." He parts my pussy with rough fingers, and then something snaps around my clit. I jerk, but there's nowhere to go. I can't see the thing either.

There's no time to figure it out. Not when he pulls a small plug out of his pocket and smears lube on it. I struggle. It's no use. Casimir holds my hips down and presses the plug against my ass and then carefully inside. I haven't done much anal, and the intrusion is strange. But not awful.

He brushes the base with his knuckles, and it shifts inside me. "I like this," he says.

"I don't."

"Mmm." His touch moves up to where my clit is pulsing strangely. Understanding rolls over me in waves. He put something on it, a clamp maybe, to restrict blood flow. It's going to hurt like a bitch when he takes it off.

Casimir lifts his attention to my face as he presses three fingers into me. I arch off the bed, the intrusion almost too much with the plug in place. He plants his free hand on my stomach, holds me down as he keeps fucking me slowly. "Like I said—your body always tells the truth."

I can't quite catch my breath. "Physical response...unintentional."

"Is that why you can't manage a full sentence?" He curls his fingers, brushing them against my G-spot. "Because you hate what I do to you so much? Give in, Ruby. Admit that you're mine, that you want me as I am, want to be with me honestly, not as watered-down versions of ourselves."

"No." I can't think. It's a blessing that I'm tied down, because I'd be riding his hand fully if I weren't. Gods, but I'm a horrible person—even as my brain is screaming at me that this man is using sex to manipulate me, that he *lied* to me, that he's going to do something to hurt my family and the city I love, there's a large part of me that simply wants to beg him to fuck me again.

I don't realize he's not holding me down anymore until I lift my hips to take his fingers deeper. His brutal smile almost makes me come on the spot. This is a game, and I'm losing.

Casimir moves before I can fully process what he intends. He unhooks the cuffs at my ankles and flips me onto my stomach. The bar my wrists are cuffed to rotates with me, though it's positioned in such a way that I still can't lift my upper body off the bed—I'm too spread out to get leverage.

That doesn't stop *him* from lifting my hips. It doesn't stop me from arching my back more to practically offer him my pussy. Gods, what is *wrong* with me? It's like he's got some kind of drug coming out of his pores that turns me into a sex demon.

Liar. You know who's responsible for your actions, and it's not him.

I'm not ready to face that truth. Not now. Maybe not ever.

But when his cock presses to my entrance, I don't try to jerk away. I just bite the sheets to keep from moaning aloud. With the plug in place, he has to fight his way inside me. He keeps squeezing my ass cheeks, spreading them and then pressing them together, making the plug shift inside me.

It feels good. Better than good.

If I'd known this is what anal could be, I would have changed my mind about trying it again sooner.

"There's my good girl. Take my cock. Just like that." His Russian accent gets thicker. He presses my cheeks together again, and this time, I can't stop myself from moaning. "You'll take me here too. Properly this time. You don't give a fuck who I am as long as I make you feel like the little slut you are. Isn't that right, baby?"

"No," I gasp. I don't register that I'm moving, squirming on his cock, until he thrusts a little. "Casimir, stop."

"Make me." He leans down to press his hands to the bed on either side of me, his chest against my back, his cock buried achingly deep inside me. And worst of all, his rough voice is in my ear, stripping me bare. "You've always been able to stop me, baby. Right from the beginning. But you never did. You aren't stopping me now. You want my cock deeper, want me to fuck you harder, need me to make you come."

It's a testament to the truth of his words that I can't find any of my own. "*No.*"

"Prove it." He reaches between me and the bed and touches my pulsing clit. Even the light stroke is almost too much. I cry out, shoving back onto his cock as much as I'm able to.

The only warning I get is a click before the clamp falls off my clit. The blood rushes back in an agonizing sensation that makes me scream. Casimir is already moving, urging my hips higher as he fucks me hard enough to shift me up the mattress.

Gods help me, but I come all over his cock.

He pulls out of me, and then his mouth is there, eating me from behind, soothing my throbbing clit with his tongue. He teases another orgasm out of me just like that.

Then it starts again.

Casimir fucks me with his tongue, his fingers, his cock, barely giving me any time to recover before he starts winding me up again. And all the while, the bastard's voice is in my ear, telling me I know how to make this stop, all I have to do is speak that one little word, how I won't say it because I'm his perfect little slut.

And I come for him. Again and again and again, until my world narrows down to his touch, to *him*.

Even as I tell him no, tell him I don't want this, I don't want him, I keep my safe word trapped firmly behind my teeth.

Which just proves my worst fear. I really am a monster.

Just like him.

13

I wake up tucked against Casimir's body.* He uncuffed me at some point during the night and is now breathing low and even. That, at least, I recognize on an intrinsic level. I've slept next to this man for two years. I know the cadence of his heartbeat against my ear, of his slow exhales and deep inhales. I don't know if it's reassuring or horrible that he can't lie in his sleep.

I lift my head and study his expression, trying to compare it to the one I knew so well. His brow is relaxed in sleep, his jaw too. It makes him look younger. More like Luke, the man I originally fell in love with. Except he isn't Luke. He never has been.

He's Casimir Romanov.

I still can't quite wrap my head around it...or the implications. Everything he's said has been focused solely on me, aside from answering that more Romanovs are in Carver City. But he can't be here because he's so in love with me. He's here at his

* HEAVY IN YOUR ARMS—Florence + The Machine

father's behest. Or worse, his uncle's. Jovan Romanov is head of the Romanov empire, which stretches the globe, and his reputation is akin to the boogeyman of the Mafia. You don't fuck with him if you want to live.

Getting out of here has to be the first priority. My family needs to know that there's something coming. Something bad.

That, more than anything, gets me moving. It's one thing to endanger myself with my choices. Hurting my parents? My aunts and uncles? Unacceptable.

Casimir's hand shoots out and closes around my wrists before I make it more than an inch from him. He speaks without opening his eyes. "The door is locked, baby."

Sure, but there's a panic button. Pushing that probably cancels the contract right then and there. The Concierge doesn't seem like someone to fuck with, and the rules of the auction are sacred. "Let me go."

He opens his eyes and sighs. "We're not past this then."

I jerk away from him, and he releases me, dragging a finger over the ring I'm still wearing. It's achingly apparent that he chose to free me. I didn't do it with my own strength. I glare. "Tell me what your family wants with Carver City."

Casimir stretches out and props his head on his arm. "The same thing we always want. Power. Territory. Money. Not necessarily in that order."

I cross my arms over my chest, which feels ridiculous while I'm naked. "That is not a plan."

"You didn't ask for the plan."

"Casimir."

His slow smile makes my heart backflip. The only warning I get is a slight tensing of his abs, and then he's on me, flipping me onto my back and settling between my thighs. "Say it again."

He's holding me down, but his expression is hardly threatening. I narrow my eyes. "No."

"So difficult."

"Answer my question. The plan. Your intentions. Whatever you want to call them. We're talking about my family's safety. I might be a fucking fool when it comes to dealing with you, but *they* are my priority."

"I know." He sighs again, as if already tired of this game. "I feel the same."

The Romanovs are notoriously clannish. Their moves make the dangers that Carver City has seen in the past look like children's games. They might marry for alliances and power, but they are loyal only to one another...and sometimes even *that* loyalty falters. At least that's the recent rumor in regard to their American cousins. The New York branch has been making moves and...

I frown. "Were you part of that stuff that went down with the New York Romanov heir?"

He catches my hands and presses them to the bed on either side of my head. "Baby, I don't want to talk about the family business right now. All you need to know is that we don't want your family dead. There's no need for war when an alliance brings the same outcome with fewer resources wasted."

An alliance.

Something is going wrong in my stomach, my chest. It feels like I'm free-falling and slamming to earth, all at once. "I see."

"Get that look off your face," he snaps.

"Make me," I snap right back.

"I'm not sorry I lied to you. If I'd told you the truth, you would have run crying to your parents, and then things would have gotten complicated. If you're waiting for an apology, you're going to wait a long fucking time, baby." His expression is so damn serious. "The moment I knew who you were, I claimed you as mine. We were always going to end up here. And I was never going to play fair."

Because I'm the fucking Belmonte heir.*

Did I think I was feeling reckless before? Well, that was nothing compared to right now. I want to scream at him, to claw at his face, to grab a gun and pull the trigger over and over until there are no bullets left. He lied to me, yes, but I'm starting to realize I was already rationalizing that away. Because he wanted *me*.

Except he didn't. He was sent to seduce and marry the Belmonte heir. If I had an older sibling, it would be them beneath him right now. Not me.

"Ruby—"

"Huntsman."

He blinks down at me as if he can't believe I just said it. Casimir eases off me but doesn't move far away. "This conversation isn't done."

No, it's not. I can't go back to Carver City with him chasing me. Even if I called in my parents, he's the *Mad Wolf*. He's a notorious killer, and while my fathers might be able to kill him before

* LAST LAUGH—FLETCHER

he hurts them…there are no guarantees. And if they succeed? I'm not ready to examine the pain that thought causes.

"I need some space."

"No."

I slide off the bed and start looking around for something to put on. The rubies on my collar slide luxuriously against my skin, and I want to rip them off with my bare fingers, but Casimir has the key, and I don't feel like arguing with him to get it back. "You don't get to tell me no. Not right now. Gods, you don't even see why I'd be pissed about this, do you? It's like talking to a wall."

He watches me with a predator's intent but makes no move to get off the bed. It doesn't matter. I know firsthand how fast he is when he wants to be. There's nowhere in this room that I can escape him. Which means I need to get out of the room.

"When's the last time you ate?"

His question brings me up short. I spin around and point my finger at him. "Don't do that."

"Don't do what?"

"Don't ask me a *Luke* question." I am notorious for getting bitchy when I'm hungry, and at some point, when we were on the verge of arguing for real, Luke learned to ask me that question. It's frankly embarrassing how many arguments died a quiet death the moment I got some protein in me.

Casimir may have Luke's face, may be asking me Luke's question, but that *can't* mean anything. Softening toward him, sharing a smile in acknowledgment that my blood sugar is probably low, letting two years of *knowing* a person make me believe his lies? Out of the question.

He watches me closely. "I'll call for some food."

"I'd rather leave the room and get it myself." I glare. "You know, stretch my legs and shit."

"You're going to run." Now, finally, he moves, easing off the mattress and pulling on his pants. "Haven't you figured it out yet, baby? There's nowhere you can run that I can't find you. I'll chase you to the ends of the earth if that's what it takes."

My stomach does that strange swoopy thing again, but I'm too twisted up to tell if it's good or bad. Maybe it really is just hunger. "Because I'm the heir."

His brows slam together. "Because you're mine."

"Tomato-tomahto." I grab the silk robe that's been left on the hook in the bathroom. It's short and slinky and leaves nothing to the imagination, but at least I'm not naked. I stalk to the door and bang on it. "Let me out. I'm done." I am not ready to cancel the contract, but surely they have surveillance—whether digital or a person lingering in the halls if something goes wrong.

"We're not done."

"I am." The lock clicks open, and I shove out into the hallway.

Casimir is right on my heels, not bothering to put on a shirt or shoes. This feels as unbearably intimate as fucking him, but I can't stop. I pick a direction at random and charge down the hall.

To his credit, he doesn't touch me. But there's no escaping his presence as my shadow. I can sense his anger growing. That's fine; mine is too.

"Ruby, stop."

"Fuck you." I hear voices nearby and take a sharp turn to head in that direction. Even now, I don't really think Casimir is going to hurt *me*, but that doesn't mean he's going to let me leave without him. I need to find the Concierge or...

I turn another corner and catch sight of the auctioneer. Reaper. That was his name. He's standing in a large arched doorway, talking to a pair of people. They move into the room behind him, and he sees me coming. His grin is sexy and a little dangerous. "Nice collar."

Help.

I open my mouth to say it, but instead, what comes out is "What's going on here?"

"This?" Reaper shrugs, the gesture toward the room elegant. "It's a little tradition among old friends." His gaze slips past me to where Casimir has stopped behind me, so close, I can feel the heat coming off his body. "Wolf."

"Reaper." There's a rumble to his voice that feels particularly dangerous. "Ruby is hungry. We're headed to the kitchens."

"I'm not hungry anymore." I peer past Reaper into the room behind him. There are couches and chairs arranged artfully around the space, and along the perimeter are a number of suspension racks, spanking benches, and other large kink equipment.

The room is full, the gathered people ranging from an older couple in elegant evening wear sharing wine on a love seat to a handful of people my age who are wearing little more than their skin.

What's great is that I don't know a single one of them.

I take a step forward, but Reaper tosses out an arm, stopping me without touching me. "Sorry, love, but the Mad Wolf is a nightmare to play with, and our voyeur ranks are filled."

"I don't want to watch. I want to participate."

Reaper studies me for a beat and then turns his attention on Casimir. "Well?"

Casimir makes another sound that's suspiciously close to a growl. "A moment." He takes my arm and practically drags me a few feet down the hall.

"Let me go," I say under my breath.

He spins me to face him. He may be manhandling me a bit, but I don't miss the fact that he's being very careful not to actually hurt me. The fool inside me wants to look into that. The rest of me wants to punish him for all the horrible feelings tangling inside me. I don't know what to think, what to feel.

"You want this."

"Sure do." I don't know if it's true, but he looks distinctly irritated. It's there in his clenched jaw and the way he holds himself a little too still.

He studies my face. "If I agree to this, you are going to sit down and hear me out at the end of it." His grip on my shoulders shifts, and his fingers start stroking up and along the rubies of my collar. "And you're going to keep this on the entire time."

"Can't really take it off without the key *you* have."

"I'm serious, Ruby. We're talking after this. No theatrics. No bullshit. No lying."

Not likely. I smile up at him and lie through my teeth. "Fine. We can talk after this."

Casimir curses under his breath. "You're lying again. Whatever. Let's go."

I step away quickly before he can guide me to where Reaper watches us with undisguised interest. As I walk back to Reaper, I catch sight of a woman kneeling at his feet. I hadn't noticed her, because he's so damn entrancing. She's a pretty white woman with long dark hair and angry blue eyes. My eyes go wide. She was the one before me in the auction, the one who sold herself for a single dollar. Was *Reaper* the winning bidder? It doesn't matter. He's my priority right now, so he gets my best charming smile.* "We're in."

"Very well."

I start to move past him, but he blocks my way again.

"Not so fast, love. If you want in, you have to prove yourself." There's a teasing note to his voice. I might be shit at reading Casimir, but I understand power plays. Casimir undermined Reaper at the auction, and now he's all but whipping out his dick to piss on Casimir's foot.

I can work with this.

"That's not—"

I ignore whatever Casimir is about to say and drop to my knees before Reaper. He's shirtless again, so it's easy enough to hook my fingers into the front band of his pants. I give him wide eyes. "Like this?"

He arches his brows, his grin downright sinful. "Don't let me stop you, love."

"Stop calling her that," Casimir snarls. "Ruby, get off your knees."

"He said I need to prove myself. So I will." I wait for Reaper's slight nod to unbutton his pants and drag down his zipper. His cock is already hard and just as impressive as Casimir's.

The woman kneeling at my side tenses, but she's not my problem.

I glance at Casimir, who's glaring at me. He says something scathing in Russian and then switches to English. "You want to suck his cock? Do it."

"I don't need your permission. We broke up, remember?" But what little hesitation I had is gone. I lean forward and take Reaper's cock into my mouth. He's attractive in the way of a fallen angel who's taken to the vices of the world, all sharp lines and sharper angles. And he *does* have a nice cock.

Best of all, Casimir is watching.

That, even more than the act of sucking Reaper's cock, gets me wet. I slide my hands down Reaper's thighs and back up to his hips as I swallow him down. I muscle past my gag reflex and give him my A game. Put on a show for the glaring man at our side.

When I glance up at Reaper, his smirk says he knows exactly what I'm doing, but he's allowing it for his own reasons. Our eyes meet in a moment of perfect understanding. He laces his fingers together behind his head, not doing anything to guide me, just allowing me to prove myself.

Okay, yeah, that's hot as fuck.

I pick up my pace, giving him everything I have. It's messy work, but that just makes me enjoy it all the more. This man is going to come, and I'm going to make it happen.

"There you go, love," he murmurs. "Almost there."

It's honestly kind of sweet that he's giving me a chance to do anything but swallow him down when he orgasms. I'm angry enough at Casimir to make a mess of myself with Reaper's come, but I want to enjoy the play party without starting out sticky.

He exhales sharply, and that's the only further warning I get. I suck harder, swallowing as he comes down my throat. I give him one last long suck before I ease off his cock and arch my brows at him. "Well?"

He laughs and smoothly tucks his cock back into his pants. "You know you've done well, you little brat." He offers his hand, and I allow him to lift me to my feet. He brushes a light kiss to my knuckles. "Don't get too settled in. The main event starts soon."

"Perfect."

He looks at Casimir without dropping my hand. "And you. If you harm a single one of my guests, I'm going to take it rather personally."

Casimir grunts. It's not words, but it seems to be enough for Reaper.

He drops my hand and waves me past him. "You're going to enjoy yourself immensely tonight, love."

I have every intention of doing so. And if it makes Casimir choke in the process...all the better.

———

"Are you happy now?"

I don't look at Casimir as I slide past two people making out. "Not even a little."

"Ruby."

Even as I tell myself not to, I glance over my shoulder at him. He's banked his obvious fury at Reaper's antics, but there's a deep heat in his pale eyes that makes me quiver. I lick my lips. "What?"

He grabs my hips and spins me around, one hand shifting to the small of my back and pulling me against his chest. It's a smooth move, so smooth that I don't have a chance to push back. Or that's what I tell myself as I find myself pressed against his heat. I plant my hands on his chest, fully intending to shove him away, but the command gets lost somewhere between my brain and fingers.

Casimir digs his other hand into my hair and presses me harder against him. He brings me so close that the rubies of my collar bite into my skin the same way they must be biting into his. "Let's get one thing straight."

"Can't wait."

He makes that sexy snarling sound against my lips. "No matter who you fuck and suck tonight, it's at *my* will."

"Whatever you have to tell yourself." My voice is too breathy, but he's unraveling right in front of me, and it feeds my recklessness, gasoline to my fire.

He nips my bottom lip, hard enough to make me gasp. "My will, baby. So have fun tonight, because when you're done playing, we're going back to that room, and I'm reclaiming every bit of you that you're all too happy to give away to others."

This isn't him threatening to murder anyone I touch. This is different. This is...even hotter.

I press on his chest, and he allows me to walk him backward

to an open chair behind him. Casimir sinks smoothly, and I follow, straddling him. His cock is hard against my bare pussy, and I can't help rolling my hips a little as I lean down to speak directly in his ear. "I'm going to fuck so many people tonight. You're going to have a lot of reclaiming to do, *baby*. Though you can't give away what was never yours."

"You were mine from the moment I saw you, Ruby." He grabs my ass and grinds me against him. I'm so wet from sucking Reaper's cock in front of him. So fucking wet and aching and... He rubs me up and down the length of his cock, the seam of his pants hitting *right there*.

Now's the time to do something, to put him in his place, but the haze of need muddies my thoughts. "No," I whisper.

"Yes." He keeps me moving at that pace, his eyes hard and hot. "No one makes you come as hard as I do. No one fucks you like I do." Casimir leans in, his breath ghosting against the shell of my ear as he keeps winding me tighter and tighter. "And no one knows what a vicious little monster you are the way I do. I've spent two years knowing you. You're selfish and petty, smart and savvy. Downright fucking *wicked*, baby. If you ever get out of your own way, you're going to be one hell of a leader for that fucking territory."

"Casimir." I don't know if I'm telling him to stop or to keep going. I can't *think*. "Please."

"Take what you need, baby."

I frantically reach between us to get his pants undone, even as I tell myself not to give him the satisfaction. I just get my fist wrapped around his length when Reaper's voice cuts through the room.

"Time to play, friends. The game tonight is a hunt, but we're doing things my way."

A chorus of laughs slams me back into myself.

What am I *doing*? I had every intention of making Casimir pay for everything he's done, but the first chance I get, I'm about to be bouncing on his cock again. I shove off him and yank my robe shut. I'm not even sure when it came undone.

For his part, he smirks and does his pants back up. The only indication that he's as affected as me is his hard cock pressing against the fabric of his pants...against the wet spot of my desire.

Meanwhile, Reaper is still speaking, projecting to every corner of the room without raising his voice. "Participation is not required, of course, but those who want to play will choose to be predator...or prey. Prey flees. Predators pursue. And if a predator catches their prey, they can have their filthy way with them. For this game, we'll follow the tried-and-true safe words. 'Red' means stop. 'Yellow' is a pause. All our lovely prey will be wearing red wristbands. Understood?"

Again, people murmur in assent. He has us all captivated. The man truly does know how to work a crowd.

He grins. "And what's a game without a prize? Whichever predator brings me the best offering will win a favor of their choosing."

"What do you mean by 'best,' Reaper?" someone calls from the back of the room.

His grin widens. "That's for me to know and you to find out." He spreads his arms. "Prey will get a five-minute head start. If you want to play foxes to our hounds, come to me now."

Participation may not be required, but if I stay here, I'm going to end up fucking Casimir again and likely not receive any answers.

Besides, when am I going to get another chance to play a game like this? Fleeing strangers who will hold me down and fuck me if they catch me? Playing kinky games without having to worry about seeing a family member participating?

I'm not missing this for anything.

14

The rules of the game are simple enough: Stay on the grounds. The participating prey have a five-minute head start, and then the predators will come hunting. Reaper will stay here with those who aren't interested in this flavor of game.

We prey gather near him at the arched doorway, accepting our red wristbands. The ones in heels are taking off their shoes, but I have no shoes to speak of. Or clothes, for that matter. The collar hardly counts, and the robe will be easy enough to get past when I'm caught.

Because it is a *when*, not an *if*. Being caught is the whole goal.

Speaking of…

I turn to find Casimir lurking a few feet away. I wish he'd grabbed a shirt before leaving the room; his shirtless chest is highly distracting.* I try to drape myself in bravado. "Better hope you find me first."

"No."

* STRUT—EMELINE

I jolt. "Excuse me?"

"You want to play games, baby? Play." His expression gives nothing away. He's completely drawn into himself, and while there's a part of me that hates his familiar face on what amounts to a stranger...the rest of me is quivering in anticipation.

He can talk all the shit he wants. He's playing. In fact...the longer I look at him, the more I start to see hints of the real him behind the locked exterior.

Because I *do* know him, at least in part. I've lived with this man for over a year, and he might have been playing a role the entire time, but there was too much intimacy that couldn't be faked. Not entirely. Not when we were living in each other's pockets.

I cross the short distance to Casimir. "Now who's lying?"

"What?"

Understanding makes me giddy. Or maybe it's excitement for what's coming. Either way, I think I finally get something about him.

I carefully press my hands to his chest and lean in, going up on my tiptoes to speak directly in his ear. "Jealousy gets you off, doesn't it, *baby*? You hate seeing me with others, but you love the frenzy that comes afterward." Just as much as I do.

And tonight, he can't kill anyone for touching me. No one is going to get hurt while we play this twisted little game.

When I ease back, he isn't locked down any longer. He grabs my hips and jerks me to him, taking my mouth in a devastating kiss. It's a clear claim of ownership, but I don't have a chance to decide how I feel about it before he steps back. "Run, baby. Run fast and run far, because when I catch you, I'm not letting you go again."

Reaper's voice cuts through any response I'd be able to come up with. "It's time. Prey, your five-minute head start begins... now."

I run.

A large part of the prey group cuts to the right, so I go left. I don't have a good map of what this massive house is like inside. I have a vague idea of finding somewhere to hide, but for now, I'm running on pure instinct. On and on and on, cutting through the shadowy halls in search of a good destination.

How long has it been? I have no idea. I'm reasonably fit because my parents insist I be capable of protecting myself, which means weekly training sessions in a variety of self-defense techniques and general fitness, but my breath sears my lungs with each inhale and exhale. The halls seem to expand and contract in the same rhythm.

In the distance, a series of calls go up, some taunting, some almost animalistic. The predators are on the move.

I need to get out of the halls. They're too open.

I veer around a corner and then another, picking the directions at random. When this started, I had a vague thought of being strategic, but there's no space for that in my head right now. I can't hide. I have to keep moving.

The next corner takes me up a set of stairs. There are more sounds now. Screams and cries of victory. The predators are finding the first wave of prey. I pick up my pace...only to stop short when I reach the top of the stairs. There's a short hallway that ends in an intricately carved glass door. The door is cracked open, a clear invitation. And where it leads...

A conservatory, but not like one I've seen before, at least not in private residences. I step through the door and look around. It's *massive* in here. A tile path leads deeper into what feels like a forest, the plants and trees pressing in on the path. It's the strangest combination of wild and restrained, of nature and civilization.

I love it.

"I saw someone come up this way."

The deep voice startles me out of my reverie. I bolt, rushing down the narrow path and deeper into the conservatory. It's a mistake.

The voice calls out again. "We've got one!"

"Now we're talking," says another.

Footsteps pursue me, closer and closer. I'm running full out now, pumping my arms, my breath sawing through my lungs, my feet pounding the tile floor. This may be a game, but my body doesn't know that. I'm not even sure my brain does. Adrenaline and fear create a toxic mix inside me, driving me faster yet.

Not fast enough.

Rough hands grab me around the waist, and then I'm lifted off my feet and tossed into another set of arms. I fight on instinct, striking wild punches until the person holding me catches my arms and pins them at my sides.

The one who caught me laughs breathlessly.* "Look at that collar. It's Wolf's girl."

"Lucky us," pants the one holding me. "She's a fighter."

"Good."

They bear me down to the tile floor, faster than I can react. They're bigger than me. Stronger. I'm fighting and cursing and

* THE DEVIL WEARS LACE—Steven Rodriguez

wetter than I've ever been. Especially when one wrenches my thighs wide and settles between them.

The one between my legs palms my pussy and presses his fingers to my ass. He laughs wickedly when I jolt. "Oh yeah, little one. I've caught you, and now I'm going to fuck this ass."

Suddenly, this isn't as fun anymore. I fight harder, but it's like fighting gravity. It takes my panicked brain longer than I want to admit to realize that this is a game and that there are rules. "Yellow!"

They pause. The guy holding my arms grips my chin lightly. "What part, honey?" His voice is suddenly kind, all the harshness drained away.

The change startles me into answering honestly. "Not anal. That's only for him."

"Do you have a problem with us fucking you otherwise?" He pauses, his eyes roving over my face. "With us coming on you?"

"No," I manage. "I want it." For the experience, yes, but also for what will come after when Casimir finds me.

"Okay." He releases me and sits back on his heels. "Let her up, Jason."

Jason obeys immediately.

I scoot away from them, my confusion making me move slowly. I clear my throat. "Um. What happens now?"

The older guy, the one who was so kind for a moment, grins, his teeth a flash in the shadows. "Run, little one. You have a chance to escape, but if we catch you a second time, we're both going to fuck that pretty pussy." He pulls two condoms out of his pocket and tosses one to Jason. "You have until we get these on to try to escape."

Oh. *Oh*. A continuation of the game, getting us back to the place where we're immersed in the chase, now with the established boundary. It makes me dizzy, and I struggle to my feet and run again. But not very fast. And not very far.

They catch me before I make it around the next corner. Jason takes me down in a tackle, somehow making it nearly painless. He pins me face down on the ground, the gritty tile biting into my bare skin. My robe is more bondage than anything else at this point, preventing me from fighting effectively.

Or maybe intentionally I'm not effective. I *want* them to fuck me here, like the predators they're playing, to take their pleasure from me, to use me. I don't know if that's fucked-up or if it's freedom, but I crave this on a level I wasn't prepared for.

Jason grabs the back of my neck, holding me down, and then his cock is there, shoving into me so hard and fast that I scream. I'm wet enough that it doesn't actually hurt, but he's not pausing to make sure. I love it.

My knees scrape against the ground as I struggle, and I can't begin to say if I'm struggling to get away from the onslaught of fucking or to get closer, to take him deeper. He abruptly pulls out of me, and I feel his knuckles against my ass as he yanks off the condom and jacks himself a few times before his come lashes my ass and the small of my back. "Fuck, but that's good pussy. Too good."

Jason moves back, and I barely have time to tense before the other guy takes his place. He's not any gentler. His cock isn't quite as long, but it's thick enough to stretch me uncomfortably. "Stop!" It's a test, an instinctive response. Not "yellow." Not "red." Just more game.

He doesn't even hesitate to fuck me harder. Three strokes, and then he pulls out. "Flip her over."

Jason does exactly that, rolls me onto my back and pins my arms above my head as his friend grabs my hips and shoves into me again. It's so dark in here that they're little more than shadows over me, fucking me roughly. I could be anyone. *They* could be anyone.

Pleasure coils inside me. I dig my heels into the ground, arching up. "Please."

His laughter has none of the kindness he showed me when I yellowed out. "Little slut pretending she doesn't like it."

"She's going to come on your cock while she cries no," Jason rumbles. He shifts my wrists to one hand and roughly palms my breasts. "Pretty tits. You should come on them. A little 'fuck you' to Wolf."

The one fucking me curses and shoves deeper yet. "Can't blame him for being homicidal over this pussy."

The way they're talking is crass in the extreme. I should hate it. Maybe. Probably. But instead, it just drives my desire higher, hotter. My orgasm surges closer.

"Jesus, Rick. Just thinking about it is getting me hard again."

"No one around." Rick's voice has gone harsher. He's close. "No reason not to go again." He pulls out of me, moving faster than he has a right to, and straddles my ribs. I thrash and twist, but there's nowhere to go as he pulls off the condom and jacks himself, quick and hard, until he comes all over my chest, all over my collar. He shifts up and wipes his cock over my lips, jerking back with a laugh when I snap my teeth at him. "Still got fight in her."

"Get her arms."

They switch positions. Now that he's orgasmed, Rick starts using his free hand to play with my breasts, pinching my nipples roughly. "You like this, don't you? Like us fucking you like this, treating you like the dirty little slut you are."

"No," I whisper, lifting my hips to take Jason's condom-covered cock again. My body is alight with a thousand little pains, and Rick's fingers on my nipples have my orgasm tightening. I'm so fucking close, Jason pounding my pussy hard enough to leave scrapes on my ass from my thrashing on the tile floors.

Movement to the side draws my attention. A shadow detaches itself from a nearby tree, shifting just enough that I know *he* knows I see him.

Wolf. Casimir.

Watching these two men fuck me. He shifts forward just enough that I can see his face, can see the murderous rage there. He wants to kill them, to slit their throats and then fuck me in their blood. Not being able to must be driving him feral.

The fact that he's watching, unable to stop this, seeing them take what he's claimed as his?

I come so hard, I shriek.

Jason curses. "Holy fuck, I'm going to—" He pulls out of me almost too late, the condom only half off when he comes all over my pussy. "Maybe we should take *her* to Reaper and have a night with her be our reward. Rushing this has me too worked up." He lets out a rough laugh and drags his still-hard cock through his come, spreading it over my folds.

"*Fuck.*" Rick has gone tense. He's seen Casimir. He releases me and rises swiftly. "Let's go. There's more prey to play with."

"But..." Jason follows his gaze and freezes. "Shit. Yeah. Let's go." They get up and jog away, leaving me where I lie on the ground, scraped all to hell and covered in their orgasms.

As their footsteps fade, Casimir steps out of the foliage to loom over me.* His gaze rakes me, no doubt cataloging every mark and bit of evidence of my being with someone who isn't him. Come all over my tits, making my collar sticky, all over my pussy.

I can't do anything but lie here. The adrenaline is still coursing through my body, mixing up the messages in my brain. He's obviously furious, but I can't quite bring myself to care right now. I can't make my body move either. Everything feels distant and spacey, almost like I'm drunk.

"Are you pleased with yourself?"

"Yes."

He sighs. "Yeah, I thought so." Casimir crouches next to me and brushes my sweaty hair back from my face. "Are you hurt?"

"I don't know."

His thumb strokes my brow. "Game or no game, if they harmed you, I'll kill them."

"Can't. It would make Reaper mad." I lean into his touch. "They were nice. And then mean. Don't murder them."

He carefully scoops me into his arms. There's a barely contained violence in his body, but that doesn't stop me from cuddling close and pressing my face to his throat. I'm sticky and sore and starting to get cold.

* WATER—Tyla

I shiver. "No murder."

"No murder," he says, his fury mixed with amusement. "You're a menace, baby. Nothing easy with you."

"Sorry."

"No, you're not." He carries me out of the conservatory and down the stairs. There's no hesitation in him as he navigates the halls. It just confirms what I already knew—he's been here before, enough times to be familiar with the layout.

We make it back to the room in far less time than I expected. Casimir walks through the space to the bathroom. He sets me down on the counter and takes a wary step back. "Can you sit there while I get this going?"

"Yep." I say it with more confidence than I feel. The adrenaline is draining away, leaving me woozy. "Probably."

He gives me a forbidding look. "Don't fall."

"Sir, yes, sir."

"Brat." He moves to the large claw-foot tub and fiddles with the faucet until the water apparently reaches the temperature he's satisfied with. Then he comes back to me and tugs off my robe. He looks me up and down and shakes his head. "You're a mess."

I follow his gaze. I'm covered in others' orgasms. There are scrapes on my knees and palms—and ass, from the feel of things. I also have a constellation of bruises forming across my body. But what catches and holds my attention is the collar. Even though it's sticky with Rick's come, it's such a clear indication of ownership that I shiver, way down deep. "Yep."

Casimir grabs a washcloth and wipes most of the come off me but frowns at the scrapes. "This will sting, but it's necessary."

Though I have every intention of processing those words, it's hard to focus when he's taking off his pants. "What?"

He takes me back into his arms and steps into the tub. The second the hot water hits my scrapes, I yelp and try to rise. Casimir clamps an arm around my waist, keeping me pinned to him. "Sit."

"It hurts." My voice comes out thick. Holy fuck, what is *wrong* with me? I suddenly feel like I'm about to cry. I press my hands to my cheeks. "What's wrong with me?"

"Subspace drop." Now that I'm no longer trying to flee, he gentles his touch and guides me to relax back against him.

The water buoys me, and his strong body brackets me. Slowly, the worst of the feeling eases. "So that's what it feels like," I whisper. I've heard about it, of course, but considering how embedded my parents and extended family are in the BDSM community in Carver City, I'd never explored anything that would have done it to me. I close my eyes. "What happens now?"

"You keep asking questions you already know the answer to." He strokes his hands over me, and if it didn't feel so good, I'd accuse him of trying to gentle me the way one would gentle a skittish horse.

But it does feel good, so I don't. In fact, I can't seem to open my eyes. My body is loose and relaxed. "Don't let me drown."

Casimir's chuckle is dry and amused and sounds nothing like Luke's ever did. "You're not getting away from me that easily, baby. Sleep. I've got you."

wake to the scent of breakfast. It takes my sleep-soaked brain a few beats to remember everything that's happened in the past few days. The murder. The auction. The chase.

Casimir.*

I open my eyes. The last thing I remember is falling asleep in the tub, buoyed by the water and held safe by Casimir's body. Safe. What a joke. But as I stretch and allow myself a few seconds to relish the ache in my body from the night's activities, I have to admit an uncomfortable truth.

I do trust him. Not with my family. Not with my city. But with my body.

He could have gone about accomplishing his goals in a thousand different ways, and I don't think I would have liked any of them. He's a *Romanov*, for fuck's sake. I never would have welcomed him with open arms.

* 1121—Halsey

I belatedly realize the shower is running and the room is empty except for a tray on the bed with a covered plate on it.

I could run.

He'd find me eventually, but I could probably get to Carver City before he caught up. Take refuge in my parents' home. Confess all the shitty choices I've made lately. Let them handle my mess.

And maybe start a war that gets my fathers killed...or ends with Casimir dead. I should want that. He's the enemy. A *monster*.

But...so am I.

Maybe it's time I faced that truth properly.

I pull the tray to me and pause when the movement doesn't send strands of rubies slithering over my chest and shoulders. I press my hand to my throat, my stomach dropping as I realize the collar is gone. Relief. That's what I'm feeling. Right.

To distract myself, I carefully lift the cover from the plate. It's my favorite breakfast: eggs Benedict. And it's hot enough that Casimir must have set it down seconds before I woke. I pick up my fork and poke the eggs. He *would* remember my favorite.

Luke was always attentive. After the jewelry misstep early in our relationship, he seemed to delight in new ways to surprise me with his knowledge of what I liked. It makes even more sense now, knowing that he's also Wolf, my fucking stalker. Or rather, he's Casimir—a combination of the two of them. Or maybe a different animal completely. That's what I can't quite figure out.

I don't register the shower shutting off, but I sure as fuck don't miss Casimir walking through the door, his skin glistening, a white towel wrapped around his waist.

"You don't have tattoos," I blurt.

"What?"

"What kind of Russian mobster are you without tattoos?"

He smirks. "One who can infiltrate any organization or association. My father chose to take a less traditional route with that shit. My uncle doesn't agree, but I'm too good at what I do for him to argue."

Too good at lying. Murder. Torture. I've heard the stories, just like everyone else. If Jovan Romanov is a boogeyman, the Mad Wolf is his pet, sent out when he wants to make an example of someone.

I take a bite of my eggs, but they taste thick on my tongue. "How am I supposed to trust you when you just told me that?"

"You'll figure it out."

I glare. "You are insufferable."

"Baby." He drags his hand through his damp hair. "How many times do you need to circle the same fucking subject before you admit it doesn't matter?"

"Trust is everything."

"Agreed." His Russian accent thickens. "When have I hurt you?"

That brings me up short. "Excuse me?"

"When. Have. I. Hurt. You?" He circles the bed, stalking closer. "Do you know what my uncle would have done if his wife fucked one of his enforcers in the middle of a bar where anyone could see?"

I register what he's saying, but my fool brain clings to one point like a dog with a bone. "I'm not your wife."

"Not yet."

His audacity startles a laugh out of me. "Even if you could convince me that you want *me*, not the Belmonte heir, my fathers would skin you alive before they let you touch me again."

"Nyet." He crosses his arms over his chest. The movement makes the towel shift as if it's about to fall. "Your old men have gone soft, just like all the leaders of Carver City. They will snap and snarl, but they'll do anything that makes their precious baby girl happy. And I do."

"Bold of you to assume blackout rage is the same thing as happiness."

He snorts. "You liked the thoughtful little shit Luke did. You liked playing the dangerous game with Wolf to the point that if Wolf had been someone else, you would have been confessing your love by the end of the weekend."

His words echo my thoughts uncomfortably and take them even further. I want to say he's wrong, but I think I've lied enough at this point. And truth be told, it's not even the lie that's sticking in my throat.

It's the fact that I could be anyone.

"Not me," I finally say. "The Belmonte heir."*

Understanding dawns in his pale eyes. "So *that's* the sticking point."

"Hard for it not to be." I poke at my eggs again before finally pushing the tray away. "You lied to me, and that's fucked-up, but

* WHAT THE WATER GAVE ME—Florence + The Machine

you have a point about there being no innocent parties in this situation. Fine. I'll agree with that. But you don't want *me*, Casimir. You're just following orders."

He barks out a sharp laugh. "Baby, the mental gymnastics you're performing right now are fucking exhausting."

"The point stands." I might be able to get past most of the shit—which is fucked-up to even contemplate, but I am who I am—except that. I'll never settle for being chosen because of the role I'll play rather than the person I am. Not when the stakes have never been higher.

Casimir eyes the tray. "You didn't eat enough."

"If I wanted your opinion on my eating habits, I'd ask for it."

He curses softly in Russian. "Fine. Let's get this out." He flips back the covers and snags my ankle. "I chose you, baby. You, Ruby Belmonte. How many heirs are there in Carver City? Five? Six? It took me all of two seconds to recognize the glint in your eyes. You're just like me." He starts to drag me down the bed toward him.

"I'm nothing like you." I half-heartedly try to kick him, but he catches that ankle too and jerks me to the edge of the mattress, then easily steps between my thighs. I prop myself up on my elbows and glare. "I might like fucking you. I might have loved Luke. That doesn't mean I'm some kind of kindred spirit."

"No, it doesn't." He strokes his hands up to my knees and slides me until my ass is nearly hanging off the bed. "But the fact remains that you *are* like me, baby. Violent and selfish and willing to use other people as your toys."

I flinch. "That's cruel."

"That's reality." He squeezes my thighs, pressing them a little wider. "Last night, you were fantasizing about me killing those two while they fucked you. It made you come harder."

I almost lie, but he'll know if I do. "Fantasy is not reality. I'm glad you didn't hurt them."

Casimir cups my pussy, his palm rough and possessive. "One day, you'll be territory leader, Ruby. Violence is part of the role, and if your parents haven't prepared you for that, it's on them."

They may have sheltered me to some degree, but I hid from the truth too. Not because I'm afraid of violence; it's more that responsibility gives me hives. What a selfish little brat I've been. I can't think with his hand on me, his fingers sliding through my folds. "What's your point?"

"My point"—he spears me with two fingers, then fucks me slowly—"is that with me by your side, you'll be safe. The pair of us will be unstoppable."

Pleasure slows my thoughts, his words and touch seducing me. "You can't just...fuck me into...submission," I finally manage.

"No." He grins suddenly, and it hits me in the chest like a freight train: that's *Luke's* smile, rueful and a little mischievous. Casimir twists his wrist and curls his fingers against my G-spot. "But that won't stop us from enjoying each attempt."

I need him to stop touching me so I can think clearly. I need him to never stop touching me, to keep fucking me until I'm wrung out and empty. "This will never work."

"Baby, it's already working." He tugs off his towel, and

then his cock is there, splitting me in half, one agonizing inch at a time. He brackets my hips with his hands, holding me down as he fucks me in shallow strokes, each one a little deeper than the last. "You loved me once as Luke. You'll love me better as I really am."

"No." But I don't know what I'm protesting anymore. My heart is all twisted, and I don't know which way is down anymore. Did I think I was in a free fall before? What a joke.

In desperation, I arch up and hook the back of his neck. He allows me to tug him down so I can take his mouth, and the moment our tongues slide against each other, it's as if I've snapped a leash that I wasn't even aware held him back.

He bears me back to the bed, his mouth harsh and demanding on me. Casimir isn't going slow now. He's pulling me to him, his hands on my neck, my spine, my ass, as he drives into me, as if he's tattooing his ownership under my skin.

I meet him halfway. I drag my nails down his back and dig them into his ass, urging him to go deeper, to go harder. It's a frenzy. There's no other way to put it. As if all the pent-up rage and confusion and hurt are distilled into this moment of fucking. Yet it's not as simple as that. This is a moment of *knowing*. Of understanding.

Of recognition.

One monster acknowledging another.*

He switches up his strokes, grinds against me in exactly the way I need. I bite his bottom lip. He squeezes my ass hard enough to bruise, his fingers finding the scrapes from

* HOW VILLAINS ARE MADE—Madalen Duke

last night and sparking new pinpricks of pain. The contrast with the agonizing pleasure of his cock sends me hurtling over the edge.

Casimir keeps my orgasm going, wave after wave crashing over me until my muscles give out. Only then does he retreat. I make a sound of protest, but he doesn't go far. He flips me onto my stomach, and there's a faint rustle as he grabs a bottle of lube. "It's time, baby."

We've never done anal before. I'd had a bad experience with a previous partner and wasn't interested in trying it again with Luke and his giant cock, and doing it right now feels like a promise I'm not sure I can keep. "This doesn't mean anything."

"Liar." He cups my ass, squeezing my cheeks the same way he did before. There's no plug this time, but my body clenches. "You didn't answer my question before."

I'm having a hard time thinking straight. "What question?"

"Have I ever hurt you, Ruby?" He presses a lubed-up finger to my ass and eases it inside. Testing me.

"You're about to." I don't really believe that though. If I did, I wouldn't be quivering with pure anticipation for what comes next. Fucking Casimir has been a life-changing experience, even though I'd die before I'd admit that aloud. We've trampled over boundaries I thought I had, and there's been more pleasure than I could have ever dreamed.

"Ruby." He stops the delicious, careful stroking. "Answer."

I curse, but he's not moving, and I want this too badly to use a safe word to end it. "Fine. No. You haven't hurt me. You bruised my pride. I hate that you lied to me for so long. But you've never hurt my body."

He resumes his careful finger fucking. "I won't hurt you this time either."

"Prove it."

He eases his finger from my ass, and then his cock is there. It feels obscenely large compared to anything he's inserted to date, and I tense.

"Relax, baby." He strokes me with his hands, soothing me even as he presses forward. His cock stretches me. Even with the lube and prep, it burns. It's not *bad* though. Just strange.

Casimir curses softly and stops the forward motion. I don't expect him to lean forward, press his body to mine. He wraps me up in him and slides one hand down to my pussy. "Relax."

"Can't," I pant. It feels like I'm being impaled. But also not. It hurts, yet there's a pressure building around that fullness that is pure pleasure. My brain can't process the conflicting feelings. Then he starts circling my clit, and it all gets so much more confusing. I moan and shake, which only makes it more achingly obvious that his cock is in my ass. But not even close to his whole length. "Casimir."

"I've got you." He's not moving anything except his fingers, the intoxicating circles causing pleasure to override my nerves. He kisses my throat, the back of my neck. "It was only ever going to be you, baby."

"What?"

He keeps up that slow circling even as his hips shift, pressing his cock a little more into me. This time, I don't tense in response. The penetration is extreme, but the more I relax into it, the better it feels. I tilt my head to give him better access to my throat.

Casimir sets his teeth there. "First time I saw you properly was at the Tower. You were on the dance floor wearing a bikini and dancing as if it was your last night on earth."

I arch a little, taking him deeper. I know the night he means. "Foam party."

"Yeah." His fingers are soaked with me, and he dips to press them inside before bringing them back to my clit. "You were drunk off your ass. There was a guy fingering you right there in front of everyone."

I had just moved out and was determined to make the most of my freedom. Up until that point, I'd only hooked up with truly safe people, and I was out-of-my-mind jealous of Michelle, who'd been going through bedroom partners the same way she goes through lipstick colors. I wanted to be wild and free, but I needed alcohol to get me there.

He strokes deeper into me, and I'm startled to feel his hips against my ass. He's seated fully inside me. I tense, but he doesn't immediately start fucking me. He allows me to adjust to the stretch of him, still fingering my pussy and kissing my neck. Still spilling low words into my ear. "You were so beautiful when you came, baby. I wanted to be the one to cause it."

I can barely concentrate past what he's doing to me. "I intended to go home with him."

"I know."

I go still. "He disappeared after that. Went to get a drink and never came back."

"Yeah."

Suspicion takes root. "Did you kill him?"

"No." He chuckles in my ear. "I just...dissuaded...him from going to find you again."

That could mean literally anything. "I don't even remember how I got home that night." I kept drinking and blacked out. Michelle was furious at me because apparently she'd turned around and I was gone. I squirm, relishing the feel of his cock inside me. "Was it you?"

"Yes. Eto bylo." He nips my earlobe. "You called me an angel and told me you loved me as I tucked you into bed."

Humiliation threatens to drown me. "I don't remember."

"That's okay, baby. I remember for both of us." He keeps circling my clit as he starts to move, easing out of me and then thrusting slowly back into my ass. "That's the night I knew you were mine. It was never going to be anyone else."

I don't know if that's really creepy or romantic, but I'll figure it out later. My body tightens with an impending orgasm even more intense than the last one. "Casimir," I moan.

"Breathe, baby. Just breathe." He doesn't pick up his pace, doesn't rush, doesn't do anything but stalk my orgasm as carefully as he's apparently been stalking me for years. "I always take care of what's mine."

I come. I don't stand a chance of holding out, and I wasn't even trying. Not this time.

Through it all, he keeps fucking me, murmuring how good I feel, how he loves to feel me come on his cock, how perfect my ass, my cunt, my body is. When I finally collapse onto the bed, too wrung out to move, he shifts back and grips my hips. Only then does he carefully pick up his pace until he's driving into my ass in short, controlled thrusts. Even after coming so hard, I can't help arching my back again, offering my ass to him, urging him to keep going. It feels so fucking good.

Everything he does to me feels good.

He pulls out abruptly and growls something in Russian as he comes all over my ass.

Then he scoops me up and hauls me to the shower. My legs are still wonky, so he sets me on the bench there as he gets the water going. I watch him dazedly. It feels like we left the real world behind, but that's probably the endorphins lying to me. "This doesn't solve anything."

He sighs. "Baby, it's simple. You love me. You're too pissed to admit it right now, but it's the truth." He continues right over my shrill protest. "And I love you too. I don't know how many fucking ways to say it: you're mine. You were from the moment I laid eyes on you."

"Casimir." I suddenly feel like crying. "Even if that were true, it will never work. I don't even know what you're trying to accomplish. Carver City will never accept Romanov rule."

He tugs me to my feet and beneath the spray. "Don't give a fuck about Romanov rule. But I'm going to marry you, baby. You're the heir. You rule. I'll be your bloody right hand. Satisfies all parties."

"Just like that."

"No reason to complicate shit." He catches my chin, his pale eyes somehow both chilled and heated at the same time. "You might not be ready to admit it, but you already made your decision. The other day. When you kept fucking me after you knew who I was. When you played primal games to taunt me. It's just your pride holding you up right now."

At this point, I don't know if he's right or not. I don't know anything at all. Instead of answering or protesting or *lying*, I kiss him.

16

Casimir tenses as if he'll just snarl at me, but then he lifts me so I can wrap my legs around his waist. There's a rush of hands and soap and rinsing each other off, and then he carries me to the bed and eats me out until I lose track of how many times I come. We fuck with the franticness of two people painfully aware of the clock ticking down on their reprieve. I can't imagine a way this will work, and he doesn't seem able to imagine a way it won't.*

There are no answers two days later, the rising sun bringing our time in this house to an end. Casimir disappears briefly and comes back to the room with our clothes and phones. We dress in silence, and fuck if I know what to do. Say goodbye? Keep arguing in circles?

I don't protest when he takes my hand and leads me through the warren of hallways to the same door through which I entered

* ARSONIST'S LULLABY—Hozier

a few days prior. It feels like a lifetime ago. There's a fancy black sports car waiting, all sleek lines and predator vibes.

Casimir opens the door for me, his movements easy and downright habitual. How many times has he done the same thing as Luke? More than I can begin to count. "Let's go."

It doesn't even occur to me to demand my own ride. I slide into the buttery leather seats and watch him walk around to the driver's side.

It's only as we exit through the gates that I turn to him. "Whatever plan your family has, it will never work. Even if I lost my mind and married you, the other heirs won't follow suit." Michelle wouldn't know commitment if it bit her in the ass. Cassim is so uptight, I can't imagine him having a whirlwind romance with an enemy. Talia is ruthless enough to slit someone's throat if they try to take the territory that's her birthright. We can't even get Kiley to come out with us, let alone lose her head enough to marry a Romanov. There's no established heir to the neutral territory that the Underworld stands in. "It won't work."

"Then you have nothing to worry about, do you?"

I glare. "My fathers will kill you."

"They'll try." He shrugs. "But if you tell them you love me, they'll pull their punches for fear of breaking their baby girl's heart."

"Stop saying that," I hiss.

"Calling you their baby girl?" He takes a corner a little too fast, a tight smile pulling at his lips.

"Saying I love you."

"You do."

I watch the speedometer creep up. If he's speeding to ensure I don't try to punch him in the face...well, it's a good plan. I'm not going to die today. "I loved *Luke*."

"It wasn't all fake. The best cover is more reality than anything else. You love *me*, baby."

I curse. "Even if I agreed with that, I cheated on you."

"Water under the bridge." He glances at me as he changes lanes. "Especially since you plan to keep doing it."

"What?"

"Ruby." The censure in his voice makes me squirm. "You get off on being bad. I get off on punishing you. One plus one equals two."

For a moment, I allow myself to picture what a future like that might look like. To be my true self, messy and bitchy and ruthless. It makes me a little dizzy to even consider. "You can't keep killing people who touch me."

He tightens his grip on the wheel. "I'm willing to...negotiate on that element of the equation."

Am I seriously considering this?

It seems like I am. I lean back in my seat and cross my arms over my chest. "Do you want to fuck other people?"

"Nyet."

"But you're okay with me doing it as part of *our* game?"

"Da." He reaches over and opens the glove compartment. "As long as you wear this when you do." He pulls out a small box and hands it to me.

It's too small to hold the ruby necklace, which is just as well. That jewelry is gorgeous and ostentatious, but there's no way I could wear it regularly. It's too over-the-top. I flip open the box and swallow down a gasp. *This* necklace is brutal in its simplicity, a chain long enough to loop twice around my throat and a dagger dangling from the end, a ruby winking in its hilt. I press my thumb to the blade and hiss out a breath as it slices my skin. "Sharp."

"Da." He sounds pleased. "A lock was tempting, but that's not your style, and someone might look at it and take it the wrong way."

The wrong way. Because I'm heir and will eventually lead the territory. Because I can't afford for anyone to think that I might be beholden to a partner in a way that would put them before my people.

The realization makes me feel strange. I choose to focus on something simpler. "Your accent fades in and out. What's up with that?"

"Habit." He shrugs. "Do you have a preference?"

The fact that he's asking me that almost makes me laugh. This is the strangest conversation I've ever had. "On whether you have an accent?"

"Yeah."

"I want what's real." I clear my throat. "What happens if your family changes their tune? Even if I were to marry you, there's no way the plan will go as smoothly for the others. What happens when the Romanovs decide war is the better option?"

He takes the exit to the airport, cutting through traffic in a way that makes my stomach swoop. "That won't happen."

"But what if it does?"

Casimir sighs. "My uncle has his hands full with Dmitri Romanov's daughters currently. Marrying you will allow me to prioritize my role here over dealing with that mess. They aren't going to buckle, regardless of what he believes. That will keep him busy long enough that Carver City will be sorted."

I can't fathom his arrogance. As if it's as simple as that. "I'm not going to keep your secrets. I'm going to tell Michelle and Zayne about Tatiana."

His jaw tightens. "Tatiana can handle her own shit."

"No love lost there?"

"She's a pain in my ass." He slashes a look at me. "She seduced you, knowing I've already claimed you. She's lucky I don't shoot her in the kneecap."

I don't know what to say to that. I don't know what to feel. No, that's a fucking lie. The truth is that I'm pulled between what I want and what I should do. I know what Michelle and Zayne would say. What my parents would say.

Kill Casimir and flee.* Return to Carver City where I'm safe and prepare for the Romanovs to strike back.

I also know what my aunt would say. She loves me, but she's sacrificed plenty for our territory. That's what good leaders do—sacrifice for the greater benefit. Marriages of convenience are common enough in our world. Marrying the enemy might be slightly less common, but it's not unheard of. As Casimir said, war is expensive.

Really, I'm just looking for an excuse to take what I want. I

* DARK MATTER—Seratones

stare at the man who's occupied so much of my thoughts for years now in one variation or another. Even with everything between us, I'm relaxed in the passenger seat, just like I have been so many times before.

"If we're doing this…no more lies. You stop pretending to be Luke. You…" I suck in a breath. "No more missions or whatever for your uncle. You can't be allied to two people, Casimir."

He pulls up in front of the airport and puts the car in park. "Baby, you know how Romanovs work."

"Yeah, I do. And I'm still drawing this line in the sand. What happens if your uncle decides this plan doesn't make sense and tells you to kill me?"

Casimir shakes his head. "He wouldn't do that."

Judging from the rumors I've heard about Jovan, I'm not so sure. He's a canny old bastard, and the Romanovs have grown astronomically in power and wealth since he inherited the rule in Russia. He's not erratic, exactly, but you're expendable if you aren't a Romanov…and sometimes even if you are.

"Maybe not, but what if the plans don't play out the way he wants here? If Carver City goes to war, I'm siding with my allies here, with my family. Not with yours."

He grins. "You've already decided to marry me."

"No, I haven't. I'm just playing through scenarios."

"Liar." He glances at the cars swarming around us, at the people exiting and entering the doors to our right in waves. "Trust me when I tell you that it won't come to that."

I might trust him, but that doesn't mean I trust the rest of his family. "What if it does? I can't say yes to you without having an answer to this. Without you giving me your word that you won't stand against the people I care about. Against *me*."

He drums his fingers on the steering wheel. "I can't avoid being called back to Russia from time to time. Regardless of anything else, family is family."

I want to argue, but he's right. No matter what happens in my life, if I somehow ended up somewhere else…I'd still have relationships with my parents.

Still. "That's not really what I'm asking you."

"I know." He sighs. "Baby, I won't hurt you. Not for anything. And you'd never forgive me if I hurt your family or friends. So I won't. The rest, we'll figure out."

It's not exactly a promise to stand with us against a Romanov invasion, but it's good enough for me. "How much time do we have before your uncle starts considering war a legitimate option?"

"I don't know. Like I said, he's distracted with New York. That will take some time to resolve. In an ideal situation, we'd have Carver City wrapped up before then."

Wrapped up. A Romanov match for every heir. The current territory leaders will never stand for it.

But this Romanov? He's mine. I can admit that now. We're two twisted plants growing toward the same bloody light, tangled with each other so thoroughly that there's no escape. More, I don't *want* to escape.

I drag in a rough breath. "We have to do this my way. My parents are going to freak out, and while we could just ride it out, that's not the best option." It's what I've been doing for most of my life. Riding the waves and pretending they aren't carrying me to a position of power. If I'd been actively training as an heir, would Casimir have approached me a different way?

In fact...if I'm going to truly step into my role as heir, that has to start now. *Before* we return to Carver City. "If you really mean to be my bloody right hand, then I have a task for you."

He climbs out of the car and circles around to open my door. Casimir offers his hand. "I'm listening."

There are people all around us, but I only have eyes for him. "I want you to secure your uncle's word that the Belmonte territory is off-limits."

His eyes widen. "A bold demand."

"If he really means to do this without war, then it should be an easy agreement." Jovan might not hold to his word, but if Casimir does this for me...it means something. I can't pretend it doesn't.

Casimir plays his thumb over my knuckles. "It will take some time. I have to go to him to have this conversation, to secure this agreement. You understand?"

He'll have to leave me, at least for a little while. I bite down on the urge to take it back, to demand he never leave my side. I guess I've made my choice after all.

But if I'm going to be a territory leader, I have to prioritize the safety of my territory over my personal comfort. "I understand. Take as long as you need."

"Not yet. I'll see you home first." He laces his fingers through mine and turns to lead me into the airport.

Gods, but I hope I'm not making a horrible mistake.

———

The trip home is shockingly comfortable. Through mutual under-standing, we don't talk private business on the plane. Instead, we watch a new action movie, and Casimir spends the entire time pointing out the foolishness of the main character as he passes me the bits of the trail mix I like—peanuts and raisins—while accept-ing the bits I don't love—cashews and M&Ms. There's a Russian accent filtering his amused words now, but this is familiar enough for me to sink into it through sheer habit.

It gives me hope. That he was being honest that not all of Luke was a lie, that maybe we fit each other even better than I could have dreamed. No more lies. No more hiding the ugly parts of myself. With Casimir, they're on full display, and he doesn't shy away from their existence. From me.

He laces his fingers through mine and lifts our joined hands to press a kiss to my knuckles. "Relax, baby. It will work out."

Maybe. Maybe not. But hope is hard to argue with. And so is...love.

Damn it.

After we land, we go back to the apartment to change and shower off the evidence of travel. With each minute that ticks us closer to telling my parents the truth, my stress grows. I'm practically vibrating by the time we head down to the car Casimir called.

I sent my parents a text so they know we're coming. The fact that I *didn't* respond to the dozens of texts from them over the past couple of days isn't going to earn me any points. I've made a fucking mess of this.

"Breathe." Casimir takes my hand as we walk toward the front door. "You got this."

"They're going to shoot you."

"Maybe."

I swing around to look at him. "What the fuck do you mean *maybe*? You can't seriously be so calm about this."

"We live in a world of blood and violence, Ruby. But they love you, and I love you, so no one is going to die tonight."

"That leaves a lot of space for pain and getting *shot*," I mutter. I dig my key out and unlock the front door. "Da."

He opens the door and tugs me inside.

If I hadn't already known my parents were worried and furious, them meeting us in the foyer would have clued me in. Mom is wringing her hands, but Dad and Da are both locked down.

Da's expression goes soft when he sees me but hardens immediately as he takes in my hands, linked with Casimir's. "I think it's time you explained yourself, Ruby."

All the words clog my throat, and I have to swallow a few times to get them in order. There are a thousand explanations and excuses lining up in my head, but it's best to rip off this bandage immediately. "Mom, Da, Dad...I'm getting married." I keep talking over their sharp questions. "To him. Casimir Romanov."

"Casimir Romanov," Dad repeats slowly. "You've got to be fucking kidding me."

"Casimir Lukov Romanov, to be most accurate," Casimir says. He's so fucking calm in the face of their growing anger.

Da is the one who moves first. He stalks to us, and there's

no warning, no tensing to indicate his intentions. He punches Casimir in the face.

The force of it knocks Casimir back a few steps. I start forward, fully intending to get between them before Casimir strikes back, but he…doesn't. Not even when Da punches him again, this time in the stomach. It bends him in half, and as soon as he rises, Da hits him again.

"Stop!"

Mom starts forward, but Dad gets there first, wrapping his arms around Da and hauling him back. "He's not fighting you."*

"He's a fucking *Romanov*." Da lunges forward, but Dad holds him back. Barely. "He came into our house and lied to our faces. He defiled our—"

"I'm going to need you to stop right there," I snap. "Casimir wasn't completely honest, and that's something he and I will deal with. You don't get to start pretending like I'm some virgin princess locked away in a tower and he stole me. I made my choices, and damn it, I'm not an innocent."

Mom looks a bit like she wants to throttle me. "You went to the Black Rose Auction. You lied to us."

"Yes." It's hard to meet her gaze. "I'm sorry I lied. I've been dealing with some stuff, and I had to do it on my own."

"You mean him." She turns her attention to where Casimir has finally straightened again. He's bleeding from his mouth, and one of his eyes is already starting to swell shut. Mom walks past my fathers to stand before him. "You're the Mad Wolf. We've heard of you. Killing you might please me in the short term, but

* EVERYTHING WE DO IS WRONG—Tuvaband

since we have no desire to bring your family down on us, tell me why we shouldn't drive you to the border of the city and turn you loose."

Casimir wipes the back of his hand against his bloody mouth. "I love your daughter. I have from the start. I knew you wouldn't give me the time of day if you knew who I really was, so I lied. But the truth is out now, and I'm only too happy to get my hands bloody standing between Ruby and the rest of the world."

"Hmm. We'll see." She glances at me. "You haven't handled this properly from the beginning. Coming in here and dramatically announcing that you're going to marry a Romanov?" She shakes her head. "Cordelia will denounce you in seconds if she thinks you're compromised. You want to marry him? Do it right."

I can barely process her words, Casimir's words. "What do you mean when you say, 'Do it right'?"

"You will move back in here for a time." She flicks her fingers at Casimir. "And you will court her properly. A little distance will do you both some good and allow you to think clearly. If this is true love like you claim, you won't have an issue proving it."

Casimir doesn't look like he likes this plan any more than I do. He glances at me and then refocuses on my mother. "Whatever it takes."

"Yes, well, we'll see." She turns back to me. "After a month or so, you can go before Cordelia and ask permission to marry. She will have final call."

"Mom!"

"This is the *proper* way to do things, Ruby. Obviously we've been too lax with you if you think you can waltz in here with a

Romanov who's been lying to us for years and proclaim you're getting married. It's time to grow up."

Casimir steps close and presses a quick, bloody kiss to my lips. "This changes nothing, baby. I'll accomplish the task you put before me and come back for you."

"You may leave now, Casimir," my mother says, her polite tone icy enough to cut him to the bone.

With one last long look at me, he turns and walks out the door. The cowardly part of me wants to flee after him, to do anything to avoid the difficult conversation coming for me. But my mother is right. It's time to stop acting like a spoiled brat.

As the door closes, I turn to face my furious parents.

Mom turns to my fathers. "Let's take this to the kitchen."

That's only a slight relief. There are two places in this house for shitty conversations—the kitchen and the study. The study is for more formal ones, for the true fuckups. The kitchen is more informal, an easier place to not feel like you're put on the spot.

"Sit."

I sit.

My parents move in a smooth rhythm that almost feels coordinated: Mom starting the kettle, Da easily shifting behind her to grab the sugar and cream, Dad pulling out the tea tins. When I was thirteen, Mom decided that talking in the kitchen over tea was the way to handle most teenage challenges. It works.

I've sat in this exact spot and spilled my heart out over crushes and fights with friends and asshole teachers and all the frustrations that arise when every conflict feels like the end of the world.

Several minutes later, we all have steaming cups of tea in front of us.

Da leans his forearms onto the counter. "You've handled this poorly."

Guilt, true guilt, threatens to suffocate me. "I know. I'm sorry."

"Take us through it," Dad says.

So I do. At least mostly. My parents don't need to know the dirty details of the sex, and they don't need to know that Casimir was playing at being Wolf to my Little Red and stalking me. But I disclose the broad strokes of the cheating, the breakup, the auction, the revelation.

"Ruby." Mom sighs. "You should have come to us."

"With all due respect, as much as I love you, I have to start dealing with stuff on my own. I won't pretend that I dealt with this well, and I *am* sorry for that, but for the first time in my life, I feel like *me* instead of a polished doll that only does the right thing all the time."

Da crosses his arms over his chest. "We never expected perfection from you."

"I know." My words get choked, but I press through. "I'm not trying to escape responsibility. I didn't want to disappoint you, so I carved off big parts of myself to fit the role that I thought you wanted, even while I dodged that role. But I've been…phoning it in when it comes to most of the stuff in my life. It's time for that to change."

"We don't have to tell you that a Romanov is dangerous. They're like cockroaches—there's never just one," Dad says. "And the Mad Wolf? He's the most dangerous of all."

"Not to me."

"Don't be naive."

"I'm not." Not anymore. I'm not ready to tell them the task I sent him on. If he's successful, it will go a long way toward proving his loyalty—both to me and my parents. "Casimir would murder the world for me. He's not a saint, but would you really want me to be with a saint?"

My parents exchange a look so filled with history that it's got too many layers for me to translate. Finally, Mom sets down her mug. "I suppose we'll see, won't we?" She rounds the kitchen island and presses a kiss to my temple. "I'm glad you're home safe." She walks through an archway, heading deeper into the house.

Da grabs the mugs and makes quick work of them in the sink while Dad watches me closely as if weighing his words. Finally, he says, "If you sneak out again, I'm cutting down every tree around the house. You want to be treated like an adult? Start acting like one."

17

The next morning, I wake to a text from Casimir.

Casimir: I'm about to get on the plane, but I'll be back in a week. Be good.

I stare at my phone for several long minutes, trying to process the complicated emotions that rise in response to the knowledge that he's leaving town. Because I asked him to. A small terrified part of me is afraid he'll be gone forever. That he's had his fun, his cover is blown, and now it's time to reconvene and figure out a new plan.

But I don't believe that, do I?*

Casimir claimed me at the auction. Publicly. I can't believe that was all part of some plan that ends with him dumping me and making me look and feel like a fool. But as the days tick by

* SAVAGE (RAIN RECORDING)—Lights

with only the barest communication, adding up to a week and then more, my resolve starts to falter. Maybe he isn't coming back at all. Maybe he's just stringing me along to keep me complacent. Maybe that awful little voice inside me is right for once.

Or, even worse, maybe Jovan has killed him and someone is using his phone to text me.

No. *No.* I cannot believe that. He's fine. It's just as he's said— it's taking longer to convince his uncle to see things our way than initially planned.

I'm going through the motions, caught in stasis as I wait for something to give. My parents' anger hasn't thawed, and my aunt isn't happy with me either. I spend every day closed away in my office, keeping my head down and diligently doing my work.

On the twelfth day after the text from Casimir, Dad knocks on my office door. Usually when I'm in trouble, it's Da who ultimately smooths things over and lets me know the worst of my parents' anger has passed. Dad isn't much of a talker. That means I can go to Dad when the world becomes too much and I just need a safe place to land. His silences are comforting in a way I appreciate more and more as I get older.

But there's little that can comfort me in my current mindset.

He looks at me for a bit, his pale eyes no doubt clocking all the signs that I haven't slept well since coming home. Even with makeup, there's no missing the shadows beneath my eyes, and I've been so stressed, I've reverted to my childhood habit of picking my nail polish.

"Let's go."

"Taking me to the firing squad?"

He doesn't bother to respond to my snotty question, which is just as well. He motions for me to follow him out the door, and I know better than to do anything else. What Dad doesn't solve with words, he does with actions, and he's not above hauling me over his shoulder and tossing me into the nearest body of water if I get too pissy for no reason. I rise with a sigh and follow him out of the room. It only takes me a few turns to figure out our destination. The sparring mat.

We walk into the gym, and he jerks his chin toward the clothes that have been neatly folded in my cubby. The gym is set up closer to a commercial gym than a home one. I don't know if it was always this way or if it was changed once Da and Dad came to live here with my mother. They certainly use it enough, even now.

"I don't want to spar."

Dad rolls his shoulders and steps onto the mat. "You may not want to. But you need to."

If Mom is good at teatime and giving me the space to feel my feelings, and Da is good at hugs and positive self-talk, then Dad is good at *this*. He's been dragging me onto the mat since I turned eleven and puberty hit me like a freight train. There were too many hormones and too much change, and my mental health took a wild free fall. Mom's words couldn't get through to me. Da's hugs didn't solve anything.

And then one day, Dad hauled me onto the mat and started teaching me how to fight. On this mat, I learned to move with limbs that had stopped feeling like mine. I don't remember learning to walk, but Mom says it happened much the same way. Dad has endless patience, and it didn't matter how shitty my attitude was, he would meet me on the mat and put me through my paces until whatever repressed emotion was rattling around my chest burst free.

And once the pain was lanced, Mom or Da would magically show up not too much later and be available for me to spew my angsty young feelings at them.

I'd like to say I have better control of myself these days, but that doesn't stop me from ducking into the changing room and pulling on my workout gear. It doesn't alter the fact that no matter how worried and stressed I am about my current situation, I know I'll feel better after this.

I step out of the changing room and glare. "I know what you're doing."

"Then you know it will help."

I step onto the mat, and it's the most natural thing in the world to fall into the rhythm of our customary warm-up. Stretching and then shadowboxing. Only once a light sweat covers my body does Dad return to me with a slight smile. "All right. Let's see how rusty you are."

I hesitate, testing him. "I really don't want—"

Just as I expected, Dad strikes out, intending to catch me unawares. I duck and attempt to sweep his legs out from beneath him. It doesn't work, but I honestly didn't expect it to. We circle each other slowly. Even when I was practicing several times a week with him, I only beat him one time out of twenty. He's always pulled the force of his punches with me, but he's never dialed back the intensity of his attacks. As much as I hate the bruises I end up with, I can't deny that I've never fought anyone as good as Dad.

I'm not in peak physical condition currently, and it's been months since we sparred together.

Within ten seconds, I land flat on my back, and my air whooshes out of my lungs. I blink dazedly up to see him leaning over me, his brows drawn together. "I knew you were out of practice, but you should've seen that coming a mile away."

I take his offered hand and allow him to pull me to my feet. "I've been a little busy."

"I know." Just that. No judgment.

We circle each other again, and as much as I want to be irritated that I'm doing this, it *does* feel good. This, at least, I understand.

It starts to feel less good after Dad knocks me on my ass five times. The last time, I'm breathing so hard that I feel a little dizzy. I hold up my hand, panting. "I'm done."

He crouches in front of me, running a critical eye over my body. "Anything worse than bruises?"

"Only my pride."* I wipe the back of my hand over my sweaty forehead. "I know I've been a giant shit, but thank you. I guess I did need this."

He drops onto the mat next to me. "Your mom and Da were born and raised in Carver City. I wasn't."

"I know the story." I've heard it enough times. About how he fought his way onto my grandfather's force and how he and Da worked the ranks to become top enforcers. About how they

* ISLAND—Miley Cyrus

both dated my mother separately before both calling it quits. And about how she managed to bring them both back into the fold of the territory—and her life. It's the stuff of legends in Carver City.

"I never once lied about who I was."

There it is. The moral judgment. I open my mouth to snap back but force myself to be silent. To consider what he's saying. My mother's words ring in my ears: *You want to be treated like an adult? Start acting like one.*

I take a deep breath. "The situation is hardly the same."

"It's not the same," he agrees quietly. "If you hadn't looked at him with your heart in your eyes, I would've killed him the night you told us he was a Romanov."

I jerk around and stare at Dad, my eyes wide. "What?"

"I'm still not sure I made the right call." I've never seen his eyes so cold. "The boy cares about you, but he *is* a Romanov. He comes with the kind of baggage that ruins lives."

"Dad, if you hurt him, I'll never forgive you."

"I know. That's why I didn't do it." He props himself back up on his hands. "I know you're too enmeshed in it right now, but look at it from our perspective. We love you. We want what's best for you. Choosing him means you'll never have a peaceful life. The Romanovs will always be looking for a foothold in our territory, and you will have to spend the rest of your years fighting to hold your boundaries. Your children will be half Romanov, which puts them in the position of having to push back against a powerful family too. That will be the legacy you and the Mad Wolf leave behind."

It's nothing more than I've considered myself. But he's not

speaking in judgment. He's merely laying out the facts. So I force myself to listen. To think about it. "I understand that."

"You think you do, but you can't ever properly prepare for that sort of thing. No one can."

I clear my throat. "What are you saying?" As much as I've begun to make my peace with caring about Casimir, with loving him, if my parents stand in our way, I don't know what I'll do. I'd have to walk away from being heir. Worse, I'd have to walk away from my parents completely. That's not a choice I want to be forced to make.

"I am saying that we've spoken with your aunt, and there are two paths forward. You cut off all ties with the Romanov right now. Or you marry him like you say you will and that's it."

"What do you mean 'that's it'?"

"I mean if you marry a Romanov, then you don't get to change your mind later. If you fall out of love or if this is just infatuation, it won't matter, because you'll be stuck. You won't be able to kill your husband without his family coming calling and attempting to raze the territory to the ground. You'd better hope he lives a nice long life too, because they won't believe a death by natural causes." He sighs. "All we've ever wanted is for you to be happy, but we obviously made some missteps along the way. You are heir, Ruby. Your choices and actions have consequences for more than just you. More than even just our family. Every single person in this territory relies on us to keep things running efficiently. To keep them safe."

"I know that," I say softly, stung. The responsibility has been drilled into me for as long as I can remember. It's why I did my best not to step outside the lines...until recently. But the more I think about it, the more I can't help feeling that Casimir and I are not in dissimilar positions. We were both playing roles that weren't our full selves for a very long time. And we both went fully toxic when the pressure got to be too much.

Reality is so much more complicated. Messy.*

Please be alive, Casimir. Please come back to me with an assurance of peace.

"Now you know that." Dad rises easily to his feet and offers me his hand. "I would give you all the time you need to make that decision, and your mom had a good point, wanting a month apart and for him to court you properly. Unfortunately, your aunt feels differently, and Cordelia is the territory leader, so her word is law. You have until tonight."

I take his hands, and he hauls me upright. Then the words penetrate. "What do you mean I only have until tonight? I don't even know if he's coming back, and you want me to make a decision?"

"Oh, he's back." He grabs a nearby towel to wipe the sweat from his face. "He showed up before I came to get you."

I stare. "We've been in here for over an hour."

"Yeah." He grabs a clean towel and tosses it at me. "Won't hurt him to wait a little longer. Why don't you take a shower before you go find him?"

I don't call Dad an asshole, but it's hovering right there on the tip of my tongue. Then again, I suppose this was a test in and of itself. For both Casimir and me.

I catch a glimpse of myself in one of the nearby mirrors.

* I OF THE STORM—Of Monsters and Men

The makeup I had on earlier is smudged from working out, and there's no saving my hair. Casimir has seen me looking messier than this, but I need a minute to think about what Dad said. "Yeah, a shower sounds good."

don't exactly take my time in the shower, but I don't rush either. It's nearly another hour later when I finally walk into the foyer.

Set up against the wall, there's an antique bench that no one ever uses. Casimir looks absurd perched on the edge of it, his elbows propped on his knees. He's not fidgeting or showing even the smallest sign of impatience. But when he looks up as I walk through the archway, his pale eyes go molten hot.

"Hey, baby."*

I chose my clothing carefully, wanted to remind him of everything he said he's been missing for the last twelve days. My short wrap dress is a deep crimson that matches my lips. I've curled my hair so it falls around my shoulders in careless waves. I look fucking *good*.

He looks even better. As Luke, he often wore suits for work, but they were always slightly ill fitting. As Wolf, he only ever

* THE DEVIL IS A GENTLEMAN—Merci Raines

showed up in a hoodie, jeans, and a skull mask, his leather gloves constantly in place. Now he's wearing a designer suit that fits him so perfectly, it has to be tailored. The dark blue contrasts with a pale-blue shirt nearly the same color as his eyes.

All I want to do is rip everything off him and reacquaint myself with his body, but Dad's warning lingers in my mind. The stakes have never been higher. If I make this choice, it's for keeps. I don't get to back out or change my mind later. I know what my heart is saying. I know what my head is saying too.

What I don't know is what Casimir is thinking.

"Did you do what I asked you?" I finally say.

"Things in Russia were a little more complicated than I expected." He gives a slight shrug. "My uncle doesn't like to be challenged, so it had to be handled delicately."

"That's not an answer, Casimir."

He reaches into his jacket and produces a paper. I accept it and unfold it, finding a letter from Jovan. It's a lot of flowery shit and doublespeak, and while he gives his word not to attack the Belmonte territory...there are obviously a lot of loopholes he left open to exploit. "This isn't good enough."

"I know." He stares at me intently. "I spoke with my father, and while he is not the leader of the Romanov family, *his* word is above reproach." He rises slowly to his feet. "If you say yes to me, then my branch of the Romanov family will stand with us regardless of whether Jovan goes back on his word. I can't speak for the other territories—they'll have to figure their shit out—but the Belmonte territory and all its people are safe from Romanov meddling. My family and I will make sure of it."

I blink, trying to process what the fuck he just said. Casimir's uncle Jovan is the ultimate ruler of the Romanov family, which means his children are the ones who will inherit that throne. If what Casimir's saying is true, then his father, the second Romanov brother, would potentially rebel if Jovan gave the order to hurt us. "How am I supposed to believe that?"

"I give you my word. Like my father's, it's less...malleable... than my uncle's." He stops in front of me but makes no move to touch me. "My father and his brothers present a united front to the rest of the world because our enemies are vast, and any sign of weakness has a risk of being exploited. That doesn't mean my father likes every choice my uncle makes. I might be firstborn, but I'm heir to nothing. My parents and siblings won't stand back if Jovan ever decides to come for us. They'll stand with us."

I should find that comforting, but all it does is spotlight just how dire the stakes are. I stare up into the face of the man I love and wonder if I'm about to make a terrible mistake. But even as I think that, I don't really believe it. Casimir *sees* me. He's twisted in just the right way to match my crooked heart. "If you try to undermine me, I will make you wish you were dead," I finally say.

His grin is slow and wicked. "Noted. We'll present a united front in public, and if I have an issue with one of your orders or policies, I'll take it up with you privately."

"Well...good."

"I don't want to rule, baby, but I'm good at getting my hands dirty, and you're going to need that skill set for what comes next. No one will touch you. I promise."*

* I PUT A SPELL ON YOU—Annie Lennox

I reach out but stop before placing my hand on his chest. "What if I want them to touch me?"

He covers my hand with his and presses it to his chest. "Why don't you tell me what you want, and we'll go from there?"

It feels strange to stand here in the golden afternoon light and speak the truths I keep most hidden. If he were anyone else, I don't think I would dare. "If I marry you, that's it. We will vow 'til death do us part. No divorce. It doesn't end until one of us is in the grave."

"Da." There's not even a flicker of doubt on his face.

Strange how that was the easy part. Asking for what I personally want is so much more difficult. I lick my lips. "That primal scene…"

"Yeah." He brushes a strand of my hair back from my face. "It made me wild to see you with other people, fucking murderous, but reclaiming you? Yeah, baby, it did it for me too."

"If we play like that, you can't actually murder people. Or not any *more* people."

He cups my jaw and smears his thumb across my bottom lip. "I know." He makes a face. "I suppose if we want more formal games, we request an invitation to Reaper's club. I think you'd like it, and it's only a short plane ride from Carver City."

I glance around, but the foyer is just as empty as it was earlier. That doesn't mean there aren't eyes on us. My parents would never let me stand here with him without being close enough to save me if things went sour. I take a deep breath. "There's no going back if we do this."

"You keep saying that. There was no going back the moment

I laid eyes on you. None of the other shit makes any difference. It's you and me forever, baby."

Gods help me, but I believe him. I carefully step back, and he tenses as if he will pull me to him, only to release me at the last moment. I wobble a little on my heels, more nervous than I expected. "In that case..." I sink slowly to my knees before him and pull the little box out of my pocket. "Casimir Romanov, we've had a relationship that you can hardly call traditional, but I've never met someone who sees me the way you do. Who loves me the way you do. I never will. You're the only one I want. I know it won't be easy, but with you at my side, I don't think there's an enemy who can stop us. Will you marry me?"

"You got me a ring." For the first time, he actually sounds shocked. "You're proposing."

"Yeah. Though if you had made me wait much longer, I don't know if I would have."

He reaches down and hooks my elbows, then lifts me back to my feet. "Liar. There's no one else for you." He reaches into his suit pocket and pulls out a nearly identical ring box. "Just like there's no one else for me." Casimir opens it, and I swallow a gasp. The ring is gorgeous and looks old as fuck. "Give me your hand, baby."

I stretch out my left hand—the first ring he gave me is still on my right—and he slides the ring onto my ring finger. I'm not even remotely surprised to find out it fits perfectly. As if he'd leave something as important as that to chance. "Now you," I say.

"It's not traditional for men to wear an engagement ring." But he does as I ask and allows me to slip my ring onto his finger.

Mine fits perfectly too. I didn't live with this man for over a year to not know his ring size.

I slide my thumb over the cool metal and grip his hand. "I don't give a fuck if it's not traditional. You're mine, and I want everyone to know it."

"I'm not about to argue." He pulls me into his arms and kisses me as if we've been separated for years instead of less than two weeks.

The first touch of his lips ignites a spark that I've been doing my best to ignore. I tangle my fingers in his and press my body even tighter against him. If we weren't standing in the middle of my family's foyer...

But we are. Which means we can't afford to forget ourselves.

I reluctantly break the kiss. "We're not getting out of here without telling my parents our decision." A couple of weeks ago, I would've said "fuck it" and dragged him somewhere we could be alone. But my parents are right: it's time for me to start acting like the heir that I am. Which means going about things the proper way.

Casimir pulls a handkerchief from his pocket and carefully wipes around my mouth, cleaning my lipstick as best he can. "Come home with me tonight."*

"Neither one of us has moved out. It's still my home too." Surely my mother won't require another two weeks of separation when Cordelia insisted we get engaged tonight.

"I know."

I catch his thumb between my teeth and bite him lightly. It's

* FEELING GOOD—Nina Simone

so damn satisfying to see his expression flip to that of the predator I crave. I lick the tip of his thumb and release him. "When we get there…I think it's time to finally decide whose teeth are bigger."

His grin is pure sin. "I can't wait to eat you right up."

BONUS EPILOGUE

CASIMIR

I've chosen my seat in the dingy bar carefully. I can see the entire room, my back is to a wall, and the low light of the place means no one is looking at me too closely.

Ruby sure as fuck doesn't see me when she waltzes in an hour later. She's in a tiny red dress that barely covers her ass and has her tits threatening to spill out with every step she takes. No surprise that all eyes in the room are on her.*

I sip my beer and watch her work. True to form, she's opening herself up to whatever trouble comes her way. She leans on the bar, and her skirt rides up. My body goes tight. There's nothing I want more than to stalk across the bar, toss her over my shoulder, and take her the fuck out of here.

That's not the game we're playing.

My hand drifts to the hilt of my knife. It's all too easy to picture blood spraying the wall from the slit throats of every single

* NIGHT CRAWLING—Miley Cyrus feat. Billy Idol

person staring hard at the hem of her dress to see if she's wearing any panties. She's not. Even the hint of her pussy is more than I want to share with these fuckers.

But we're not playing that kind of game tonight either.

It's a couple who catches her interest, because my girl does nothing halfway. The white woman is petite and even shorter than Ruby, a pretty brunette with a wicked smile and wandering hands. Her man is a white guy who's muscle for the Sarraf family. I don't know his name off the top of my head, but I've seen his picture in the dossier my family compiled before coming to Carver City. Nothing of note there, which means he keeps his head down and does his job.

I suppose there are worse options she could choose.

They take her to the round booth that's a step up from the main floor. High enough that I can see under the table without trouble. Jealousy sinks into me, rooting through every part of my body as I watch the woman kiss Ruby's throat and delve her hand between my woman's thighs. The shadows are too deep to see her part Ruby's pussy and press her fingers deep, but there's enough movement visible that I know that's exactly what she's doing.

Ruby's gaze cuts to the door, looking for me. Smug in the way of a brat up to no good. My cock is so fucking hard, I'm having trouble keeping still. I want to cross to her, flip the table, and... Nah, I want to fuck her *on* the table. To claim her in front of every single person here.

The enforcer cups her jaw, and she covers his hand with hers. The giant ruby on her ring finger has me relaxing my grip on my knife. I promised no violence, promised to play the game we both enjoy, but fuck if it's as easy as I expected.

I am who I am.

Watching my wife come at the hands of another does something to me, *for* me. She's having the time of her life, but she keeps looking for me, anticipating the moment I put a stop to all this. A little game we've played out many times since she put on my ring and we exchanged vows.

Sometimes, I let them fuck her—or her fuck them, more accurately. Not tonight. I'm too fucking restless. But she hasn't orgasmed yet, and I'm content to...

The enforcer reaches for the front of his pants and withdraws his cock. Without a godsdamn condom. "Motherfucker."

I push to my feet and reach their table in seconds. All three of them freeze. The enforcer goes pale and holds up his hands. "We didn't know."

"My ring on her finger." I have my knife in my hand without intending to. I promised I wouldn't spill blood, but *fuck*, it's hard not to sometimes. "You." I point my knife at the woman still plastered to my wife's side, her hand still under Ruby's dress. "Back off."

Ruby shivers, her blush deepening even as she raises her chin. "Hey, baby."

"Up. Now."

The little brat doesn't bother to do things the proper way. She just climbs onto the table, flashing her cunt at the poor assholes who thought they'd get a taste of it tonight, and crawls to me. Then she stands on the table and hops into my arms, wrapping her legs around my waist.

"Are you pleased with yourself?" I cup her ass and walk away from the table, ignoring the soft cursing of the enforcer. He's not going to do shit, and we both know it.

"I am." She digs her fingers into my hair and her heels into the small of my back. "Fuck me, husband. Hurry."*

I carry her through the bar to the bathroom. The lock is broken on the door, but neither of us gives a fuck. My wife will come all the harder if someone does walk in on us. I set her on the counter and shove up her dress. She's so wet, she's glistening.

"Always so determined to give away what's mine," I murmur. The words are true enough, but I say them now because they get her off harder. I pull down her dress until her tits pop free. "No bra. No panties. You came here to fuck someone you weren't supposed to."

"No..." She's breathing so hard that her breasts shake. "Maybe."

I press close, enjoying the way she melts against me. It takes no time at all to get my cock out. She's so damn sure she's getting her way, but if there's one thing we both love, it's when I put my woman in her place. So I don't take her mouth, despite her offering it to me. I don't press my cock to her entrance and shove into her, reclaiming what she enjoys giving away.

Ruby reaches between us, but I grab her wrist and push it aside. She curses. "Hey!"

In response, I grip her jaw hard enough for my fingertips to dent her skin. "Baby, you know it's not going to be that easy. Just like you know how to make this stop. Nod if you understand."

* ANIMALS—Nickelback

Her eyes are wide and downright delighted. She nods, and I loosen my grip enough to allow the movement.

"Good girl," I murmur. "Now, you've pissed me off something fierce, and you're going to make it up to me. You know what I want."

She moves with me as I ease back, sliding to her knees before me. I keep my grip on her jaw while she pulls my pants down farther and wraps her fist around my cock. Only then do I move my grip to her hair, gathering it away from her face.

I love it when she sucks my cock. She always goes down on me like she's mad at me, like she wants to suck my soul right out. This time is no different. Ruby takes me into her mouth in one long movement until I hit the back of her throat. That doesn't stop her though. She hums a little, and then she takes me deeper.

But even as pleasure gathers in the base of my spine, tightening my balls, I don't want this to end. I never want to stop fucking Ruby, but these nights are something special. Something forbidden and fucked and perfectly *us*.

So no, I won't be satisfied fucking her mouth until she cries. Not when her pussy is still dripping for someone else.

I haul her up, ignoring her protest, and lift her. Ruby squirms but makes an eager sound when she realizes my intention. We end up with her knees on my shoulders, her pussy right in front of my face as I hold her upside down. She wastes no time taking my cock into her mouth until her lips meet my base.

Damn woman is going to make my knees buckle before I have a chance to taste her orgasm.

I cover her cunt with my mouth, relishing her taste even as

I try to muscle down my threatening orgasm. She doesn't relent, almost as if she knows exactly how close I am. Brat.

My back hits the door. Fuck, didn't mean to do that. I'm lost in the slick feeling of her on my tongue, in her needy clit begging to be stroked. My hands are full, keeping her in place, so I thrust my tongue into her, earning one of her sexy little whimpers.

I give her one long lick and growl. "Come for me, wife. It's the least you can do after the trouble you caused."*

"Make me." She sucks me so deep, she gags herself, but that doesn't stop her.

It's a fucking race. I'll punish her for this later, but right now, I need her to come. I suck on her clit, working it with my tongue in the way I know she loves. Her thighs shake on either side of my head, and she's moaning around my cock. There, *there*. She practically takes my head off as she orgasms, squeezing so tightly, I see stars.

This time, my knees really do buckle as I come down the back of her throat. Only by wedging myself against the door do I keep my feet.

Ruby gives me one last long suck that makes me shiver, and then she eases off my cock. "Are you going to put me down?"

"I'm thinking about it." I lick her pussy again. "But I have this sweet little cunt in my face, and it's distracting as fuck."

"Casimir!"

"Baby, if you're trying to convince me to put you down long enough to take you home, saying my name in that tone of voice isn't going to get it done."

Instead of answering, she keeps wiggling until I'm fucking

* MOVEMENT—Hozier

obligated to make her come twice more. Only then do I set her back on the counter.

She looks a fucking mess. Her dress is wadded up around her waist, her hair is tangled, and her lips are swollen from sucking my dick. Best of all are the tear tracks on her face and her sexy little smirk. "Fuck me, husband."

Godsdamn it. I give my cock a rough stroke. After her second orgasm, I was ready to go again, but I really did mean to take her home. Oh well.

I shove her legs wide and spear her with my cock. Ruby moans loud enough to be heard over the music playing in the main room. She clings to me as I fuck her roughly. "Yes," Ruby moans. "Take your pussy back."

"Never let it go." I loop my arm under her hips to raise them so I can get deeper, as if I'll ever be deep enough inside this woman. "It was mine all along." Gods help me, but I'm a fucking sap for this woman. I grip the base of her neck with my free hand and nip her earlobe. "Come for me again, wife."

She spasms around me, her pussy pulsing. "Say it again."

"Wife." I grind into her, rubbing her clit against my pelvic bone. "My wife. Forever."

"Yes!" She digs her hands under my shirt, scratching the shit out of my back. It only makes me fuck her harder. Giving us what we both need. This time, when she orgasms, I don't bother to fight my own. I pump into her, filling her with my come.

I pull out of her and allow myself a few seconds enjoying the mess I've made of her. I drag my finger down her center. "Someday...someday, we'll do the baby thing."

Ruby startles out a laugh. "Too soon, Casimir."

"Yeah, I know." I kiss her and tug her dress back into place. It's not enough though. She's still too fucking exposed. I pull my shirt off and drag it over her head. She huffs, but I don't miss the way she dips her head to inhale the scent of me.

Ruby hops off the counter and laces her fingers through mine, the gesture sweet as shit after the filthy fucking. She presses against my chest and grins. "But I suppose you could start practicing if you really wanted to." She laces her fingers in my hair, and I let her tug my head down so she can speak directly in my ear. "Put a baby in me, husband."

Before meeting her, I wouldn't have said that I had a breeding kink, but fuck if she's gone and proved me wrong. I pick her up and toss her over my shoulder, chuckling when she squeaks. "We're going home. Right fucking now." I reach for the door but pause before opening it. "I love you, wife."

She hugs my torso from behind and upside down. "I love you too, husband."

ABOUT THE AUTHOR

Katee Robert (she/they) is a *New York Times* and *USA Today* bestselling author of spicy romance. *Entertainment Weekly* calls their writing "unspeakably hot." Their books have sold over two million copies. They live in the Pacific Northwest with their husband, children, a cat who thinks he's a dog, and two Great Danes who think they're lap dogs.

Website: kateerobert.com
Facebook: AuthorKateeRobert
Instagram: @katee_robert
Threads: @katee_robert
TikTok: @authorkateerobert

The End of

WICKED PURSUIT

and the Beginning of

DIVINE INTERVENTION

Every book in the Black Rose Auction is meant to be read as a duology. Now that you've reached the end of *Wicked Pursuit*, simply close the book, flip it over, and start *Divine Intervention* from the beginning. Happy reading!

The End of

DIVINE INTERVENTION

and the Beginning of

WICKED PURSUIT

Every book in the Black Rose Auction is meant to be read as a duology. Now that you've reached the end of *Divine Intervention*, simply close the book, flip it over, and start *Wicked Pursuit* from the beginning. Happy reading!

ABOUT THE AUTHOR

R.M. Virtues is a bestselling Afro-Indigenous, Two-Spirit author of romantasy and horror romance best known for his high-heat, high-stakes retellings and reconstructions of mythology, fairy tales, and folklore. He currently lives in Nevada as a guest on Nuwuvi (Southern Paiute) land with his family and Funko Pop horror collection. When not writing, R.M. can be found watching horror movies, playing fantasy video games, or falling down a research rabbit hole.

Website: rmvirtues.com
Instagram: @rmvirtues
Threads: @rmvirtuees
TikTok: @rmvirtues

DIVINE
INTERVENTION

Welcome to the

BLACK ROSE AUCTION

In **WICKED PURSUIT** by Katee Robert, a Little Red Riding Hood remix, a mob princess with a taste for doing things she shouldn't acquires a stalker who will kill anyone who touches what's his...

In **DIVINE INTERVENTION** by R.M. Virtues, a Goldilocks remix, a witch must work with her ex's father (who she betrayed) and an angel to steal a magical chalice from the auction floor. But things get scorchingly complicated when all three agree that revenge is best served in the bedroom...

ALSO BY R.M. VIRTUES

A SERIES OF SACRILEGIOUS EVENTS
Sing Me to Sleep (Companion novel)
Pin Me to the Wall by My Longing (Companion novel)

THE GODS OF HUNGER SERIES
Drag Me Up
Keep Me Close
Let Me In
Love Me Now

STANDALONES
What Are the Odds?
Claiming Mrs. Claus

The

BLACK ROSE
AUCTION:

DIVINE
INTERVENTION

DIVINE
INTERVENTION

R.M.
VIRTUES

sourcebooks
casablanca

Published by Sourcebooks Casablanca, an imprint of Sourcebooks
P.O. Box 4410, Naperville, Illinois 60567-4410
(630) 961-3900
sourcebooks.com

Originally self-published in 2024 by R.M. Virtues.

Cataloging-in-Publication Data is on file with the Library of Congress.

Printed and bound in the United States of America.
LSC 10 9 8 7 6 5 4 3 2 1

For all the sinners who aren't sorry and
every angel willing to fall.

FOREWORD

When we set out to create the Black Rose Auction series, we knew we wanted it to be luxe and dangerous and sexy! The premise is that there's an annual auction, presided over by the mysterious Reaper, where anything can be purchased for the right price. It's a place to make statements, to auction off the services of some of the world's most exclusive sex workers, to find priceless artifacts that the general public has only heard rumors of. Within these books, you'll find dangerous men, powerful women, and a heist or two! Be sure to check out read.sourcebooks .com/blackroseauction or scan the QR code to get an introduction to all six authors and their work!

    We've been fans of R.M. Virtues's work for ages, so we were so freaking excited when he joined the project! We've been basically shoving Sing Me to Sleep into people's hands since it came out (SLEEP PARALYSIS DEMON HERO, ENOUGH SAID), and we're so delighted that

he returned to that world and continued to expand it with Divine Intervention. *He said, "Goldilocks?" and we said, "YES, PLEASE AND THANK YOU."*

Buckle up, friends. Let us introduce you to Goldie, a woman who's been backed into a corner by angels and is done playing their games. She's at the Black Rose Auction to steal a magical chalice and, oh hey, her ex's dad is also attending, and sure, she might have stolen from him in the past, but there's tension *still…almost as much* tension *as there is between her and a certain angel.*

What could possibly go wrong?

Jenny Nordbak and Katee Robert

CONTENT GUIDANCE

TROPES: Ex's dad, supernatural polyamorous romance.

TAGS: Ex's dad, polyamory, Two-Spirit leads, Black love, Black romance, consensual nonconsent, primal play, sex on tape, what are you willing to do for forgiveness? Everything, blasphemy, nonhuman parts, queer monster romance, A Series of Sacrilegious Events, *Sing Me to Sleep*, angels and demons and witches oh my!, welcome to the dark side, betraying Heaven, is it business or pleasure? Both, fallen angels, sacrilegious acts, blasphemy!, sharing is caring.

CONTENT WARNINGS: Explicit sex, daddy kink, consensual nonconsent, sex on camera, violence, bodily harm, threats, harassment (antagonist), threats, brief/vague discussion of assault and harassment, religious imagery, sacrilegious acts and blasphemy, death of loved ones (mother and wife, past, off-page), discussions of grief, nonhuman parts depicted in sex scenes (i.e., biblically accurate angel wings).

PLAYLIST

Throughout *Divine Intervention*, you'll find footnotes referring to songs that inspired a scene, might be playing in the background of a scene, or may otherwise enhance your reading experience. We encourage you to queue up these songs so they're ready to play whenever you see them referenced. For a handy Spotify playlist tailored to each book, go to read.sourcebooks.com/blackroseauction or scan the QR code below and search for *Divine Intervention*.

ON MY MAMA—Victoria Monét

I AM HER—Shea Diamond

GO GO GO—Jorja Smith

BLOODY SHIRT (BASTILLE REMIX)—To Kill a King

WAY DOWN WE GO—KALEO

BOA—Megan Thee Stallion

SHEISTY—Trinidad James, Kamaiyah, and Hope Tala

BETTER OFF ALONE—Jenny Plant

HEAVEN IS HERE—Florence + The Machine

WAIT A MINUTE!—WILLOW

OH MY GOD—Adele

ANGEL OF SMALL DEATH AND THE CODEINE SCENE—Hozier

WILD SIDE—Normani feat. Cardi B

I WAS THINKIN'—Reggie

SHOT CLOCK—Ella Mai

I AM—Michaela Jaé

DREAM GIRL EVIL—Florence + The Machine

SAINTS—Echoes

WATER SLIDE—Janelle Monáe

EFECTO—Bad Bunny

WHEN I WATCH THE WORLD BURN ALL I THINK ABOUT IS YOU—Bastille

WHEN WE—Tank

GLORY AND GORE—Lorde

FROM EDEN—Hozier

ANGELS—The XX

STOP THE WORLD I WANNA GET OFF WITH YOU—Arctic Monkeys

HUMAN—Of Monsters and Men

GOOD PRESSURE—Shea Diamond

A LITTLE DEATH—The Neighbourhood

THE FRUITS—Paris Paloma

LA NOCHE DE ANOCHE—Bad Bunny and ROSALÍA

BETTER—Khalid

STRANGERS—Ethel Cain

NIGHTS—Snow Tha Product feat. W. Darling

QUÉ MALDICIÓN—Banda MS de Sergio Lizárraga and Snoop Dogg

I NEED MY GIRL—The National

LOVE LIES—Khalid feat. Normani

TONIGHT YOU ARE MINE—The Technicolors

WE HAVE IT ALL—Pim Stones

SNOOZE—SZA

I'M BLUE—Faouzia

EAT YOUR YOUNG—Hozier

CHANEL—Frank Ocean

GIRLS AGAINST GOD—Florence + The Machine

WASTELAND, BABY!—Hozier

TLALLI

Grassy hills stretched over the landscape before Tlalli, cradling the sprawling mansion like gentle hands.* It was an impressive estate for the area, and though she had seen so many places now that it was hard to keep them all straight, she would always find some gratitude for even the most mundane creativities of humankind.

It was difficult, though, to enjoy anything with Anthony prattling on at her shoulder, his grumbled words about something that had happened at least an hour ago taking away from the fresh air and pretty pillars. She did her best to pay him no mind, ignoring every mention of her name for attention or otherwise. She was over it. She was over everything he and the Dominion had ever brought into her life.

"Come on, Goldie. Help me out!" Anthony called.

"I'm not your nanny, Anthony. Help yourself," she cooed back condescendingly.

* ON MY MAMA—Victoria Monét

That had not been his name when she met him. That was the name Michael had given him the day Anthony officially joined the angels' elite ranks, which was the more shocking aspect of this situation. While plenty of other mortals—with and without magic—had aided the angels over the centuries and continued to do so, few had ever been officially inducted into the Dominion itself, much less been given audience with its governing body— the archangels, Michael, Raphael, and Gabriel.

And the worst part? Anthony had done so little to earn it.

It was Tlalli who had planned and carried out the heist at Anthony's estate—or rather Anthony's *father's* estate—and it was Tlalli who had endured dating Anthony to do so. It was Tlalli who had made his father, Cahuani, trust her until that trust was a weakness, and it was Tlalli who had ensured that Anthony was able to escape the home he swore was a prison. And had she not done all that, he never would have made it to the Garden of Eden, much less into the Dominion.

Still, the moment they reached the Garden, it became quite clear what Michael's motives had been for using her. It wasn't because he respected her or her abilities. It was because he had planned to offer her to Anthony as a prize for betraying his family.

Michael held to that intent even now despite Tlalli making clear that she wanted nothing to do with Anthony.

For the past four years, Anthony had been as insufferable as he was inescapable. Michael continued to pair them up, regardless of Tlalli's demands and pleas, and by now, disenchantment had taken root in her chest. This wasn't what she had signed up for—playing sidekick to a selfish, arrogant mortal playacting as

an angel. After all the flak the angels had given her for having a Nahualli for a mother, watching them put this jackass on a pedestal was like taking a shot to the chest. Every single day.

Like Anthony and her mother, Mecati, Tlalli was also one of the Nahualtin, ancient sorcerers native to the land that settlers now called Mexico. Once she joined the Dominion, she was forbidden from utilizing her Nahualli magic except, of course, when it benefited the angels, something Mecati had been mortified by. Tlalli wondered if Anthony had been given an exception for that too, although she doubted he would take one anyway. He had done everything in his power to leave his old life behind. Meanwhile, Tlalli had done everything to cling to hers.

She had been unwilling to relinquish her name first and foremost. It was one boundary she had warned Michael that he would never be allowed to cross. He had respected that for a good while. Then Anthony had come along.

When Anthony first met Tlalli, he and his shameful lack of creativity had nicknamed her "Goldilocks" because of the golden locs she often donned in human form. She could grin and bear it at first when they were alone on Earth, but once they returned to Heaven, it became increasingly unbearable once the other angels began to join in. No matter what she said now, they merely whisked it away, adding their own variation of the name to the tune of Anthony's incessant laughter. That was when she realized her fate amid the angels had been sealed. They would always see her as nothing more than a toy, the gift Michael had given Anthony for turning on his own. And if she remained in Heaven, there would be no way to change that.

Of course, she could not simply leave. There was no "leaving" Michael and therefore, really no "leaving" Anthony. She doubted she would just slip away anyway. She was too petty, too spiteful, too angry, to just walk out and let them think they'd scared her off. No, when the time came for her to leave, she would not do so quietly. However her escape came about, she would ensure that it shook Heaven and the Dominion to its core.

She simply had to find a way to do that.

When they reached the mansion, the ornate front doors opened before them, permitting them entry into a spacious hall. Though she was not looking forward to spending several days surrounded by mortals and demons, she figured it should be easy enough to lose Anthony in this place. At the very least, she'd enjoy the distance from Michael.

Given that the auction they were attending was on neutral territory, the archangels and the Puri—governing bodies of the angels and demons respectively—had certain stipulations for the duration of everyone's coexistence here. One of these stipulations was that the governing bodies were not allowed on the premises, and they could not be in direct contact with their representatives. This meant Tlalli and her little team would have no help from Michael or the other archangels. They were on their own.

Though Tlalli had insisted she could do this alone, Michael had been adamant about sending not only Anthony but also Elias, one of the oldest angels. Tlalli had always felt that it was a bit of a cheat to send Elias on any team mission when he could probably take on a whole legion of demons on his own. Yet Elias had long since lost his lust for the work, so he acted as a glorified

babysitter for Anthony—and, by extension, Tlalli—a role that he was taking on more and more frequently. Rather than making her life easier, this made everything worse.

Of course, the most infuriating part about this job was the fact that Anthony didn't have to be here at all. He had nothing special to offer, but he kissed so much of Michael's ass that he got to tag along on all Tlalli's trips as he pleased. She had pleaded with Michael to keep Anthony in the Garden. With so many mortals attending the auction and a demon delegation inevitable, she thought Michael might see how much of a liability Anthony would be. He hadn't. He never did when it came to Anthony.

She was sick of it. She was sick of all of it.

"I'm gonna need you to lose the attitude, like real quick." Anthony's voice was so close to Tlalli's ear that she nearly jumped.

"I'm gonna need you to learn what personal space is," she shot back coldly. "Like *real* quick." She could hear his teeth grinding.

"Don't forget what you are, Goldie."

"Of the two of us, only one has forgotten what they are, Anthony, and it's not me."*

Before he could retaliate, the Concierge came into view alongside a few other mortals that Tlalli became acutely aware of all at once. She rolled her shoulders, trying to get used to this skin again.

Though she had been born and raised in her human vessel, tailored for her at birth, she had spent a substantial amount of time in her "divine form," as the angels called it, the past several

* I AM HER—Shea Diamond

years. Since her mother passed, she had continually limited the use of her human form, and now it felt like a coat that no longer fit as well as it used to.

She ambled along the edge of the lobby as Anthony and Elias checked them in, taking in the guests who had already arrived. She could sense the presence of demons but could not pinpoint their location, meaning they were likely not down here at the moment. Still, they had arrived first, meaning they already had the upper hand.

Tlalli didn't know much about this ancient chalice they had been sent to retrieve, but she knew it was important. Michael had made that quite clear. To her at least. Failure could very well be a death sentence.

Anthony's hand landed on her ass, and on instinct, she whipped around with her fingers curled into a fist.

"I swear, Anthony, if you put your hands on me one more time—"

"Don't act like you don't know who you're talking to," he said, his grin spreading wide.

Like his name, the vessel he now inhabited was not the one he had when she met him but one fashioned for him by the Dominion, one he had been allowed to customize. The pale skin, the ice-gray eyes beneath his shades, the slick brown hair... It was even more unsettling to be touched by this body. She was basically being touched by a stranger.

"I know exactly who I'm talking to. Do you?" Though immediately, she decided she was done with the conversation. "You know what? I need some air." She turned and decided

to head in whatever direction her feet fell first, then search for an exit.

"You better be in the room the moment I say so," he called out. "We have things to do, baby."

She waved him off with a flick of her wrist, disregarding the demand altogether. She would get back when she got back, when her skin no longer felt so tight and his face didn't look so punchable.

Once she made it back to the lush grounds, she felt much better and began taking in the scenery at her own pace. She took her time in the gardens, and once she wandered out of those, she indulged in the breeze coming off the lake before heading for the boathouse and dock just down the slope from her.

Mecati used to talk about living a simple life in a cabin by the sea. Even when Tlalli was older, they would sit at the table for a cafecito with fresh pan dulce and talk about doing it. *A few more years, just a few more years*, they would say. A few more years, and there would be peace between Heaven and Hell. A few more years, and Tlalli could return to Earth full-time.

They both knew it was a lie.

And eventually, a few more years was all Mecati had, and time went by far too fast for them to ever make it to the sea. Mecati was taken by a mortal illness that Tlalli failed to contain alone. In her desperation, Tlalli had run to Michael to beg for his help despite how the Dominion abhorred all mortal magical practitioners. She'd wanted to believe he would make an exception. She'd wanted to believe she was worth one.

Yet Michael denied her. He denied her and spat on her

mother's name all in a single breath. She could still hear his response clear as day in her head.

Every breath a witch takes upon the Earth is a gift they do not deserve.

Maybe that had been the beginning of the end of her belief in them. Maybe that was when she'd realized that she was just as expendable as her mother, no matter how devoted she'd been to the Dominion. If not, she had surely realized it after being all but bound to Anthony. Either way, the lesson had been learned. She had done her best to deny the decay of her belief the past few years, but she could do so no longer. Now she just needed a way out.

The sun began its descent far too quickly, and eventually, she knew she could not stall any longer. She was hoping she at least had her own room in the suite, but she would not hold her breath. Despite prior threats she'd made regarding the sleeping arrangements, she didn't trust Anthony to be so polite.

Even in the Garden, he failed repeatedly to respect her boundaries, invading her space and pushing his luck. In one of the most recent incidents and one of the final straws, he'd attempted to let his hands wander, and he caught *her* hands in response. Of course, as soon as he recovered from her retaliation, he ran off to tell Michael, who had the audacity to scold her. Now she spent most of her free time attempting to put as much distance as possible between her and Anthony.

She no longer felt comfortable sleeping in the Garden, finding reprieve only in stasis, where she could briefly step out of existence, where the only ones able to summon her were the

archangels. Sometimes, she wished she could stay there for good, if only to escape Anthony's overwhelming entitlement.*

She decided to stop for a drink in the lounge before she continued upstairs, but she came to a halt the moment she crossed the threshold.

At the long bar counter on the opposite side of the room sat a familiar face, slightly obscured by the brim of a black cowboy hat. It was a face she hadn't seen in four years, one she had hoped to never see again, yet one she would never forget. It was the face of a man she had betrayed.

It was a pretty face nonetheless. In fact, Anthony's father, Cahuani, was the upgraded and improved version of Anthony in almost every way, even before Anthony took on his new form, so much so that Tlalli had almost regretted having to rob Cahuani. With his flawless dark brown skin and matching eyes that seemed to peer into your soul from beneath enviably long eyelashes, he'd pinned her in place with one of his looks on several occasions. He was slightly shorter than her, with a solid build and a smile that could knock you back a few feet, a smile he likely hadn't flashed in a while. He hadn't just lost his only son in the past four years. He'd lost his wife too.

That, Tlalli luckily wasn't responsible for. At least she didn't think so.

Both of Anthony's parents had been Nahualtin too, powerful ones, who had—according to Michael at least—sold their souls to the devils. All Tlalli had known about them before for certain was that they had been well-known in Heaven, and she had

* GO GO GO—Jorja Smith

assumed that was how Michael and the Dominion knew who to target for the heist. She had also assumed that Anthony having a treacherous heart was merely a stroke of luck. It wasn't until after the job was done that she realized that couldn't be true. Michael had known what Anthony was long before Tlalli entered Anthony's life, and he had already promised her to Anthony before she ever decided to seduce him as part of the heist.

That thought alone made her blood boil.

From what she could see, Cahuani was alone, sipping his glass of dark-colored something and scrolling through his phone with his eyebrows knitted. She could still remember the anger in his face as she disappeared from his estate with not only his son but also a priceless item entrusted to him by the Puri. Meaning she and Anthony had not just robbed his father but the Puri as well.

She had always figured it would catch up to them eventually, especially when Michael cared so little for their safety, but today was not the day. She knew without a shadow of a doubt that Cahuani was the last person in either faction who would violate the truce. And the longer she thought about it, the more he looked like an answer to her prayers rather than a consequence of her actions.

Maybe it was desperation. Maybe naivete. Either way, she was beginning to think that this could be an opportunity. This could be her way out. If it was, she had to reach for it. If there was a chance, she had to try. After all, what did she have to lose?

Apparently not enough.

Licking her lips, she smoothed out her dress and made her way to the bar.

CAHUANI

Cahuani didn't *want* to be here. Greed had known that. Greed had even been slightly reluctant, but he'd sent Cahuani anyway.*

"You're our best chance of success," Greed had said.

Greed wouldn't have lied. He knew lying wouldn't have swayed Cahuani's attitude, because at fifty-five years old, Cahuani was resistant to charm, and flattery would have ricocheted off his spite first anyway. And the job was crucial, meaning there was no room for error. Meaning no room for anyone but their best.

Nevertheless, the auction was a rather straightforward endeavor. Cahuani had been to many before, though usually, mortals with no magic—the Puri had come to call them orfani or "the orphaned," since they had been abandoned by their god—were the minority. Additionally, the tensions between Heaven and Hell had never been so palpable.

* BLOODY SHIRT" (BASTILLE REMIX)—To Kill a King

For the past seven months or so, angels had been carrying out more attacks on demon strongholds, wreaking havoc in places they had once agreed to steer clear of. The Puri had been reluctant to strike back, fighting off assaults when necessary and remaining strictly on the defensive. Cahuani didn't know how long that would last though. The situation was on the verge of becoming dire.

Nonetheless, the Puri were more concerned with artifacts like the one Cahuani had come for than attacks on their terrain, so that was where Cahuani would maintain his focus. At least for now.

Cahuani and his companions, the demons Xaphan—whom the angels had actually injured in one of those recent attacks, putting him out of commission for over a month—and Acheron, had come for a cup. More specifically, they had come for a chalice.

The orfani zealots who the Puri had initially gifted it to called it "Noli Oblivisci." The Latin translated to *forget not*, although when Cahuani had asked Greed the meaning, Greed said he would tell the story only once the chalice had been returned, because it was safer that way. Cahuani didn't question him. He rarely did. He rarely had to.

From what he understood, items with magical properties like the one he was after would be viewed and bid on separately from whatever the orfani salivated over. A good thing too. He knew inanimate items weren't the only things on their pedestals, and the thought of that made his stomach churn.

Though Cahuani was flattered—and honestly quite relieved—by the faith that the Puri still had in him after his son's betrayal, the work no longer held his interest the way it once had. Nor did the cause hold his heart as it used to.

That wasn't to say his loyalties weren't ironclad, because they were. He still believed in the Puri. He just...wasn't sure he was what they needed anymore.

But they were certain he was, and that was what mattered, so here he was, trying to brace himself for the very real possibility of having to face his son for the first time since he'd robbed him and left his family with nothing but pain and confusion.

That wasn't the only thing that had Cahuani on edge, however. The number of orfani, angels, and demons all in attendance was a fragile entanglement, and if he still knew anything about his son, it was that Tec—*Anthony*—loved a ticking time bomb. More than that, Anthony loved to speed up its clock.

Sometimes, Cahuani let himself remember just how excited he was to be a father even before he transitioned. Finding out that transitional magic would allow him to procreate without the aid of western medical practices had been the biggest blessing. Never once had he considered the possibility that his child would grow up to see his lineage as a curse.

Cahuani took another slow swig from his glass before checking his watch. Xaphan and Acheron had left him here alone while they scoped out the premises, and he considered going to find them. This lounge was way too open for his liking.

Yet something kept him rooted to the chair—a feeling, a sensation, an assurance from the ancestors that he was meant to be here in this room on this spot at this time today. Whatever it was, he tuned out as much of the rest of the world as he could and focused on his drink, scrolling aimlessly through his phone when that wasn't enough, just to give his hands something to

do. It was a riveting way to spend an afternoon in a remote mansion.

All at once and without warning, alarm bells began to go off in his head. He straightened in his seat, but before he could scan the room, someone sat down beside him, neglecting the many empty stools across the bar.

He knew for a fact that it wasn't Xaphan or Acheron. Both of them towered over him, and while the person beside him was slightly taller, they were certainly nowhere near as tall as his demon companions. He kept his eyes on his phone, paying them no mind, but his reaction was visceral just beneath the surface. He knew exactly who it was. Her voice only confirmed it. Even after four years, he hadn't forgotten it. And he hadn't forgotten *her*.

"Is there such a thing as arriving to these things too early?"

Leaning on his apathy, he lifted his glass and took a slow drink even as the memories flitted across the forefront of his mind. Why wouldn't they? The first time he met her, she was sleeping in his son's bed.

"It sure feels like it," he returned after a time.

He had expected angels. He had even expected Tlalli. However, he had not expected this level of audacity, certainly not on day one.

Though he supposed he should've. The last time she had befriended him, she had done it at his kitchen table over oatmeal every morning for weeks while intending to rob him. What was starting a conversation in an open lounge?

Regardless, whatever scheme she and his hardheaded son had put together this time, he wasn't about to entertain it at the risk

of his own job. No matter how much he still loved his son, whatever name he went by now.

"Are you here on your own?" Tlalli purred. "Or is someone keeping you waiting?"

"A little of both at the moment, I think," he said.

He knew she was waiting for him to really acknowledge her, to look at her, to *see* her. It had been evident to him that she liked attention from the moment they met, and that hadn't seemed to change. Though what *had* changed was the demeanor with which she propped herself up. She was no longer selling the innocent, inconspicuous role—always helpful, always doting, always checking in on him. Now, the fangs were on full display.

Not that he would ever need the reminder of how dangerous she was again.

"Me too," she said, her smirk audible. "Though I admit I'm not as alone as I would like to be."

He caught sight of her profile out of the corner of his eye as she leaned over to order a drink. She hadn't changed much. She was still beautiful of course, but that beauty seemed more otherworldly, as if it no longer fit inside her human vessel, instead spilling out around the edges of her skin.

Her characteristic golden locs fell around her slender shoulders, framing her sharp face. Her deep-brown skin, only a few shades lighter than his own, glowed differently, a product of who she was, *what* she was. Like hazard lights.

Still, she looked comfortable in that human skin, working every inch of it to her advantage. He wouldn't be fooled by it

again though. He made a habit of knowing his enemies, no matter what form they took.

"These walls got ears," he pointed out, sitting back in his seat. "You sure you want them to hear you talking to me? And so openly too."

There was a brief pause before she said, "I might have companions, but I have no keeper."

He shrugged. "I guess it wouldn't matter much if it was your keeper who put you up to this."

She paused for a few seconds before responding. "So you do remember me."

He chuckled. "How could I ever forget *you*, Tlalli?"

Six weeks. For six weeks, she had lived with his son under his roof, eating at his table and walking in his gardens, enjoying the lush life supplied to Cahuani by her enemies. Not only that, she had dragged Tec—*Anthony. His name is Anthony now, dammit*—away from him faster, hardening the rogue ideology Anthony had fallen into and weaponizing his son's hatred and disdain for how he practiced his trade.

Of course, Cahuani could acknowledge that Anthony's betrayal wasn't entirely on her. He had seen the signs of his son's changing ideology long before she came into their lives. Cahuani still couldn't pinpoint why or how or who had led his son down that path. He only knew that Anthony had been eager to run along it, straight past the point of no return. And it never had anything to do with angels or demons. It only had to do with power.

Anthony had called Cahuani and Aliyah, Anthony's mother, weak for being willing to work under the Puri. He wanted his

own power. He wanted to be more. Though in his attempts to become so, he had clearly started to internalize a hatred for who he was and thus for who his parents were. Besting them apparently became more important than being good, and by the time Anthony met Tlalli, he was already gone. A chance to hurt Cahuani must have been too good to pass up.

And here was the angel who had offered his son that opportunity, smiling in his face like it had been some chance meeting all those years ago and not a coordinated attack.

He would not fall for those big doe eyes again. That he vowed.

"You sat in my kitchen drinking my coffee," he went on after a sip from his glass, "had me grieving your mother with you nine months to the day of her passing, and you still had the audacity to play in my face. That's not something I can forget."

Or forgive, if he had it his way. Her mother had been a Nahualli, like Cahuani, and in their culture, they always held their fallen in the highest esteem. For Tlalli to use Mecati's passing as a way to get to him, to weaponize her grief, whether it was genuine or not, so that he lowered his defenses in order to console her, to grieve with her... If he held rage for nothing else against Tlalli, he would hold rage for that.

He could see in her face that he had struck the nerve he'd aimed for, although she was doing her best to pretend that he hadn't. Any guilt he may have felt about it was buried beneath that thick layer of apathy and his commitment to his purpose here. This was business. Whatever happened in this massive house had to qualify under that title and that title alone. Personal emotions, both his and anyone else's, had to be pushed aside.

She recovered much quicker than he anticipated, and just as he put his glass to his lips again, he was forced to bite down on its edge. Her lips were no more than a centimeter from his ear when she spoke.

"I didn't come over here on anyone's command, Papa Bear," she purred, dipping the long acrylic on her pinkie finger into his glass, then licking the whiskey off it.

He breathed out slowly through his nose. "Then why risk it?"

"I imagined you would be civil in such a public place."

He made a show of looking around, taking in the entire two other people now, including the bartender, who currently occupied the old-fashioned lounge draped in wood grain.

"I think they'll be fine as long as I keep it quiet," he concluded.

"You wouldn't hurt me."

"And how do you know that?"

"Because you follow the rules, and you honor the truce, even if the rest of us wouldn't." She had him there. "Besides, I'm not here lookin' for trouble."

"And what else did you expect to find with me?"

"I'm here to talk business."

"There is no difference when it comes to you, Tlalli. That's what you're forgettin'."

And frankly, he didn't have the time for it. Though…okay, he could admit that he was still trying to figure out how she managed to get one over on him to begin with. He'd been around the block more than a handful of times. He knew how the world worked and how it didn't. And above all, he had known how to protect his household, his family. Well, back when he had one.

Aliyah never blamed him for the loss of their son, but their final two years together had been tense. In fact, Cahuani was convinced they would have ended up separating if she were still here, an opinion that was contingent on his denying that they had already done so in a way. After all, she had neither allowed him to try to cure the illness that had seized her nor relinquished her soul to the Puri so that they could be reunited.

She constantly assured him that she still loved him, up until the day her spirit left this plane, and she still visited every Day of the Dead. Yet each and every day since Anthony left, it was clear that most of her had followed right behind him.

The ache remained, of course. The last two years had been void of so many things he had once thought eternal. He himself was a ghost, walking the halls of their ancient family estate, which sat on land on the southern New Mexico border that his ancestors had fought to protect for ages. And though he still owned that land, he could not help but feel as if he had failed those ancestors. He doubted that feeling would ever subside.

Tlalli was a reminder of that failure, even if she was no longer the main source of his ire. When looking at her, he saw the archangels and their thievery, not of the amulet they had taken from his safe but of what he valued most in this world—his son, his family.

He threw back the remaining contents of his glass and straightened his tie just as a big burly man with umber skin entered—Xaphan.

Xaphan met Cahuani's eyes and halted just beyond the doorway, then dramatically raised a brow and gestured to Tlalli. Cahuani only rolled his eyes, pulled a roll of bills from

his jacket, and put down enough money for the tab and a generous tip.

"Let us make this clear so that there are no *inklings* going forth," Cahuani stated, standing up. "You do not have business with me nor I with you." He looked at Tlalli, his eyes sharp. "And if you manage to forget that again, I will not be so gracious."

Tlalli snorted, turning in her seat to look at him properly. "Okay, let's not get wild with the veiled threats, Papa Bear. Say what you mean." She stood up too, invading his personal space. "And say it with your chest."

This time, he smirked and leaned in to whisper in her ear without hesitation. She didn't know who she was dealing with, but that was all right. He would remedy that.

"If you don't find a way to keep your distance from me, I'm gonna send those pretty little angel wings nestled under this pretty little skin back to your employer in a box, truce be damned."

He stepped around her then, patted her shoulder, and moved toward Xaphan and the door. Xaphan's loud ass was already asking questions before Cahuani reached him.

"Okay, who the fuck is that, and where did you find her?"

Cahuani grabbed Xaphan's shoulder and steered him down the corridor toward the elevators. "Sorry, brother, you'd have to go all the way to Heaven for someone like her, and I would not recommend it."*

3

TLALLI

Tlalli's heart thudded in her chest as she made her way up the floors, feeling as though the elevator was going half its normal speed. She had briefly traded smiles with the woman in the opposite corner, then kept her eyes on her own gold-tipped toes sticking out of her sandals. Try as she might, she couldn't determine what she was feeling, whether it was rage or fatigue or fear or sadness or disappointment or panic or...lust.

Oh yeah, Cahuani was just as smooth as he'd always been, but he was different too. More specifically, he was *cold*. That chill hit her like a brand against her back.

And she liked it. Fuck, she liked it. She liked it, and she didn't know how to cope with that.

But that wasn't the point. The point was that she had put far too much faith in him. She'd seen the first opportunity—which wasn't really an opportunity at all—to escape, and she'd taken

it like a naive child. What did she expect? That he would simply forgive her in this gaudy old lounge after four years of nothing? Maybe she had hoped that by now, he may have realized that she had a job to do, and given the Puri let him live, he might've gotten over it. But no. No, he was still angry. Honestly, if she didn't know any better—and she didn't…she never did—she would say he was even angrier now.

Yet that only made her more eager to persuade him. Maybe she really did have a death wish. Then again, death didn't seem so bad if the alternative was Anthony and the Dominion.

As if to remind her of this, Anthony's voice boomed around the room the moment she entered, causing her to recoil.

"Where have you been! I told you not to wander!"

"And I told you I didn't care," she shot back.

"You know," Elias drawled from where he sat on the couch, "your behavior is very unbecoming of your position, Goldie."

She hated that she couldn't tell whether he was mocking her or Anthony with that bored, monotonous tone.

"We are here to conduct a very serious business that has no room for error," Elias continued.

Never mind. He was definitely being sarcastic.

"Look, I can do my job just fine," Tlalli retorted. "If I couldn't, I wouldn't be here. And if you don't think I can, tell Michael to send someone else. Otherwise, my free time is mine."

She could see the agitation on Anthony's face, but before he could initiate another tantrum, she slipped into the bathroom and slammed the door, then spelled it shut. The door handle shook

violently once Anthony reached it, but she paid it no mind. After all, they had somewhere to be.*

Tlalli took her time in the shower, allowing the hot water to alleviate some of the tension built up in her neck and loosen up this skin. Anthony banged on the door a few times, but she ignored it until her hands had pruned and the steam was too much.

Still, she made an event of getting ready after, taking at least long enough for the fog to start lifting from the mirror that she kept trying to wipe clean. She thought of the mornings she would get up and find her mother already seated in front of her vanity mirror, applying her favorite eyeliner beneath tattooed brows. To this day, in all Tlalli's years alive with and without her, she still found Mecati the most beautiful person she had ever seen.

Mecati had been a quiet woman who wielded her magic in service of their people, their community, rather than the Puri or the Dominion. There were many witches from various factions, such as Brujas and Curanderas Tlalli had grown up around, who did the same. They were all categorized under the title of "witch" by angels and demons, but they had their own internal names, and the magic differed from group to group, as did the way they chose to utilize it.

The Nahualtin's identifying trait was the ability to shift into a second form, usually an animal. This form was known as their Nagual, and when mastered, it could even be manifested outside their body like a companion.

Mecati, whose Nagual had been the coyote, never had the chance to teach Tlalli how to fully take her second form before

* BOA—Megan Thee Stallion

the angels laid claim on her, but some nights, Tlalli still dreamed of the jaguar.

Mecati had raised Tlalli on the banks of the Rio Grande in southern New Mexico, cultivating Tlalli's love for the land and their people. Tlalli's father had never been around. She'd only met him once when she was really young, and she didn't find out he was an angel until Gabriel himself swept into their humble living room, demanding Tlalli fulfill her duty to the Dominion. She was sixteen then and an adversary of humility, so despite her mother's fears, she agreed to join them because she thought she had something to prove. It would forever be her greatest regret.

Mecati had explained that while she knew Tlalli's father was an angel—procreation between humans and mortals, which could only happen at will and not by accident, was severely scrutinized but not entirely outlawed—he had made it clear he didn't want Tlalli knowing. Mecati believed keeping it a secret would protect Tlalli from the Dominion. It hadn't.

Instead, in their efforts to build an army that could finally stomp out their enemies, the angels had apparently made the decision to utilize any and all angels they could, even those born from the witches they loathed so deeply.

Not that this prejudice had ever stopped the Dominion from using witches of all backgrounds for their own gain before then. That was their thing though—hypocrisy and double standards.

Right before Mecati passed, she and Tlalli promised each other they'd honor the code of their people. They could see each other once a year during the Day of the Dead but not visit or

summon each other outside that. Basically, with the utmost reluctance, Tlalli had agreed to let her mother go.

Some days—well, actually a lot of days—she regretted that too.

When she at last exited the bathroom, dressed in a formfitting emerald-green dress, Anthony was nowhere to be found, but Elias was still on the couch, twisting a fresh cartridge onto his vapor pen. Angels who descended from the Garden and its subsidiaries tended to pick up some number of human habits after initially attempting to use them to fit in. Something in the air, she supposed.

She wondered if the vape had any effect on him or if he had to do something to the oils to make them stronger. She wondered if angels like Elias felt any weaker here on Earth, the way she felt away from it.

"You know he *will* throw a tantrum in front of all these mortals if y'all keep at this, right?" Elias deadpanned, sitting back in his seat.

"Where is he?" she asked, ignoring the comment altogether.

"Dunno. He just said to meet him in the lobby."

"And to make sure I got ready?"

Elias only shrugged.

Though the body he occupied was only forty years old or so, he was an ancient angel, one Tlalli had been taught about as a child. After actually spending time with him though, any starstruck admiration she had more or less bled away rather swiftly, and she found that although he was more tolerable company than Anthony—when he was alone at least—Elias was a dry conversationalist with very little care for anything other than the small bits of joy he could supply himself with in this realm.

In truth, Tlalli was almost certain that he was damn near as disenchanted as she was with the Dominion. Especially now that Michael and Raphael wanted a war, there was very little fun to be had and very little peace to be found.

He sighed. "I'm just sayin' to keep the peace."

Anthony's peace, he meant. Unfortunately, Tlalli was not invested in Anthony's peace.

Instead, she asked, "Why did you agree to come babysit him anyway, Elias?"

He didn't answer straight away, instead exhaling a thick cloud of vapor and tugging at the coarse black curls of his thick beard. He slouched in the corner of the couch, his eyes to the sky. Did he still see something when he looked up there, or had the light gone out for him too? Would he pretend it hadn't if she dared to ask?

"I don't know if 'agree' would be the word I'd use," he replied. "But let me tell you. With the way shit is now, it's best for all of us to spend as much time as we can down here. The farther from Eden, the better."

"I'm sure the demons would let you visit if you ask nicely," she teased.

He didn't respond, instead taking a long drag of his pen, then springing to his feet and grabbing his evening attire from the opposite chair. His suit was, as always, a simple black-tie ensemble. Comfort was his goal, but Tlalli would never deny it looked good on him.

Subtle as it was, there was in fact a charm to Elias's disinterested disposition. What a shame Tlalli was only just noticing that charm now.

Or maybe ignorance was a blessing. After all, if she did eventually leave Heaven, she would rather not have anything to miss.

Elias pulled off his shirt and tossed it at her in his version of a truce, and she caught it with a narrowed gaze, taking in his carved shoulders, muscular chest, and soft round belly. She found herself amused by the fact that while Cahuani and Anthony could shift from man to bear, Elias was a bear of a man in human form.

She sometimes wished Elias would give her more. She knew he didn't owe her that, but it didn't keep her from wanting it anyway. They could be friends if he weren't so damn neutral all the time, so damn eager to stay in line. It would be nice to have an ally. Or at least someone who felt the same indignation she did.

He had been a little warmer with her after her mother passed. Then again, he was also the only angel to show any kind of compassion to her, minuscule as it was, so the bar had been low to start.

"Ready to go?" he asked.

She looked up, and he was already in his suit, looking as comfortable as she expected, the fabric loose in some places but tight in others. A reminder that he was the muscle here.

"What is the point of this thing tonight anyway?"

She was convinced rich mortals liked to have parties to flaunt their hoarding problems, and she wished they would have one standard party and not all these different types of events. She would never be able to tell you the difference between a gala and a banquet or a charity banquet and a ball, but she would show up and serve.

"To get a look at the items beforehand and, you know, mingle."

"With mortals we will likely never see again?" she quipped.

"It's not about us. It's not even really about them. They treat parties the way they would treat us if they ever proved we existed."

"And how is that?"

He smirked and fixed his coat. "Like a spectacle to cash in on."

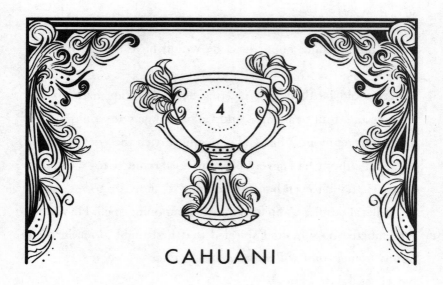

CAHUANI

Xaphan and Acheron had not allowed Cahuani to back out of the gala. And Cahuani knew that if he tried, they would track him down, then even if they didn't drag him back to the party by his arms, they would irritate him so badly that he would end up dragging himself. So he stood before the full-length mirror in his suite against his will, straightening his tie, then smoothing it down into his black vest.

Once he was satisfied, he donned his cuff links and black felt cowboy hat. The scent of his sandalwood beard oil soothed his senses, and he inhaled it deeply. He was going to need all the help he could get tonight to remain composed. Even after all these years of learning to mask his emotions and conduct himself with some semblance of charisma, he still struggled in a crowded room. The biggest threat in those places was always sensory overload; the air never sat right in his lungs.

He focused on his breathing during the elevator ride down,

trying not to think about how he would have to see Anthony tonight.

It would be their first meeting since Anthony had left the Reyes estate four years ago, and Cahuani knew it would not be a pleasant reunion. While Cahuani still carried the grief of losing his son, Anthony had never once expressed remorse for what he'd done. He hadn't even had the decency to show up to his mother's funeral despite Cahuani's direct summoning spell. He vividly remembered how he had spiraled that first night alone in their family home. *Am I still a husband? A father?*

He still didn't know.

The elevator stopped and opened on the second floor, and to Cahuani's abject horror, there stood Anthony, buttoned up in a plain black suit and tie. Even in that hideous skin, Cahuani would know his son anywhere. He could sense Anthony always, his phantom limb. Their spirits would always be joined. Until Anthony's betrayal, Cahuani never thought the connection would feel like a curse.

The air in the elevator seemed to plummet below zero. The way Anthony's lips curled when he looked at his father was a nightmare come to life. No surprise, no shock, no shame on his face. Only that Cheshire Cat grin as he stepped inside.

"Hey, Papa Bear."

Surprisingly, the sound of the old title on Anthony's lips made Cahuani's stomach churn. He had thought it would've bothered him more earlier when Tlalli had used it, but no. It had glanced off him then. Now, it made him want to climb up the fucking walls.

Anthony had been Little Bear once upon a time, the two men sharing a second form. Not many Nahualtin inherited either parent's Nagual, and those who did usually received it from the parent that carried them. Yet Anthony hadn't taken the hummingbird form of his mother. Instead, he'd inherited his father's form. That had always seemed special to Cahuani.

It apparently hadn't meant a damn thing to Anthony.

"Come to buy something else you can't hold on to?" Anthony jabbed.

Cahuani slid his hands into his pockets. Pained as he was about seeing his son, he would not let Anthony goad him into anger—not here, not now. This was business. Personal shit had to be set aside.

"I'm surprised they didn't skin you, honestly," Anthony went on with a chuckle. "You must have done a whole lotta crying and pleading, huh?"

"When you are respected as I am respected, you get to make a few mistakes," Cahuani returned, his voice level. "Maybe you'll get there one day."

Anthony howled with laughter. "I don't need anyone else's respect." He moved to stand in front of his father, then looked down at him. "And I don't make mistakes."

"Hmm." Cahuani nodded politely. "But if you did make a mistake, particularly here at this auction, what would happen to you?" He met Anthony's sharp gaze. "What can you buy with none of your own money and no one else's respect?"

Anthony clenched his jaw, thin-skinned as ever, his eyes flashing with raw rage. That made Cahuani feel a few inches taller. It

reminded him that he was the father, not the son, and certainly no Holy Spirit.

"You have no idea what I got," Anthony spat back. "You don't know who I am now, old man."

"I know exactly what you are. I'm not impressed."

Anthony snorted. "You couldn't handle me at your worst, Papa Bear, so—"

Cahuani took a quick step forward and reveled in the sight of Anthony's spirit recoiling at once even though Cahuani had not struck him. He never had. He never believed he needed to. Instead, he reached up and straightened Anthony's tie, then tightened the knot at the top.

"You have never seen me at my worst, *Anthony*." He gave the tie a firm tug before releasing it. "Do me a simple favor this weekend, yeah? Be a good boy and stay out of my way. Oh, and while you're at it, make sure your girlfriend does the same. I'll tell you like I told her earlier. This is your only warning. I'm not tellin' either of you again."

Cahuani smoothed his hands over Anthony's shoulders, gave them a firm squeeze, then moved around him and out as the doors slid open. He could almost feel the steam rolling off Anthony's back, which soothed him some, though he also felt a tremendous amount of guilt for taking any comfort at all in his son's lack thereof. But this was where Cahuani drew his boundary. This was how it had to be. His boy was gone, his name erased. And the monster who had killed him had not even kept his face.[*]

At least that made it easier to pretend he was someone else.

* SHEISTY—Trinidad James, Kamaiyah, and Hope Tala

Cahuani found Xaphan and Acheron standing opposite the Concierge's desk, looking through an archway into the hall where the gala was being held. People were already filling the hall fast, and Cahuani felt sweat collecting on the back of his neck.

"Wow, you clean up nice," Xaphan stated, clapping a hand on Cahuani's shoulder.

Though Xaphan and Acheron had human vessels that looked much younger than his, they had been alive for centuries. However, from what Cahuani understood, Acheron was quite new to working here on Earth and in a human vessel. He was originally what was known to mortals as a sleep paralysis demon and worked in the sleep realm that existed not simply between Earth and Hell but between life and death.

"You two as well," Cahuani returned with a tip of his hat.

"Was that...uh...?"

Xaphan gestured toward Anthony's departing form, and Cahuani nodded, attempting to hide any ill feeling that may have been left behind on his features.

"I'm not seein' the resemblance there, boss."

"I think that's his intention."

"So the angels are here already?" Acheron asked, saving them from an awkward silence.

"That's right," Cahuani replied. "But I don't know. Something feels off."

"No, I'm with you," Xaphan said. "No offense. I'm sure your son is top-tier to them, but they sent him to get this thing? On his own?"

Cahuani shook his head. "He isn't alone. They sent Tlalli as well—"

"Wait, the one who *robbed* you?"

"Yep."

"Is that the woman you were talking to at the bar earlier?"

Cahuani nodded with a wince, Tlalli's eyes flashing behind his own for a brief moment. Acheron whistled, and Xaphan barked a laugh. Cahuani appreciated their levity, although he couldn't bring himself to participate.

"Well, they must've known the Puri would send you," Acheron pointed out.

"And they're expecting me to drop my guard," Cahuani agreed. Or at least he wanted to, but that felt too simple.

"Exactly." Acheron clapped once. "So as long as that don't happen, we'll be good, right?"

Cahuani smirked. "That's definitely not going to happen."

Nonetheless, he still felt as if he were missing something, and he didn't know how worried he should be.

"Just keep vigilant," he said at last, gathering his wits. "Anthony is many things, but he is still my son. I know him better than he knows himself. It's the woman he's with I am concerned about."

"We got your back," Xaphan assured him. "With them and everyone else."

"I would hope so. Otherwise, what use are you?"

Cahuani smiled after a moment, and the demons did the same before the three of them headed into the large hall.

It was immediately evident to Cahuani that Xaphan could

work a room, though Cahuani supposed that should have been a given. Xaphan was a member of the Anima Dae, reaper demons that collected souls for the Puri. Like other factions such as the crossroad demons of the Crucis Dae and the infiltrator demons of the Obscurus Dae, the reaper demons worked on Earth and knew how to deal with people. Xaphan himself had been a reaper for centuries, and it showed. Cahuani was grateful the Puri had sent him. It allowed Cahuani to resign himself to silence for the most part.

Soon enough, Acheron was more comfortable in the crowd as well. Cahuani had never been able to adjust so quickly, despite his best efforts. He no longer looked at this as a character flaw though, instead learning to play to his own strengths.

Though others flocked toward a first look at the auction items, the trio abstained. After all, the chalice they had come to claim would not be on display. It would be concealed until the night after, and even then, they need not see it. They knew what they had come for. Cahuani imagined the angels did too, but that was irrelevant. Nothing would help the angels succeed this time.

The chalice itself seemed quite ordinary in appearance according to the description Sloth had provided. It was a simple golden chalice that the Puri had apparently given to a pope they neglected to name for a purpose they neglected to share, and it was supposed to have been returned to them upon his death. Unfortunately, it had been "lost" for centuries inside Vatican City, one of the few places that the Puri could not penetrate. At least not on their own.

The few members of the Obscurus Dae that had been able to infiltrate Vatican City's walls had come up empty in their

searches until just a few weeks ago, when they found that the chalice had been moved and was now on auction. Cahuani had no idea who had brought it here or how, but that information was inconsequential to his role. His only job was to make sure the cup made it back to Hell, a much easier task than sharing space with Anthony for three days. Cahuani's team had a secret weapon, one the angels could never possibly compete with.

Cahuani managed to make it through two drinks before he laid eyes on his son once more. And Tlalli, who stood at his side looking positively...miserable?

Cahuani observed her for a moment too long with far too much concern for his liking. In the few seconds—okay, maybe minutes—he'd stared at her, she'd turned her head to scowl at Anthony at least a dozen times, her lip pouting out farther each time. Cahuani still wasn't convinced her behavior wasn't an act, but her expressions made him truly consider what Anthony had become in the time since leaving his father's home. Tlalli may have succeeded in conquering Cahuani's safe, but that did not mean she had been as successful in doing the same with his son. Cahuani did not know if that was a blessing or a curse.

The moment Cahuani had an opening, he made his way up one side of the dual staircase that stood in the center of the room. He was already popping his knuckles halfway up, counting each crack. It was something he often did to help calm his mind.

"Ce, ome, eyi, nahui, macuilli..."

By the time he'd escaped onto the balcony overlooking the room, he felt more in control, now able to see and comprehend the bigger picture. This was his place. This was where he thrived.

"You good?"

Cahuani nearly broke his fingers, crushing them together as a voice exploded behind him. He whipped around but then registered Acheron and berated himself for being so easily startled. He was off his game. He had to get it together.

"My bad," Acheron said with a wince, offering Cahuani one of the drinks in his hands.

Cahuani took it, catching a whiff of bourbon as he brought it swiftly to his lips.

"I'm still working on my inside voice," Acheron said. "You don't gotta be though. Good, I mean. I know I'm not." He chuckled and sipped his drink while tugging at the collar of his shirt.

It was terribly obvious that he still wasn't comfortable in his human vessel, but his composure was steady, and Cahuani could admit he was impressed. He had seen demons struggle in their new vessels the way he did in his own human skin, sensitive as he was to the many sights and sounds of a world that had not been made with him in mind. It was why he cracked his knuckles while counting in his native tongue of Nahuatl, why he kept a pair of earbuds—though he preferred the chunky headphones that covered his entire ear, it was best to be discreet in places like this—close at hand. They offered him control that his magic could not.

"I can't tell, which is more than good enough at this point," Cahuani replied.

"Well, I *can* tell that you're not, so what's up?"

"You can literally *hear* emotions. Of course you can tell."

"Oh, this has nothing to do with my skills and everything to

do with the amount of tension in your jaw. That shit hurts. Ask me how I know."

Cahuani chuckled into his glass. "Spoken like a demon who recently learned that the hard way."

"Exactly, so..."

Acheron said nothing more, patiently waiting for Cahuani to give him something. Of course, Cahuani didn't know what he had to offer, especially when they hardly knew each other.

Was it tough seeing his son? Of course. Was it tougher seeing him as the enemy? Absolutely. However, those were simply facts that he had to factor into his plans for the duration of this auction, the same as every other variable he was up against. They had to be.

When Cahuani failed to reply, Acheron continued. "You know, this is the farthest I've ever been away from home."

"From Hell?" Cahuani asked, his brows knitting together. He didn't think the distance changed between there and any place on Earth.

Acheron laughed. "Naw, my—my soulmate."

"The orfani woman." The words passed Cahuani's lips before he could bite down on them. He remembered the story that Xaphan told him about *why* Acheron had come to work topside.

But Acheron only laughed again. "Yeah, Penelope," he confirmed. "She—I mean, since we met, I've either worked in Hell or in Sin City, and I'd get to go home to her right after work, no matter where I was assigned. I guess it would be more accurate to say this is the *longest* I've been away from her..."

Acheron's eyes went somewhere else as he trailed off, and his nails tapped the side of his glass. Cahuani softened at the sight. Yeah, they were more alike than he'd realized. At the very least, their humanness was.

"The rules of any truce on neutral ground always have to be pretty strict," Cahuani offered, trying to refocus Acheron's attention. "Even if the level of enforcement tends to fluctuate."

"Can you list our rules for me again?" Acheron asked quickly, seemingly not because he didn't know them but because he recognized that they both needed the distraction.

"No member of the governing bodies, the Puri and the Dominion's archangels, is allowed to step foot on the premises designated neutral for the duration of the treaty," Cahuani recited in his most comforting cadence. "They are not allowed to communicate with any representative of either faction on neutral territory directly, whether telepathically or otherwise. No representative is allowed to leave the designated premises for the duration of the truce, in this case three days. No acts of aggression or violence are permitted between the representatives in attendance, and no magic is to be performed in view of any orfani, mortals with no magical or spiritual connections. No orfani is to be injured or harmed in any way by either faction. Any such acts are to be treated as an act of war."

Acheron's eyes at last met Cahuani's again. "And that's usually enough?"

"It has been. Back before the Puri had so much power, the angels may have been a bit less...*civil*, but they know better now."

At least he thought they did, but sending Anthony here was certainly a choice.

He could see in Acheron's eyes that he was having the same thought, so when the demon asked his next question, Cahuani wasn't entirely surprised.

"What happened to him? I mean, why did he join the Dominion?"

Cahuani leaned against the railing, suppressing the desire to search the room for his son and instead looking down at his boots.

"He thought his mother and I were weak for working beneath the Puri despite our power. A few years before the betrayal, my wife, Aliyah, and I were offered positions on the Council of the Imbued." At Acheron's confused look, Cahuani smiled. "That is the head council of all magical practitioners. Every denomination of practitioners has its own council, and usually we would have had to serve on the Council of the Smoking Mirror, our faction's personal council, before being offered positions, but they wanted us."

"But you were already working for the Puri, right?"

"Yes, and I imagine that had a lot to do with the accelerated offer. However, we weren't interested."

"Why not?"

Cahuani winced. "The Council is a neutral party, and I'd been working with the Puri and against the Dominion long enough to know that remaining neutral was not an option. Aliyah agreed."

"And that made your boy angry?"

"Anthony wanted us to take the positions because he believed we would be able to use them against the Council itself, to steer them away from their neutral position and into an offensive one."

"And you were against that."

"Honestly? I knew it was what I would've done if I'd taken the position. I would've tried to show them neutrality wasn't actually an option, and I would've pushed them to side with the Puri."

"And your wife?"

Cahuani smirked now. "She *was* against it. She wanted them to see the error of their ways, but she knew we would be villainized by our own people if we forced it, and I realized she was right. We could keep educating willing members, but they had to come to the conclusion on their own. But Anthony thought us cowards for denying ourselves that opportunity, and after that, that's all he cared about—power. How to get it, how to take it, how to rob anyone else of it. And I tried to sway him, to talk him down. I tried everything I could. I never thought he'd outright betray us. I certainly never thought he'd side with the angels of all beings, but…"

"But he's his own person, and there was nothing you could've done."

In his heart, Cahuani knew that. He knew that just like the Council of the Imbued had to make its own decisions, Anthony had to as well. That fact didn't make any of this any easier though. It didn't make the reality hurt any less.

He took another deep drink from his glass and turned back to the room below. At once, he felt a gaze on him, and he scanned the room until he met Tlalli's eyes. The moment he did, she quickly averted her gaze.

She was quite the actress. He would give her that.

Yet the longer he looked at her, the more curious he found himself. What could she possibly expect of him? What plan had she and Anthony laid out in their minds? How could either of them believe he would play into it?

Just then, as he watched Tlalli's golden head make a beeline for the exit after another exchange with Anthony, he decided he wanted to know. He trusted his instincts, and his instincts were telling him this was worth investigating. After all, he had all the faith in his own team's plan. There was nothing to worry about.

"I'll catch up with y'all," he told Acheron.

Ignoring the fresh confusion on the demon's face, Cahuani handed Acheron his glass and hurried down the stairs and out of the hall, giving chase.

ELIAS

Elias truly wished that the champagne, endless as it was, could do more for him. At least as much as it seemed to do for the mortals around him. But no, he was still far too sober for the scene Anthony was currently making in the center of the gala.*

How funny—they were meant to deflect attention from themselves, and here was Anthony, favored pet of the Dominion's archangels, gathering as much of it as possible. And although Elias consistently reminded himself that Anthony was, in fact, not one of them, it hardly helped. He couldn't say that he had ever seen a witch act up like this either. Tlalli was both, and despite the angel wings, she still had some common fucking sense.

He could not say the same for her peers back in the Garden. In reality, Anthony fit in with them far better than Tlalli and Elias ever had. Michael was orchestrating a chaos that was building to impossible heights, and the angels in his employ were eager to hit

* BETTER OFF ALONE—Jenny Plant

that final note, whatever it may be. It wasn't the war either. Elias knew that for certain. He had seen many wars, on Earth and elsewhere, and the greatest struggle wasn't in the blood and bullets. It was in what came after. In the rebuilding, the recovery.

Elias wasn't sure Heaven ever actually recovered from the last battle it witnessed. It never recovered from the Fall.

Stop it. He had been doing this a lot lately—questioning everything he thought he knew about both his own faction and each of their sworn enemies. Things had stopped adding up and making sense a long time ago, but Elias wasn't one to stir the pot or kick up dust. He was just trying to get through the day.

But get through to what? He didn't know. Eternity had looked exactly the same for ages, and there was nothing to look forward to. The younger angels thought the war would bring great reward. Elias knew better. Because what had been hidden from them—the lies, the deceit, the hypocrisy, the revisionism— could not be hidden from him. He had been there at the beginning of the world and through every stage of its history, and he would be there at the end.

"What the fuck did you say to him, Tlalli!" Anthony barked again, drawing another round of disapproving and disdainful looks.

Truth be told, Elias liked mess, although he never showed it. He had perfected the art of casual disinterest. Yet he wanted to hear all about whatever Tlalli had talked to Anthony's dad about. That curiosity was only heightened when Elias saw the infamous Cahuani Reyes himself, looking like every sin Elias had ever been warned against. And every temptation he had ever been told to fight.

Therefore, he was invested in whatever story Tlalli had to tell. However, he doubted Anthony's tantrum was going to get them any legitimate answers, so Elias would have to enforce his babysitter role.

"Anthony, maybe we can use our inside voices for right now, huh?" Elias said, allowing his voice to take on the slightest lilt of patronization. "People are starting to look at us funny."

"I don't give a fuck what these people are looking at!" Anthony snapped back. "I want a fuckin' answer!"

"And I do not care," Tlalli said slowly with both her mouth and her hands, her fingers appearing to tap each word in midair as she said it. "I don't know how many times I have to explain this to you, but I literally do not have to explain shit to you, Anthony. You are nothing to me but a coworker."

"And this is work!" he bit back so hard that Elias was now actively considering an exit. "If you're risking our fucking plans talking to the enemy, I gotta know about it!"

"And you think if she were, she would tell you that?" It came out of Elias's mouth before he could stop it, and Anthony was immediately huffing and puffing. Ugh, Elias swore mortals were a full-time job in and of themselves.

Well, Anthony certainly was. Elias was beginning to feel real guilty for expecting Tlalli to put up with him when even Elias himself, known in Eden for his patience, was at his wits' end with him on day one.

Every other trip before this where he'd been forced to babysit Anthony was starting to take up more space in his brain than he cared to admit. None of this was fucking sustainable.

Before Anthony could explode again, however, Tlalli stormed out of the hall, leaving the two of them there to field the glances they were still getting. Elias was certain the security guards near the door were going to come over at some point, and he wasn't really all that interested in being subjected to that conversation.

"Go find her," Anthony snapped at him.

Elias had known anger. Of course he had. It was a by-product of existence, as a mortal or otherwise. But it had never come so swiftly. Apparently, Anthony had tested his infamous patience long enough, because he was thoroughly overwhelmed.

"Um, let me remind your ass that I do not work for you, Anthony," Elias said coldly, stepping closer to the man and eclipsing him once he swelled to his full size.

He was certain Anthony could see his divine form bristling just beneath his flimsy vessel, the outline of it blooming from his back like a dark shadow. Elias had no qualms about providing the reminder: Anthony was beneath him. Anthony would always be beneath him, and no amount of kissing Michael's ass was gonna change that. Anthony was beneath Tlalli too. It was time he accepted that.

"You don't get to demand anything of me. You don't get to expect me to clean up after you."

Anthony chuckled. "You know damn well you're not the front man here, Elias. This is *my* job. I call the shots."

"Not to me." Elias wouldn't back down, no matter how large Anthony tried to make himself seem. "And whatever this dramatic shit is needs to wait. No, matter of fact, it needs to die. ASAP, and I'm so serious. Leave that girl alone, or I'll call *both* of

your daddies, the one Upstairs and the one in this house, and tell them you're being a fucking child."

Anthony's face screwed up in petulant rage, but Elias only straightened up further, letting his power bleed lightly from his pores. After a moment, Anthony grunted and stalked off toward the door as well, no doubt to find Tlalli. Elias trusted that if she didn't want to be found though, Anthony wouldn't have much luck.

Though Elias knew he loathed Anthony, he never really knew how to feel about Tlalli. Or at least he never inspected those feelings. Sometimes, he felt sorry for her. Sometimes, he wished he knew how to be an actual friend to her. And sometimes, he wished he knew how to be something more.

But none of that mattered, because none of that was possible. They were coworkers trapped in an endless cycle of exploitative servitude, and he could offer her nothing beyond what she already had. Besides, they worked well together, likely because of how detached they were from everything and everyone else. It would be foolish to try and fuck up the flow. The work was all that mattered. The work was all that could.

Scrubbing a hand over his face, Elias headed for the bar at the other end of the room in search of something stronger than champagne. It wasn't that he was completely immune to the alcohol. This was a human vessel, and he felt everything there was for it to feel. However, it took more to affect him, a lot more, and that was the issue at the moment.

A few minutes later, he sat glaring at a glass of straight tequila in front of him. The bartender had given him periodic glances of

concern as he filled it, but Elias instructed him to keep pouring until he was told to stop.

"Try some of this," a voice said from the other side of him.

Elias looked up to see a familiar but not entirely welcome face. Though if he were being honest, this face was far more welcome than Anthony's right now. Or ever.

Xaphan slid an ornate silver flask across the bar to him before moving closer. Elias smirked.

"I imagine it's filled with Gluttony's bourbon," Elias quipped.

"And it will never run dry," Xaphan said with a nod.

Elias had met Xaphan on several occasions, in situations such as this, where interests overlapped but courtesy was still maintained. Xaphan had always been one of the more pleasant rivals to be around, but Elias still held his guard up at all times. One could never be too careful, and the demons were always scheming. Kind of like the angels always were.

Although the demons did seem to have given up trying to persuade him to join them. He almost regretted that development.

Elias picked up the flask and took a large swig.

"There's no reason we can't be civil with one another," Xaphan said when Elias handed it back.

"I suppose not. Especially when you're confident in your work."

Elias didn't truly believe Anthony's claim that Tlalli was working with the demons, but the more he thought about it, the more he realized he didn't much care. All this, every instance of tension between angels and demons, felt so...forced. The angels *wanted* a rivalry. Otherwise, they would have destroyed the archdemons

a long time ago, torn them out from the root. Instead, they'd sent them away to a place where they could thrive. And grow stronger.

Hell was a monster of Heaven's own making, and regardless of the cost, the Dominion would never admit that. Like a mortal comic hero and their favorite archnemesis, they needed each other. Or at least the angels needed the demons.

Xaphan chuckled but said nothing, merely glancing toward the entrance. When Elias looked at him, really looked at him, he thought he could make out the outline of his true form, equipped with massive corkscrew antlers and stone-gray skin. If he couldn't, he must have been imagining that Xaphan looked similar to his creator—Lucifer, Prince of Pride, Head of the Puri. Or just "Pride" in most places. Someone Elias knew very well.

In fact, he knew every member of the Puri. Much better than anyone could—or would—ever know. And much longer too. He was there before they fell.

Elias himself wouldn't call it a fall, but that was neither here nor there. Those lies had been born, bred, and built into an entire belief system by now. And there was no use fucking with a system he couldn't beat.

He could admit it. He was a follower. He always had been. He had no interest in being anything else. He didn't know how. So he made peace with what that entailed. He *had* to. He had to believe there was nothing he could do. Otherwise, all this shit would suddenly feel so much more miserable, and he wasn't equipped to handle that.

"Greed knew it would be you," Xaphan went on, taking a drink of the flask.

When the bartender gave Xaphan a questioning look, he let his eyes flash red, which quickly sent the mortal skittering off in the other direction, no doubt immediately forgetting what he was running from in the first place. Elias gave the demon a disapproving look, but that did about as much as anyone would expect, which was nothing at all. Xaphan merely shrugged.

"Well, you can tell *Mammon* I say hi," Elias returned, making sure to emphasize Greed's given name. Or at least the one given to him by the Righteous God all those ages ago. He knew it wasn't fair, but existing wasn't fair. None of this was, and they all had their roles to play.

"Oh, I will. Don't you worry. But I'm actually wonderin' why your boys sent you down here with those two."

"You know why Anthony is here, Xaphan."

Xaphan chuckled. "To throw his old man off."

Elias nodded.

"I just figured that was a bit...childish for the likes of Michael and Raphael."

"Now I know you're just bullshittin' me."

Xaphan laughed harder, and Elias's lips twitched. Michael and Raphael could throw tantrums that put even Anthony to shame, and Elias's stomach turned every time he thought about it. Because their tantrums usually had an astronomical body count. Ironically, that was what usually made them worthy of praise to their devout followers on Earth. Such was the life of the Righteous God's favorite angels, Elias supposed.

"What did you really want?" Elias now asked, turning to face Xaphan fully. "I mean, you obviously didn't expect me to

run my mouth about what we're doing, and you definitely didn't have to come down just to share a drink, so..."

This time, Xaphan's laugh was something much darker.

"You forget that I know you, Elias. And I'm not one of those young demons who think the war is a fun idea. I know what it costs, and so do you."

"So you came looking for a kindred spirit."

"Naw, I came to remind you that when you're ready to do the right thing, we'll be there."

Ah, so they hadn't given up on him. "I'm sure Greed told you to pass that along as well."

Xaphan nodded without hesitation. "He did, but I mean it just the same." He clapped Elias's shoulder briefly. "And I'm here if you need a break from your babysitting gig with another drink too. 'Til then, have a good night, Elias."

Xaphan disappeared, leaving Elias to sit there with a full cup of straight tequila and a heavy feeling in his stomach.

It was difficult to remember all the losses Elias incurred the day Heaven went to war with its own. When Pride fell, all the heavens shifted, and what *was* and *would be* changed irrevocably. The weight of those memories alone had kept Elias from forming any new relationships, especially with the younger angels. Especially with Tlalli.

She had been alive for only a few decades, her devotion forged from a history rewritten a thousand times by then. He could never let her in. He could never hand her the truth and expect her to carry it upon her shoulders. It wouldn't be fair, and it wouldn't be smart. And Elias would never be capable of

opening himself up wide enough to gain her understanding, much less grant her any in return.

Ironic, considering that the wound left by that day still felt wide-open most of the time.

The Puri hadn't just been Elias's companions. They had been his friends, Greed and Lust most of all. But he had always been adamant about his position, because what was the alternative? Admitting he had wasted years trying to convince himself they had been wrong?

No, absolutely not. He couldn't. Not now, not ever. The lines had been drawn. Elias had chosen his side. They may have been friends once, but they were no longer. They were the enemy. Greed was the enemy. And Xaphan by extension.*

After knocking back the entire cup of tequila in one swift motion, with a few whistles from his impromptu audience and a gasp from the bartender, Elias pushed away from the bar and headed for the door. He needed some air.

TLALLI

Tlalli hated to admit when she was wrong. She had been wrong about a lot of things, though she denied just how many. But of all the things she had been wrong about, she had never been more wrong than she'd been about the Dominion. And she could no longer lie to herself about it. Nothing they had ever done or could ever do for her was worth the trouble of working with Anthony.

He was pushing her to the edge, wedging his brand of vitriol between her logical mind and her basic instinct. And she did not care that he knew she'd spoken to Cahuani. It had been inevitable, given her carelessness. Her very intentional carelessness.

At least that was what she told herself. Otherwise, she would have to admit she was desperate, and Tlalli did not do desperate. Her mother had raised her better than that.

However, Mecati taught her never to run from a problem either, and here she was, pacing some random hallway in this labyrinthine mansion, trying not to bash her fists into something.

Being the bigger person was only growing more difficult the longer she paced, however, Anthony's smug face refusing to leave her be. She was going to kill him before long. She was going to kill him, and she was going to enjoy it.

A figure appeared at the end of the hall just as she turned around again, but she didn't allow her surprise to cloud her features or disrupt her step, and she kept her head down. Then their voice fell over her shoulders like a sudden wave, nearly knocking her clean off her feet.

"That was quite a show you put on."

It took only a moment to aim all her ire at Cahuani. She turned on her heel at once, then stalked toward him. "Listen, I'm not in the fuckin' mood, all right, Cahuani?"

She could hear her mother in her voice right now, her sharp cadence and the dregs of her accent echoing through the corridor. Still, she expected Cahuani to do what Anthony would do, continue pressing and probing until she broke and the hall was assaulted by rain and lightning...

But no. He didn't. He didn't press. He didn't probe. Instead, he halted in his steps, his features morphing from quiet amusement to genuine concern.

She almost hated that more. *Almost.*

Rather than asking what was wrong or demanding to know details, he merely...stepped around her and walked toward one of the rooms. After taking a key from his pocket, he unlocked the room and stepped inside, then held the door open for her.

"Are you gonna come in?" he asked, raising his brow when she only gawked at him.

"This is your room?" The question fell from her lips without her permission.

"It is. I assumed that's why you're up here."

"How would I know what floor you're on?!"

"Same way I know what floor *you're* on. It's part of the job."

He looked sincerely confused, which helped her pull back from the edge she was teetering on just a bit. Though the problem with doing that was that it cleared her vision, most notably her vision of him. Going into that room was a bad idea.

He had to know what he was doing in that suit and cowboy hat, and if he didn't, he was doing it very well regardless. Silver glinted in his thick beard where the hallway lights caught it, but the rest of him was bathed in shadow, an omen of what was to come if she accepted the invitation.

But she was angry and reckless and set on revenge, and she wasn't sure she could stamp that out in the next few minutes.

"If you weren't waiting for me, that's fine," he said, his tone neutral. "My mistake. Good night, Tlalli."

She watched helplessly as he stepped farther inside the room, releasing the door behind him. *Don't do it, girl. You'll wake up to regret it no matter where you are by then.*

Although...maybe she was giving herself too much credit. It wasn't like Cahuani, of all people, would let her do something reckless. Not that it was his job to keep her in check, but she trusted that he would at least prove to be a voice of reason. Maybe. Probably.

And even if he wasn't, what the fuck was she afraid of again?

At once, Anthony's face manifested behind her eyes, smirking

and guffawing. She balled her hands into tight fists, her long nails threatening to either snap in half or go straight through her palms.

Hatred propelled her forth. This was a bad, horrible, terrible idea, and nothing good would ever come of it. He had to know that as well as she did, so the invitation was more likely to be a setup than an actual conversation of any type. After all, just this morning, he'd demanded she keep her distance. Why would he change his mind now just because she was upset?*

It didn't matter. It couldn't matter. Because nothing could justify her walking through that door. *Nothing*.

She caught the door just before it closed and pushed her way inside.

As if he'd already known she would follow, Cahuani did not look up when she entered. He stood at the small bar on the opposite end of the room, pouring two glasses of wine, and she tried not to take offense at the assumption.

"Trying to get me drunk then?" she blurted out, attempting to reclaim some semblance of control.

"Trying to be a good host," he returned easily. "And I don't have enough wine to get you drunk anyway, but if you're so worried about what I might do to you, why come inside?"

She scowled. "Well, if you were so worried I was here to do something to *you*, why invite me inside?"

"I wouldn't. If I still believed that. Just so we're clear."

Okay, now she was twice as confused.

"How the fuck do you just flip that fast? This afternoon, you were convinced I was out to get you."

* WAIT A MINUTE!—WILLOW

He chuckled. "Are you complaining?"

"No, I wanna know—" But then it clicked. "You talked to Anthony."

Unless Anthony knew the mortal tending the bar in the lounge, which she highly doubted, that had to be the case. The two must have already run into each other. Cahuani must have been the one who snitched on her.

"I am not about to apologize for having suspicions *you* willingly gave me upon *your* betrayal. Don't blame me for what trouble it caused you."

"Oh, I don't." She was acting on instinct at this point. All she knew were barbs and defenses. "I promise you that your son is trouble at all hours of the day, not just when he has to see you again."

She blinked and he was standing before her, holding out a glass of wine. She took it, if only to give her hands something to do.

"Regardless, whatever the trouble may be, you better find a way to refrain from taking it out on me, or I can send you right back to him."

She scoffed, prepared to pop off on him again, but for one quick second, his eyes glinted like a sharp blade, and the warning was so dense that she lost her breath. Irritated, she took a drink from her glass.

Nonetheless, she did have to figure out a way to stop forgetting who she was talking to. This wasn't Anthony. This was Cahuani, who was everything Anthony would never become. Anthony was a storm, but Cahuani was the calm sea before it.

He was seemingly always in control. Anthony had his control panel right on his sleeve. She could press his buttons by accident. Cahuani was an enigma far too complex to be so easily manipulated. It angered her just as much as it relieved her.

"So you weren't trying to set me up." He stated this as if they were in a debriefing while taking a seat on the couch and placing his hat on the seat beside him. "But you said you had business with me."

"Didn't you bring a demon or two with you? Can't they tell you if I'm lying?" she asked, exasperated. She still had a mortal heart after all. It was not immune to their inquest.

"They could, but I don't need them, nor do I want the help." He leaned forward. "You have something to present to me, be my guest, but the warning I gave you earlier still stands."

"You said to stay away. That was the original warning, remember?"

"Then let me formally update it." Cahuani's eyes burned into hers, and she felt as though they were crawling down her throat. Or up her belly. She couldn't tell. "If you lie to me, mislead me, fuck with me or my job here at all, that warning stands. And remember, I said the *wings* would be sent to your employer. The rest of you? Oh, I'm sure you've been many places, but there is no place like the one you will end up. And in that place? You're nothing but prey."

"You won't—"

"I've waited four years, Tlalli. I can wait out a truce for two more days."

She narrowed her eyes, but the act held little weight. Even

sitting down, he was every bit as commanding as always, and she had no doubt he meant what he said. Obviously, he was worth something if the Puri didn't kill him after the robbery. The Dominion surely would've killed her if she had failed. Michael had told her that at least a dozen times just before she left. Though she was certain Anthony still would have been welcomed with open arms. She didn't understand it, but Michael seemed to have a bigger plan for him.

She thought of what Anthony must be doing right now, what he must be thinking, if he was freaking out. Goodness, she hoped he was freaking out. She'd left her phone in the hotel room earlier that night, and she'd made damn sure to keep their telepathic line closed, so any hope he had of getting in touch with her was all but lost. Unless he came to visit his father. And how ironic would that be?

It made her positively delighted.

"So you're gonna help me," she said, trying again to find footing in this conversation. She sat in the chair angled toward him beside the couch.

"I said I was gonna hear you out," he corrected.

She bit her tongue.

"Whether I help you will depend on a few things, but right now, I wanna know what it is you need help with, Tlalli."

Now *she* wasn't sure if this was what she wanted to do or not. It seemed too easy, too simple. She had complete faith that he would help her once she told him, but what would it cost? Would she just end up in someone else's cage?

Even with that thought at the front of her mind, her alternative

did not become any less horrendous. She was tired of Anthony. She was tired of the Dominion. She was tired of all the lies and broken promises. She needed an escape, whatever that looked like. She would deal with whatever came next however she had to.

"I want out," she stated plainly. "I want out of the Dominion, and I want away from Anthony."

She expected him to say he told her so or point out that she had put herself on this path by coming into his son's life. She even thought he might scoff and ask her what the fuck she expected him to do. Instead, he merely stared at her, stroking his beard with those thick fingers.

"Have you been thinking about this long?"

"Since not long after we left you."

"Did something happen?"

"A lot has happened, man." She sighed, not really wanting to offer specifics. "You wanna know if I made this decision on a whim? I didn't. I've tried to make it work, to remain rooted in my purpose, but it isn't there. It isn't *with* them anymore."

"And what? You wanna trade sides?"

"I—Look, I don't know about all that. Right now, I don't wanna be on anyone's side. I just wanna be—"

"Free."

She looked at him, and his eyes were doing that thing again. Looking deeper into her than she was prepared for. She couldn't look away. It was as though she were in a trance. Especially when he licked his lips real slow and leaned back, propping his ankle on his knee. Ain't no way he wasn't doing this shit on purpose.

She sat back and crossed one leg over the other. "Yes, free," she said at last.

"And how are you expecting this to go exactly? I mean, you may be able to persuade *me* emotionally, but you know who I work for. You know who you robbed. They won't forgive a betrayal like that so easily."

"I know." She nodded. "I figured I help you get whatever y'all came here for, and you help me get away from the angels and live to tell the tale."

"That won't be enough, Tlalli. We're getting that chalice with or without your help, I can assure you. But they'll want information. They will want things to win a war: data, numbers, *names*."

She didn't hesitate. "And I will supply whatever I can."

"Do you have no ties whatsoever to anyone in Heaven?"

She looked down at her lap. Elias appeared behind her eyes, but he was there and gone in an instant. They weren't friends. They weren't anything.

She had a few *close* acquaintances Upstairs—people who warmed her sheets or supplied her information every now and again—but she didn't spend enough time up there to make lasting bonds. She was often on extended missions, like the heist at the Reyes estate, and after her mother passed, she let a lot of other bridges fall into disrepair.

She wasn't about to explain all that to him though.

"No, I don't." She took a drink of her wine before continuing. "Not anymore."

"One more thing then. And I *do* expect an answer."

She braced herself but maintained eye contact.

"What happened between you and Anthony? What changed?"

After a moment, a nervous laugh left her. "Are you gonna punish me for breaking your baby boy's heart or something, Papa Bear?"

"I might have if I thought he had one."

She gaped at him a moment longer, trying to convince herself that this was a tactic. He was not yet an ally, and Anthony was still his son. She had to tread carefully.

Yet caution did not come to her. Instead, there was only agitation. "Then why does it matter to you?"

"Because he is the enemy now, and inevitably, I will have to face him. In order to do that, I have to know what he's become."

"How can I tell you that when I don't think I knew him to begin with? I... It's not like I loved him, Cahuani."

"Do you have to love someone in order for them to hurt you?"

She pursed her lips, and just like that, a dozen memories flitted across the forefront of her mind.

"I never intended to stay with him," she said softly, the words unspooling from her tongue of their own volition. "It was part of the job for me. Seduce him, get into your house, steal the amulet. That was what I agreed to."

"With Michael?"

She nodded. "But apparently, Anthony and Michael had an agreement of their own."

Cahuani shifted in his seat, and she bit her lip.

"I don't know if they had already met by then or if Michael had just heard of his...*aspirations*, but either way, they played me same as I played you. When I got back to Eden, I didn't get a

promotion or even a pat on the back. I got told that I belonged to Anthony. I was his prize for betraying you."

"Why would Michael do that?"

Tlalli shrugged. "Anthony asked. All he had to do was ask. I don't know what grand plan they have for him, but Michael is... They treat him like a king up there. And nothing I said mattered. Not to Michael and not to Anthony. I can't even sleep in the Garden with the other angels anymore, because Anthony would keep coming to my bed every night and demanding I fuck him."

"Did he—"

"No." The word held so much venom. She wouldn't let him ask. She couldn't. The implication was enough. "I'm still stronger than him, and I don't care what Michael says; I don't belong to anyone." She deflated some then. "But I know that I can't fight either of them forever, and now that Michael makes us take all our missions together, I just never have a break."

He stared at her for a long time, and eventually, her pride alone could not keep her eyes on his. She looked away, down at her wineglass.

The silence settled around them, not quite comfortable but not entirely unwelcome. It was only disturbed by what she believed to be the sound of his knuckles cracking. She remembered him doing that often when she lived in his house, all the while muttering under his breath. She could hear the words clearly too. He was counting to ten in their mother tongue—Nahuatl.

Eventually, he breathed out a heavy sigh.

"I'll help you, Tlalli, but I am not playin' games with you, all

right? You do as I say. Regardless, I cannot make any promises about what the Puri will or won't do."

She shut her eyes. "I don't care. I'm telling you, I just want out."

"Okay. Then we'll get you out."

She heard him swallow more wine, which made her swallow hard in turn, and she gulped down the rest of her glass in one go. Why the fuck was she afraid? For so many nights during her six weeks' stay in his house, she'd sat mourning her mother in his kitchen, letting her guard down when she should have been working to lower his. What could possibly be scarier than that? Why…?

Oh. Maybe that wasn't fear. Maybe that was shame.

As if compelled to ask, she blurted out the words before she could think twice. "So you forgive me then?"

She looked up just enough to catch him smirk. It made her head spin. *Bastard.*

"Oh, I ain't sayin' all that."

She rolled her eyes. "Then what do I have to do for that?"

"Why do you want it?"

"Because I am sorry. Not for the robbery but for—for hurting you in the process. For lying to your face. I'm sorry, so just… tell me what I gotta do for your forgiveness."

He cocked his head to the side. It almost made her regret asking. "Depends, I guess."

"On what?"

"What are you willing to do?"

Bastard.

The man who had just said he wasn't playing wanted to play.

He was committing to it. And here she was trying to be the bigger person, the better person. The apple may have fallen a little closer to the tree than she'd initially guessed. At least that was the best-case scenario. Worst case was that Cahuani was something else entirely, something she had no clue how to deal with.

And that thought…well, it did things to her she didn't know how to cope with. Things that weren't entirely bad.

The sudden thrill that went through her stopped Tlalli's heart for a moment. But only for a moment. She was still angry, and she was still reckless. He was the worst possible decision she could make right now.*

Unfortunately, he was also the only decision she wanted to make.

* OH MY GOD—Adele

CAHUANI

W here is Anthony now?"

Cahuani didn't ask because he particularly cared but because he was suddenly acutely aware of what he'd just asked her. To say his prior question was inappropriate would be an understatement, but worse than that, he didn't know if he meant it to be or not.

She made him nervous. To what extent, he did not know, but he could no longer deny it. It was best he at least show his full hand to himself before this continued, lest he find himself in deeper trouble than before.

He set down his drink and rested his arm across the back of the couch, trying to bury the lust that had begun to sprout like weeds along the inner lining of his skull.

"Upstairs," she said slowly, her eyes downcast. "Or... downstairs? Who knows. I didn't stick around to find out, remember?"

"Where do you think he would be?" he attempted, but she huffed.

"Cahuani, I don't care where he is. Why do you?"

"I just wanna be prepared in case he decides to come up here—or down here—looking for you. Not that I—"

"Uh-uh. Don't try to change the subject."

He blinked, and she was standing much closer than should have been possible, her glass left on the coffee table.

"You asked me what I was willing to do."

"And you failed to answer."

"I was trying to quantify."

"And are you done quantifying?"

"I can't stand you."

"Yet you're still here."

"I can see where your son gets his charm from."

"And you fell for that charm, didn't you?"

"I bet he got everything from you."

He stood abruptly too, and her eyes widened in surprise. He tilted his head back enough to look at her, his eyes climbing up the slender column of her neck on the way there. Hell, what was he doing? Was he really so weak as to fall into this trap, knowing damn well how it would end? Even if he could convince himself he was the one setting it, the outcome would be the same. He would wind up choking on the blood.

Yet he could not find the will to care.

"My son got many things from me, but don't get it twisted." He stepped impossibly closer, yet somehow, there remained the barest break between their bodies. "He is not me. And I am not him."

She searched his face. For what, he had no clue, but her eyes were diligent in their observation, though he gave nothing more away.

"Then show me." Her voice was breathless, the words brushing his lips before they dissipated.

"What do you want me to show you?"

Her lips twitched. "That you're not him."

He stared at her for a long while, and she stared right back; neither betrayed their intentions or intuitions. How far was she willing to go? How far was *he*? And where had this been going to begin with?

These were questions he always collected answers to *before* he stepped in a room with someone and certainly long before he stepped into business with them. Yet this improvisation did not scare him the way it should. Instead, it enticed him. It had been a long time since he'd been enticed.

Nonetheless, he had to be responsible, if not entirely respectable. Because he was not his son. He was still good.

"You do not need my forgiveness to be deserving of escape, Tlalli," he stated, the silence shattering so fast that *he* nearly jumped. "I already said I would help you. I don't go back on my word, and I will not—"

"If I wanted you to take it easy on me, Papa Bear, I'd ask." Her eyes darted toward his lips and back again. "And I haven't asked."

He swept his tongue along his bottom lip, unable to suppress the act. "So you want to earn my forgiveness then."

"I do."

"But you never answered my question." His hands brushed hers. "What are you willing to do for it?"

She accentuated every word. "Whatever you feel is the necessary level of punishment, I want you to give it to me, and I will gladly take it."

"Mm." He tilted his head, and he could feel her breath on his lips again. "Are you sure you want all that tonight?"

She hummed and looked up in thought. "It doesn't all *have* to be tonight, but if you want it to be, it will be. If not, then...in the next two days at least."

Right. Before she disappeared and he returned to his empty home in the desert until he was needed once more. Another reason this was a bad fucking idea on top of all the other reasons it was a bad fucking idea. He cared too much. He had already cared too much. Long before they saw each other again. As deep as he'd tried to bury that, the fact remained. If he fell on this sword, it would cut him all the way through and hurt twice as much coming back out.

And that was if this wasn't still some elaborate plan his son had put together to get rid of him. It wasn't as if Anthony would care if it started a new war as long as he won his.

But what did it matter anyway? War was coming one way or another, and Cahuani's fate was sealed. Hell had his soul on layaway, and once he shed this human vessel, he would be remade into something else. The only things he would have left to mourn were his ancestral magic—exchanged for the magic of the demons—and his home with no heir, but once he made peace with that, there was nothing else to fear. Until then, he might as

well embrace his fragile human existence and do as he pleased. Anthony certainly had.

"You're serious about this," he said slowly.

Though this time, he did not merely take her word for it. His hand was around her throat before she had the chance to inhale, pressing into the hollow, then adjusting until he found her pulse. She gasped but did not move, her hands remaining stiff at her sides.

"You aren't setting me up."

She met his gaze, her eyes blown wide. "No, Cahuani, I am not setting you up."

It wasn't foolproof. To lie was built into her training. But in times like this, in a gravity like hers, he was only a mortal man. He let that be the only thing that mattered now.

Releasing her, he took a step back. "Then get out of that dress. Quickly."

He waited patiently for the pushback, for the realization of what she had just agreed to, for the panic. He should've known better. She had traipsed through his house unbothered, knowing very well what she was getting into, and she had never once let him catch on. What would be so different now?

"I do have a condition," she said instead.

"And what condition would that be?"

"I want you to film it."

He had not been expecting that. Not in the slightest. Anything but.

"Do you?" His tone was a bit too weak for his liking.

"I do." She slid the single strap of her dress from her shoulder. "I also want a copy."

"Is there any particular reason?"

She rolled the dress down to her hips, then her knees, where she released it. It fell the rest of the way on its own, leaving him with a near unobstructed view of her gentle curves and thick thighs. Only a sheer red thong and two pasties stood between him and the fruit of Eden.

Then those barriers magically began to fade into nothing.

"You will have evidence of my double cross in case this really is a setup, because we both know even if Michael was in on it, Anthony never would agree to *this*." She went on. "And I'll have a souvenir."

"I told you—"

"I know what you said."

Yet she still wanted it on tape. He had no qualms beyond the legitimacy of her consent. After all, he'd already crossed his own boundary. There was really no use lying about that now.

And though he did wish to ask why she wanted a souvenir, he thought better of it and turned his focus to the task at hand. Because it *was* at hand. And now that it was, he needed a game plan. He had to try to fit everything he wanted to do to her into three nights.

"I got the tripod, Papa Bear. Don't worry."*

He had no clue where his mind had been when she said that, but it was right here bouncing off the walls now. He was unable to evade the shiver that moved down his spine at the name. In its wake, everything clicked.

Because fuck it. What did it matter that she'd dated his son?

* ANGEL OF SMALL DEATH AND THE CODEINE SCENE—Hozier

She wasn't dating him anymore, and she wasn't dating Cahuani either. This was what it was: something to do, something to keep them both from letting the situation overwhelm them.

As for Anthony, he'd made it clear the day he joined the Dominion that blood meant nothing to him, and Cahuani would be a fool to believe that anything he himself did or didn't do in this room tonight would change that. Anthony had made his choices. And Cahuani was free to make his.

With that, any apprehension he'd held fell to the floor beside her dress.

All at once, a tripod the same height as Tlalli materialized beside her. She gestured to it, and he made quick work of positioning his phone on it while she collected her dress and placed it on the chair.

"You are completely overdressed," she pointed out.

He turned around and took hold of her face so fast that she gasped and her eyes sharpened. He could feel her body come alive, her divine form boiling just beneath this thin skin, waiting to be unleashed. He did not relinquish his hold.

"Let us be clear about who is in control now," he whispered against her lips, watching her glance down at his. "You want to escape? You do everything I say outside this room. You want my forgiveness? You do everything I say inside it. Is that clear?"

"Yes, Papa Bear."

"Do you have a safe word?"

Her tongue moved over her lower lip. Then she met his eyes. "*Apostate.*"

He couldn't help but smirk. Then he claimed her mouth with

his, burning away the last barrier standing between them and discarding the ashes like confetti. She sagged against his body, and he curled his other arm around her waist in time to keep her upright, but the world was spinning faster, and the air was growing thin. Soon, they would both be nothing but dust.

He welcomed it.

8

TLALLI

Tlalli lost her religion somewhere between when Cahuani first kissed her and when he drew the first orgasm out of her, his hands not even touching her as he pressed her against the living room wall with his body. With one of her legs hooked around his waist, the grind of his hips against hers was more than enough to inspire a near-unbearable hunger, and the way his mouth ravaged her neck set everything ablaze. She couldn't have held out if she wanted to.

Her knees buckled the moment the orgasm dissipated, but Cahuani didn't let her fall. Of course he didn't let her fall. Although the way he cupped her pussy nearly turned her to ash.

"What's wrong, princess?" he cooed. "Too much? Or perhaps too little?"

She shook her head, but only once. It was still spinning. "No, Papa Bear," she managed, not entirely sure what she wanted to say but saying exactly what she felt nonetheless. "Just right."

She could *hear* him smile. "Good girl."

Then his hand was around her back, and she was being steered away from the wall before she could fully open her eyes.

"Kneel on the couch," he commanded. He released her, then snapped his belt in his hands, and she all but stumbled onto the cushions. "Grab the back."

"Yes, Papa Bear."

"Don't let go."

She nodded, for a moment forgetting the instruction he'd given earlier, then arranged herself on the couch.

"Sorry? I couldn't hear you."

She inhaled slowly. "Yes, Papa Bear."

"Good girl."

The belt whipped across the center of both her ass cheeks with acute accuracy. It landed twice before she managed to choke out a cry in response.

"Did that hurt, princess?" His voice was warm honey down her back.

"Yes." She couldn't help but confess. "But I liked it."

"I'm sure you did. You want me to fuck you the same way, don't you?"

She whimpered.

"You want it rough because you want it to hurt. And you want it to hurt because you think you deserve it."

It would've been insulting if it weren't so damn disarming, the ease with which he played her body like an instrument he'd long mastered. Her pussy was still spasming, her thighs glistening

with arousal and trembling in anticipation. And he hadn't even taken his fucking pants off!

Why had she put a clock on this? In what world was a weekend going to sate her when she was already prepared to beg just to have him touch her? She would only leave here with more longing in the end.

She definitely made the worst possible decision she could have tonight. And yet, she did not regret it at all.

She shivered as his voice filled the air again, this time so much closer than she expected. He was standing directly behind her. When she began to turn her head, he snapped the belt once more, causing her to abruptly abandon the effort.

"Eyes ahead, Tlalli," he growled.

"Cahuani—" she breathed.

"You want to atone, don't you? You want to be forgiven for your sins?"

Her body shook hard in response. He knew exactly how to deconstruct her very being and turn her own body against her, wielding it for his purpose. And she had no qualms about it. Tlalli had never wanted to be dominated. Yet tonight, she wanted to be conquered. By Cahuani and Cahuani alone.

"Yes, Papa Bear."

She shut her eyes in surrender and let her head hang forward. There was movement behind her, and she braced herself for another strike of his belt, eager to feel the burn of the leather across her ass again. Instead, the sofa cushion beneath her shifted, and then the head of his cock was tracing the seam of her ass.

She whimpered again in spite of herself, but before she could

bite down on her tongue hard enough to suppress anything else, his hand was on her neck, bending her forward, and his cock was entering her cunt none too gently, stretching her walls.

"Cahuani!"

It was a broken cry at best. Her hand floundered as she reached back to grab him and failed. He was quick to reach down and guide that hand right back to the couch.

"What did I say, Tlalli?" he hissed. "Let go of this couch again, and you can go back upstairs. Or downstairs. Wherever Anthony is waiting for you."

The threat was far too real and far too disconcerting to challenge. And had it been anyone else, Tlalli certainly would've challenged it. Also, she'd promised to listen to everything he said, to follow every direction and instruction down to the letter if she wanted his forgiveness.

And she did want his forgiveness. But the fact of the matter was that she wanted him to fuck her *more*.

The camera peered at them from a few feet away as he eased into his strokes, finding a rhythm he liked and leaving her little time to adjust to the fullness he provided. She didn't mind it. She would take whatever he offered her eagerly. He seemed to know it too, positioning her to his liking without so much as a word. He was the only one who could get away with some shit like that. Anyone else would have been dust by now.

Instead, she was the one disintegrating beneath his touch.

His hands moved along her body like a sculptor's, caressing every inch and applying pressure where necessary. He wrapped a hand around the front of her throat, loosely at first. Then, with

a firm squeeze, he plunged deeper inside her, and her eyes rolled hard in her head.

"Oh God," she gasped.

"I think it best we not draw his attention," Cahuani returned.*

Tlalli couldn't concentrate long enough to care who or what she might summon to the site of her sacrilege, at least not once Cahuani's hips started hammering against hers like a battering ram. She stretched out over the couch, spreading herself open farther, and he took advantage like she knew damn well he would. He wasn't new to this. He read a situation and handled it with efficiency. Fucking her seemed to be anything but an exception.

At some point, he was standing again, one hand holding her hips in a bruising grip and the other gripping the back of her neck, keeping her bent forward with no hope of escape. *Thank goodness.*

Heavy as her eyelids were, she managed to catch a glimpse of the camera once more and imagined that Cahuani was staring at it too, envisioning what he looked like pounding her. The image she herself conjured made her hips buck back against his and her teeth sink into her lower lip.

Maybe she would send the video to her phone as soon as they finished this round. Maybe that phone would chime from its place in the bathroom drawer and alert Anthony to its presence. She really only used it to communicate with him and Elias, so she had never bothered to lock it. All he had to do was swipe up to see it. Maybe she should let him. Maybe she even wanted him to. If he started a war over it, that was on him, and at least then

* WILD SIDE—Normani feat. Cardi B

Michael could no longer pretend Anthony was anything but a burden, more trouble than he was worth.

But that would be so terribly reckless, wouldn't it?

"Oh God!" she called out again as Cahuani switched up the angle, which earned her another sharp slap on the ass.

"You want forgiveness, princess?" Cahuani said. "You better address your prayers accordingly."

And she did. Of course she did, because she was a good girl who did everything he said.

"Fuck, Papa Bear!" Reward came swiftly. She bit down on the end of the last word as she sailed over a precipice, her body in a free fall she couldn't see the end of.

Her legs quaked, and her fingers clung to the back of the couch, although they did little to anchor her. The world seemed to split open beneath her as another bloomed from its crust. Was this what it meant to be born again? To be made anew?

She did not have time to ponder that. Cahuani, who had pulled out of her at some point during her devastating orgasm, was spinning her around and dragging her down to the floor. She parted her lips to try to force air into her lungs. His cock went down her throat instead.

His balls slapped her chin twice before her nose was pressed flush against his groin, then his feral roar filled the room as he came. She gulped him down on instinct, her eyes screwed shut.

"That's my good girl," he muttered, patting her cheek none too gently and sending another spasm through her pussy. She was elated she would have all this on tape.

When he at last pulled out of her, she gazed up at him through

heavy lids. His molten brown eyes were already on her, his tongue sweeping over his lips.

His words came out in a huff. "Congrats, princess. You're not beyond forgiveness after all."

Part of her hoped she was. She would rather spend an eternity atoning like this.

9

CAHUANI

Cahuani awoke with a start as a pounding erupted through the room, his heart hammering in alarm. He rubbed the sleep from his eyes until his vision cleared, then pushed himself out of bed. Glancing over his shoulder, he saw the sheet on the other side of the bed collapse. Moments before, the outline of Tlalli's form had been visible beneath that sheet. The pounding must have awoken her as well.

He bit his lip but then hurried toward the door when the banging grew louder.

"Come on, Cahuani!" It was Anthony's voice penetrating the wood. "Get—"

Cahuani threw the door open before Anthony could slam his fist down once more, then swelled to his full size in the doorway. Anthony immediately recoiled, taking two steps back and gathering his composure—or at least the closest thing to composure that he possessed. Then he rushed toward his father only to

be roughly yanked back. It was only then that Cahuani realized Anthony wasn't alone. The angel Elias was at his side.

"What do y'all want?" Cahuani asked. "It's six in the fuckin' morning."

"We were wondering if you'd seen our companion." Elias spoke as though this were a friendly visit and not a raid. "Little taller than you, gold braids, a snarl on her face probably. She—"

"No, I ain't seen Tlalli. Why the fuck would I be tryna see Tlalli when I specifically told this boy to keep her away from me yesterday?"

Elias merely stared at him as if trying to determine if Cahuani wanted a legitimate answer to the question or not. Cahuani gave him ample time to figure it out before fixing his eyes on his son.

Cahuani pointed his finger directly at Anthony. "You keep forgetting who you're talking to, and I'll start doing the same. You won't like it, son. I promise you that."

"We don't want any trouble," Elias assured him, although he was looking at Anthony again. Cahuani realized he must be the babysitter. He almost felt sorry for Elias. "We *all* know a disturbance will reflect poorly on both our employers, and that is the last thing we need right now."

"I'm sure. Maybe next time, you should check these things on your own, Elias."

"I'm gonna do my best, I assure you."

Anthony took another step toward his father anyway, and Cahuani clenched his fists at his sides. Though he knew what lay beneath the mask Anthony donned, that mask was begging to be hit square in the jaw.

"You better stay away from her," Anthony spat.

"Thank you for the reminder, Anthony. I really needed it at the crack of dawn." Cahuani tried not to roll his eyes. "Go get yourself cleaned up. You look a mess."

They stared each other down for what felt like a decade, Cahuani fighting off regret while hatred crusted Anthony's gaze. At last, the younger retreated, turning and stomping back down the hall like a child. Cahuani could hear multiple doors shutting quickly. Embarrassing.

Once Anthony had disappeared into the elevator, Cahuani turned back to look at Elias, who had not moved. Instead, the angel was eying him with an expression Cahuani could not decipher.

Though he had heard of the angel—Greed spoke of him on several occasions with a reverence that had always intrigued Cahuani, albeit not enough to ask for elaboration—this was the first time they had actually interacted with each other. Yet the air between them felt charged. Like Elias knew something Cahuani didn't know. Or at least like he knew more about Cahuani than Cahuani knew about him.

Elias was several inches taller than him and had broad shoulders, a barrel chest, and a round belly outlined by the fabric of his white T-shirt. He wore a pair of equally round glasses, and Cahuani wondered if he actually needed them. He was handsome, with his tight black curls and honey-brown eyes. When Elias ran his hands over his own thick forearms, Cahuani's attention was drawn to the veins there, defined against his dark brown skin, which glowed even in the dim hallway lights. Or maybe those lights were just dim in comparison to Elias.

"Sorry about this," Elias said. "I tried to stop him, but... Well, I'm sure you know your son."

In spite of himself, Cahuani chuckled. "I do. Sorry you've been reduced to playing his guardian angel."

Cahuani felt the urge to inform Elias that he'd heard great things about him, but he didn't know if that was an appropriate thing to say under the circumstances. After all, this was *not* a friendly visit. They were not friends.

Elias shrugged. "Eh, it has its pros and cons, I guess."

He didn't elaborate further, and Cahuani couldn't bring himself to ask him to, so the two simply stared at each other as the silence pressed in. If Cahuani didn't know any better, he would have said that the look on Elias's face was one of intrigue. Though even that didn't seem to sum up the expression, and something about it made his stomach flip. Like he was being excavated right here in the hall. Yet rather than wanting to retreat and shut the door, Cahuani yearned to offer Elias better tools for the digging. And that would be fucking foolish.

"Is that all?" Cahuani forced out, suppressing the urge to squirm.

Elias seemed to snap out of his own trance. "Oh, shit, yeah. Yeah, my bad. Uh, have a good morning, Cahuani."

Suddenly, Cahuani's skin felt too tight, too hot, too constricting. Enemies were not meant to speak your name like that—like they enjoyed the taste of it on their tongue. Then again, Cahuani couldn't say for sure that Elias did. He had always been good at mistaking tone and other social cues, especially with strangers. This must simply be a reminder that the weakness persisted.

"You too, Elias."

With that, Cahuani stepped back into the room and shut the door, ignoring the overwhelming feeling that the conversation was unfinished.

"You'll need to go back eventually," he said softly as he approached the bed. "We need to keep up the ruse. What will you tell him when you return?"

A cocoon of shimmery golden light formed atop the sheets, then grew until it dissolved into Tlalli's divine human body. Fuck, he wanted to be between those legs again right now, his tongue so deep in her pussy that he could feel her heartbeat.

"That I was in stasis sleeping off my anger," she returned with a shrug. "Which was where I had planned to stay to begin with, because he refused to get me my own room."

Ignoring the second part for the moment lest he lose hold of *his* anger, he focused on the first. He had forgotten that the angels could do that, just step out of existence and away from all realms. What a privilege that must be. Yet another that the angels monopolized while villainizing everything and everyone else forced to live in the world they created.

"Can't he sense you here?" Cahuani countered after a moment. He needed to be sure. He couldn't risk the job.

"He can only do that if I allow it. I don't allow it unless it is absolutely necessary."

"What qualifies as 'absolutely necessary'?"

"Not right now. I will tell you that."

He could not think of what to say to that, nor did he wish to argue. He had already committed to trusting her. There was no point feeding into his own anxiety now.

When he said nothing, she turned her head to look at him, pouting playfully. "You tryna get rid of me already?"

"And when did I say all that?" he shot back.

"Why are you staring at me like that?"

"I'm tryna figure out which hole I wanna use first."

Her lips parted and her tongue poked out, then she rolled over to stretch out on his side of the bed.

His eyes scraped over her from feet to head, taking in every inch of her and committing it to memory as he dropped his boxers to the floor again.

"Do you need some help deciding?" she purred.

"If you would be so kind."

"Well..." She trailed her hand down between her thighs and pressed against her clit, releasing a whimper before sliding her fingers upward again. "I'm still kinda sore down there, Papa Bear."

He suppressed a shudder and moved closer to thread his fingers gingerly through her braids and guide her head to hang over the edge of the bed.

"And you haven't had breakfast yet," he pointed out gruffly.

She glanced up at him. "Neither have you."

"Then I guess we should handle that first and foremost."*

If she had planned to offer a response of any kind, he wouldn't know. The moment her lips parted again, he pushed his cock between them, and she took it in with a delighted moan. He watched in elation as her throat expanded around it, and he ran his palm over the bulging skin before squeezing it. Whatever

* I WAS THINKIN'—Reggie

sound she tried to make vibrated through him in the most delicious way, and he had to fight not to push deeper.

Though he didn't need to in the end. Tlalli's hands wrapped around his thighs and pulled him closer until her lips were against his groin.

He pumped slowly to start, pulling out every now and again when she tapped the side of his thigh for breath. He let her get comfortable in that rhythm, her tongue and teeth adding various sensations that had him goading her.

"Fuck, that's a good girl." He pushed out a breath, leaning farther forward.

Memories of the night before flooded his head, his mind drawn to the reminder of the footage that now lived in his phone. He had looked into the camera's eye several times the night before, reveling in its hungry gaze as he fucked her and yearning to see it all play out on screen. She would be immortalized there, a perfect picture of desire on his massive television at home. He could not wait.

Okay, that wasn't true. He could wait, as long as waiting equated to having the real thing. And if he had to choose, he would hold off watching forever in exchange for fucking her like this every day.

Still, just the sight of her could make him cum if he let it. But no, not yet. He had to return the favor.

With his hands, he spread her thighs. With his fingers, he spread her folds. Then he began to draw soft circles around her clit until she was moaning around his cock again, pushing him away and pulling him deeper in quick succession. The pattern only intensified when he replaced his fingers with his mouth.

Like an artist with a brush, he was particular about each and every stroke of his tongue, so he flattened it against her clit before resuming his circular motion. Tlalli's nails bit into his thighs, and then she pulled off his dick completely, but before he could check on her, she was sucking his balls into her mouth, sending his hips jolting forward and his shaft sliding through the valley of her breasts.

"Fuck," he groaned, then gave her pussy a firm slap.

She whimpered beneath him but didn't change course, her hands moving up along his ass to squeeze and knead the flesh.

He slipped a hand between the two of them and grabbed hold of his dick, then searched out her mouth until she once more granted him entry. He did not leave her to her own devices this time, however. Instead, he began thrusting into her throat at once. A moment later, he buried his face in her folds.

Her body arched and bucked, coating his lips and cheeks in arousal in mere moments as she careened toward an inevitable climax. He was sloppy with it, ravenously slurping and sucking and biting wherever and whenever he could as he devoured the sweet fruit of Eden. Even when he pulled out of her airway every now and again, he didn't let up. Cahuani took great pride in everything he did, in every task he undertook, and in every job he committed to. Tlalli was no different.

He was going to ruin her for anyone else.

He had only just sunk two fingers into her pussy, his lips wrapped firmly around her clit, when she screamed around his cock and graced his tongue with the excessive fruits of his labor. Eagerly, he licked her clean. Then he pushed himself up and out of her mouth.

He had to keep her on her toes; he refused to let her get too comfortable. Her pussy was still spasming when he climbed atop her and slid his dick into it. He wouldn't last long, but that hardly mattered. Her body shook beneath him, her nails scratching wildly at his shoulders as he thrust.

It had been a long time since he'd had this much energy to offer, especially for sex, but she made it easy. In fact, she made it impossible to be anything but insatiable.

She didn't need to know all that though, at least not right now. With a hand around her throat and his teeth scraping her jaw, he rutted into her until his own orgasm crashed down around him like an avalanche, rattling him to his core. The ecstasy was almost unbearable in its force, but he rode it out all the same.

"Cahuani..." she breathed, her eyes dazed and far away.

He answered by claiming her lips, first with his own and then with his teeth, biting her lower one hard enough to break skin. She only kissed him harder.

"Oh, you *really* want forgiveness," he managed against her mouth.

"Fuck," was all she muttered in return.

"What's wrong, princess? Too hard?"

She shook her head slightly.

He chuckled. "Too soft?"

"No... Just right."

TLALLI

So what is their plan then? The angels."

Tlalli caught Cahuani's gaze in the mirror in front of her as he ironed his shirt, his dark curls still dripping and his inked bare chest slick with moisture. She bit her lip, her fresh coat of dark-red lipstick staining her teeth.

Focus, Tlalli. She blinked as she caught up to his question.

She had forgotten they hadn't discussed that yet; she had been prepared to tell him every single detail since she saw him in the bar.

After standing up from the vanity, she turned and moved toward him until she could whisper in his ear. Not because she wanted to be near him or anything but because these walls talked, as he'd pointed out the day before. "They're planning to swap it out."

He stopped abruptly, and she had to pull his hand that was holding the iron away from his shirt before the fabric started to burn.

He set the iron down with a grunt, then turned to her fully. "When?"

She sighed. "The plan was to do it just before the auction closed... Well, Elias's plan was to do it just before the auction closed, and Michael was in agreement with that when we left. Anthony's plan was to wait until you had it so that he had a reason to attack you and your demons."

Though she found no sign of hurt in his face, she could still feel the emotion whirling around him like a growing storm. She tried not to think about the fact that if she could feel his emotions like this, it meant he had truly—and willingly—let her in.

Yet after a moment, she realized that while hurt may have been there, another emotion she might have expected was surely not—fear. What *was* this plan he was so confident in?

"Given that, I would say it's best you and I take it sooner rather than later," she suggested carefully, trying to see if he might give her some details of the plan willingly. "If Elias feels like he has to do it sooner himself, he will. My question is will you be able to tell the fake from the original if they do manage to get it?"

He nodded. Then his eyes met hers, and she knew what would come next. It occurred to her then that she might be more terrified of this mutual trust than he would ever be.

"The item was designed and crafted by one of the Puri," he explained after a beat. "The one they call Sloth. Acheron, one of the demons that came with me, was created by him as well. Acheron would be able to tell if it came from their shared creator or not."

"Really? I never knew that about demons."

"And until you are free of the angels, you still don't."

He gave her a wide smile, as if to apologize for having to say so, but she understood. And she wouldn't betray him again. She knew that. Even if the sex weren't as good as it was, she still wanted out of the Dominion. Although the sex did make her want out *more* because, well, sex with Cahuani felt a lot like freedom.

Either way, she wasn't leaving here with Anthony. She refused.

"Regardless," he went on, picking up the iron again, "there's no need to worry. Neither Elias nor Anthony will be able to retrieve that item before us."

Again, his confidence was solid and unyielding, and it piqued her curiosity.

"How can you be so sure?" she finally asked outright.

He glanced up at her, his eyes glinting. "Because in order to retrieve it, they would need to be able to see it while it's cloaked, and they cannot."

It all clicked into place. "But Acheron can."

"Exactly."

He didn't seem at all worried that she might let that slip to Elias or Anthony either; she wasn't sure if that meant he did trust her now or the plan was that foolproof. She decided to leave that designation to him and him alone.

"I know Anthony will have his suspicions for the duration of this outing," he went on, "but what about Elias? Do you think he'll know?"

"What, that I'm getting out?" she asked.

He nodded.

"Now who's forgetting who they're talking to? The reason I have been around this long is that I am *very* good at hiding things

from everyone." *Including myself.* "I know what I'm doing, and I can assure you, I can handle those two."

He stared at her in that way he did when he was trying to determine what route to take from whatever she'd just said, and something about it...well, something about that pause felt so much like the grace she had constantly been denied by even the most gracious. It was like he was actually listening to understand and not just to respond.

"Then I believe you can do it."

He started to lean in but then seemed to think twice, pulling back and focusing on his ironing again. She didn't think twice, however, gripping his face and turning it toward her to smother his lips with her own.*

The shirt did burn this time, but it was a much quicker fix than the larger mess at hand would be.

She was still walking on clouds when she left his suite, projecting herself down to the grounds outside so that she could come in through the front door. Not that it mattered. She had already told Anthony she had no intention of sharing a suite with him this weekend, and although she had planned to step out of this realm altogether as opposed to sleeping in Cahuani's bed, Anthony need not know the details.

She was happy to find that her human skin fit far more comfortably than it did the day before, and the soreness in her throat and between her thighs only served as a reminder of the gift she had received last night. And this morning. And fifteen minutes ago.

Fuck. There was nothing Tlalli had ever experienced, in

* SHOT CLOCK—Ella Mai

Heaven or elsewhere, that could contend with what Cahuani had put her through in the past twelve hours. Her human body was sore, but her celestial spirit was stronger than it had ever been, and she quickly concluded that she would have done anything for Cahuani's touch if she'd known it was this good beforehand.

Shit, if she would've fucked him back *before* she robbed him—which could have certainly been the move if he hadn't been happily married at the time—she might have called the whole thing off and told him the angels' entire plan. *That* was how good he had it. That was how much Cahuani differed from Anthony.

But it wasn't just the sex, loath as she was to admit it. It could never just be the sex. That man cared, and that scared her more than anything Anthony could ever do to her.

So she focused on the fuck because the fuck was the easiest thing to focus on. She knew damn well her little souvenir was not going to be enough, no matter how many times she watched it. She needed at least six months just to sit on his face, because the way he flicked his tongue right before—

"Okay," she huffed to herself, stepping into the elevator.

Of course, it was easier to keep her mind off Cahuani once she was back in Anthony's suite.

Anthony went off the moment he saw her, while Elias sat on the couch looking miserable, his head resting against his palm and his fingers twisting subtly in his hair.

"Where the fuck were you, Goldie!"

"I told you already, Anthony." She sighed, dropping onto a chair. She supposed it had been too much to hope for a different line of questioning at the very least, something she could actually

engage with, something that would make her angry rather than just...tired. He was so boring with his bullshit. "And I'm not gonna tell you again, because I didn't have to tell you at all."

"You're lying!"

"Even if I were, it's none of your business!"

"Anthony, we got a fuckin' job to do," Elias finally snapped, surprising Tlalli. She'd never heard him sound so...*affected*. "You been at this all damn night. You want me to tell Michael you can't do your job, let me know, but I'm not letting you jeopardize this. I'm not taking any licks for you again."

"Oh, fuck you, Elias," Anthony shot back. "I'm asking where she's been because she's been talking to my father! And how do you know she isn't plotting on us to get back at me for whatever she's mad about now!"

Tlalli looked at Elias, who looked back at her before they both burst into laughter. This was why she wasn't worried about him. They might not be friends, but they understood each other. They were the same type of person. They put their heads down and did their work, and they didn't ask too many questions. The difference was that Elias had been there so long, the disenchantment simply became part of the charm for him. He probably wouldn't know how to believe in something new. This was his safe place. He would never leave. And she could never stay.

For the first time, she was grateful they weren't friends.

"You gotta get over yourself, Anthony." Elias sighed, removing his glasses and drying his eyes.

"No, for real," Tlalli said, "because I'm not new to this, and

I'm not you. I don't do foolish shit just because you piss me off. I don't let anybody have that much power over me."

"Oh, really?" Anthony scoffed. "You think Michael would like to hear that?"

"You wanna go tattle to your sky daddy, fine by me." *And I'll tell my daddy* was what she wanted to say, but she thought better of it. "Until then, if you're not talkin' business, you have no business talkin' to me."

Anthony pointed a finger at her. "You keep it up, Tlalli, and you won't leave here with me."

She had to fight not to laugh. "Don't threaten me with a blessing, Anthony."*

"Go get yourself a drink downstairs, Anthony, huh?" Elias replied. It was evident that his attitude wasn't just about Tlalli. The giddiness and energy Elias was acting with right now told Tlalli that he was just as fed up with Anthony as she was. "Let the adults talk for a bit."

Anthony looked like he wanted to argue, but then he always wanted to argue. He seemed to change his mind at the last minute, instead fixing his shirt and storming toward the door. Only then did Tlalli realize why she felt so disappointed. He hadn't mentioned seeing the video, which she had definitely sent to her phone first thing this morning despite her better judgment. Guess she'd left the ringer off. Shame.

"How did you end up dating him in the first place?" Elias groaned once the door slammed, pinching the bridge of his nose and shutting his eyes. "Like, it was all for the heist, right? It had to be."

* I AM—Michaela Jaé

"I wish I could say it was," she returned. "I mean it was to start, but... unfortunately, he played me better than I played him for a while there. He wanted out as much as I wanted in, and I hadn't planned for that."

Just like Cahuani now. She tried not to let herself go down that road, but she couldn't deny the truth. She was doing to him what Anthony had done to her, and though it was inconsequential to her, she could not imagine that Cahuani had failed to see that.

She was using him again. Except this time, he was not only aware of it—he was giving her permission.

And yeah, he was getting something out of it, but Tlalli wouldn't call it an even trade.

"Don't worry," she said, trying to lighten the mood. "I regret it every single day."

"Don't worry," he echoed with a wry smile. "I know."

They stared at each other for the longest time, a moment stretched out into an eternity where she saw things in him, about him, that she had never been privy to before. She had the sneaking suspicion that he was seeing the same, the energy around him more electric than it had ever been and the smile on his face more genuine than she'd ever seen. She liked it. She vowed to commit this specific image of him to memory before she left.

But there was something else too—like he was holding back or biting his tongue to keep from saying something she couldn't even begin to guess at. If it had him this excited, however, she naturally wanted to know. Badly.

Elias rubbed his hands on his knees and suddenly sat forward before she could ask. "Look, I'll let him calm down, and then I'm

back on him at all times. And if I have to make a move to make sure we get this thing out of here without bloodshed, I will."

She stared down at the ground for a while, not letting herself respond too quickly. It was imperative she not give herself away right now. "Well, if that has to happen, promise you'll keep me in the loop, all right? If I gotta run interference, I'll do that, painful as it might be."

"Oh yeah, of course. I'm not gonna cut you out. This is as much your job as it is mine, and I'm not interested in taking credit, as you might know."

"Oh, really?" she quipped. "I never would have guessed."

"Fuck off." They both laughed, but after a moment, his face turned more serious. "Do me a favor though, will you, Gol—Tlalli?"

She froze, the soothing salve of her given name settling upon her shoulders like a warm shawl. She could not remember him ever saying her name. Fuck, she wished he never did.

"What's that?" she managed, refusing to look at him.

"If I do gotta, you know, put my foot down with him again, and it gets ugly, just—promise me you'll get as far away as possible."

No. No no no. Her heart clenched in that torturous human way that made her want to tear her skin off. How dare he ask this of her. How dare he act this way now. It was too late! Too late to be friends. Too late to be anything.

She smirked, shoving at his shoulder, although the shove was half-hearted at best. *Fuck, Elias.* "Don't tell me what to do, Elias," she shot back playfully. "I'm not promising anything of the sort."

"Well, I figured I had to try saving your hardheaded ass," he replied after a beat.

"I am who I am."*

"I know. And I appreciate you."

She realized that might have been the first time any angel had ever said that to her, but before she had the time to fully process that, he disappeared into the bathroom and turned the shower on. Although showering wasn't something they had to do, it kept their human skins malleable and comfortable. Their magic was indeed limited within these vessels, but it could still cleanse them both inside and out, which was why they also didn't have to worry about most mortal diseases and physical illnesses. Nonetheless, it was easy for human skin to become stiff and suppressive. Because of this, Tlalli was even more grateful to Cahuani.

Had she actually needed to escape out of existence and into stasis, she would have had to shed her skin and don it again in the morning, which meant she would have once more had to adjust to it. Although she had worn it since birth, each time they were parted, even for a brief while, she was forced to adjust to it once more. A by-product of the angels' magic and their rejection of its limitations.

It wasn't just the skin either but everything that came with it—the emotions, the motor skills, and the cognitive processing. Adjusting was always a struggle that left her miserable for far too long, especially when compounded by Anthony's abrasive presence. Then it was like one thousand needles poking into her skin.

* DREAM GIRL EVIL—Florence + The Machine

She wished now that she could run right back upstairs and hide between the sheets, wrapped around Cahuani, pinned down by his body and his charm. Though she quickly shut that fantasy down, already feeling the warmth in her belly begin to heighten.

But in that moment between fantasy and reality, the sound of the shower made its presence known again, and suddenly, Elias and his bare torso populated her thoughts as well.

Oh, she was wildin'. She needed to get her damn head on straight.

She stood up just as the bathroom door opened again and a cloud of steam formed and parted to give way to Elias's head. And half of his bare torso.

"By the way," he said quickly, not quite meeting her gaze as he pointed across the room toward his bed. "I put your phone under my mattress. It...uh...went off this morning, but I got to it before Anthony woke up."

He didn't wait for a response, and she wasn't sure she could've given him one. He disappeared back into the bathroom, and despite how softly he shut the door again, the click of it seemed to ring out like a gunshot. She gawked at where he once stood, blinking rapidly.

Had he seen the fucking video?

She needed out of this suite at once. She decided it best to be productive and find out what Anthony was doing with his anger. Shutting her eyes, she reached out to see if she could locate him remotely, and to no one's surprise, she found that the channel that connected them was still open on his end. *Typical.* He wanted control so badly, yet he had no clue how to

wield what little he was given. A weak motherfucker through and through.

He was stalking through the lobby when she got eyes on him, looking every bit as pissed off as his spirit felt. She veiled herself from his vision, her magic sparking around her like electricity before it quieted. Then she posted up near the Concierge desk, where the Concierge was trading information with the many attendees flocking in and out of the entrance hall.

"He's looked like that for the past fifteen minutes."

At first, Tlalli didn't realize they were talking, much less talking to her, so it took her a moment to answer. The energy coming off them was certainly not like any other mortal's, although she couldn't quite pinpoint why.

"Has he caused anybody any trouble?" she asked.

The Concierge shrugged, making it look as though they were simply exhaling as Anthony turned around again. "Only whoever he was hissing at on the phone a few minutes ago, I imagine. Other than that, everyone has steered clear of him."

"I'm assuming you couldn't hear what he was saying."

They only stared at her then, searching for some sign of incentive no doubt. With a good-spirited roll of her eyes and a snap of her fingers, she made a few bills manifest on the counter. They were there and gone with a flick of the Concierge's wrist.

"I did hear that he said something about wanting to 'make it happen tonight' and 'making it special.' I'm assuming you have no clue what he was talking about."

She feigned exasperation. "Yeah, he's pissed at me. I turned

down his proposal, and now he thinks he can find something for sale here that might change my mind. It won't."

"That's good news. You deserve better."

"Thank you for saying that."

The Concierge nodded curtly before turning their attention to an incoming patron.

Tlalli turned her eyes back on Anthony. He was still pacing, but his eyes were on his phone. He wasn't calming down, it seemed. Instead, he was getting anxious, and usually when he got anxious, he would come looking for an outlet. He would come looking for Tlalli.

She closed off the connection on her end, at once cleansing herself of Anthony's rotting energy and exhaling in relieved comfort. Rolling her shoulders, she watched as Anthony tapped the screen of his phone and then put it to his ear. His back was to her now, and she moved closer, then came to a standstill near one of the plants flanking the exit. It was easier to evade Anthony sensing her magic if she was standing still.

"Michael, we gotta talk," Anthony growled into the phone.

Michael. He really was taking this above Elias's head. The bastard. And not only that, he was breaking the fucking truce to do it. He really was looking for a war.

She was about to confront him, stop him any way she could, but then he spoke again, and she realized that...Michael wasn't on the other line.

"Call me back," Anthony snapped. "ASAP. I'm serious. If I have to make a move myself, I will, but it's not safe. For all we know, they have it already."

He seemed to hang up, shoving his phone in his pocket, but Tlalli hardly felt any relief. What happened if he did get in touch with Michael? Or worse, what if this wasn't the first call and he'd been in touch already? And...what if Michael had agreed with Anthony's plan all along?

She had doubted the Dominion plenty of times over the past couple of years, but this...this was the first time she realized she no longer trusted Michael at all.*

* SAINTS—Echoes

ELIAS

Elias loved a hot shower. It was one of the select human comforts he had found himself especially attached to, alongside hamburgers and comic books and vaping. No one knew about any of these interests, but he cradled them in his hands nonetheless, a small respite from the endless white noise of his existence. And one of his favorite things about a shower was his ability to let his mind wander in it.*

Could he gather almost any and every type of information with a snap of his fingers? Perhaps, but it was such an overlooked luxury to just be able to wonder, to think of the world as it might be, as it could be, rather than simply as it was. Elias did not care to be all-knowing. He wanted to be able to wonder whenever he pleased.

He wondered what the first shower, both natural and mechanical, had felt like to humans. He wondered how many different kinds of showerheads there were in the world, and he wondered

* WATER SLIDE—Janelle Monáe

about the various bathing rituals each culture had. Then he wondered how mortals had continued to evolve these shower designs into works of art in many places. High-end hotels had been rather impressive to him each time he'd had a chance to visit them.

He also wondered how mortals had decided that fucking in a shower was a good idea. Though that thought may have had something to do with the sounds coming from the other side of the wall currently.

He tried to tune it out, more for their privacy than his own annoyance, but that proved quite a task. Soon, his mind had simply threaded the sounds along the path it was currently following, and his thoughts descended into more...*dangerous* areas.

Like Tlalli and Cahuani.

It turned out Anthony had been right about them. Elias knew because he'd seen them fucking. He hadn't meant to, really. He'd heard Tlalli's phone go off that morning, and he'd dashed into the bathroom to grab it before it woke Anthony. He'd swiped up to quiet it, and before he could process what was happening, the video was playing, and he'd been unable to look away. Now, he couldn't stop thinking about it.

And the longer he stood there under the spray of the water, trying to block out the sound, the clearer the video played in his mind. Tlalli's full breasts bouncing against the couch, her face screwed up in pleasure, Cahuani's bulky figure slamming into her from behind, and her moans spilling out into the space, intoxicating him in a way mortal champagne never could.

Then, without warning, the scene began to change, evolve, and Elias was there with them too...

"Fuck..."*

Powerless to fight it, Elias wrapped a firm fist around his hard dick, biting down on a whimper that threatened to scrape his throat raw due to how sensitive the shaft was. He wasn't easy to impress, to affect, to rile up. He prided himself on his ability to remain neutral and nonplussed. Yet Tlalli and Cahuani had both imprinted on his brain in a way he couldn't quite explain, and inspecting why would take far more energy than Elias was willing to spend.

But he was good at picking up bad habits. He enjoyed making himself more human than he had to be. And there was no sin Elias would ever be more guilty of than hedonism.

He pumped his cock hard and fast, muttering and mumbling and cursing under his breath. His consciousness whipped out of the frame long enough to wonder if Tlalli was still sitting on the couch outside, but that consideration only made him more desperate. He pressed his forearm against the wall, then leaned forward and bit down on it to muffle his groans.

Someone on the other side of the shower wall screamed in climax. Elias came with a sharp howl into his own skin, painting the gray shower wall in broad white strokes. His knees nearly buckled with the force of it. It had been a long time since he'd let himself indulge. He'd had a few partners in Heaven every now and again, but it took a lot to seduce him, and he preferred to entertain himself in other ways that required less effort. Still, he could admit it. He'd forgotten how good it felt to cum.

Shame began to collect on his skin, but he quickly washed it off

before climbing out of the shower. His head spun with the possibility that Tlalli was still right outside the door, and suddenly, without warning, the overwhelming urge to see her and tell her what he'd done was at his neck. It was the kind of guilt that dragged mortals to the confessional. He wanted to bathe in it.

Though when he did finally leave the bathroom, the room was empty, and disappointment fell into his stomach like the heaviest stone. He didn't let it fester, however. He never let it fester. It had been a mistake to picture her, to think of her like that at all. It had been a mistake to watch that video for any length of time.

He and Tlalli weren't anything. They weren't even friends. The only thing they shared was this cursed existence and the bleak future the angels envisioned.

Plus, trying anything with her, especially right now, would only bring Anthony's wrath down on him, and nothing in this world was worth listening to that boy cry and whine about some shit that was none of his business. Again, Elias had better ways to spend his time. That was half the reason he hardly indulged in the other people in the first place. It was always too complicated and more trouble than it was worth. With Tlalli, that would prove true tenfold.

Those thoughts alone cleansed Elias of whatever melancholy he had invoked a moment prior, and he left the room with a clear head and the desire for a new indulgence.

TLALLI

It didn't take long for Tlalli to find Cahuani. Dangerous as it was to seek him out in the open, she had been too impatient to try to contact him to set up a proper meeting, especially when she hadn't bothered to retrieve her phone from under Elias's mattress. She couldn't really explain that particular choice, but she wasn't about to try either. There were more pressing matters to tend to.

Cahuani stood at the very back of the large conservatory that branched off the main house, staring out the window, his hat concealing half his face, and his hands in his pockets. He wore a glen plaid suit stitched with lines of black, blue, and white. A blue tie tucked between a white dress shirt and a black vest completed the outfit, which was perfectly fitted to his form.*

It was unfair how fucking good he looked at any given moment, how smooth he was without saying a word, how warm

* WHEN I WATCH THE WORLD BURN ALL I THINK ABOUT IS YOU—Bastille

even from a distance. She watched with unwavering attention as his hands came out of his pockets, admired the stretch and curl of his thick fingers, the umber skin that encased them. How was it possible to make the simplest of movements so erotic?

He turned when he heard her shoes on the marble, raising his head and giving her a smile that made her belly twist into knots. She only realized that he could see her, that she had let him see her when still no one else could, in the moment before he brushed his thumb over her lip. The movement was so sly that she doubted anyone who might have entered would have caught it.

She wondered what else they could get away with.

Though before she could give in to her own recklessness and find out, his expression changed into one of concern. Always the responsible one.

"What are you doing here? Were you followed?"

He didn't say it aloud, instead allowing her access to the words inside his mind. Oh, he really was trusting her now. She offered the same in return, letting him read her mind.

"Nope, the only one that can see me right now is you," she returned, her lips pursed.

"Oh, really?"

"Mm-hmm. Don't worry, Papa Bear. I know what I'm doin'."

Although she wasn't entirely sure she did.

He scanned her blatantly from head to toe, licking his lips before looking away. Yet somehow, *she* was the one left breathless.

"Did you speak to Elias?"

"I did. He's prepared to make a move sooner if he has to, meaning he likely doesn't know about the cloak on the chalice."

He ran his fingers through his beard, his teeth sinking into his lip, and a chill ran down Tlalli's spine. She had to *fight* to keep her head on her shoulders and out of the gutter.

"And...Anthony?"

She ignored the pause in his words, instead trying to figure out how best to explain that particular situation to him. She had to tell him about Anthony's call to Michael. Cahuani might not immediately report it to the Puri, given the danger that would put her in, though if that was the case, what was the point of telling him?

He was trusting her though, and omitting information was not a good way to honor that. She had to let him decide what he did with it.

"The tantrum didn't last as long as it could've, but..." She sighed. *"Look, I don't know if it's something to worry about or not, but Anthony was trying to call Michael just now in the lobby."*

At once, Cahuani straightened, narrowing his gaze, which pinned her in place.

"And I don't know if it's the first time," she added softly.

"You think he wants to start something," he said.

"Oh, I know he does, Papa Bear." She didn't miss the way his jaw clenched at the name she had been screaming only hours before, but she kept her focus this time. *"And I can't say there is anything he won't do to get it."*

"And you're sure Michael was in agreement with Elias's plan?"

"I mean, that's the plan he pitched to Elias and me when we went in."

"And Anthony wasn't there?"

She huffed. *"Naw, but he rarely is. He's like the younger*

sibling we're forced to take everywhere even though he always swears he's running the show."

His lips twitched. She wasn't sure whether to be relieved or concerned by that, so she sidestepped the thought altogether. She was just happy to see him amused.

"So it's possible then that Michael had his own agenda all along." He seemed to be speaking to himself more than her, so she said nothing. *"I knew something wasn't right. I knew it in my spirit."*

"What do you mean?"

"Did Michael tell you why he wanted you to retrieve this item? Or even the amulet you took from my home?"

She opened her mouth but promptly paused midbreath, realizing that...no. No, Michael hadn't explained. He rarely explained anything anymore. They were at his disposal, puppets hanging from his strings, and Tlalli had stopped fighting that fact. What difference would the reason have made anyway? The job was the same, and that was all she cared about.

"Michael had to have known he didn't have a chance of retrieving the chalice," Cahuani said, taking her silence as confirmation. *"Even if the other angels don't know about the demons' ability to locate items they share a creator with, Michael and the Dominion would at least have a hunch by now. How many times have they tried and failed to get to one of those items? It's why you had to rob me in my home, because they tried to get the amulet before and failed."*

She tried not to wince at that, but she wasn't sure if she was successful. He didn't seem to notice either way. Cahuani had begun to pace a few steps in either direction, his fingers

alternating between combing through his beard and fiddling with the buttons of his waistcoat. Then he began to crack his knuckles, and the familiar muttering under his breath followed soon after.

"Why did they leave you with the amulet?" she blurted out loud before she could stop herself, overwhelmed by the influx of questions flooding her mind and feeling guilty for his overstimulation. She gave him an apologetic look the moment she heard herself aloud, but he merely smiled.

"It turned out that I had been set up on both sides."

"Wait, what?" She gaped at him. "What do you...? Do you mean the Puri set you up?"

"Well, not entirely on purpose, but...they had a hunch that the Dominion was attempting to recover artifacts made in Hell. They weren't sure why, as the objects' powers cannot be wielded by the angels, not even the Dominion, but they had to know for certain. I learned after that they'd started entrusting the items to witches throughout this realm to learn not only if the angels were looking for them but if they could actually find them."

"And we did."

He nodded. "But they didn't expect—" He paused a moment, seeming to change his mind about what he wanted to say. "Well, a heist. Nor did they expect Anthony to betray us, which was really the main factor. No offense."

"None taken, trust me."

"But that was why it was so easy to make amends with them. I still...have my guilt over losing the amulet, but I know they still trust me, and that's been enough."

"So why would the Dominion be going after these artifacts if they can't use them?"

He shrugged his broad shoulders. "No idea. We have gone over every possibility, but we've come up short."

"You think Michael would let Anthony start a war here? In a mortal's mansion?"

He barked a laugh, and the sound was both damning and distracting. "If you're asking me, we might be in bigger trouble than I thought, princess."

She pouted at him. "Well, it isn't like they tell me much anyway. Anthony is definitely farther up Michael's ass than I've ever been though, so if you think he's here on a completely separate mission, I'm not gonna be the one to tell you otherwise."

Panic scraped along the inner lining of her belly, but she stifled it the moment she recognized it. She was not about to lose her head. This had always been inevitable. The Dominion had been yearning for a war, and they were stooping to the lowest possible level to get it. Maybe that had been Anthony's purpose all along: to be the trap they would set for Cahuani, making Cahuani either have to kill his son or sacrifice himself to Anthony's cause. She could not bring herself to ask Cahuani which he would choose.

"So what's the plan?" she asked silently, stilling herself.

"I'll talk to Acheron and Xaphan as soon as I leave here," he replied. "We'll grab the chalice just before the viewing. We have a replica that will pass well enough until it gets back Upstairs."

"I doubt Anthony will care if he's here to start a fight."

"We have to anticipate that, but we cannot act on that hunch.

*We cannot be the ones to start a conflict. We have to treat this as
a routine recovery mission."*

"So you're not gonna tell the Puri about Anthony calling
Michael?" She had to ask.

"And have Michael and the Dominion figure out you've
turned on them before I can get you out of here? Not a chance,
princess. I made a promise, and I'm going to keep it."

"Even if it starts a war?"

"If it isn't this, it'll be something else. You and I both know that."

Indeed, they did.

"Look, we just do what we came here to do, all right?" he said
aloud and yet just above a whisper, his hand taking hers gently and
pulling her closer to him. "My priority is to get you out of here."

"And the cup or whatever?"

"That'll be Acheron's priority."

She smiled up at him, although his eyes remained on their
conjoined hands, his thumb running across her knuckles repeatedly. All he'd been through, and he was still soft. Even to her.
Even to someone who didn't deserve it.

"I suppose you should get back," he said. If she didn't
know any better, she'd say he sounded just as disappointed as
she felt at the idea. "Make sure Anthony stays out of trouble
for a bit longer."

"What's the rush?" She moved to stand in front of him. They
could afford a few more minutes. If they were right, this was all
going to end the same way whether they spent a little more time
together or not. "We still have a few hours to kill before things
get tricky."

"Yeah, but I have to find Acheron and let him know the move. Then I got—"

"Just give me, like, ten minutes, hmm?" She ran a hand down his torso to his belt.

"Now, you know we don't have time for that, princess."

"Didn't you miss me?"

"That's irrelevant at the moment."

"Is it? I don't think so." She committed to moving now, circling around to his back. "Just act natural for me, Papa Bear. I promise to make you feel real good." She leaned closer to his ear. "Real fast."

He clenched his jaw as she unbuckled his belt and slipped her hand inside his trousers to palm the growing bulge within. Her slender fingers pressed and squeezed, kneading and massaging him through his underwear. Soon, his cock was hard and he was putty in her hands.

"You're not being a very good girl," he breathed out, his eyes fixed beyond the window as he braced a hand against the glass. "And we had an agreement."

"Oh no. Does that mean more punishment, Papa Bear?" She moaned.

He chuckled, although the sound turned into a hiss when she at last moved her hand to the interior of his boxers and wrapped it around the base of his shaft. After carefully folding it upward, she began to stroke.

He glanced over his shoulder, not at her but toward the door to see if anyone was approaching. She didn't worry too much. The entrance itself was obscured by furnishings and foliage,

so they had more than enough privacy. But she knew him well enough to know that he hated any kind of attention, so she didn't drag it out as long as she'd have liked to.

"Fuck," he muttered under his breath, his fingers curling against the window and his breath fogging up the glass when he leaned his head closer. "Tlalli..."

"Yes, Papa Bear?" She sped up.

"Punishment does not even begin to encompass what you have waiting for you upstairs when the day is done."

She pressed her thighs together. They were already slick with want, and each time he pulsed in her hand only added to that.

"Mm, I'm sure it doesn't," she said. "But that's for later. For now, *I'm* in control."

She kissed his neck, then ran her tongue along the skin behind his ear before moving back down toward his shoulder. Her free hand ran up his stomach to his chest and felt the way it rose and fell more rapidly by the second. He was close. She could feel it...

But she never got him to climax.

Without warning, Cahuani gripped the hand in his pants, pulled it out, and used it to drag her in front of him so that she faced the window. Then he pinned her there. Her squeak of surprise was muffled by Cahuani's rough hand against her mouth as he yanked her dress up and her panties down.*

Before her head could stop spinning, he was buried inside her, thrusting upward with enough force to push her onto her tiptoes. She screamed hard into his hand until she couldn't scream anymore, her eyes rolling back in her head and her lungs frozen in

* WHEN WE—Tank

place. He was already moving, picking up speed with each thrust, and giving her everything she needed and then some.

She couldn't even begin to imagine the image they created at the moment, what someone would stumble upon if they wandered back here, but he no longer seemed too concerned, so she damn sure wasn't gonna be either. She would take her licks as he saw fit. Wherever and whenever he saw fit.

The hand not muffling her mouth dipped between her thighs, and fingers found her clit with such adept accuracy that her knees buckled without a shred of resistance. He held her upright just long enough to shove her over the edge.

She slapped a hand against the glass, crying out as her legs trembled beneath her. Then he picked her up off the ground fully, leaving her weightless and floating into oblivion.

Until she was crumpling to her knees on the floor.

"Turn around," he said roughly.

But he didn't wait for her to obey. With his hand at the back of her neck, he guided her to face him until his throbbing cock was mere inches from her face. Her arousal encased his shaft, and she shuddered again, the aftershocks making her dizzy.

"Come on, princess," he growled. He no longer sounded like himself. Or rather he sounded more like himself than ever before. Right now, she could hear the beast beneath his skin, and she yearned to draw it out. "Open your mouth."

She was helpless to deny it, all but unhinging her jaw to take him. He did not wait, jamming his cock down her throat and following up with short thrusts that had her clawing at his thighs but refusing to tap out. His hand was the only thing keeping

her head from slamming into the wall, but he guarded it with unyielding devotion despite how hard he was fucking her face.

At one point, he pulled out far enough for her to inhale, and she used the split second to reorient herself. When he pushed back in, she swallowed hard, and her throat expanded just as his other hand came down to grip it. He pumped vigorously, his grunts growing wilder by the moment despite his best attempts to muffle them, and she savored every sound. Her pussy was still spasming, her fingers aching to graze her sensitive clit.

Though before she could, his hips were flush against her face, his back rigid, and his dick swelling in her throat. He leaned his forearm against the window, then bit into it to smother the roar that left him as he came. She sucked him deeper still, reveling in every ounce of energy leaving his body and entering hers. She pressed her tongue against his balls before she slowly pulled off and away. He shuddered as her mouth detached entirely with a pop.

Again, he recovered before she anticipated, dragging her up to her feet and pressing her into the window with both his hands on her hips and his mouth on hers. She groaned against him, aching in every place he was not touching, winding her fingers in his curls.

"Mm," she sighed when he finally pulled away. "Am I still in trouble, Papa Bear?"

"I guess you'll find out tonight," was his only response.

She pouted, but he merely smoothed down her braids before fixing his state of dress. Once he finished, she ran her hand over his trousers to iron out the wrinkles with a touch of her magic,

and he gave her another kiss on the cheek in thanks. The warmth that radiated from the spot made her weak.

"What's your next move?" he asked silently after they had fully disengaged from each other, lest they lose another hour in this conservatory.

"I'll have to be civil with Anthony, at least for a bit," she returned. *"It's the best way to keep tabs on him. It's easier to keep him in the dark if I'm close...but I'll still be able to talk to you now, right?"*

She tried not to sound desperate or worried, but the thought of losing this newfound connection made her feel...out of sorts. It was harder to go back into the lion's den when she had something worth ditching it for out here. Even if she would only have it for a little while.

"Of course," he said, his eyes softening. *"You need me, you reach out, all right? I'm gonna go find Acheron and Xaphan. I'll keep you updated."*

She nodded and pressed one more kiss to his lips, a kiss that was far too soft for her liking and far too short to sate her. She began to turn away when he grabbed her hand.

"And, Tlalli?"

"Hmm?"

She looked over her shoulder at him, only to find him biting his lip. She shivered.

"Think carefully about what you're wearing tonight," he said, the words snaking from her head down to her belly. *"The moment the viewing is over, I'm coming to find you, so whatever is keeping you from me is likely to get torn up."*

Oh, this was gonna be a long afternoon.

"*Yes, Papa Bear,*" she said, offering one last smile before she forced herself to leave, fighting every urge to turn back.

CAHUANI

Cahuani met Xaphan and Acheron near the boathouse behind the main house. The two demons had answered his summons almost at once. Although they could've met in his room, he decided he needed some air, so rather than lead them into the boathouse, he made his way toward the tree line. He got several feet beyond it before he turned to look at them.*

"What was wrong with the boathouse?" Xaphan asked.

"Saw a couple of folks go in there a bit ago," Cahuani said with a shrug. "Didn't wanna disturb 'em. Or vice versa."

Xaphan chuckled, leaning against a tree. "So what's up? What have we got?"

Although the demons were still in human form, Cahuani allowed his own eyes to see them for what they were, two hulking forms, one onyx and one stone gray, with vast horns that mirrored those of their creators. Xaphan's horns resembled an

* GLORY AND GORE—Lorde

enlarged version of a ram's, spiraling around themselves twice like a screw, just like Pride's. Acheron's, a vast rack of thick antlers like those of an elk, mirrored Sloth's.

"*We need to do this tonight,*" Cahuani said bluntly, though not aloud. They couldn't be too careful now. "*Before the viewing.*"

"*Why? What happened?*" Xaphan questioned, following Cahuani's lead.

"*It seems that Michael and my son may have...hidden motives for their presence here, and it's best we get the chalice as soon as possible just in case.*"

The two demons gave Cahuani a puzzled look, no doubt seeking a better explanation. They deserved one too, but it was difficult to repeat. To do so meant to continually confront the fact that his son, whom he had loved and raised, loathed him. And loathed him enough to kill him.

"*You think they're gonna start some shit?*" Xaphan asked gently, seemingly reading the struggle on his face. "*Did your little angel say something?*"

"*She said Anthony's been calling Michael. She doesn't know if Michael's answered, but—*"

"*So they're breaking the treaty, right?*" Acheron asked. "*That's it?*"

"*If I call the Puri and they come up here, it could all be a trap. And if that's the case...*" Cahuani bit his lip, looking down at the ground. "*I promised Tlalli I would help her escape. I cannot jeopardize that on a hunch. So we get the chalice before the viewing, then we keep up the ruse until the auction closes. Then, at least if we have to get clear of orfani*

quickly, we don't gotta worry about it... And if you're worried about Tlalli—"

"Hey, look, I trust you," Xaphan immediately cut in. "So if you trust her, that's enough for me. It would be enough for Greed too."

Cahuani grunted. Greed was not his creator but was more than his employer. They were friends, family, kindred spirits. And Greed owned his soul. Cahuani had handed it over shortly after his wife passed as a means of ensuring he could help the cause even if his mortal body died. He didn't want to fade away. He wanted to fight. He wanted revenge for the loss of his son.

By giving Greed his soul, Cahuani gave the Puri an eternal soldier and gained life after death. It wasn't quite the immortality that the angels had. He would still have to endure whatever death awaited him, and his soul would have to go through the painful transition into something demonic. Sloth would construct him a new vessel, and though it might be nearly identical to the body he inhabited now, it would be different too. And of course, his Nahualli magic, including his second form, would be lost. He would inherit the magic of the Puri, and while that was surely nothing to scoff at, his loss would indeed be tremendous. He would still be able to shape-shift, but it wouldn't be the same. His ancestral magic tied him to this land, his ancestors, his people. And as far as he knew, that wasn't something that could be preserved.

But now was not the time to think about that. His next life was a long way off, and he still had more years to look forward to than any of the orfani—so long as the angels didn't kill him at least.

"So before the viewing then?" Acheron asked, signaling his agreement.

"*Yeah, that way, the angels will see the replica and think it's still there. Once the viewing passes, who knows what they'll do or when they'll do it?*"

"*And if something does happen?*" Acheron's voice grew quieter in Cahuani's head. "*Like…let's say they already set a trap for when we make a move.*"

"*Then you send out a signal, and I'll come for you,*" Xaphan assured him, gripping his shoulder. "*And, Cahuani, you get Tlalli out of here.*"

Cahuani quickly shook his head. "*I can't leave y'all here. I—*"

"*You're not leaving us. You're taking another role in the backup plan. We'll get the angels away from here. You get her away from them. You keep your promise. Because the moment they know she's betrayed them, she becomes a liability.*"

Cahuani could not argue with that, and Tlalli had already said she didn't want to be on anyone's side right now. She just needed out. And he had promised her that.

At last, he nodded, and Xaphan gripped Cahuani's shoulder too. The three of them stared between one another. Cahuani could see it in their eyes: they wanted to ask about Anthony. And Cahuani wanted to ask too. He wanted to plead for his son's life just as much as he wanted to grant them permission to do what they had to, but he could not bring himself to do either.

When the time came to make a decision, Cahuani would remind himself that Anthony had already made his. And if he was willing to start a war, he was already a liability. And even if he wasn't, he was already lost. There was no more protecting him.

"All right, just make sure we stay in touch," Cahuani concluded, turning to look back toward the house.

The mansion spread out before them, the sun sinking at its back, the world feeling so much smaller than it ever had. Though Cahuani had always known in his heart that he would one day have to face Anthony, he had kept the thought at bay, telling himself it would be years before they saw each other on a battlefield. Now that he knew his son was set on accelerating that engagement, he doubted he could hold it off for much longer himself.

He didn't want to have to kill Anthony, but he knew whether he'd have to was up to Anthony. And if the demons had to, Cahuani would not fault them. Instead, he would be grateful that Anthony's death did not have to be at his own hand. He could be petty. He could be vengeful. He could even be callous. But he did not wish to take the life he had created only by the grace of his creator. It would be more an insult to them—and to Aliyah—than to the angels anyway.

Once the sun was fully eclipsed by the house, the three headed back up the sloping grounds to prepare for the viewing. And the heist.

As they understood it, items of a *magical* disposition were viewed separately from those that were shown earlier in the day. Cahuani could not be certain what other niche items would be present at this viewing, but he didn't dwell on it too long. He was only concerned with the Noli Oblivisci.

Yet even after Acheron retrieved the chalice, the trio would have to attend the viewing so as to keep up appearances,

meaning Cahuani would have to see both Anthony and Tlalli, and he would have to give nothing away. Usually, stoicism came easy to him. However, every time he thought of Tlalli now, he thought of her mouth around his dick and her legs around his neck. Meaning this was gonna take some effort on his part. He'd never had to look his son in the face and pretend he wasn't fucking his ex-girlfriend.

They reached Cahuani's suite just forty-five minutes before the viewing.

"*Can you feel it already?*" Xaphan asked.

"Yeah," Acheron said. "*This won't take long at all. I'll meet y'all downstairs once it's secured.*"

Cahuani wasn't entirely sure how the magic worked, but he knew Acheron would be able to conceal the chalice once he had it without having to leave the estate, and after that, the only ones who would be able to find it would be him and Sloth.

"*You send the signal if there's any trouble, all right?*" Xaphan asked. Acheron nodded, but Xaphan kept his gaze, the way Cahuani used to keep Anthony's when he needed to make sure his words landed. "*I mean it, Acheron. Do not try to take on an angel here. Especially Elias. He looks fragile in his human skin, but he's even older than we are, so—*"

"*I got it. I promise.*"

The two nodded to each other, and Acheron disappeared into nothing.

Cahuani moved to the mirror, straightening his tie.

"So what is it with this girl anyway?" Xaphan asked,

plopping down on the couch with his flask. "I mean, I know she was dating your boy or whatever, but...you don't hate her?"

Cahuani smirked at his own reflection before turning to face the demon. "Naw, I... It's hard to explain. I guess I can see that she really wants to change, you know?"

"Yeah, but you genuinely care about her. I can feel that. Is it just because you're from the same people?"

"To some extent, I guess, but...when she was living in my house, there were nights when I couldn't sleep, and I'd come downstairs, and she'd be sitting in the kitchen. We would talk, and although I know she lied about what she was doing there, I don't think she lied about everything else. Don't get me wrong. I'm angry that she made me care despite knowing what she was gonna do, but..." He shrugged his shoulders while picking his hat up from the coffee table. "She'd just lost her mother, and I was fighting to keep my son. I never told her that. I think if I had, I couldn't forgive her now, but we bonded over that fear of losing the connection to our ancestors, to the land."

"Did you know she was an angel then?"

"Oh yeah. I mean, I wasn't sure she could tell I knew, but I could see it. She never used that magic in my house though, at least not in front of me. She used our magic, Nahualli magic."

"Don't the angels forbid that?"

They both exchanged an unimpressed look before Xaphan laughed at his own question.

"They do tend to make exceptions when it benefits them, huh?"

"Well, at the very least, they turn the other cheek." Cahuani put his hat on his head and gestured toward the door. "All

right, let's go. We should get to the lobby the same time as Acheron."

"Yeah, but hold up."

Xaphan approached him, holding out something. It was a coin, large and gold, and there were distinct markings etched into each side. Although he'd never used one, Cahuani immediately knew what it was. It was a ticket straight to Hell.

"If you and Tlalli need to get out, you use this and get back to the Puri," Xaphan said. "We'll handle the angels until they send backup."

"And you think they'll let a rogue angel into Hell?" Or any angel for that matter. To take an angel into Hell or a devil into Heaven was considered an act of war, and that wasn't just during the auction. It was part of the larger treaty that was to be honored at all times, even in demon strongholds and other places mortals were aware of divine existence. A treaty the angels of course had broken on multiple occasions. Cahuani wondered why they negotiated truces at all anymore.

The Puri had never fully retaliated however, at least not yet, and Cahuani wasn't sure why.

Nonetheless, while the universal rule did specify that it was only disallowed if the move was "against the will of the being," Cahuani knew better than to believe the angels would believe this consensual. And Tlalli would not be there to tell them otherwise, even if there was a chance they would believe her.

"If she's in danger of being attacked by angels? Yes, they will," Xaphan answered. "If an angel wants out, the Puri take their word for it."

"And they always just accept angels?"

Xaphan smirked. "They were angels once, remember? They fell too."

Cahuani could not argue that. He nodded, taking the coin and placing it carefully in his breast pocket. The words that would activate its transport magic tickled the underside of his tongue.

As they boarded the elevator, nervous energy flooded his system, the lights too bright and the bell too loud. He began to crack his knuckles, but before he could start to count, Tlalli's voice filled his head. It was a much sweeter sound than his own voice.

"Everything good, Papa Bear?"*

She could no doubt feel his emotions the moment she reached for him, her magic transmitting them like a song over a radio, and although he lacked such capability, he need not feel hers. He could hear the concern baked into her words.

"Yeah, everything is good," he managed after a moment. *"I'm on my way down. Where is Anthony?"*

"He's right here." Concern was replaced by annoyance. *"But Elias hasn't come down yet, so just make sure Acheron stays alert."*

Cahuani disengaged her long enough to send a quick message to Acheron, letting him know they did not have eyes on Elias. Just as he finished, Tlalli reached out again.

"How long 'til you get here?"

He smiled. *"Why? You miss me?"*

"If you want me to behave tonight, you won't make me answer that."

* FROM EDEN—Hozier

"*I don't see how one has to do with the other. I asked a simple question.*"

"*You don't ask simple questions, Cahuani. You don't know how.*"

"*Now that's a damn lie. I absolutely can.*"

"*Then prove it, because that wasn't one.*"

"*What color panties are you wearing?*"

She went quiet, and at first, he assumed she was just giving him the cold shoulder now to avoid the question. But just as they reached the first floor, her voice filled his head again.

"*None now. But you might wanna check your little pocket square in whatever suit you've decided to torture me with tonight.*"

He paused, knitting his brows together before cautiously looking down at the aforementioned pocket. He expected to see his neatly tucked red pocket square, and for a moment, he thought he did, but the longer he looked at it, the better he knew.

He laughed inside and out, ignoring Xaphan's side glance and raised brow.

"*How did you know what I'd wear?*" he questioned.

"*It's the last viewing, and you're supposed to be a distraction. Not just for me either. I knew you'd want to look and feel your best, so...a suit with a pocket square.*"

His mind whirled with the question of how she knew any of that, how she could be so sure of herself, how she could know him so well. But he had no idea how to express that, so instead, he said, "*The power dynamics of this connection are severely unfair. And I got the short end of the stick.*"

"*Does that mean I get the long end?*" she purred.

He smirked and licked his lips, patting his pocket. *"I guess we'll see later. I'll see you in a minute."*

"Well, act like you don't. For both our sakes."

"I got you."

"Yo, I know you weren't just mind sexting right next to me," Xaphan grunted as the doors opened.

Cahuani merely smiled wider and patted Xaphan's shoulder before stepping out into the lobby.

14

TLALLI

The antechamber outside the viewing room was a mess of whispers and hunched figures, and tension hung like a thick cloud over it. Tlalli tried *not* to turn toward the door every time someone new entered, berating herself for her unyielding desperation. It was embarrassing for real. She wasn't trying to be out here investing herself in the whereabouts of a grown-ass man literally old enough to be her father. In fact, she shouldn't have been investing herself in him at all. Especially when he would continue to get older and she would not. She'd vowed after her mother passed to keep her distance from mortals, and she'd renewed that vow after Anthony. There could be no exception. Not even Cahuani.

The doors in front of them opened, at last admitting patrons into the viewing room.

"Stay close," Anthony growled.

She didn't bother answering him. It would be easier to get

through the evening if she simply let him think he had any control left where she was concerned.

There didn't seem to be too many people participating, and the room itself was arranged to create an air of intimacy that warmed Tlalli's skin. As they strolled along the carpeted floor, she took in the vast variety of rare items arranged upon pedestals around them.

"Where the fuck is Elias?" Anthony hissed, turning back toward the door abruptly and forcing the people behind him to quickly reroute. Tlalli stepped to the side, eying him warily in spite of herself.

He was anxious, and Tlalli hated when he was anxious. When he was anxious, he was reckless, and when he was reckless, he was dangerous. She could overpower him if need be, but she would put it off as long as possible. She could not promise she wouldn't kill him, and whether Cahuani had accepted that possibility or not, she wasn't sure how he would look at her if Anthony fell at her hand.

Nevertheless, Anthony's outburst did seem like enough of a justification for her to reach out to Elias and see where he was.

"Hey, where are you? He's asking."

She waited as patiently as she could, feigning interest in a diamond necklace on one of the nearest pedestals. The design was nothing special, and soon, Tlalli found herself more focused on a blue dress in another case, one that pulsed with something she nearly recoiled from.

When she drew closer, she noted the negative energy and obvious magic bleeding from the expensive fabric. Definitely a

curse of some kind, a good one too. Nonetheless, Tlalli broke it with a quick wave of her hand if only to cleanse the atmosphere of its effects. No mortal should be fucking with a curse that bad.

She moved on down the line past a few more items, her eyes eventually coming across a petite form on a pedestal down the way. It was a mortal with red hair, pale skin, and a very proud look upon her face. Though before Tlalli could move any closer, Anthony gripped her arm, and she had to focus on not swinging on him. She might've done it anyway if he hadn't immediately let her go.

Regardless, with each passing second, she grew more anxious, wondering if Elias was trying to get the chalice at this very moment. Had he come across Acheron, the demon thief? Were they fighting each other for it?

Though she assumed if two ancient beings were raging anywhere in the house, there would be some kind of sign *she* would be able to discern even if the mortals could not.

And if that were the case, she didn't know what her next move would be. She would want to get as far away from Anthony as possible, but she wasn't willing to leave Cahuani behind either. He had changed his plans so as to help her escape. She would pay him back for that at least.

It was then she realized that checking the door for him had been pointless all along. She could *feel* him the moment he entered, not in the way she preferred but in a way that *mattered.*

Her heart began to beat faster. Her wings, buried beneath her skin, fluttered. She could not get enough air into her feeble lungs. She nearly let out an audible noise when a voice suddenly echoed

* ANGELS—The XX

in her head, although she realized a moment later that it wasn't Cahuani's. Strangely, she wasn't disappointed.

"*I'm on my way in,*" Elias replied. "*I was—I tried to see if I could maybe get to the chalice before the viewing, see if I couldn't create a temporary replica of it to put on display, but there's a concealment charm on it. A very good one.*"

"*So you couldn't find it?*" She tried not to let her smile bleed into the words.

"*Naw, so we'll stick to the plan for now.*"

"*Do you think the demons would be able to find it if they looked? Even with the concealment spell?*" She couldn't help but ask.

"*Honestly, I don't know. It is their creation, their magic, but I mean, we'll know for sure in a bit. If it is on display, we'll put a locator spell on it, so I can find it later even if it's hidden.*"

Instinctively, she looked toward the door, but it was Cahuani's eyes she found gazing back at her. Weakness stung her knees like nests of angry wasps, and she only remained upright by sheer power of will.

He looked as impeccable as always beneath his black cowboy hat, his beard freshly trimmed and his red and black suit accentuating his muscular arms and chest.

She was instantly transported back to his estate on the eve of winter, watching a massive black bear, larger than any common bear, race toward the woods from the back of the house. She imagined if she saw that same bear now, his fur would be streaked silver, and he would still look like the most powerful animal in existence.

Though even in his human form, Cahuani commanded the

room in a way she could not deny. The demons flanking him only emphasized the power he wielded. It was beautiful.

But she could not stare for too long, as moments later, Elias appeared behind him, throwing a glare at the demons. He quickly recovered and instead searched for Tlalli, who waved him over.

"Who the fuck are you—" Anthony began before he saw Elias approaching.

"Have y'all seen it yet?" Elias questioned, saving Tlalli from having to decide whether to scold Anthony this time.

"No, we were waiting for you," Anthony shot back. "Good job waiting for the fucking demons to get here. What, did y'all walk down together?"

Elias didn't even answer him, instead turning his attention toward the row of pedestals nearest to them. He read down the numbers until he came to the correct casing, then looked in at the Noli Oblivisci.

To anyone else, it was a simple chalice, golden in color, with red jewels set into the sides. Some kind of intricate writing in a language she couldn't discern from here was inscribed on the handles, and the base was studded with smaller black stones. It wasn't all that unique or interesting on its own, but even at this distance, she could feel the power that coursed through it.

Or was that merely the strong scent of bait?

It would seem safe to assume the demons had already retrieved the real chalice, given that Acheron was now at Cahuani's side. Acheron also didn't look particularly disappointed, but of course, she did not know the demon well enough, meaning she could not see his true face. And who knew what was etched there?

So she focused on Cahuani again, telling herself it was strictly business but refraining from reaching out telepathically anyway. She didn't trust her expressions this close to Anthony, and she didn't need him causing a scene.

Cahuani too seemed to be masking his emotions, his jaw tight and his lips pursed. Yet amid all this regal formality, Tlalli caught sight of his breast pocket, a familiar piece of red lace sticking out in a way that maybe *could* be mistaken for a pocket square. If you weren't her and hadn't put those panties there yourself at least.

She hid a smile behind her hand and turned back toward Elias, who was still inspecting the chalice.

"Is it the one?" Anthony asked, sweat beading along his temple.

"Yeah, feels like it," Elias stated. "Can you feel it too, Tlalli?"

"Very much so," she returned dutifully. "That has to be it."

"Not that she would tell you the truth anyway," Anthony sneered.

Both of them ignored him.

"Go 'head," Elias encouraged her.

"Naw, I got it," Anthony said, but Elias put a hand on his chest before Anthony could move toward the chalice.

"Absolutely not," Elias said sternly. "Go 'head, Tlalli."

Tlalli didn't hesitate, moving around both of them and quickly placing a locator spell on the cup. It was over and done in a matter of seconds, and the three of them moved away.

"I'll grab it the moment the house goes quiet tonight," Elias said.

"And what if it's a trap?" Anthony shot back. "What are the odds the demons won't get it first? Or that they haven't already gotten it? We should just wait until—"

"I'm not doing this with you again, Anthony," Elias returned immediately. "Our job was to get the chalice back. As far as I'm concerned, it's right there. We stick to the plan."

"Fuck the plan. We—"

"Unless Michael calls me to tell me 'fuck the plan,' we're sticking to it."

Anthony mumbled something under his breath that sounded a lot like "we'll see," but before Elias or Tlalli could question it, he was storming back toward the exit.

"What do you think he's gonna do?" Elias asked her.

"What can he do?" she replied. "He can't stop you from taking it, Elias, and as soon as you have it, it won't matter. So stick to the plan like you said."

"Right." He paused. "But aye, don't... Just steer clear of him tonight, all right?"

Again, he sounded legitimately concerned, and again, it took everything in Tlalli not to have a visceral reaction to that. She had been in this vessel too long. The emotions it held were beginning to weigh on her more the longer she stared into those kind brown eyes behind his circular glasses. His tongue moved across his lips, and she remembered her phone was under his mattress. Somehow, in this moment, his care felt more intimate than the video on that phone, and she had no means of explaining that. Her fingers twitched at her side.

She took a step back.

"That was always the plan," she assured him. "But you send a signal if you need me. I'm so serious right now, Elias."

He gave her a weak smile. "I will."

She didn't believe him. Yet what could be done? Truth was she was more set on believing that Anthony wouldn't try anything. He had to know going against Elias would be a death sentence, rendering all that glory he had been fighting for null and void. Elias was likely one of the only beings in existence who could kill Anthony and not be shunned for it by the Dominion.

Plus, there was no reincarnation for angels, and she doubted the Puri would welcome Anthony back to Hell for anything other than punishment, so Anthony would just be dead. Not even Michael could save him from that outcome.

Tlalli supposed everything boiled down to whether Michael was involved. If he wasn't, Anthony would either get himself killed or give up and go home when the auction ended. If Michael was involved though and he decided to come to Anthony's rescue, well...it wouldn't matter because none of them here stood a chance against Michael. It would be up to the Puri to intervene.

Tlalli never knew how exactly she felt about Michael, just like she never really knew how she felt about his god. His god never felt like her god, especially when she had never once interacted with Him.

It wasn't a question of belief or faith. Those were the woes of mortals. When angel blood ran through your veins, it felt like solid proof of His existence, especially when angels, demons, and everything in between had a name for Him.

Still, Michael had always seemed to be the one in charge. Maybe he had bullied his god into submission too.

Or maybe the Righteous God did exist, and he had simply lost interest in the toiling of mortals and monsters, no longer willing to pull the strings only to watch them cut into his own fingers. Whatever it was, Michael held the reins, and that was more than enough for Tlalli to distrust the entire system. There was no one in Heaven who would save her from Michael, meaning there was no one who would save her from Anthony. She would have to save herself.

As she turned away from Elias with that thought in mind, she once more caught Cahuani's eyes piercing into her from across the room. Her heart fluttered into her throat, causing her breath to stagger. Without thinking, she reached for him.

*"You wanna get outta here?"**

He answered straightaway. *"I'll meet you at my door in seven."*

"Make it six."

"You got a deal."

Though she did hesitate. Something in her held her in place a moment longer than she had meant to stay. Her gaze was drawn back to Elias, who was staring at the chalice with soft eyes. Why did this feel like the last time she would ever see him? And why did that bother her so much all of a sudden?

At last, she tore herself away from him and left the room, then made her way back up to the main house and sought out the nearest stairwell. From there, she projected herself directly to Cahuani's door, only then remembering that she would have

to wait for him anyway. It was shameful how impatient she was, but she needed to be cleansed of the evening as soon as possible. Including the rot of Anthony's energy and the soft lilt of Elias's voice.

She hated to celebrate prematurely, but she felt she had won. She would be free of Anthony, of Michael, of all of it, in just over a day, and no matter what came next, she could at least say she had made her own decision and stood by it.

Cahuani came upon her suddenly, pressing her into the door and knocking her out of the fantasy of the very thing that was coming to pass. He kissed her neck and ran his hands down the fronts of her thighs until he turned his fingers inward. They grazed her bare pussy before she could brace herself, and she moaned against the door.

"That was longer than six," she managed.

"You'll get your six." He grunted.

Then they were falling through the open door.*

* HUMAN—Of Monsters and Men

CAHUANI

Cahuani watched in vibrant awe as Tlalli tugged at the invisible bindings that secured her wrists and ankles to the bed. He wet his lips, then moved his gaze to the folds of her glistening pussy as her knees fell open farther. This was certainly a sight worth damning Heaven for.

"You just gonna stare at it, Papa Bear, or you gonna somethin'?" she growled.

His smirk spread slowly across his lips, his eyes already alight with concentrated mirth. "You know better than that, princess," he crooned. "You can't goad me."

"But I can sure as hell try."

She tugged at her bindings again as he looked up at her, baring her teeth, but he still took his time undressing. Through the slow unbuttoning of his shirt, the careful unknotting of his tie, and the measured unbuckling of his belt, his eyes never left hers. With each piece of clothing that hit the floor, he

could see her hunger growing until it was a monster all its own.

He had been torturing her for quite a while now; he had been intent on savoring this. If their time was running out, he wanted to make it count in whatever way he could, and thus far, this plan had been foolproof. Now, she was at his mercy, and though she struggled against her bindings, he could see it in her eyes: she was just as excited as he was.

He doubted she would ever admit it aloud, but it was obvious to him that she needed this. She needed to be taken care of, but she also needed to be put in her place. She was so used to biting back and defying orders, being unruly and ungovernable. But with him, she would have to learn to admit defeat. At least when she was tied to his bed.

"How are those bindings, eh?" he questioned. "Too loose? Too tight?"

She gave them another tug, her chest rising higher into the air. He could see the snark forming on the edge of her sharp tongue, so he didn't wait to make his next move.

He climbed atop her, then straddled her chest and took hold of his cock, which was already throbbing with need. Her lips parted in anticipation, but he didn't guide the shaft to her lips just yet, instead admiring the dilation of her pupils and the curl of her tongue against her gorgeous mouth.

"Mm," she hummed, her eyes fixed on his erection. "I'd say they're just right."

"Yeah, that's what I thought you would say," he returned. "Now be a good girl for me and open that pretty mouth more."

She didn't hesitate, and neither did he, pushing past her parted lips and forcing her jaw open instantaneously. She tried to glare up at him, but it must have been difficult, because tears had already begun to cling to her lashes, and her eyes were rolling back as his tip hit the back of her throat.

He reached his hand toward the bedside drawer, opening it and retrieving his phone.

"Can I put this on tape?"

She shivered almost audibly, and her cheeks hollowed as she nodded.

Biting down on his lip, he pulled up the video camera and hit Record.

And Tlalli didn't shy away. Instead, she put on a show.*

Cahuani quickly found it difficult to hold the camera with the way she was bobbing her head up and down his cock, making up for her lack of hands with what he was certain were more *tongues*. He couldn't find the words to question it, nor did he want to, and eventually, whatever the camera caught was in the hands of the universe, because his head was thrown back and his eyes were screwed shut.

Once he was flying too close to the sun, he tossed the phone on the bed, pressed his hands against the wall, and pulled himself out of the warmth of her mouth. She whined in rebellion, but not for long. Her complaints fell silent as soon as her hands came free and his mouth found hers.

He then dragged his tongue down the length of her body, taking his time to trace the perimeter of each nipple and the area

* GOOD PRESSURE—Shea Diamond

around her navel. He kissed along her thighs until her moans hit the right note, and he lapped at her clit until her fingers twisted so hard in his curls that his scalp ached. And it needed to ache. Otherwise, he was doing something wrong.

He didn't intend to be soft when he slid his dick inside her this time, but he was anyway. He wasn't sure if it was because of the look of awe in her eyes or the tender way she cradled his face on that first thrust. Regardless of the reason, he couldn't bring himself to seek justice or vengeance or atonement right now. He only wanted to feel her come alive beneath him.

And he soon realized she was bringing him to life as well.

"Cahuani..." she breathed, her eyelids starting to flutter.

"*No*," he said sternly, giving her cheek a light slap. "I want you to look at me."

She struggled to keep her eyes open, but she obeyed nonetheless. Power poured into him, striking like lightning in the center of his gut. He sped up, fucking her harder, faster, stronger, by the second. The silence was again broken by her boisterous moans, her fingers scrambling to find a perch on his back.

Oh, he wondered what Heaven would do if it were to see what he had done to its angel. Hell, he wondered what Anthony would do if he were to know Cahuani had won.

Ah, there was that pettiness, that callousness he often held at bay. He liked the bite of it against his skin, this need to get even rather than get hurt. What did it matter anyway? Soon, they would be at war, and the only thing they would have was what they chose to do now. And he chose to live again, not to die with his wife or flee like his son. To live. Preferably between Tlalli's thighs.

"Yes!" she shouted, at last able to form the word as her hand gripped the back of his neck. "Cahuani, please!"

"Please what, princess?" He pressed his forehead against hers. "Tell me. Say it."

"I—ah!"

But she showed him instead, careening through her climax, her gaze piercing his until it could no longer hold. By then, he was following suit, incapable of reprimanding her, the two clinging to each other as the bed shook and the world tilted. Her head fell back, and his mouth fell to worship the expanse of her throat, the golden glow of divinity beneath her skin warming his lips. And yet all he wished to do was corrupt it.

"So I assume Acheron was successful." Tlalli sighed once she at last caught her breath. "If you're in such a good mood, I mean."

Cahuani rolled off her onto his back, and she quickly burrowed into his side.

"He was," he said, running his fingers down her back, "and he'll be able to keep it safe until we can leave here. Xaphan will make a few bids to keep up appearances, and that will be that."

"And the mimic? Is it...? It was a really good copy."

"It is an exact replica, and there is just enough of Sloth's magic in it to make it glow until they get back to their golden gates. We'll be long gone by then."

"What's the plan? I mean, how far can you take me?"

He sighed, turning slightly to look at her. "You and I are going underground. Like, all the way underground. Hell, specifically."

She immediately rose, turned to prop herself on her elbow, and looked at him.

"Excuse me?" she said. "Hell? How—"

"It's the only place we can go right now where you will be safe. Where we'll both be safe."

"Yeah, I get that, but, Cahuani, you know the angels will use that against the Puri. They won't ever take their word that I *wanted* to go there, no matter what I do."

He pushed himself up to meet her gaze head-on. "We'll figure it out, but I made a vow, and I know the Puri. They'll help, and they'll let us stay there for as long as we need to."

"We?" She raised a brow.

"Yeah, we."

"You're going to stay?"

"Do you wanna stay down there alone?"

"Well, no, but—I mean…"

"Look, don't get it twisted. You said three days, and I'll take three days, but I can't just go home either if Anthony decides he wants to escalate this. He wants a fight. He wants to prove he's better than me, and I—I am not ready to face him like that. If I can avoid it, I will."

He hated just how vulnerable he sounded, but he was trying to be honest. More honest than he had ever been.

She stared at him for a long while, and in the end, he was the first to look away, lying back down. She moved closer still, cradling his cheek in her palm.

"I'll go anywhere with you," she whispered. "As long as you can promise me that we'll both be safe."

His gaze sharpened, and he raised his hand to cup her cheek. "I promise we'll both be safe."

She nodded slowly. "But I wanna stay here for as long as we can, at least until more of the mortals leave. If we leave now, we leave everyone else here vulnerable to Anthony's temper tantrums, and I won't do that. I'll fight if I have to."

He chuckled lightly after a beat. He couldn't say he was surprised. He knew better than to think she wouldn't differentiate between escaping and running away. And she was right. He hadn't said anything to Xaphan earlier, but the truth was that Cahuani also couldn't just leave Anthony to be anyone else's problem when it was his to solve.

He nodded. "Then we'll stay until it's over. But remember, the truce officially expires at the end of the third day. If we stay beyond that, we have to be very careful."

"It would be pointless for Anthony to attack once the truce ends though. Right?"

As much as he wanted to agree, he couldn't without any doubt. "One would hope, but we can't be sure."

"Well, there's that party tomorrow night, remember?"

He nodded. There had been information on the play party with his auction invitation, an engagement meant to round out the auction weekend, but he had intended to leave long before that. Now, the party was even more reason to stay. As much as Cahuani wanted to believe Anthony—or Michael for that matter—wouldn't put the mortals in danger, he could no longer be too cautious. It was best they stay and watch over the party. Discreetly of course.

"Nonetheless," he sighed, "if Michael does come here, if he's in on Anthony's plan like that, we'll have to go. I'll have to get to

the Puri, and you and I will only be a liability to them and everyone else if we stay."

She inhaled sharply, but whatever argument she had seemed
to die on her tongue. Instead, she nodded, then turned her head
slightly to press a kiss to the inside of his palm.

He could see worlds in her eyes, galaxies and solar systems
alight with forgotten pasts and neglected futures. Their own world
came into stark clarity, brighter than it had ever looked. All at
once, everything mattered more than it had yesterday. And then in
the next moment, none of it mattered at all. Nothing except Tlalli.

Though he was soon hit with the harsh reminder that this
could never be more than what it was right now. He had already
been given his happiest possible ending, sad as it was. He was
meant to finish out the epilogue alone.

Tlalli had her entire life ahead of her, eternities at her feet.
He would only grow older, fading into the dust and clay he had
been formed from. Sure, he would be reborn in Hell after, and life
would begin again, but he highly doubted she wished to shackle
herself to him or Hell for an eternity. She'd nearly done that with
the Dominion once already. Now, she wanted to be free, and he
wasn't sure if he could ever truly give her that.

In fact, he wasn't sure what he could give her beyond this
little arrangement. He didn't know if he had anything left to give.

"I want you to know something," she said, tearing him from
his thoughts. The words came out of her in a breath, like she
hadn't entirely meant to say them.

His eyebrows knitted together. "What's that?"

"I—I didn't plan on using my mother's death against you.

I never would've done that. I thought I could hold it together by then. I knew Michael wouldn't have cared whether I could or not. The consequence would've been the same if I failed, and honestly, I was fine until..." She looked down at his chest, her teeth wrapped around her lip. "Being in your house brought so many memories back. It was so much like our house. The music, the magic I got to use again, the coffee in the middle of the day, and—Aliyah's baking too. Especially her baking. It was hard."

Cahuani's heart clenched, a million thoughts and words and memories of his own cascading down the back of his neck. But he didn't let them petrify him. Instead, he let them hurt as much as they needed to, then soothe him instead.

He took her chin between his fingers and guided her eyes up to his again.

Maybe he was foolish for being so quick to forgive her. Maybe he was foolish for wanting to forgive her at all. Nonetheless, he had been clinging to this bitter rage for so long that it had scraped his hands raw, and he no longer knew how to hold it. Certainly not when she looked at him like that, like there was still something worth looking at. Maybe he was just tender right now, but he was willing to take a risk for that look.

"I'm sorry for what I said at the bar about your mama," he said. "I was tryna hurt you, but... Yeah, I did wanna believe you were just that conniving, that you would use her against me, against both of us, because it would be easier to hold a grudge, to hate you. But please don't think I ever regretted caring about you, Tlalli, even back then. I would've done it all again if it meant being there for you however I could be."

"And you were. You were the only person who was there for me most of the time. I had no one to turn to after she died, no one to tell about her. And I was so scared that if I had to carry her on my own, I'd fail eventually."

"You won't." He leaned closer, pressing his forehead to hers. "I promise you that you'll never have to carry anything on your own again if you don't want to."

She immediately shook her head. "You can't promise me that, Cahuani. Don't—"

"Girl, I'm a grown-ass man. Of course I can."

They both laughed, though hers sounded a bit more watery than his. "Why, after all I did to you? To your family?"

"Because even if the anger is righteous, it's never too late to put it down. And I'm too tired to carry it anymore."

She nodded. "Well, you don't ever have to carry anything on your own again either if you don't want to."

His lips twitched just as she brushed hers against them briefly. Then she was pulling back entirely, and his eyes snapped open wider.

She had a look of concern on her face. "Can I ask you a question?"

"Yeah, of course," he replied.

"How did...? What happened to her? To Aliyah? Did I...?"

"No," he said quickly, shaking his head. "Um, she got sick. We didn't really know what it was or how it happened, but it did, and when it got real bad, she made me promise to just let her have her final days in peace. She was tired of fighting, and I figured I owed her that much, so..."

"But did she get sick because Anthony left? Because of what we did?"

"I can assure you that wasn't it. It was hard, yes, and she wanted him there, but, Tlalli, nothing you could have done would have stopped him from betraying us. You realize that, right?"

"I mean, I guess…"

"Come on now. You've met him. He don't listen to nobody."

She smiled only when she saw him smiling, and then she nodded in acceptance, allowing him to press a soft series of kisses to her cheek and jaw.

"Mm," she groaned. "One more thing though."

After pulling back again, she cupped his cheek and ran her thumb along its curve.

"I really am genuinely sorry for what I did. I thought it was right, that we were doing the right thing and fighting the good fight. Even so, I could see what Anthony was, and I could see where it would lead. That alone should have been enough."

"Don't apologize for none of that. What's done is done. And besides"—he leaned in, biting his lip—"you're more than making up for it. You've been taking all your licks like such a good girl."

Her lips curled upward before they met his.

He was gonna milk every moment they had together. He'd made up his mind. Maybe they were two lonely people using each other to make themselves feel less alone. Maybe there had been a connection formed somewhere along the way. Whatever the case, all this was temporary. None of it would last.

But he still felt possessive when she climbed on top of him.*

* A LITTLE DEATH—The Neighbourhood

She braced her hands against his chest, grinding her bare pussy down on the length of his cock, pinning it between her folds and his belly. His hands bracketed her hips, a grunt leaving him as he helped her pick up speed.

He pulled her down toward him and nipped at her nipples with his teeth before tenderly sucking them in turn. Tlalli bucked against him, her clit glancing off his shaft, and expelled a heavy moan from her lips. She failed to recover before he lifted her and slammed her straight down onto his erect cock.

He gripped her ass and bounced her up and down with relative ease.

"Take it," he said between curses in every language he knew, impatient, *insatiable*.

She threw her head back, then continuously jammed her hips down to meet his at the height of every stroke he delivered. Wave after wave of pleasure rolled through his body with every touch. She cried out into the open air, careless with the way the sound carried, a song he would never grow sick of.

He dragged his eyes open to look at her and lost his breath when he saw the sight before him. Tlalli was still stretched out before him, her human hands still on his shoulders and her neck exposed to his ravenous mouth.

But that was not what ultimately conquered his attention. No, it was the massive powder-white wings that erupted from her shoulders and eclipsed the rest of the world. Dozens or hundreds or thousands of eyes stared down at him, fluttering in time with the feathers they adorned. He had quite literally never seen anything more divine. And he had never wanted to possess anyone more fiercely.

For only a moment, he wanted to be honest, so painfully and brutally honest. He wanted to confess to her his shameful truth. He wanted her to know that these few days were not enough, that he wanted to keep her for longer, as long as humanly possible. And that even then, when he had no time left on this Earth, he would resign himself to yearning for her in Hell.

But then she was dragging him up to sit, her hips gyrating against his and his mouth chasing hers. They clashed at the center as feathers dusted his shoulders and claws sank into his sides. Her pussy clamped down around his shaft, and his body was no longer his. It was an extension of her own, a modification made for her pleasure. And he wasn't mad about it.

Together, they moved, climbing toward climax with great strides until his head was nothing but a fogged chasm. And for the first time since his wife died, he thought that perhaps this existence wasn't so bad. Perhaps there was still more to discover, still more to experience.

Perhaps it was all just Tlalli and the endless list of things he wanted to do to her on every surface made by man and god alike. Either way, opening his heart again might be worth consideration. Because either way, they were damned.

TLALLI

When she entered the conservatory again, Tlalli had to fight to ignore memories of the day before. This time, she was meeting Elias rather than Cahuani, although she had just left the bed of the latter no more than a few minutes prior. Elias had summoned her so suddenly that she was certain something must be wrong, but his signal did not harbor the agony of an angel's call for combat help, so she tried not to think the worst just yet.

Nonetheless, she was sure Cahuani was somewhere close. At the very least, he was up and alert. He feared this was a trap, and while she may have assured him Elias wouldn't do that, she wasn't entirely sure herself. She also knew that even if she was sure, there was no use arguing with Cahuani.

Outside, the clouds were wringing themselves out along the countryside, the storm that had started the night before still lounging about. The rain had lightened as the sun rose, but Tlalli

knew a downpour would arrive by the evening. She supposed the play party had been a good idea on the mortals' part, given they likely couldn't leave the estate until morning anyway.

She confirmed the lack of a life-or-death situation when she found Elias leaning against the back wall, embarrassingly close to the corner Cahuani had pinned her in yesterday. She took a deep breath and came to stand beside him. It was obvious at once that although Elias wasn't in mortal peril, he was not entirely all right. His jaw was so tight that she feared he might shatter his teeth at any moment.

"What's going on?" she asked.

"The chalice is gone."

No. No, this couldn't be happening. How on Earth could he have figured it out so fast? Cahuani assured her that the copy would hold. Every move they'd made had been backed by that assurance.

"You're sure?" she managed, although her mind was still reeling.

"Yes, I'm sure," he bit back. "I went back last night like I said I would. It was gone. Just…gone. No echo, no imitation, nothing. I left one, enough to fool the mortals, but…we don't got it. We don't have the cup, Tlalli."

"Maybe they concealed it again. Maybe—"

"You know damn well who has it."

Her blood ran cold, as did his eyes.

"And so do I."

For a long time, she had no idea what to say to that. Any misstep and she would implicate herself in a betrayal worthy of

death. She had no clue how much he already knew, and his eyes offered no indication of where he was actually aiming his ire. So all she could do was stare at him in hopes it became clearer.

At last, he showed her mercy.

"The demons wouldn't just take the chalice without leaving something behind," he said. "Not when they're still here."

"So then what?" Tlalli croaked.

"Come on, Tlalli. Only one person coulda removed that locator spell."

She'd all but forgotten about the locator spell she'd placed on the false item, but once she remembered, the rest of the picture became clear. She could follow Elias's path of thought, and she had to admit she was almost ashamed that she hadn't seen it coming.

Anthony had disabled her locator spell and taken the fucking chalice.

"Have you tried to get in touch with Michael?" she asked, her throat hoarse.

"Yeah, nothing yet. I don't know what the fuck we're supposed to do. I can't find Anthony anywhere."

"What do you think he's planning?"

"In all honesty, Tlalli?" He let out a mirthless chuckle while running a hand through his dark hair. "I have no idea. But we both know what he wants."

"Yeah, he wants a war."

He was always going to want a war. Anthony would go searching for a war until the day he died. Or the day Cahuani died.

She wanted Anthony dead.

This was the first time she had blatantly admitted it to

herself, but it was an easy truth to accommodate. The disgust that plagued her each time he was in her line of sight had numbed her to any guilt she may have felt for the thought. She realized maybe that was all the proof she needed: even if the angels were what they claimed to be, she no longer fit that mold. All the lessons, all the laws, all the beliefs—all of it was a lie, and none of it meant anything to her anymore.

"You wanna know what worries me most?" he asked, crossing his arms over his shoulders as he stared out the window. "I don't know how long the Dominion will wait to intervene if he does try something. All they've been seeking for years now is a reason for war. If they let the demons kill him, they'll have it."

"You honestly think they're willing to start a war here? Out in the open?"

She didn't know why she was asking. She already knew the answer. Maybe she felt protective of Elias's lingering faith. Or maybe she just didn't trust him to believe the truth from her lips. Either way, she bit down on what she actually wanted to say and hoped he would find his way there himself. He had to. Otherwise, he would never know peace. He deserved peace.

"A year ago, I would've said no, Tlalli, but...you and I both know shit has been going sideways for a while now."

She scoffed. "Yeah! I know! Yet not two days ago, you were telling me to suck it up and keep the peace."

"And I'm sorry, all right?" He turned to look at her now, his eyes sincere. "But what did you expect? I've... This is my purpose, the basis of my entire existence. What other—"

He looked away from her abruptly, and she knew she need

not ask what he was going to say. Because it would be a lie. He'd had a choice, the same choice the Puri had, and he'd chosen to side with the Dominion, to maintain their rotten regime.

Any other day, she would have pointed that out, spat it in his face and given him no choice but to swallow it. But today, everything was different.

"I don't know anymore," he said instead, "but if all this falls apart…" He stared out the window and far off into a place she could not see.

She eyed him for a long while, contemplating what to say. As much as she wanted to believe he was saying what she thought he was saying—or that he would at least consider it—she could not be certain. And even if he was, she could not know for sure that he was being honest. This could be a setup. If he was at all suspicious about her or if he had realized the real chalice had been stolen earlier, he could be trying to get her to reveal her role. And if she did that, she not only put herself at risk, she put Cahuani at risk as well. She wasn't willing to do that.

She needed more time with Cahuani, much more. She didn't care how fleeting what they felt for each other might be. She just wanted to keep feeling alive for as long as she could before they were once again swept up in the inevitable war between good and evil where no one knew who was who until someone won.

She really hoped that war would not come tonight, but if it did, she would fight beside Cahuani. Until the end of it.

One way or another, this auction would be her grand finale as one of Michael's angels. She did not care what the angels told themselves about her when the blow landed. She would gladly be

the villain in everyone's tale. At least then, she would get some fucking credit.

Still, she didn't want Elias's blood on her hands.

She wondered if maybe Elias was starting to warm up to her because he was afraid for her. Maybe he didn't believe she would survive this war. Or maybe he was just afraid that *he* wouldn't. Though she supposed the more sensible reason was that he was afraid neither of them would, that no one and nothing could withstand the collective wrath of Heaven and Hell colliding.

She was inclined to believe that too. They were immortal but not entirely invincible. Still, she was just too damn stubborn to simply lie down and die, and if he decided to, she was glad she wouldn't be there to watch.

The look of defeat had become so ingrained in Elias's expression that she almost forgot that was what it was. But it served as a reminder that he was already lost to her, no matter how close she thought they were getting right now. He didn't care for her enough to fight. He couldn't. He didn't even care for himself enough to try, so how could she possibly save him? It was obvious he didn't want to be saved.

Whatever she may have felt for him, whatever she was capable of feeling for him, he could never feel it in return. It would never suit his brand of hedonism.

"So what are you gonna do?" she asked him.

He shrugged again, turning around to slide down the wall and sit on the floor.

Without thinking, Tlalli did too.

"Hope for the best, I guess. But if Michael thinks I'm gonna

go up against the demons for Anthony, for anybody, with all these mortals around, he's terribly mistaken. If Anthony challenges them, he's on his own."

"Agreed."

That gave her some relief. Though she hated for the demons to have to endure Anthony, she could not help but admire the idea of all their immediate problems being solved. All of which held him at their root.

Yet no matter what happened, she couldn't protect Cahuani from the impact. He would lose his son again, and even though he knew that, having known would not make it any easier. She had known she was going to lose her mother before it happened, and the wound was still too large for her to close.

"You gonna go to that party tonight?" Elias asked after a time. "With the mortals? I hear it's some kinda massive orgy or whatever they call it."

She snorted before throwing him a pointed look. Although she and Cahuani were staying for the duration of the party, she wasn't about to tell Elias that. "Now, you know I have no business rolling around with mortals, especially when Anthony might show up and split one in half for even looking at me."

"Yeah, I guess that's true."

There seemed to be something else Elias wanted to say, but he held fast. She wouldn't be surprised if he had his suspicions about Cahuani, because she didn't do much to hide her feelings. Anthony was gonna ask and believe what he wanted to, but Elias...he didn't ask people questions. He hardly ever cared about the answers.

"Why? Did you wanna go?" she asked, both to tease him and to shift his attention.

He chuckled. "No, I did not wanna go."

"Because I mean, that's the last place Anthony would probably look for you. It's okay to wanna see how things work down here, Elias."

He rolled his eyes. "You know angels fuck, right? Maybe not as openly as mortals, but we do."

"Yes, *we* fuck. I did not know that *you* fuck."

He shrugged. "I've had my share of experiences is all I'm sayin'."

"Okay, whatever you say, player. Just make sure you know what you're getting yourself into. The mortals are very creative when it comes to this stuff."

"I'll make sure to prepare a safe word."

She gave him a purely impressed look against her better judgment. "Imma be honest. I did not expect you to know what a safe word was."

He realized what she'd said and shoved her shoulder, and she burst into laughter.

"Hey, I'm just bein' honest!" she returned. "There's nothin' wrong with it! But I know you don't really involve yourself with other people, so I figured you just prefer other indulgences. I mean, when we're down here, all you do is vape and talk shit."

"I indulge just enough, okay? Damn."

And by now, he was laughing too. She had never realized how joyous the sound was. It wasn't condescending like Raphael's laughter or bitter like Michael's. It was infectious. It was worth saving.

Fuck, she hated herself right now.

Once he sobered though, he looked down at his hands. "Do you got a safe word?"

She smirked now and gave him a dark look. "Trust me. I have many things I keep from you for your own good, Elias."

"Oh, come on now. Telling me your safe word ain't gonna scare me off."

"So you say."

"Well, now I gotta know what it is."

She eyed him warily, but he merely cocked his head, urging her to go on. So she leaned in close, closer than she needed to, and brushed her lips against his ear. "Apostate."

She felt the shudder that ran through him as she whispered the word against his skin. The power it imbued her with was as intoxicating as his renewed laughter. Maybe even more so. Oh, she could break him into pieces if she so pleased.

"You play too much," he said after a beat, although his laugh sounded nervous.

"Who said I was playin'?" She snickered.

Still, she immediately turned to get up, because whatever had passed between them in that moment, whatever electric current had shot to her core and attempted to root there, she couldn't act on it. And she wanted to, badly. But she couldn't be the one to make this harder than it had to be. She wasn't that brave.

"It's okay, Elias. I don't think any less of you just because you're probably the most vanilla muhfucka in—"

Though apparently *he* could act on it. Before she could get to her feet, he was atop her, pinning her face down to the ground

with his body over hers. She heard his wings erupt from his back, then felt the feathers fall over the two of them, concealing them from all else.*

"You wanna bet on that?" he whispered, his mouth flush against her ear. "I'm happy to prove you wrong."

She froze, trying to determine whether he was serious. Then she felt the thick bulge of his cock as it began to harden against her ass.

Oh, he was definitely serious.

And if that were not enough, he let her *in*. All at once, they reached for each other, and all at once, she felt his desire burning into her back and filling her lungs. And mixing with her own.

She thought of Cahuani. They weren't a thing. At least not a whole thing. They were likely not going to be a thing when he had fulfilled his promise to get her out. Even so, this had nothing to do with that. This had everything to do with Elias, who she was going to abandon without so much as a word. Elias, who could have been her friend or something more if the circumstances had lined up sooner. Elias, who she had never seen so alive before this moment.

And suddenly, this seemed like the only appropriate way to say goodbye.

"What are you gonna do, Elias?" she said, feigning boredom. "You gonna take me?"

"You think I can't," he bit back.

"I think you won't."

"Say the word."

* THE FRUITS—Paris Paloma

"You don't have it in you."

"Say your safe word, and I'll let it go."

"I don't need to say the word, because you ain't gonna do shit."

With a quickness, he shoved up her dress and yanked down her panties. Lust flooded her belly and tinted her vision. It was only then that she realized how badly she wanted this, how eager she was to see him at his absolute worst.

"Say the word, Tlalli," he urged again. "Say the word, or I'll take you, right here, right now. I'll show you just how vanilla I can be."

"Fuck you, Elias."

Before she could breathe in again, he shoved every inch of his erection unceremoniously into her folds, and she knew at once—he was about to fuck her like he had a whole lot to prove.

Tlalli cried out but was quickly cut off by Elias's hand. He held the position for only a beat, giving her little time to adjust to his girth before his hips were rocking against hers. His thighs trembled almost audibly. He had been yearning for this. There was no doubt in her mind.

And now she realized just how much she had been too.

ELIAS

E lias had no idea what he was doing.

Well, he knew he was fucking Tlalli, and judging by the sounds she was spilling all over the conservatory floor, he knew he was fucking her good, but apart from that, he had no clue.

He had no idea what had come over him; he hadn't thought too hard about it. Maybe it was the finality that had begun to outline their conversation. Maybe it had felt too much like an ending. Either way, now was a hell of a time to start catching feelings, physical or otherwise, for Tlalli. War was inevitable, and they had been abandoned here on Earth with Anthony and his desire to trigger it himself.

Of course, these developments may have been the driving force behind his boldness. The end of the world was on the horizon, and Elias was tired of constantly looking back at his existence and wishing he'd done *more*. He did not need another regret, and he would have regretted not trying to give Tlalli something that

might symbolize the truth. He cared for her. He always had, but he never felt like he'd been allowed to do it out loud. That hadn't been fair to her, and had she turned him down now, he would've understood. He would have been horrified too if she'd turned him down, what with the way he'd gone about it, just jumping her like that, but...

Well, he couldn't quite explain it, but something in her spirit had pulled at his, and he'd trusted it. He'd trusted it so deeply and so desperately that this, like war, had felt inevitable.

He pushed two fingers into her mouth and pressed down on her tongue, then reveled in the sudden sound of her gagging. He sped up his strokes instinctively, digging into her deeper and deeper, until his name dotted the air amid her string of moans. It was jarring to think he'd never known Heaven until this very moment. All that time spent Upstairs, and yet this was the closest he had ever been to a god. How lucky he was now.

And how damned.

"You...bastard," she spat once he removed his fingers, even as she bounced her ass upward into his stroke, keeping the game alive.

"But you didn't think I'd do it, right?" he shot back, more animated than he'd been in a while. "You didn't think I could."

"I still ain't seen nothin' new."

"Admit that you wanted this, Tlalli." He grunted.

"No."

"Say it."

"Fuck—"

"Confess your sins."

She expelled a long moan, one that shot through him like a blast of hot air.

Between her little movie with Cahuani and her choice of safe word, he'd known the moment she said it what games she liked to play, and he had realized just as quickly that he was willing—even eager—to play them too.

"I know you want to," he said. "You've *been* wanting to. You wanted me to punish you. You wanted me to shove this dick inside you."

"Get over yourself."

"You wanted me to fuck you until you begged me for mercy."

"I don't!"

"Then say the word!"

She wouldn't. He knew she wouldn't. She had let him in. He could hear every thought and feel every emotion pulsing through her, and he could see every vivid fantasy her mind was stringing together in quick succession, like a movie made just for him. She wanted this as badly as he did, and he would be sure to deliver.

"I don't want it," she lied half-heartedly. "I don't want *you*, Elias."

How funny they had both truly believed that not an hour ago.

"And when you cum for me?" he growled. "Then what?"

"Never."

"We'll see."

He pushed himself up onto his hands, drawing his knees up and driving impossibly deeper until she was trying to claw her way up the floor. Her attempts were of no consequence, however. He kept her in place, pinning her face to the tile with one hand

and her shoulder down with the other. Then he folded his wings back beneath his skin and began drilling even harder into her pussy with every intention of ruining her right there for anyone to see.*

He could have pulled them out of the room, out of existence, into a void only they could navigate. But no. He was petty and possessive, and part of him wanted someone to see, to know he could be a monster too. That he wasn't just Michael's lapdog or Heaven's dull blade. That he was still more powerful than Anthony could ever hope to be in Heaven or on Earth. He had teeth and claws and needs and wants, and all of them yearned for Tlalli now.

No matter how this ended or what happened next, he vowed to leave his mark on her.

She didn't bother muffling her screams, and neither did he as his hips clapped violently against hers. His legs pushed hers farther apart, and her pitch changed with every new angle he managed to hit in stride. Yeah, this wasn't his first rodeo by any means, and he was pulling out all the stops for her. Whatever had clicked in his mind the day before was firmly rooted in place now, and he wasn't about to act as if he weren't dedicated to keeping it there. He didn't know what would happen when they went back to Heaven. All he knew was that he didn't ever want her to question his admiration again.

Though he imagined that might be a bit hard when this felt like anything but an intimate fuck.

She whined as he pulled out of her and whipped her head

* LA NOCHE DE ANOCHE—Bad Bunny and ROSALÍA

around to scowl at him. Before she could form an audible question, he had hold of her ankle, and he flipped her onto her back none too gently.

Her legs remained spread before him, making it easy for him to slip right back inside, but a shift in the air was undeniable. She stared up at him in awe, her lips parted and eyes glittering with flecks of divine gold. He couldn't explain to her what was transpiring between them—inside him—right now, so he hoped she wouldn't ask. The slow stroke he delivered must have given her at least some semblance of an answer, because suddenly her mouth was at his throat and her nails were at his back.

He wanted to tell her that she need not claw her way in. She had already done that.

He'd been trying to figure it out, what it was he saw in her, sought in her. The answer hit him now as he threw caution to the wind and relinquished his hold on his last lingering inhibitions: it was the image of who he wanted to be, who he wished he would have been.

She would have done the right thing all those ages ago. She would have followed her friends into the fire. No, she would have followed her own conscience. She would have rebuked the future she saw in the Heavens and burned it all down with the speed of her descent. She would have been braver than him. And for that, she deserved better than what the Dominion would ever be willing to give her.

He knew he couldn't offer her anything more than the Dominion, but he wanted to show her that he would if he could. He didn't know if this was the best way to do it, but it was what

he had, this last little piece of him that had not yet become jaded. He hoped it was enough, even just for a moment.

When everything became too real, he sped up again, and she urged him on with her hands, firmly gripping his ass.* Their sounds skittered across the floor, strained and staggered and so very human. He felt both powerful in this skin and vulnerable when he touched hers. And he knew that whether he ruined her or not, she would certainly leave him in ashes. He would never be the same again.

She came with a cry that she tried and failed to muffle against his shoulder, the outline of her own wings bursting out beneath her with a blanket of shimmery light.

"Elias! I—"

She convulsed against the cold floor, her eyes rolling back as his hand wrapped around her throat. As much as he wanted to make this last, he knew it was coming to an end, and he intended to greet that end on his terms, to make it count.

His grip tightened as he kept pumping into her, and his mind homed in and fixated on every constriction of her pussy around his cock. This was all he knew now, the only thing he could discern in a world of muddled colors and white noise. He could drown in the bliss of knowing her like this. In that moment, he truly wanted to.

"Fuck!" he snarled against her cheek as he buried himself to the hilt again, once, twice, three times, before he tumbled over the edge and into oblivion. His eyes rolled back then too, his body seizing as his back arched. Her hands were on his ass again,

* BETTER—Khalid

then her legs around his thighs, milking him eagerly until he'd emptied his seed inside her. He shuddered once more before collapsing atop her, struggling to catch his breath. Her fingers tangled in his hair; her lips brushed his temple. It was so soft that he wanted to cry.

How foolish an idea this had been. How was he ever supposed to recover? This was why he'd run from it in the first place. Coming wasn't the only climax after all. This was his peak, and he would never reach it, much less reach past it, again.

This was how to kill a mortal—douse them in longing.

TLALLI

Yeah, Elias was *definitely* fucking in Heaven. That was all Tlalli could think right now as she attempted to get her lungs to work properly again. She was (only slightly, of course) irritated that he had never fucked her before, especially given the fact that he seemed to have learned her body in a matter of moments following first contact. Every sweet spot and soft target, he'd hit, and he'd done so with the kind of fervor few had ever offered. In fact, other than Cahuani, she couldn't name anyone who had fucked her so thoroughly.

Maybe if she could just convince Elias to come with her—

No. No, that was not possible. This was where it ended. There was no room for false hopes like that.

The peaceful quiet the conservatory had known prior to their encounter was restored once they gathered their bearings. She imagined that if anyone had come in here, they had likely fled the moment they heard the screaming, and if not, well…she couldn't

find it in herself to care. If someone had stumbled upon the show, she only hoped they appreciated it. After all, it was one afternoon only. She wished she had recorded it.*

To her horror though, she found herself reluctant to leave Elias, taking her time to work up to it. Yet eventually, she had to get back to Cahuani and tell him about Anthony. They had to be prepared for anything, and right now, Cahuani was sitting upstairs unaware. That thought put her on edge as soon as the lust cleared from her mind.

She still wasn't sure if she should tell Cahuani about this little engagement with Elias. She doubted it would matter. It shouldn't at least, but...well, it mattered to her. She had promised to be honest with him, and although that oath likely didn't extend to something like this in his mind, it did in hers.

But Cahuani's feelings weren't exactly her concern at the moment. No, it was *her* feelings that were giving her pause. Feelings she would've sworn did not exist an hour ago. And what the fuck was she supposed to do with that?

"All right, so we split up and steer clear." She sighed, carefully concealing her ulterior motives, although that now felt like pulling teeth. "Stasis is probably safest. Whatever Anthony's going to do, let him deal with the consequences. We already did our parts. He has the chalice. He knows the job is to deliver it. If he fails to do that, that's on him."

Elias nodded as he stared out the window. "Just..." Suddenly, he turned back to her, his eyes intense. "You promise me you won't go lookin' for him."

* STRANGERS—Ethel Cain

"I want nothing to do with him, so I promise you that," she returned quickly. She had plenty more fun things to do than go looking for that kinda trouble. "Let me know if you hear from Michael. You know he won't call me directly."

He nodded, gripping her shoulder, then squeezing it once before letting go. He was about to leave when he suddenly turned back to her again. "And listen. You're worth a thousand of Anthony, all right? I'm gonna make sure you get the credit you deserve when we get back."

She didn't have the heart to tell him it was too late for that.

She waited a few minutes in the conservatory before she too left, projecting herself back to Cahuani's room. He was sitting on the couch with a cup of coffee in his hand, his ankle propped on his knee and his tablet propped against it. All at once, her heart swelled. The room grew smaller, yet the distance between them remained far too large.

"Everything all right?"

He must have seen something alarming in her face, because he quickly set his tablet and coffee down on the end table. Before he could stand up, she was mounting his lap. Then she took hold of his face and pulled it to hers.

She kissed him hard, swallowing the breath he had been unable to expel and demanding more with a probe of her tongue. His hands grasped at her thighs and back and arms, eager to pull her closer as she tried to melt into him completely. Again, she was renewed by a drink of his mouth. Again, she was restored by the touch of his hands.

When she pulled back, he followed, eyelids heavy. She held

his face at a reasonable distance. Eventually, his eyes fluttered open fully, but before she could speak, he did.

"I hope that wasn't an apology."

Her brow furrowed. "What would I be apologizing for?"

He shrugged. "I may have passed by the conservatory to make sure things were going well, and they did in fact seem to be. I didn't stay long though, I promise. Only a moment or two."

She blinked and tried to find another meaning to the words, only to reach a dead end. He smirked at her, his fingers coming to dust along her jaw.

"As I said, I hope it wasn't an apology."

"You're not angry?" It was the only thing she could think to say.

"Why would I be angry? I don't own you, princess, at least not outside this bedroom. And I'm not saying I don't care either, so don't go getting it twisted. I just mean I want you to have everything you want."

She licked her lips and relaxed her hands against his neck, but she still couldn't find words. Not because she was ashamed or embarrassed that he'd seen her fucking Elias but because she now had to grapple with the fact that she and Elias were over, that the conservatory was likely the last time she would ever see him.

Cahuani would be enough. Of course he would be enough, but she was selfish. At least right now, in this moment, she wanted more than enough.

Cahuani softened, both of his hands cradling her face even though she could not look at him. "You care about him, don't you?"

A laugh absent of amusement trickled down her chin. "I

didn't think I did three days ago. I didn't even think he liked me until an hour ago, so…" She shrugged it off quickly. She couldn't do this, not now. There was too much at stake. Forcing herself to meet Cahuani's probing gaze, she took a deep breath. "But it doesn't matter anymore. We had our moment. The moment's over. I'm not looking back."

She wanted to know what was going on inside Cahuani's mind. Sure, she could poke around if she wanted to, but that felt like a violation, so she wouldn't unless he allowed it, and she didn't have the courage to ask. Because she knew he was telling the truth when he said he wanted her to have everything she wanted, and the last thing she wanted at the moment was for him to be worrying about how to get that for her.

He seemed to accept the finality in her tone, nodding and pressing another kiss to her lips. When he pulled back, a soft chuckle left his lips.

"What's so funny?" she asked, desperate to shift the mood in the room if not the one inside her head.

"You're not very good at behaving."

Her lips curled slowly. "Don't act like you didn't already know that, Papa Bear."

"Oh, I certainly did." He shook his head slowly, his eyes twinkling. "Mm, what am I going to do with you?"

"Oh, you've proven very creative in that department thus far. I'm sure you'll figure it out."

"Well, the bondage seemed to do wonders."

She licked her lips. "For both of us… Though if you were in need of inspiration, there *is* that party tonight."

He tilted his chin upward, surveying her features. "You want to go?"

She shrugged. "I mean, we don't gotta get *completely* involved. We'll give the mortals their space, but watching over them shouldn't mean we can't have any fun." She paused a moment. "But I know parties aren't really your thing, and you didn't actually say you wanted to go when you mentioned it, so...I mean, we don't have to go. We can absolutely stay here and get creative ourselves. The storm will likely pick up again anyway, and besides, a competition feels like a waste of your skill."

"And I cannot imagine a greater prize than watching you come." He licked his lips, and her eyes trailed after the motion of his tongue. "But if you wanna go, it would be a shame to waste the opportunity. Besides, we deserve to enjoy our last evening here. We'll just do as you said, keep a bit of distance between us and the other partygoers. It's a very large estate. I'm sure we can find a stage of our own."

She fought to keep her smile from faltering, but when it proved too much, she burrowed her face into his neck. She knew she still had to tell him about the rest of the meeting, specifically what had happened with Anthony. He had to know, but the words refused to form on her tongue. They felt like a bad omen in and of themselves, like whether she spoke them was irrelevant.

That wasn't true, of course. Whether she spoke them was the difference between a prepared Cahuani and a Cahuani caught off guard. The latter would do no one any good.

Well, no one but Anthony.

"Anthony stole the chalice," she blurted out. Easing into it felt

pointless. "The fake one, of course, but...Elias thinks it's the real one, and he thinks Anthony might try to use it to start a fight."

"Well, that won't work," Cahuani replied, allowing the subject to change without pause. "We know it's fake."

"But we can't find him, Cahuani. If he thinks he has the real one, don't you think he'd be rubbing it in our faces? And why would he take it if he wanted y'all to so he had a reason to attack?"

"Maybe he wanted Elias to think we did take it, so Elias might back him. I mean, that's the mission, right? Get the chalice by any means necessary?"

"He had to know better. He had to know Elias wouldn't simply take his word for it, and...I don't know."

She went quiet, trying to discern what it was that was putting her on edge now that she was focused on the mission once more. He was right. The demons had the real chalice, and Elias was safe and sound. They were already wary of what Anthony might do, so what more was there to worry about?

"What are you thinking?" he asked softly.

"I'm thinking we still don't know Michael's role in all this. I'm thinking that maybe he knows more than we think he does, and not just about Anthony." She bit her lip. "Honestly, for all we know, we all just walked right into their trap."

By now, that seemed to be the only real explanation for Anthony's ability to act in the fashion he had since arriving. Like he was always going to be the point of impact. And why would the Dominion even attempt to honor the treaty when they had been attacking demon strongholds for months now? The demons

had kept them at bay and let it be, refusing to be goaded into a war, but that would only last for so long. The angels had to know that too. And here, in a neutral zone...

Fuck. The angels didn't even have to kill the demons. They only had to kill the Puri's beloved Nahualli sorcerer. They knew this because the Puri had spared Cahuani after they stole the amulet. The demons could excuse an amulet. They could excuse a few critical wounds and destroyed buildings. They would not excuse the death of Cahuani.

"Anthony came here for me," Cahuani concluded aloud for both of them.

She met his eyes and saw her despair reflected at her, a despair that deepened as more pieces fell into place. Michael was not just expecting the war to start here—he had sent Tlalli and Elias with the man he'd hoped would start it. He hadn't cared if Tlalli and Elias got caught up in this family feud. He had deemed them disposable too.

That fact didn't matter so much to Tlalli, of course, because the mission had given her a chance to escape, but Elias... She had no clue what he would do when he finally realized that.

"Forget the party," she said abruptly. "We should leave."

Cahuani slowly shook his head. "No, we aren't gonna leave."

"Why not?"

"If we leave, I run, and if I run, I only delay the inevitable."

"But this isn't about you. This is about the entire world. And every mortal here."

"That is why I must stay. What if we leave and he attacks the mortals to get us back here? No, we have to stay until this ends,

even if the truce expires first, and when the time comes, I'll face the monster I made."

"Cahuani—"

"If he kills me, he starts a war. If I do not kill him, I do."

She opened her mouth but quickly closed it again. It took her a moment to understand what he meant, but once she did, she realized he was right. Because it was the same logic she had used to justify her own aims. If they did not end Anthony's plans tonight, they would only grow bigger, stronger, more dangerous to more people.

Cahuani couldn't be held liable if Anthony attacked first even once the auction truce ended. In fact, if Anthony attacked after the truce ended, it was Cahuani's duty to stop the aggression. If Anthony failed to kill Cahuani, Michael would either have to let it be or start the war himself. And Michael might just do that, but that would still be better than letting him manipulate the Puri into becoming the aggressor.

Elias used to say that when the war started, the most important thing to each side would be the optics. Tlalli finally understood what he meant.

"Okay." She expelled a heavy breath. "But then I have to find a way to formally leave the angels. It would all be for nothing if you defeat Anthony and they still use the accusation of my 'abduction' as a reason to attack." He seemed to only just realize this too, but before he could back out, she gripped his face firmly. "You're right, Cahuani. We have to do this the right way. It was foolish to even consider anything else, and... Look, I know the Puri are used to being the villains in stories, but we cannot let

Michael win. We cannot let him get away with trying to play the victim again."

Cahuani was already nodding as if he'd been thinking she needed to leave this way all along. He likely had been but had been so devoted to keeping his promise to her that he'd tried to ignore it. She could appreciate that, but she was done trying to flee. The war was inevitable, yes, but it did not have to happen here. It did not have to happen *to* her. She had a choice.

"I'll talk to Xaphan," he said after a long silence. "As soon as the truce ends at midnight tonight, we'll put the Puri on alert. They can find a way to ensure you get the audience you need to leave properly without having to step foot in the Garden even if Anthony doesn't make a move."

"And what about tonight? What if Anthony just shows up here and tries to start things off in the hallway?"

"We just have to steer clear of him until the morning. If the orfani are in danger, we act, but otherwise, we evade Anthony at all costs."

It took Tlalli a moment to remember *orfani* was the Puri's word for mortals without magic.

"If we're lucky, the mortals will leave here in the morning without any issue," Cahuani continued. "At least then, no matter how things go with Anthony, we don't have to worry about them. It'll be fine."

Now she had to laugh, not because of how confident he looked but because of how easy he made it for her to feel just as confident.[*]

* NIGHTS—Snow Tha Product feat. W. Darling

"And you're good with him finding out about this?" she asked, tilting her head.

"What? That I'm fucking you?"

She snorted. "That *I'm* fucking *you*."

"Mm-hmm, whatever you say, princess. Regardless, it's of no consequence to me. I don't really give a damn what he thinks anymore. The only angel whose opinion I care about is yours."

She grinned. "That's a good answer."

"Yeah, I thought so too. Now"—he pulled her closer and ran his hands down her thighs—"about this party theme…"

ELIAS

Elias knew he should be taking Tlalli's advice, disappearing from existence to hide away from whatever chaos Anthony decided to rain down upon the Earth. Elias didn't owe anyone anything, least of all Anthony, but that didn't negate the fact that Elias was still an angel. Or rather it didn't negate the fact that Elias still had his morals and his values regardless of what he was, and he couldn't bring himself to abandon the mortals he had helped raise, helped create.

Additionally, the thought of hiding from Anthony made his skin crawl in a way that it had not in a long while. Even sitting up here on the roof of the estate felt like a cowardly position. Elias had freed himself from the limits of his own pride many ages ago, yet after an hour with Tlalli, that pride had reared its ugly head again.

Or maybe it wasn't pride. Maybe it was simply caring, an act he had too easily slipped back into as he slipped inside Tlalli.

Maybe she had managed to do the worst possible thing and bring out the best in him.

If that was the case though, Elias was more of a liability than anything.

He hadn't confirmed it outright to Tlalli, but since Anthony had stolen the chalice and disappeared, Elias was convinced that Michael had some hand in Anthony's current rogue antics. After Elias and Tlalli fucked, he found himself afraid for the first time in his life, afraid of the future. Since then, he had been rethinking and second-guessing everything, replaying every interaction between him and Michael prior to leaving for the auction and forcing himself to face every red flag that went up. By the end of it, the truth was so glaringly clear that it hurt.

Elias had been lied to in Michael's office the day they left for the mansion. Whatever the Dominion's plan was, Elias was now certain it differed from the plan given to him and Tlalli, and while he still couldn't discern what that plan was, he did come to a worrisome conclusion. He and Tlalli hadn't just been abandoned. They had been sacrificed.

Yesterday, Elias would have laughed at this revelation and welcomed whatever glorious end befell him. Now? That wasn't an option. Not for him and not for Tlalli.*

The sun had long since set, meaning the party downstairs was in full swing. A small sliver of Elias had wanted to go and check it once it began, but after this afternoon, he doubted anything or anyone there would hold his attention.

Instead, he decided to search the house and grounds for Xaphan,

* QUÉ MALDICIÓN—Banda MS de Sergio Lizárraga and Snoop Dogg

hoping to find him quickly despite the storm that was once again picking up outside. He had no clue what he would say to the demon, but finding him was the only thing he could think to do now. While Elias knew Tlalli was fucking Cahuani, he had no idea if she was conspiring with demons. He had been putting off thinking about it quite easily the past twenty-four hours. If he followed through with this plan of his, he would have to confront her. And he would have to tell her the truth about what he knew and how he knew it.

He figured it was always going to come to this. Xaphan had said so himself, that Greed was still waiting for Elias to do the right thing, and as hard as Elias had tried to deny that the Puri were the ones interested in "the right thing," the time for denial had passed. The Dominion could not be trusted, and everything was at stake.

Nonetheless, as he made his way out onto the muddy grounds, he found his heart once again at odds with his head. He no longer wished to seek out Xaphan. He wanted to find Tlalli. He wanted to tell her first.

He was reaching for her before he could think twice about it, then letting the steady pulse of her being guide him in the direction of the tree line. She had left the connection open, and judging by the strength of it, she was still here in this realm. Apparently, she hadn't taken her own advice either.

As he neared the tree line, however, he found his path blocked by a familiar figure: the one he had been looking for before.

"What are you doing out here?" Xaphan grunted, crossing his arms over his chest.

Elias rolled his eyes. "Looking for you."

Xaphan seemed genuinely surprised at that response, but he softened nonetheless. Then a smirk fell across his features. "And what can I do for you?"

Elias wet his lips while glancing around consciously. He definitely hadn't thought this far ahead, but there really wasn't much else to say apart from the truth, so he started there. "Anthony got to the chalice," he said.

Intuition had long ago told Elias the demons had already gotten to it first, but his award-winning denial had held up right until this moment, when Xaphan's face screwed up in what Elias would call confused guilt.

"The chalice you put in place of the real one," he tacked on sheepishly.

Yet Xaphan's features didn't change much, and the longer they stood there staring at each other, the clearer the picture became. Xaphan already knew. He knew what Elias was gonna say, all of it, which could only mean one thing. Tlalli had told them. She had indeed already made the decision to betray Heaven.

Elias could admit he was hurt, but the pain only lasted a moment before Xaphan dragged him back to the matter at hand.

"Is this you doing the right thing?"

There was only the slightest hint of smugness in Xaphan's voice, but it was more than enough to make Elias's blood curdle. Still, Xaphan stared hard at him, as if willing the confirmation to form in the air around Elias's lips.

"I don't know?"

"It's really simple at this point, Elias. You know what's gonna happen, and you know your angels have left you to the wolves.

You know how this ends. Now, you can die for that loyalty you're so proud of, but I think you know you deserve better. Otherwise, you wouldn't be out here looking for me."

Elias clicked his tongue. "What am I supposed to do? Just... throw it all away? Run and never look back?"

"Naw, that ain't possible. You have to look back. You have to look and see and tell the Puri everything you can, because otherwise, everything you've put your faith in is gonna destroy all that you helped build. And then all of this was for nothing."

"And if we fail?"

"Then at least you can show up in Hell and say you did your damn best to be good, even when you were given every permission to be anything but."

There was no denying who Xaphan's creator was. Lucifer, the Prince of Pride himself, had been every bit the orator that Xaphan was now. And Pride had been so close to securing Elias's loyalty all those millennia ago, yet Elias, who had still believed so strongly in the way of the Righteous God, despite the calamity that had brought them together in the first place, had fought him.

He'd watched Pride lead his angels out of Heaven to rebel against the Dominion's warped idea of creation. Then he'd watched the Dominion become everything Lucifer had warned they would, and Elias had numbed himself to the reality since. Not anymore. There was no going back. There was no buying time. He had to make a decision, and he had to make it now.

And if Tlalli was leaving, what else did he have in Heaven worth staying for? Even if she wished to leave him behind, even

if she had committed to cutting ties, he still had to make a choice for himself.

"She didn't tell you, because we didn't trust you," Xaphan said. There was nothing particularly cold about his statement. It was just a fact. "We wouldn't have allowed it whether she asked or not. We couldn't risk sabotaging ourselves, so we had to wait for you to come to us yourself. But you know the Puri keep a place for you."

"And even after all this time, they really still want me on their side? After I—I called them liars and turned my back on them?"

He smirked now. "You keep mistaking devils for angels, Elias. We aren't gonna damn nobody for making a very logical mistake, and y'all got history. Fact of the matter is you're useful, and they know that if you come to us, you mean it. That's good enough for me, so you wanna do this, we got you."

Elias chuckled, running a hand over his beard. "You make it sound so easy."

"I mean, it really is at this point. Besides, think of it this way." Xaphan put a large hand on his shoulder. "You get a brand-new pair of wings that are much cooler than those chicken feathers you're sporting now."

After a beat, the two cracked matching smiles, and their laughter climbed up the trees and into the canopy of leaves above. The rain fell heavily around them, but Elias was undisturbed. He felt lighter than he ever had before.

Elias took a deep breath once the laughter subsided, then looked out into the dense forest behind Xaphan. His desire to see Tlalli was renewed. In fact, it was stronger now, and as he

recalled the few seconds he'd seen of that little video, so was his desire to see Cahuani. Since he was being brave and all, he figured he might as well do all the things he'd been wanting to do this weekend. Or at least try to. If they rejected him, so be it, but at least he could start anew without question about where he stood with them.

"I assume they're in there," Elias said, nodding his head toward the woods. "You're the bodyguard, right?"

Xaphan smirked and rolled his eyes. "I'm making sure things remain calm out here. Acheron is on duty inside. He's got a bit of an advantage that lets him stay...*unseen* in public places."

As much as Elias wanted to ask what that advantage was, he decided to believe it could wait.

"Let Cahuani know I'm coming," Elias went on.[*]

Xaphan raised a brow. "I don't think—"

"I know what they're doin', and I'm not asking them to stop on my account," Elias interjected. "Just let him know."

Xaphan shrugged his broad shoulders and nodded, then stepped aside and gestured deeper into the wood.

Again, Tlalli pulsed beneath Elias's skin, guiding him along the path, but there was another light too, growing before his eyes and burrowing into his ribs—Cahuani. It had to be.

He heard her first, the familiar moans he had strummed from her body earlier that day wafting through the air alongside the patter of rain against the ground. Then he registered a bass line of grunts and groans that were at times more animal than human—Cahuani's second form making its presence known

* I NEED MY GIRL—The National

when it could. Chills ran down Elias's spine. Yearning gripped him by the throat.

He found the two in a small clearing that could hardly be called a clearing, rain coming down hard around the canopy of Tlalli's wings. The golden light of them reflected off the trees, and Elias lost his breath. In comparison... Well, there was no comparison. Heaven could never hope to hold the divinity that this clearing did now. Nothing could, not even Michael and all his angels.

He was glad she'd chosen herself. The Dominion did not deserve her. Elias didn't either.

Though before he could abandon this endeavor, their bodies shifted, and Cahuani's head appeared over her shoulder, the silver streaks in his beard catching the light of Tlalli's wings, black curls plastered to his forehead. His dark eyes were filled with a ravenous hunger as they locked on Elias's, and every dark and devastating thought the angel had ever had—every dirty idea he had refused himself—erupted in Elias's mind. The world grew brighter, and the trees leaned in. They whispered words of wanting in his ears. This time, Elias heeded them.

TLALLI

Predator and prey.

Those were the roles Cahuani and Tlalli had adopted upon entering the play party hosted by the one they called Reaper. Tlalli had been surprised to find Reaper was actually not a demon, contrary to her assumption, but he proved quite adept in his line of work regardless. He could certainly plan a party. Tlalli almost wished she and Cahuani could fully join it, but she had faith that playing out the theme on their own would be just as fun.

As she ran, Tlalli pictured the bear barreling through the forest in search of her, eager to tear into her supple flesh. She could feel Cahuani's heart thudding alongside hers, his excitement strumming her veins like a most familiar instrument. All that power pulsed between them, and the faster she moved from place to place, the more certain she was that he would catch her.

Oh, how badly she wanted him to catch her.

"You run as if you're not aching for my cock inside you."

His voice was a low growl in the back of her head, knocking half the breath from her lungs. Michael's god had never spoken to her, but she could not imagine anything or anyone sounding more divine than Cahuani did in that moment.

"But you want to pretend, don't you?" he went on. *"You want me to take it from you. You want to play the game for real."*

She whimpered and faltered in her stride. She hadn't really inspected her extended interest in the theme of the party, nor had she questioned the ease with which she opted to call herself prey. Although her willing vulnerability was for Cahuani and Cahuani alone, there was an admission of sorts that came with the choice. One she was not yet prepared to say outright.

And...well, it wasn't for Cahuani alone, was it? Because this desire to be taken had stemmed from her earlier entanglement with Elias, and while she'd refused to acknowledge the small part of her that wanted *him* to catch her out here in this forest, she knew it was there. It reared its ugly head every time she turned a corner.

"Yes," she confessed in spite of herself.

"Then I will," Cahuani said. *"I'll take it from you. Just remind me: What's the safe word, princess?"*

She nearly tripped trying to squeeze her legs together as she dashed down a row of trees and through a small clearing. It felt as if the walls were closing in. *"Apostate,"* she repeated.

"Good girl."

The moment his voice cut away, she suddenly felt trapped, like if she looked over her shoulder, she would see him there with a switch in hand. The image brought her as much fear as it did pleasure.

Yeah, she really did like this. For too long, her fear had been weaponized by others. Now it was hers alone, wielded entirely for her pleasure.

Suddenly, she collided with a massive object that she assumed was a tree. Until she realized that the massive object had actually collided with *her*—a mountain of dark fur, streaked silver in the moonlight. It was damp from the rain, but it smelled only of Cahuani and the soft earth she now lay in beneath him.

By the time she turned over, Cahuani's form was human again, his bare skin slick with rain and sweat alike. His cock stood at attention between them, a threat and a promise, and Tlalli's stomach twisted into a sea of knots she knew damn well he could work out if given the chance.

Still, she stuck to the game and started to scramble away from him. He took a firm hold of her ankle and dragged her right back, his inhuman strength and ancient magic overpowering her vessel with ease.

"Where are you goin', princess?" he asked slowly, his voice low yet strong enough to overcome the storm swirling around them.

She didn't answer, instead twisting around and attempting to claw her way across the ground. She kicked her free foot at him, but he grabbed that too, then yanked her closer until he could press a hand between her shoulder blades. The head of his cock pressed against the seam of her ass, and she bit down hard on her tongue to suppress the moan that bubbled in her throat. How could she even pretend she did not want this man to possess every inch of her that he could?

Another moan cut through her lips as he swept his fingers

through her folds, collecting her arousal on the tips. Then he leaned close enough for her to catch those fingers disappearing into his mouth. Her hips rolled against the ground of their own volition, the ruse in peril. She was ready to beg if he asked. Luckily, he didn't.

"You wanna say the word?" he said softly.

She spat into the dirt beside her head. He only chuckled before ramming the full length of his shaft inside her eager cunt.

The game fell apart pretty soon after, her praises of him filling the air until they conquered the rush of rain assaulting the clearing. He was rough, so very rough, but there was always that unrelenting assurance, a reminder that he was not Anthony and she was safe under Cahuani's dominion. It was all she'd ever wanted, and this man handed it to her with an unmatched ease.

If she'd known this was what it meant to be damned, she would have fallen long ago.

She was only just claimed by her first orgasm when he slid out of her, turned her around, and pulled her up into his lap. He slipped right back into her pussy with ease and was welcomed with warm hugs and sharp spasms that had him pumping up into her eagerly. She would've thanked him for how thorough he was if she'd been able to get any breath into her lungs.

Though once her eyes rolled back into place and she could take him in, she was again speechless. His focus was evident despite the pleasure contorting his beautiful features. He slapped a hand against her ass and bounced her higher in his lap, hitting every spot he knew he needed to and then some. All she could do was wrap her arms around his neck and hold on for dear life, her legs still

too numb to help out in any meaningful way. Not that he seemed to need aid.

All of a sudden, she could feel eyes on her, piercing her skin in a way she had never quite known. It was so intense that at first, amid the feelings Cahuani was already inciting, she could not tell if it was good or bad. The cordial mixture of fear and thrill in her convinced her Anthony was there, that he had finally been able to track them down and catch them in the act. Part of her reveled in the possibility. Part of her loathed the idea of an interruption.

After forcing her eyes open, she saw Cahuani's eyes fixed over her shoulder, and she was certain he'd seen Anthony. She reluctantly prepared to move into fight mode. Then Cahuani spoke.

"Come to see my good girl in action, Elias?"

"Honestly?" Elias returned, sending chills down Tlalli's spine. "I came to take her."

"And why would you feel the need to do that? If you want a go, you need only ask."

"Why would you want to share with me?"

"I think it's more the fact that she does not mind being shared."

"Is that right?"

Cahuani picked Tlalli straight up off him and turned her around in his arms to face Elias.

Elias's eyes were on her as he stepped out from the shadows. The grotesque scarlet glow of his lust twisted around the base gold of his aura. Everything about him looked exactly the same, and yet...everything about him had changed.

His features were sharper, though his true form also seemed

to be spilling out on all sides, the edges of his majestic white-gold wings growing more visible by the moment. Selfishly, she took off her proverbial rose-tinted glasses and gasped as she was graced with clarity. His divine form bloomed before her, his wings outstretched. And she realized his human eyes were not the only ones fixed on her. All of them were.

"Tell him your safe word, princess," Cahuani hissed in her ear.

As if he'd pulled a string, it came fluttering from her lips at once. Elias acknowledged it with a nod. She doubted he'd forgotten since this afternoon regardless. He seemed to mouth it in time with her recitation.*

Another gasp of surprise escaped her as Cahuani moved backward and laid her down on the ground before him. Though once she realized what he was doing, she eagerly parted her legs, a personal invite that Elias was acutely aware of, given the glint in his eyes.

It was then that Tlalli realized just how badly she wanted this. All of it, everything. Elias was here, and Cahuani was too, neither of them asking her to choose between angels and demons, mortals and the divine. They were handing her the whole world without any demand for payment, and she would be a fool not to take it.

She did not allow herself to question what it meant that Elias was here, nor would she entertain the idea that Cahuani had known this was coming. Instead, she took this for what it was, giving herself over to them and this fantasy they had begun to weave.

* LOVE LIES—Khalid feat. Normani

Still, she couldn't help but hope as Elias approached her, his clothes falling away and his wings fluttering at his back: maybe he did want out. Maybe she could save him.

"Go on," Cahuani urged. "Have a try."

Elias's eyes remained on hers as he sank to his knees between her thighs. "What about a taste?"

She was nodding before she could think about it, and then his head disappeared between her thighs as his wings brushed against her skin and brought her to life. The connection between them was suddenly ablaze with information, secrets and sensations that felt like tiny electric shocks across her skin. She could feel it all: his need and desperation, his infallible gratitude. All the feelings she had thought him incapable of played like a song in her head, ages of emotions uncorked inside him, inside her. It felt like praise. It felt like worship.

No one who stumbled across them would see their divine forms illuminating the space. Yet anyone who came across them would see Elias devouring her pussy with an eager tongue and agile fingers.

Her back arched as she called out, but Cahuani kept her shoulders pressed to the ground, her luscious moan bouncing off his barrel chest.

"Is that enough for you, princess?" Cahuani questioned before lowering his head beside hers and brushing his lips along her forehead. "Or do you need more?"

"More," she grunted as she reached down and tangled her fingers in Elias's curls.

"What do you say?" Cahuani asked.

"Please!"

Elias met her plea with haste, his tongue elongating and swelling inside her, the bridge of his nose pressing against her clit. She bucked wildly, Cahuani alone keeping her rooted to the ground, as Elias pushed her toward the precipice and robbed her of all control. When Elias's tongue pulled out, Cahuani slapped her clit, the two of them falling into sync with such ease that she was almost convinced they had planned this beforehand.

"How's that?" Cahuani asked when she had become nothing more than a mess of moans. "Too much? Too little?"

She tried to shake her head, but it was so heavy with lust. "Just—right."

"Mm, good girl."

Then Elias pushed two fingers into her wet cunt, and when she opened her mouth to cry out, Cahuani leaned over her and shoved his cock down her throat.

ELIAS

The forest was now hallowed ground, consecrated and christened by the sweet song of pleasure hanging from the branches. Elias could hardly focus on the stroke of his own fingers when his eyes were hooked on the expansion of Tlalli's throat each time Cahuani thrust into her mouth. Her fingers held Elias's hair in an iron grip, her nails digging into his scalp. He took her clit into his mouth, then circled it with the point of his tongue as he continued fucking her with his fingers. She gagged and groaned around Cahuani, her body writhing with desperation, until climax seized her in a punishing grip.*

"Oh, you need more, don't you, princess?" Cahuani crooned, slapping her clit again when Elias pulled his mouth away, cheeks glistening with the fruits of her orgasm. He needed more too. "Come on. Let's see just how much you can take."

* TONIGHT YOU ARE MINE—The Technicolors

Cahuani pulled out of her mouth, took a fistful of golden locs, guided her up onto her knees, and then gestured to Elias.

"Lie down," Cahuani's deep voice whispered in Elias's head.

It was so easy to let Cahuani in that Elias hadn't even noticed he'd done so until now, but he had no regrets. He obeyed without hesitation, lying back on the bed of damp moss beneath him.

In the dark, it was not much different from the Garden of Eden, the scents and sounds of nature cradling him in soft arms. In fact, he imagined the Garden would be much like this without its oppressive atmosphere.

Tlalli climbed atop him, then moaned as she lowered herself straight down onto his hardened shaft. His hips bucked upward instinctively, desperation twisting the coil in the pit of his belly. He knew that one night would never be long enough to do all the things he imagined, and he still wasn't ready to consider whether he would have more time after. He was too enamored by the sight of Tlalli above him to think about it anyway, her hands firm against his chest as her hips moved in swift figure eights around his dick. Then she was crying out in time with a roll of thunder as Cahuani entered her from behind.

Cahuani's veined forearms draped over her thighs further fractured Elias's focus, and he almost forgot what he was meant to be doing. But once their eyes met, they were trading strokes as if they'd done it a thousand times before.

Tlalli collapsed against Elias's chest, another orgasm no

doubt threatening to overtake her, although she'd started trying to fight them with all she had. It was endearing to say the least, but she wouldn't last. They wouldn't let her.

"Fuuuuck!" she called out, clawing his chest open only for the skin to close in the wake of her nails. "Please!"

"What is it, baby?" Elias crooned breathlessly, running his hand through her braids even as his hips thrust upward hard and fast. "Too much? Or not enough?"

Cahuani leaned over them, then took hold of Tlalli's shoulders and slammed up into her. Though in this position, with Tlalli's face buried in Elias's neck and Elias's eyes on Cahuani, it almost felt like Cahuani was fucking them both.

Elias shuddered. Cahuani licked his lips.

"No," Tlalli breathed.

"Say it," Cahuani urged. "What is it?"

"Just right."

It was an affirmation and an incentive all at once, and the two of them reacted in tandem, speeding up their ministrations until her body convulsed between them, the warmth of her nectar spraying Elias's thighs once more.

Would he ever get enough of this? He highly doubted it. So just like this afternoon, he would fuck her like it was the last time and hope it tided him over. Though he knew that just like this afternoon, it wouldn't.

Elias watched as the Nahualli slid a hand over his own cock. Cahuani's magic glowed blue around it like a sleeve before dissipating. *Lubrication.* Cahuani then signaled him to roll over, and Elias had never been so swift to follow a command in his

life, immediately wrapping his arms around Tlalli's waist and rolling them both over so that she was now beneath him. She clung to his shoulders, even as tremors continued to rack her body. He found himself unable to help leaning down to kiss her shoulder and her neck, then nipping at the skin of her jaw and the lobe of her ear.

To his surprise, she fumbled for his head, then pulled it toward hers and captured his lips with her own. If the sex hadn't ruined him, this certainly would. His heart collapsed in his chest only to begin hammering against his ribs a moment later. *Oh no.* A kiss made it real. A kiss made him tender. Did she have any clue how irrevocable this was? Was she at all aware of the power she had over his very human heart?

And would it matter when the sun rose again?

Before he could offer himself any kind of answer, he was gasping as Cahuani wrapped a hand around his throat and pulled him up until his back hit the witch's chest.

"Be honest with me," Cahuani hissed in his ear, causing Elias to shiver *hard*. "You didn't just come for her, did you?"

"No." The answer fell from his lips, as simple as a breath. Ironic since he could hardly breathe right now.

"Good. I'd hate for you to have to miss out."

The swollen head of Cahuani's thick shaft slid between Elias's cheeks, and Elias simultaneously tightened up and tried to relax. Being with Cahuani had been a mere far-fetched idea just a day ago—Cahuani had been a gorgeous man with a gorgeous aura but far out of Elias's reach. Yet now, as he slid inside Elias, it was as though this too had been inevitable, the stretch so good that Elias

could've wept. Elias's emotions only intensified when Tlalli took his dick in her mouth.

Now it was the two of them moving in perfect synchrony, tearing the last of Elias's reservations from his skin. He grasped Tlalli's head, reveling in the way her tongue laved over his shaft and the lewd sound of her gagging when he hit the back of her throat.

Cahuani wrapped an arm around his chest and pulled Elias tighter to his own, the thunderous clap of his thick thighs against Elias's rivaling the thunder that rumbled above the trees.

"Oh, fuck!" Elias bellowed, reaching back with one hand to claw at Cahuani's leg.

"Yeah, you were lookin' for this, huh?" Cahuani groaned in Elias's ear.

"Yes." He had no shame about it anymore. "Yes! Fuck!"

In the solace and seclusion of the wood, they indulged in this hunger that now bound them together by the throat. Elias had never skimped much on his hedonism, but he had never thought to reach for something quite like this. This level of fulfillment was dangerous after all. It was the kind of fulfillment that would ruin you for anything else. He never knew it possible, to be so fulfilled, even by two people. Yet Cahuani and Tlalli were servicing every need he never knew he had, and he was grateful. Oh, fuck, was he grateful. So grateful he almost wanted to pray.

His eyes fluttered open when Tlalli's mouth left his dick, and a chill wind cut through the leaves as rain splattered his heated skin. Tlalli turned herself around and backed her ass up against him, then ground it into his cock. He took her hips

in a bruising hold without a thought, but he didn't push inside her just yet, letting her whimpers dot the air for as long as he could while Cahuani kept fucking him, kept bouncing Elias between them.

"Haven't you had enough?" Elias asked, knowing the answer.

"Not even close," she purred, tangling her fingers in the wet carpet of grass and moss.

"What more could you want?"

"For you to fuck me until I can't walk in this vessel anymore."

"You sure you can handle that?"

"I'm willing to try."

Her yearning was even sexier than her faux reluctance, but he wasn't about to say that. He would keep both if he could.

He thrust inside her with a strained howl that was buried by the cry that left her lips. Then his hands were on her shoulders, shoving her down into the grass and mud while he swung his hips between one lover and the other, desperate to unravel them both.

Cahuani was quick to match his urgency, his hands taking hold of Elias's shoulders and pushing him down too, until his chest was against Tlalli's back. She flattened against the ground, and again, it was as if Cahuani were fucking them both, leaving little room for Elias to set his own pace. Not that Elias minded. Cahuani knew what he was doing, and Elias, who was usually a giver rather than a receiver, had never been this strung out before. He would be worried if he hadn't already accepted this fate after his first fantasy featuring Cahuani.

They were nothing but a tangle of moving parts on the forest

floor with a cloud of euphoria encapsulating them. Cahuani bit down on Elias's neck. Elias scraped his teeth against Tlalli's shoulder. Tlalli sucked Elias's thumb into her mouth. Nothing ever seemed to be enough, but they kept feeding the beast anyway, searching for a release, yet longing to make it last.

This time, it was Cahuani who came first, as signaled by the sharp thrust of his hips and the harsh bite of his teeth in Elias's back. Elias cried out, but the sound was nothing compared to the one he made when he felt Cahuani's seed fill his ass, the warmth spreading through him with a quickness.

He leaned over Tlalli, fucking her with frenzied strokes as his own climax grew near.

"Fuck!"

He had no clue who had said it—or at least who'd said it first—but Elias couldn't worry about that now. The world was going white, and his lungs were growing heavy.

"Cum for me," Cahuani snapped, already seeming to recover from his orgasm despite the breathlessness of his voice. "Both of you. Right fucking now. Cum for me."

"No!"

That was Tlalli, who was shoving at the ground with weak hands.

"Then say the word, princess."

"No!"

"Say the word, or take his fucking dick and cum for me."

"N—"

She didn't get to finish. At least not her words. Elias dropped against her and reached beneath her to grip her ass as he drilled

into her pussy, devoted to making her come, hell-bent on making Cahuani happy.

Cahuani's hand whipped across Elias's ass, the witch expelling a gruff laugh as he kept his cock sheathed inside Elias. It had hardly softened, still spasming inside him, which only made Elias more eager to please him.

Tlalli's moans grew louder until they cut off abruptly, her mouth still agape but the sound lost to the world. Her nails broke skin along Elias's shoulders, but he didn't stop. He wouldn't. Not until he got what he needed.

"Be a good girl now, princess," Cahuani urged. "Cum for Papa Bear."

Elias and Tlalli both came at once, clinging to each other with bloodied nails and broken cries, their hips rutting out of rhythm as they rode out a rigorous climax. Cahuani pressed his hips flush against Elias's, sending another round of shock waves through the angel.

Nothing else would ever please Elias again. Nothing else would ever compare.

They must have lain there for ages, Elias and Tlalli holding each other while Cahuani caressed Elias's hips, the rain slowing to a gentle lull that could've put Elias to sleep if Cahuani's touch didn't. Before that could happen, they at last disentangled, a shared bliss falling over them as they came back to Earth.

They gathered their bearings in a comfortable quiet, soft touches passing between them with little thought. It was Tlalli who finally shattered the silence with the loudest question she could've asked, her eyes fixed on Elias's.

"So does that mean you're coming with me?" She paused. "With us?"

Elias smiled bashfully, looking down at his feet. "If you'll have me."

Cahuani smirked.

Tlalli rolled her eyes. "What the fuck do you think we just did?"

TLALLI

Tlalli was awoken by violence, transmitted telepathically and tearing her apart from the inside, a shrill, unyielding thing that scraped along her insides and sent her falling out of bed screaming. A bed Elias was notably missing from, although she knew for sure she hadn't dreamed him falling asleep beside her. She had been nestled between him and Cahuani all night. Yet the sheets were cold and her body felt as though it were on fire.

It was him. It was his signal terrorizing her. Elias was sending an SOS.

She still only came into full consciousness when Cahuani managed to get his hands on her and push cleansing magic through her body in hopes it would purge her of whatever force was causing her harm. It did no good.

She could feel his magic coursing through her blood, but the alarm continued. She could take the agony no longer, and she could not find the words to explain it to Cahuani, so she did the

only thing she could think to do. She took herself and Cahuani to the source.*

The pain stopped abruptly as they hit the ground in a disoriented tangle of limbs. Shouting echoed around them just as water hit her face from above. *Rain.* They were outside again, and it was pouring again.

They were on the lakeshore just shy of the tree line, the mansion quiet behind them and the sky still dark, although the horizon was a milky gray. At the very least, the rain and fog concealed them from view of the house, but she had no clue how long that would last.

Tlalli managed to get herself up, then pulled Cahuani to his feet once she was able. He was still in his boxers just as she was still in only his dress shirt and her panties, and the fabric was already plastered against his thighs. Unfortunately, she could not spare the image any admiration, because from one moment to the next, he was running, and his skin was disappearing beneath a thick layer of black fur.

Down the slope, illuminated by a long web of lightning, was Elias, battered and bloody amid a shower of loosened white feathers and locked in combat with a massive bear. Not quite as big as the bear running toward them now, but a big one nonetheless. *Anthony.*

"*I have to get Anthony away from here.*" Cahuani's voice pushed through the chaos of her thoughts, setting some of them to rights.

"*Go,*" she urged. "*We'll follow.*"

Tlalli was still trying to process the scene when Acheron and

* WE HAVE IT ALL—Pim Stones

Xaphan appeared from nowhere and followed Cahuani. He must have summoned them the moment she awoke screaming.

And they were all running straight into the fray. Exactly what Anthony must have wanted.

She would've liked nothing more than to take her divine form but knew that could endanger Cahuani. Even in his second form, he was still mortal, and mortals couldn't handle being fully exposed to an angel's "true" form. Besides, as far as she could see, Anthony was on his own in his fight, and he was only mortal.

Cahuani reached Anthony first, despite the demons using their wings, and tackled him to the ground with a roar that shook the forest around them. Then the two massive predators and Xaphan disappeared into thin air, though she could still feel Cahuani in her bones. She would find him. As soon as she took care of Elias. And he and Xaphan could certainly handle Anthony.

So long as Michael doesn't show up…

"Fuck," she muttered. They had to go.

Tlalli caught Elias just before he collapsed to the ground, his hands gripping her arms in desperation. There was so much blood, and she could not pinpoint a single wound, gashes marking his skin every few inches. Anthony should not have been able to kill an angel. Even if Michael had made an exception and let him use his Nahualli magic, which seemed to be the case, a single mortal could not take an angel down on their own. Not unless they had the means—very specific means—that were locked away in Heaven under Michael's own eye.

Yet the poison Tlalli sensed beneath Elias's skin could not be mistaken. It was a poison that could only be found at the tip

of a specific blade. And only another angel, more specifically an archangel, could've given Anthony such a blade.

The anger that shot through her felt like a cold blade itself. She wanted nothing more than to make that bastard bleed too.

"Hey, come on. Stay with me," she breathed against Elias's hair before cupping his face.

Shutting her eyes, she focused on healing him. A shadow fell over her, but nothing touched her, and she soon sensed the other demon, Acheron, beside her. He was acting as a shield.

"Come on, Elias."

Elias coughed and gagged against her chest, but soon, his hands were tightening around her biceps, growing stronger with every second, and she knew it was working. But it was taking so much more than it should have, and she was growing weak.

Acheron must have seen that, because he put his hand on her shoulder. When she met his gaze, he nodded.

Still, she paused for a moment. She had never pulled power from a demon. She had never had to. Nor could she use her angel magic to do so. She would have to use her Nahualli magic, the magic of her mother.

Oh, what would Mecati think of all this trouble?

After closing her eyes again, Tlalli focused on the point of contact and homed in on the dark current of Acheron's power. Slowly, she threaded it through her own until the two were fully entwined, and then she used this power like a bucket in a well, emptying the poison from Elias's veins. This worked much more quickly, and within minutes, Elias was able to speak.

"What happened?" she asked.

"I... Something felt off when I woke up this morning, and I couldn't go back to sleep, so I was gonna go looking for Anthony. But he was at the door. I think he was trying to get in. He grabbed me. I don't think he knew it was me. I think he thought it was his...Cahuani."

"And he brought you out here?"

"Naw, I...I projected us out. I didn't... I was trying to get him away from you, but I—I couldn't... He has one of the blades, Tlalli."

The confirmation robbed Tlalli of her breath. She stared back at him in both fear and disbelief. He could only mean an Ashen Blade. It was a blade infused with the kind of poison that a mortal could use to kill an angel, a blade that was supposed to be under lock and key in Heaven with the others of its kind. Tlalli had never seen one before, and for the longest time, she'd assumed they were nothing more than a myth. After all, why would the angels invent something that could kill them? Now she understood why. And if Anthony had one, it meant she and Elias were right. They had been set up from the jump, and Michael was in on it.

"I'm sorry," Elias croaked. "For...calling you. I—I couldn't handle it."

She gave him a stern look. "You realize if you *hadn't* called me, I would've killed you myself?"*

He rolled his eyes, a good sign somehow. "He wasn't... He shouldn't have been able to kill me."

"And he shouldn't have been able to kill the two of us if you'd let him in that room, so—"

* SNOOZE—SZA

"But he could've killed Cahuani." Suddenly, his voice was quieter. He dropped his gaze.

Tlalli had no response for that, because she knew he was right, which only reminded her of the fact that Cahuani was now somewhere grappling with Anthony and they had no idea what other tricks Michael had sent Anthony with. Or whether Michael was somewhere lying in wait.

"We have to go," she said.

She and Acheron helped Elias to his feet before she reached out for Cahuani, finding him with relative ease as his emotions erupted inside her like a shaken bottle of soda. They filled her so suddenly that she went rigid against Elias, and he had to adjust swiftly in order to support her weight. Before he could ask, however, she was projecting the three of them away from the mansion, toward Cahuani.

When the world came into focus again, it seemed as though nothing much had changed, though the lake that spread out before them was slightly smaller and undisturbed by rain. The sky was darker though, and the house that rose atop the hill was the color of adobe. She knew this place well, but the memories of it were tarnished. They were at the Reyes estate.

The calamity halfway between the house and the lake drew her attention. Two bears rolled around on the slope, fighting for dominance. For survival. At the moment, the larger bear had the advantage, but the pendulum continued to swing as roars colored the early morning air in sorrow.

Xaphan hovered above the bears but made no move to interrupt. Again, Tlalli reached for Cahuani, though deeper this time,

trying to understand what was happening. But she already knew the answer, and it nearly brought her to her knees.

Cahuani had accepted the reality. He knew it had to be him to take Anthony from the world just as it had been him who brought Anthony into it. Who had the actual chalice had never mattered. This outcome was inevitable.

She looked down at Elias just as he looked up at her, and before she could even ask, he nodded. His smile was rueful and apologetic as his eyes glossed over and the bruises around them shrunk. He knew it too, same as her—this had always been the plan, but it wasn't Anthony's plan. It was Michael's.

And they had been expendable pawns all along.

"I should've let you kill him on day one," Elias managed, sitting up.

With that, she could not argue. However, she knew without a shadow of a doubt that it was fated to end like this. Cahuani was always going to have to defeat his son. It had to be him. Anything less was not justice.

Once Tlalli pulled Elias to his feet, they stood beside Acheron doing the only thing any of them could do—watch. Watch and wait.

Watch and wait and hope.*

* I'M BLUE—Faouzia

CAHUANI

The high-pitched howl that left Anthony as Cahuani bit down on his neck felt much like a spear through Cahuani too. This was his son, his child, who he had brought into the world in an act of revolution, only by the grace of the magic his gods had imbued him with, defying every belief and expectation the zealots held about people like him.*

Cahuani had demanded Xaphan stay out of this despite the demon's prior promise to handle Anthony so that Cahuani did not have to. Cahuani had realized that he would never forgive himself if he allowed someone else to bring harm to his son. Killing Anthony would leave a wound all its own, but Elias knew better than anyone that though Anthony—Tecolotl—would always be a piece of him, Anthony was also his own person. And Tecolotl was gone.

Cahuani and Anthony both had their own lives and their

* EAT YOUR YOUNG—Hozier

own fates, and they had each made a choice that brought them here. Cahuani did not regret a single moment he spent loving his son. He only regretted that it hadn't been enough.

Cahuani flung Anthony across the ground, and the latter shrank as he rolled away from his father, until his human form lay sprawled on the grass. Cahuani shifted back as well, paternal instinct overriding that of survival before he could reconsider. He approached cautiously just as Anthony shoved himself up onto his knees.

Blood ran down Anthony's face, but the skin of his forehead and neck was already stitching itself back together. His eyes flashed, looking between Cahuani and something behind him.

"Traitors, both of you!" Anthony spat, and Cahuani knew then that Tlalli and Elias must be there. "I knew it! I knew you couldn't be trusted!"

"A lot of good that did you," Elias tossed back, his voice as nonchalant as ever.

Cahuani would've laughed if his blood weren't boiling beneath his skin.

"What, Elias? Were you fucking my father too?"

"Wasn't that obvious when I opened the door to his room this morning?"

"You fucking—"

"Actually, it would be more accurate to say your dad was fucking *me*."

"Both of us actually," Tlalli quipped. "At once."

"And it won't be the last time either," Cahuani added, his own spite propelling his tongue.

Then Anthony was on his feet, racing toward them, his form

shifting once more into the bear. Cahuani was just as quick, changing midair, then slamming his body into Anthony's. The ground shook beneath them as they landed. Anthony's claws tore open Cahuani's snout, but Cahuani managed to wrap his teeth around the front of Anthony's throat again. This time, Cahuani opened a wider gash, and Anthony was unable to make a sound as he shuddered beneath Cahuani.

"*I will do better in the next life,*" Cahuani said in his head. He doubted Anthony would let the message in, but it had to be said. He would keep that promise. Of that, he was certain. "*But I must accept my failure in this one.*"

With all his strength, he kept Anthony pinned down while he used his massive paw to tear through flesh and fur, to burrow down into Anthony's chest and up into his rib cage. Then Cahuani wrapped his paw around Anthony's heart.

"*I will bury it with your mother.*"

"Cahuani!"

It sounded like lightning cracking across the land and thunder rolling across the plain. Cahuani looked up to see a massive figure walking through the fog, emerging from the tree line, shrouded in shadow. Yet that shadow was distinct. From its top protruded a pair of vast antlers like those of a reindeer. Though soon, the form began to shrink and transform into one of a man, and the antlers morphed into a cowboy hat quite similar to Cahuani's, which was back at the auction house. It shuddered out a breath.

It was the Prince of Greed himself.

"Acheron," Greed called while waving his hand toward Anthony. Immediately, Anthony was bound with a glowing red

rope. "Take Anthony to the Helix. They'll treat his wounds there before we show him to his new home."

Although Cahuani wasn't entirely sure what was happening, he gingerly removed his hand from Anthony's chest, leaving his heart in place. Cahuani then shifted back to his human form just as Acheron swept the wounded bear into his arms.

"What are you doing, Greed?" Cahuani questioned. "You— you don't have to do this."

"I know that," Greed assured him with a wink and a smile.

In human form, Greed was still imposing, large and muscular with a sharp smile and dark eyes wrapped in dark brown skin. He was the most charming of the Puri and also the most hospitable, meaning it was more difficult to piss him off than even Lust, who was known for being pretty laid-back himself. Cahuani had always been grateful for that.

"They'll call it kidnapping," Cahuani pointed out. "They'll call for war."

"They called for war the moment they sent him to that auction," Greed returned. "Look at this. Does this not look like a setup? Killing him won't change that. The whole reason they recruited him was for this purpose. I think you know that, Cahuani."

Cahuani stared at him, the last of his resolve beginning to crumble. Yet only when Greed gripped his shoulder did Cahuani begin to break.

"If he hurts...anyone else..." Cahuani breathed, trembling. "If he costs us—"

"We'll keep him safe," Greed assured him. "And we'll keep

him out of the way. But his soul is going to the same place. Might as well give him a chance to repent."

Cahuani chuckled. Tears streamed down his face.

"Two angels?"

Cahuani looked up again at Greed's words only to find that Greed was looking over his head. Cahuani turned around to see Tlalli and Elias approaching.

"Wait a minute now," Greed said, leaning dramatically as if to get a better look. "Is that who I think it is?"

"Mammon," Elias called back good-naturedly with a wave.

Cahuani found it odd to hear someone other than the other archdemons call Greed that, but he couldn't pick apart that thought at the moment. He also wasn't entirely convinced that Greed had only just realized who Elias was, but he said nothing.

"Well, I'll be damned."

"Will you still give them refuge?" Cahuani questioned.

Greed nodded after a beat. "Of course we will."

"Thank you so much."

"Don't worry about it. I'm just tryna be a more charitable guy."

Cahuani managed another soft chuckle. "Of course."

"You should head inside though, collect whatever you need. I already had folks grab some of your stuff from that mansion. Sloth and Lust have your place cloaked, but once the angels realize what's happened, I doubt it will hold long. It's best we keep with the plan and take y'all back Downstairs for now."

Tlalli and Elias reached them then, and Greed tipped his hat with that million-dollar smile of his on display. Cahuani

was more interested than ever in whatever history Greed and Elias shared, the looks they traded dripping with old wounds and untold stories. Now was not the time, however. They had to get moving.

"Here," Xaphan said, reaching them as well. "Anthony dropped it back at the mansion. I figured we shouldn't leave it behind."

He held out a dagger with an intricately carved ivory handle and a curved silver blade that seemed to glow a faint blue.

"I managed to knock that out of his hand, and then he shifted like a fuckin' coward," Elias filled in, nodding to the weapon.

Cahuani had never seen anything like it, but he could feel the aura the blade gave off. It was rancid, and it sent a chill down his spine. The discomfort only intensified as what looked like anger blanketed Greed's expression.

"He had that?" Greed asked.

"Yeah," Xaphan returned with a wince. "And as someone who's been stabbed by a Dominion blade before, I can say without a doubt in my mind that this? This is some other type of shit."

"And you're absolutely right," Greed said grimly.

"What is it?" Cahuani asked, unable to take it anymore. If he understood Xaphan's meaning, this was a different type of blade than the one that almost killed the demon several months back. And not just different but worse.

"An Ashen Blade," Tlalli stated, her eyes fixed on the dagger as if it might fly at her of its own volition. "The only thing that can kill an angel."

"Well, not the only thing," Greed said, his southern American accent thick, "and it wouldn't kill an archangel, but it does allow for an angel to kill another angel. Or for a mortal to. And they were likely the prototype for the Dominion blades, the ones the other angels carry around that nearly took out our dear friend Xaphan here."

Cahuani recalled the story of Xaphan being attacked by the Dominion and nearly dying from his wounds. However, he'd never asked exactly how or what he'd been attacked with.

"How do you know all that?" Cahuani wasn't sure he'd asked aloud until Greed looked at him.

"Because we, the Puri, were forced to help invent the Ashen Blade. It's one of the first things we disagreed with the archangels about."

"Can it kill a demon?" Cahuani questioned.

Greed turned back to Xaphan and glanced down at the blade still in his outstretched hand. After pulling a handkerchief from his own breast pocket, Greed carefully wrapped the dagger and stowed it inside the lining of his jacket.

"This particular model wasn't intended to, no," he answered. "There were no demons when it was created, but who knows how their older weaponry has evolved since our departure given what their new weaponry is like. I'll have Sloth check it out when we get back."

"But that's proof, right?" Tlalli stated, then bit her lip. "Michael was intending to let Anthony kill us."

It was obvious that she knew the answer already, but Cahuani suspected she needed someone else to confirm it. He could

understand that need. He'd had it when Anthony betrayed him too. It wasn't easy to watch your whole world crumble before your eyes and not think you're missing something.

"I'd say so, darlin'," Greed returned with a sympathetic look as he clapped a hand on Cahuani's shoulder. "But we'll talk about all that back home. Xaphan and I are gonna go check in with the others while y'all pack up."

Greed and Xaphan disappeared then, and Cahuani took a moment to look out at the estate. He committed it all to a fresh memory—the gardens at the rear of the house, the Lake of Cuetlaxochitl fanning out beyond them, and the warm red walls of his ancestral home. At once, he felt entirely himself. He tried not to think about the fact that this might be the last time he saw it for a while. And maybe even the last time he saw it like this at all.

With a soft breath, he turned back to Tlalli and Elias, only to find that Tlalli now stood alone a few feet away. He gave her a questioning look, but she merely gestured toward the lake. He turned to see Elias walking toward it.

Before he could think too hard about it, Cahuani turned back to Tlalli.

"Why don't you go inside, see if there is anything you'd like to steal while you're here again?"

She gave him an unimpressed look, but he shooed her along anyway with half a smile. Eventually, she rolled her eyes but took the hint and headed into the house. Cahuani then made for Elias, who had seemingly collapsed near the shore and was looking out at the water. From here, he looked entirely human.

Cahuani sat down beside him.* "Having second thoughts?" he asked, only half joking.

Elias snorted softly. "I can't afford second thoughts."

"Then what's going on?"

Elias laughed again, but this time, the sound was overrun by a potent anger. A dark-red glow emanated from his skin and grew stronger with every word. "They set me up. I have spent my entire existence, thousands of years, trying to uphold their regime. I gave them everything, and this is what I am worth? A fucking scrap in the middle of the woods?"

Cahuani could do nothing but listen. He wished to reach out, but he didn't know how or if it would be wise. Emotions had never been his strong suit, although he had gotten better for Anthony. Not good enough but better. It seemed he would have to learn once more.

"That is what they do," Cahuani stated, deciding it best to be logical if nothing else. "That is what they have always done, Elias. And I know. I understand your loyalty, and I commend it, but you have a chance now to start over."

"Yeah, in Hell." Elias snorted. "How the fuck am I supposed to do that?"

"It won't be forever, and you can do whatever you want when all this is over."

"If we survive."

"Tlalli and I will be right there with you. And she's starting over too. We all are really. But these are our lives, some of which are going to last a very long time. Maybe we should start actin' like it."

* CHANEL—Frank Ocean

Elias looked at him now. "And you—you're willing to die for this? This cause the demons have."

"Survival? Yeah, I am."

"The angels are supposed to be protectors, lovers, friends. Yet every angel I know, the ones I still trust, are tired. They're exhausted, and they're...they're fed up."

Cahuani wet his lips. He had so many questions. He always wondered just how much the angels who worked beneath the Dominion knew about the Dominion's dealings on Earth. He wondered how many would choose to fall too, if given the opportunity. Thus far, he'd seen two in a day, which seemed quite high for a single incident. That told him more than enough about the Heaven that took his son.

"I remember when the Puri left," Elias said, his voice growing suddenly softer. "I remember the agony the Righteous God was in. But things were good for a while. Until they weren't. And everything changed after Michael and Raphael took over officially, and...and the—"

He seemed to catch himself, and there was a look of shocking revelation on his face. Like he'd just connected two devastating dots.

Cahuani did not wish to push him. It would do neither of them any good, and Cahuani knew that eventually, the Puri would get all the information they needed from Elias. Cahuani could wait. Right now, he only wished to get his lovers somewhere safe.

"Look, you don't have to make all the decisions right now," he said at last. "You don't have to parse fact from fiction in the

span of a day either, Elias. So just...come with us. We'll figure it out from there, and the moment you say you want out of Hell, I'll get you out. I promise."

"You can't promise me that, Cahuani."

"You underestimate my influence."

Cahuani's lips curled, and Elias laughed. It sounded absolutely joyous, the most pleasant thing Cahuani had heard today. Almost as pleasant as Elias's moans mixing with Tlalli's the night before. In a matter of hours, he'd gone from grateful to greedy. These few days with Tlalli wouldn't be enough for him, and one night with Elias wouldn't be either.

As if Elias had gone to the same place, he said, "I can see why Tlalli likes you."

Cahuani waved him off. "Please."

"No, I can feel it. She really does like you."

"Well, to be fair, she really likes you too."

Elias chuckled, but the sound soon ended in a frown. "Three days ago, she couldn't stand me. And I really told her just to suck it up and take Anthony's shit. I never should've told her that."

"Now you're giving yourself too much credit," Cahuani pointed out. "Tlalli was never gonna listen to you anyway."

They both laughed, and Elias shook his head. "I mean, yeah, but I still should have supported her."

"We all got lessons to learn, Elias. Better late than never."

"I just... Look, I want you to know that whatever y'all got goin' on, I'm not trying to interfere or anything."

"You won't. You haven't." Cahuani picked up a flat stone and rubbed it between his fingers. "But you have feelings for her."

It wasn't a question, and Elias knew it. "Do you?"

"I don't know what I feel." Cahuani sighed. "That's not on her. I've been…numb for a long time to a lot of things, and emotions like this not least of all. I'm still learning to feel like that again, but she makes me want to. Does that bother you?"

Elias glanced at him. "No, actually. I just—I want her to be happy. And she seemed really happy last night."

They shared a smirk. Then Cahuani said, "Yeah, but that had as much to do with you as it did with me."

"Does that bother you?"

Cahuani allowed himself to truly consider the question, but the outcome did not surprise him. He had already been thinking about it for as long as they'd been talking. He had been trying to figure out what he could offer to both Tlalli and Elias. He didn't want to be the decent man and just bow out, nor did he want to be the possessive man who put his desires first.

Right now, all he wanted to be was the man who loved. And maybe Elias was just as integral to that as Tlalli was.

"No," Cahuani said honestly. "In fact, it makes me proud. It makes me think that if we worked that well together for one shared goal, why couldn't we work that well together again? And if so, helping each other start over becomes a thousand times easier."

"Yeah, I suppose it does."

"And maybe it doesn't work forever. Maybe it only works for now, but what's so wrong with that?"

"I don't see anything wrong with that. No shame in taking what we can get."

"Exactly."

"Are y'all plotting on me?"

The two looked over their shoulders to see Tlalli coming toward them, still in nothing but Cahuani's wrinkled dress shirt.

"What else would we be doin'?" Elias shot back.

"Mm-hmm, thought so."

"Speaking of which though...I should tell y'all both something." Elias looked between Tlalli and Cahuani with an expression that bordered on embarrassment. "I sorta...may have seen y'all's little video."

Tlalli made a strangled noise in her throat. "What?"

Elias huffed. "Well, when I found it in the bathroom, I swiped up on the screen to turn off the sound. You're the only being in existence who still sets a full ringtone for a text message by the way."

"Okay, hey now."

He ignored her. "But when I swiped, the video just...started playing."

There was a long beat of silence, Elias seemingly bracing for impact, before Tlalli burst into laughter.

Cahuani chuckled quietly, pinching the bridge of his nose.

"I'm assuming that was *before* we met in the conservatory?" she asked.

"Well, obviously," Elias replied. "Sorry?"

She rolled her eyes. "Honestly, I'm just kinda disappointed that Anthony *didn't* see it now."

"I mean, we could always make a new one, and if they need help torturing him..."

Tlalli smirked at him, and even Cahuani gave him an impressed look.

"You're gonna do just fine in Hell, I think," Tlalli assured him.

"I concur," Cahuani agreed, though his expression cleared after a moment. "Did Anthony say anything? Before y'all started brawlin'?"

"Naw," Elias said, "but he looked very, very surprised."

Cahuani stood up with another soft laugh, patting Elias's shoulder one more time. Cahuani and Tlalli shared a knowing look, and he figured he need not say anything else for now. He kissed her cheek as he passed and headed up to the house to collect the rest of his belongings. It wouldn't be long before the angels did whatever they were gonna do.

Of course, he really only cared to take one thing. It was the only thing he could not under any circumstances leave behind: a porcelain box on his dresser in which his wife's ashes were held. He might be ready to start over, but that did not mean he was leaving her behind.

TLALLI

'm sorry," Tlalli blurted out the moment the silence got the best of her.*

It had been poised on her tongue since Elias had shown up in the forest the night before, but she hadn't been able to say it aloud.

Elias waved his hand dismissively. "You don't gotta be sorry, Tlalli. It isn't like I gave you a whole lot of reasons to trust me with your escape plan. I'm just glad you made that decision for yourself in the end."

She stared at his profile for a long time. She wasn't sure what she had expected or what she would have wanted him to say, but it wasn't this. Maybe she wanted him to be angry. Maybe that would be easier to dismiss.

This whole emotion thing never got easier, did it?

"Okay, what the fuck is this?" she snapped.

* GIRLS AGAINST GOD—Florence + The Machine

He whipped his head around so hard that she feared it might come off his shoulders, his brow cocked and his eyes filled with confusion.

Guilt mocked her from just behind him, a monster he could not see even as it clawed at her viciously.

"What is what?" he asked slowly.

"Were you already planning to leave yesterday when we fucked in the conservatory?"

Her filter had been fried, and she had no use for tact anymore. This shit was messy, and they were on a clock.

A wry chuckle left him as he looked back out toward the lake.

"Naw," he answered simply. "But if I'd known you were gonna leave, I would've given it more thought."

"What does that mean, Elias? What...what does any of this mean?"

"I don't know, all right? I never—I didn't let myself look at you like that. See you that way. I was already a lost cause, and you...you were angry enough to do something about whatever the Dominion was heading toward. I knew that, and I knew I wouldn't be able to stop you. Eventually, I knew I wouldn't want to, but I also knew I wouldn't know how to help you, so I stopped thinking about it. I stopped thinking about a lot of shit, Tlalli."

"Don't I know it." She huffed out a breath, pulling her knees up to rest her arms and chin atop them as she too stared out at the water. "You never seemed to care about anything, Elias, least of all me."

"Yeah, that was by design. I'd cared too much in the beginning. I lost...I lost everything for it."

She turned her head slightly, inspecting him again. There was a stark grief that blanketed his features, one that permeated the air around him and reached out for her too. He seemed to rein it in some when he realized he was being studied, but she didn't let it go. "Tell me what that means."

It wasn't a demand but an invitation, and to assure him of that, Tlalli reached out and took his hand in hers. It was cool to the touch, his heavenly light dim beneath his skin.

"Obviously, you have a history with the Puri," she went on. "I knew that a long time ago. You're... You've been in Heaven forever, and the few times you'd talk about it, I could see it in your face. Something hurt you."

Something between a smirk and a wince lined his lips, but he didn't answer right away.

All of a sudden, she was acutely aware of Cahuani's approach, his energy growing stronger in her blood. She assumed it was why Elias wouldn't answer, but then, once Cahuani drew closer—and Tlalli realized he wasn't alone, although she didn't know who was with him, nor did she risk turning to see—she realized Elias wasn't shutting down. He was waiting.[*]

Cahuani came to a halt a foot or so behind them, and Elias at last offered an answer.

"I was there at the beginning," he said, his eyes far away. "I was there when the Puri...fell. I'm sure Greed could tell you the whole story better than I can—"

* WASTELAND, BABY!—Hozier

"We'll tell it together when the time comes." Greed's voice came from beside Cahuani, confirming that it was he who had accompanied the Nahualli back down here.

Elias nodded and continued. "But they were my friends. We were friends long before the Garden, before the Dominion, before the Righteous God was known as the Righteous God."

"How is that possible?" Cahuani questioned, voicing Tlalli's own thought.

"In time, brother," Greed repeated.

Elias chuckled. "But I doubted them. I doubted everything they believed in, all that Lucifer said. I doubted them, and I was wrong for it. I made a mistake, and I paid for that this entire time. And so did a lot of other angels who listened to me when I said to suck it up and trust in the Dominion." He turned to Tlalli then, his eyes soft as flower petals. "I never should have told you to trust them. I'm sorry for that."

"You already apologized for that, Elias," she said. "And I already told you not to. It's behind us now. All of that is behind us, and I'm just really glad you're here."

They stared at each other for a long while, and although they said nothing, she could feel everything he felt, hear everything he was thinking. And it made her heart swell. Oh, she was so damn glad he was here. She had been quick to deny it before, but leaving him...it would've broken something inside her she never could have repaired, not even with Cahuani there to help.

"On that note..." Greed sighed as if this had been his conversation all along. Tlalli was gonna have to get used to him. "All I wanna know is if you're finally coming home, brother."

Elias stood then, pulling Tlalli up with him before he released her hand and faced Greed. Years of history passed through a singular glance, and she really hoped Elias didn't expect her to just be waiting on the scoop. She was gonna grill him again as soon as they got home. Wherever that ended up being now.

"Yeah, I think it's time," Elias said.

Greed grinned the biggest grin Tlalli had ever seen and placed his large hand on Elias's shoulder. Then he moved it to Elias's neck and pulled him into a bear hug. Okay, maybe it wouldn't be too hard to get used to him.

"I missed you," Greed admitted while pressing his mouth to Elias's temple.

Elias playfully pushed at Greed's chest but didn't actually try to break away. It was endearing to say the least.

"Yeah, yeah," Elias grumbled as they pulled apart. "Just remember that when you start putting me to work."

"Don't worry," Greed said. "We offer vacation time, unlike your last employer. Speaking of which, there is no way in Hell I'm calling you Elias."

Tlalli snorted in spite of herself, and Elias rolled his eyes. Though eventually, he nodded.

"Then you can call me by my name," he returned. "The one I came into this world with."

"That, I can do."

"But," Elias said, holding up his hand, "only after you've dealt with my wings."

Greed nodded and hugged him again, and Tlalli accepted that now was not the time for questions. Regardless, she was

more excited about this whole starting-over thing than she had been yesterday. The world didn't seem so strange anymore. She had Cahuani, and she had Elias, and that was more than enough for her. She didn't care if they ended up in a cell in Hell so long as they were together. Maybe that was what her mother had always wanted for her—contentment.

"Ready to go then?" Greed asked them.

The three of them nodded. Tlalli slipped between Cahuani and Elias, taking each of their hands in hers.

"All right," she sighed. "Let's get a look at this place of eternal damnation everybody's always talkin' about."

Greed's massive grin returned. "Oh, I am gonna enjoy this."

From one moment to the next, they disappeared from the mortal realm, Tlalli shedding all that she could of Heaven on the grounds of the Reyes estate. Whatever the angels found there, they could have. She was theirs no longer. She was her own.

Though she could admit she was looking forward to sharing with Elias and Cahuani.

ACKNOWLEDGMENTS

I would really like to thank Katee Robert, Jenny Nordbak, and Bonkers Romance for inviting me on this wild journey that has been more exhilarating than I could've imagined. I loved writing this book more than I expected, and I am so proud of what it has turned out to be!

Writing this book specifically has meant so much to me, and it was a labor of love. To be putting out a romance with two Two-Spirit leads is such a phenomenal and empowering experience, and I could not be more thankful for the opportunity! And thank you to everyone who has given this story a chance! I really hope you've enjoyed it as well, and I cannot wait to invite you back to this universe very soon!